Praise for *ENGLAND'S LANE*

' lay well be his masterpiece . . . [The] world of the Fifties
lovingly and perfectly evoked, the sin seething under the
  rface . . . Connolly unfolds a rich and compelling drama of
 fe that is anything but everyday, with Dickensian attention
  letail, trademark black humour and a genuine love for his
   tions'   *Daily Mail*

  eph Connolly specializes in sardonic period melodramas
  . Borrows several cups of sugar from that grand house of
   rary experiment, *Ulysses* . . . There are moments when
  gland's Lane* poses a national portrait . . . He knows exactly
   at he's doing, in an immensely contrived, sophisticated and
   sfying game'

                                            Adam Mars-Jones, *Observer*

' le is arguably Joseph Connolly's stock in trade . . . as the
a   or of vibrant tragicomic slices of cosmopolitan Englishness,
.   The story is a high-brow soap opera, set half a century
     What brings *England's Lane* to life, however, is the carousel
o   oices that Connolly sets in motion'

                                                    Independent on Sunday

'Connolly captures the eponymous street . . . between the
end of war-time rationing and the rise of the out-of-town

supermarket, and relishes the paraphernalia of London in the late 1950s. He is a writer who specializes in convoluted social comedies with a dark undertone'

Gerard Woodward, *Guardian*

'*England's Lane* features a gallery of grotesques – repulsive men, duplicitous women, and not-so-innocent children – in a story of secrets, lies and brutal murder . . . This atmosphere of repression and taboo is the perfect culture for Connolly's dark novels'

Daily Telegraph

'*England's Lane* is a novel of voices. Of voices shaped by time and place and class . . . Connolly has a keen sense of the hushed emotional tenderness of English life and our silent shattering pain'

Sunday Telegraph

'It's the depth of detail that makes the book shine: from the period brand names to the clothes, make-up and language. A darkly humorous, colourful and deliciously indulgent carica-ture of a rampant postwar England'

Time Out

'The best novel I've read this year . . . you can smell the wood shavings and tobacco smoke, taste the boiled sweets'

Richard Littlejohn, *Daily Mail*

About the author

Joseph Connolly is the critically acclaimed and internationally bestselling writer of eleven novels, as well as eleven works of non-fiction. He lives in Hampstead, London.

By the same author

Fiction

POOR SOULS

THIS IS IT

STUFF

SUMMER THINGS

WINTER BREAKS

IT CAN'T GO ON

S.O.S.

THE WORKS

LOVE IS STRANGE

JACK THE LAD AND BLOODY MARY

Non-fiction

COLLECTING MODERN FIRST EDITIONS

P. G. WODEHOUSE

JEROME K. JEROME: A CRITICAL BIOGRAPHY

MODERN FIRST EDITIONS: THEIR VALUE TO COLLECTORS

THE PENGUIN BOOK QUIZ BOOK

CHILDREN'S MODERN FIRST EDITIONS

BESIDE THE SEASIDE

ALL SHOOK UP: A FLASH OF THE FIFTIES

CHRISTMAS

WODEHOUSE

FABER AND FABER: EIGHTY YEARS OF BOOK COVER DESIGN

JOSEPH CONNOLLY
ENGLAND'S
LANE

Quercus

First published in Great Britain in 2012 by Quercus Editions Ltd

This paperback edition published 2013 by

Quercus Editions Ltd
55 Baker Street
7th Floor, South Block
London W1U 8EW

A CIP catalogue record for this book is available
from the British Library

PB ISBN 978 1 78087 721 1
EBOOK ISBN 978 1 78087 720 4

10 9 8 7 6 5 4 3 2 1

Typeset by Ellipsis Digital Limited, Glasgow

Printed and bound in Great Britain by Clays Ltd, St Ives plc

To Patricia

In the Beginning . . .

I am a capable woman. And no, I don't really believe that it's vain of me to say so. Coping, when your own life and that of everyone around you is daily in danger, is really not so very terribly admirable. I am a capable woman, yes – but so very many of us had to be, during the long dark days of the war. We had to have strength. Rather surprisingly, it grew within you – the mind and body, I think, they come to sense its necessity. I drew upon it very largely in order to try to overcome the loss of my sister, who was dearer to me then than anyone on earth. This, though, all of this, it came a few years after. At a time when I foolishly believed that death and dying were over and done with. And I needed even more strength then, and of quite a different sort, to deal with the strangeness that emerged from her terrible passing – so very unexpected was this bright new love that ripened and burst inside of me (so shocking, and just unstoppably) for Paul, the little boy, hardly more than one year old, whom she left behind her. The pain from loving him, from knowing now that to me he is just quite utterly everything there is in the world, can simply stop my throat, and yet somehow it is charged with such sweetness. The agony of anxiety for his every moment fills me with warmth, a wash of warmth in which I nearly luxuriate, so happy am I to have it: and then I feel guilt for that.

Yes: guilt for that – and I suppose . . . no, not suppose, I don't suppose it, of course I really do know why. Because I carried within me the knowledge that never would I have that, a child, and then suddenly one came to me, so how could I ever deserve it? Eunice, my sister, he was lost to her, and so was her very own life. That must have been the worst of her dying – she had had time to think of it, I know. That must have been the worst of her dying – knowing that soon she must leave him. And now he's mine. So yes: guilt for that.

To me, the war itself was not really so appalling as afterwards – everything that happened, all that I felt, when finally it was over. I had married Jim in 1940 when he was home from leave – one day he had been given, just a one-day pass – and I am being neither flippant nor wilful, please do believe me, when I tell you that I really can't remember exactly why I did that. The reasoning behind it. Not love. No – not love. Well obviously no, not that. A few of us, quite a few of the girls who were working in munitions, were happily doing it. Sounds so terribly silly now – a gang of young women who barely even knew one another debating and then deciding between themselves that on the whole they might as well go ahead and do it: get married. There never seemed to be a shortage of eligible young men, most of them soldiers. One girl, Una — she married a boy she had only just met. At a dance. Eighteen, the two of them were. And then the following weekend they had gone to the pictures. Next thing we heard, she was engaged. She had a Woolworth's ring on her finger which she waggled in our faces while hitching up her skirt and parading up and down the canteen as if she were, oh . . . I don't know — as if she were a Norman Hartnell model at a West End fashion show, or something. We did laugh. They married the very same week, and then the boy — can't remember his name — was stationed in Africa, Egypt it might have been, and that, I am afraid, is the very last she heard of him. A more common story than you'd like to think. She didn't really seem to be too put out. Her main concern appeared to be whether still she would pass as virginal to the next young man who came along. It makes her sound so terribly awful, doesn't it? But she wasn't. It was just how people were. How they came to see things. Nowadays . . . what is it . . . ? Fifteen, eighteen years later, it all just seems so utterly unthinkable. But then — well, life was hanging on a thread, you see. This is what you have to remember. So fine a thread. Everyone — and particularly the young and untried — was terribly aware of that.

Jim, well . . . I had known him for a little bit. Not too

long. Later, he used to say to me 'Do you remember? Ay? Do you? Ay? That evening we met, Mill? That were an evening, ay?' Yes, I'd say – course I do, Jim. But I didn't. Had no recollection of it at all, and normally I'm very good about that sort of thing. Observant. Very retentive. But there. Speaks volumes, I daresay. Anyway – Jim, he was what my mother, had she still been alive at the time, would have dismissed as common. And she would have been right, of course. He still is. It seems unbelievable to me now, but I'm not at all sure that I noticed at the time. The way he spoke. His table manners, or the total lack of them. The unspeakable things he would do with his fingers. And, of course, the fact that we had no interests whatever in common. Or more to the point, the fact that Jim had and continues to have no interests at all that I've ever divined, beyond his ironmonger's shop. Beer and budgerigars, if you count such things. I am sure he has never read a book. I mean in his life. I really do mean that. He called me Mill. Never Milly, just Mill. Which I absolutely hated, and I told him so. Made not a blind bit of difference. And still he persists with it. But . . . he was quite good-looking in those days, I suppose, in a roughish sort of a way. I thought if we married, we'd at least have beautiful children. And he had this way of cocking an eyebrow that for some reason or another would always make me laugh. In the manner of a budgerigar, conceivably. It doesn't now, make me laugh. I'm not even sure if still he does it. Couldn't tell you.

Anyway, he was amusing enough. He must have been. We

4

had one night, just the one night together before he had to get back to barracks. He never did leave these shores though, Jim. Never was posted abroad. Something to do with his feet, he told me. Or his ankles. Something. But that night, though – that one single night . . . oh dear God, that I well remember. How could I ever forget it? It had only been a Registry Office wedding – over before it got started. Eunice was there – can't remember who else. Some rather awful friend of Jim's. Very few, though. And Jim, he had booked this room, little room, above a pub. The smell of stale ale rose up through the floor. The bed, it nearly filled the whole of the space – though still, I remember thinking, it did seem very narrow. For two people, I mean. It creaked, the metal frame, even when you so much as touched it. Jim was down the corridor 'attending to nature', as he called it. He still does say that: 'Won't be a jiffy – just got to attend to nature.' Oh dear Lord. Anyway – I sat on the corner of the bed . . . not sure there even was a chair . . . and I felt so cold. In every sense, really. There was a draught from the grimy window, there was linoleum on the floor – no hint even of a bedside mat. And within me, of course, I was utterly frozen. I had thought about this moment – women do, I think. And you wonder. Well you go through very many moods, I suppose: curiosity, dread . . . embarrassment, chiefly. A sort of excitement, just possibly. But not in my case. Here was simply something to be got through: we were good at that, during the war – getting through things. There was rarely any choice in the matter. So here, I thought, was just one more little thing to be endured: couldn't last for ever, could it? Everything comes to an end. And it wasn't going to kill me. Was it? He still smelt of beer when finally he came to me. He told me to be brave. 'Be brave,' he said to me, as he fooled around with his braces. And I had to laugh. What a buffoon, I thought: what an utterly perfect buffoon. Bravery was not required, which is just as well. I still am not quite sure that he even managed what I would say to be penetration. And then he was snoring, and hogging the eiderdown. Anyway, I thought, with not inconsiderable satisfaction: it is done. I have got over it. As I knew I would. For I am, as I say, a capable woman.

On the small table in that vile little room, I had set out all of my things. Coty powder and lipstick. A little bottle of scent that Eunice had given to me – Paris Soir. I still have the bottle, kept it all these years. There is a tiny very dark residue at its base, and the label now is yellowed. My brand-new nightgown – so terribly pretty. Pink, with little satinette bows at the neckline and a sort of ruching to the cuffs. Saved up coupons for, oh – it seemed like just ever. I didn't even get to putting it on. He just came at me, Jim. He still was wearing his boots. This was not, I remember thinking, how Clark Gable would generally go about things. Anyway – never mind: it was over.

Up until this time, I had been living with Eunice in a couple of rooms with kitchenette and shared bathroom above Amy's the hairdresser in England's Lane. She had begged me not to do it – marry Jim. But I didn't listen. I don't know why I didn't listen – hers was the only opinion I would have respected, and always I knew how very much she loved me. It's not as if I even wanted to, particularly. She didn't have a boyfriend, Eunice – and that was very surprising in itself, because she was always the better-looking of us, and by a good long way. Two years older than I, and quite the beauty. All the mashers would give her the eye – but it was always me she linked arms with, me who went with her to the Odeon, the Gaumont, the Empire. I only realised – how very stupid I was – I only realised after my ridiculous wedding that I would be living apart from her, that no longer would we be able to share our sisterly little rituals – and that instead I'd be with Jim, in the flat above his ironmonger's. In the very same street – that was the funny thing. Maybe that's how we came to meet . . . ? I honestly can't remember. Anyway, the ironmonger's was all boarded up for the duration, and he was away in the army, thank God. So I did go on living with Eunice. It was all as if nothing had happened. 'Yes,' she said, 'but when the war is finally over, it'll be different. I'll lose you. When Jim comes home.' I looked at her with love. I took her hand and touched her hair. 'Well,' I said. 'Maybe he won't.'

But he did, of course. Many didn't, so very many didn't, but Jim was only in Minehead, you see. And so he did. But before all that of course, there was the bombing. God knows we had already had to withstand so very much ceaseless bombardment. It is really so awfully hard – impossible, really

– to explain to anyone who has not themselves been through such a thing . . . but after a while, when you've had night after night of it, there comes upon you a sort of peace, an inner serenity. Sounds so mad – but I talked to Eunice about it, one of those terrible nights, and she agreed with me, Eunice, she agreed with what I said. At the very start of the war, back in '39, we all of us were quite terrified, of course. Even on the day that Chamberlain told us that now we were at war with Germany – beautiful morning, warm summer sunshine, it's not at all a day you could ever forget – within hours the blessed siren was setting up its wailing. Londoners, I think, they all thought that their number was up. Nothing happened, though – nothing happened for a good long time, and that's when people started laughing about it all. Calling it 'the phoney war' and saying that the blasted politicians had worried us half out of our wits, and all for nothing. I knew quite a lot of people – Marion, who sometimes worked in Mr Levy's greengrocer's, Eunice's friend from work, and another woman I used to meet most mornings on the train – who straight-away went to collect their children from wherever they had been evacuated to, and only just a few weeks earlier. But soon it started. There was nothing phoney about it then. And once it had begun, no one could ever see an end to it. Except when London would be engulfed in a firestorm, and all of us must die: it's only a matter of when.

I suppose, though, that it was the very regularity of the bombing that after a while made us see things quite differently. We had got through another night somehow – well hadn't we? So who's to say we can't do it again? There entered into our standard resilience a reckless sort of bravado: Come on Hitler! Do your worst! We can take it! All that sort of thing. Which I think, on reflection, is far from healthy, overall. When the Blitz took grip, Eunice and I, at the first great mournful rising moan of the siren, would pick up the battered old suitcase that we always kept packed with all our little essentials, and hurry to the cellar. It was, of course, quite awful down there. Well it was where we kept the coal, after all, and all sorts of broken chairs and other bits of rubbish you never have time to get rid of. We had put down a few blankets and there was a hurricane lamp and a paraffin heater that always made me feel so very queasy. And piles of old *Woman*s and *Woman's Own*s from the salon just above us. I may be painting a cosy little picture, but believe me, it was very far from that. We really hated sitting down there – and more often than not it would be for the whole of the night: only at dawn would you hear the all-clear. And so one evening, later than usual, when it all started up again, Eunice and I, we just looked at one another, and I think we must have had exactly the same thought at the identical moment. 'Blow it,' she said. 'I'm not going down. I just can't face going down there again. I'm staying here. If they get us, they get us.' I had just washed my hair, I remember, and was trying to dry it with a towel in front of just the one bar of the fire – that meter, I am telling you, it just ate up the shillings. And so we didn't. We simply stayed upstairs, trying not to wince at the whistle and then the crumping of bombs, some of them falling really rather close. At the summit of Primrose Hill, you see, which is awfully near, there were anti-aircraft guns, and always these were a target. And from that night on, we never went down to the cellar again. So you see what I mean: reckless, very, and goodness we were lucky, because Mr Lawrence, the newsagent, he took a direct hit, completely took the roof off, and he's only just three doors down. He wasn't hurt, though – just a few scratches miraculously, thank the Lord.

We were very different, really – my sister and me. Well we were in some ways, anyway – mentally generally in tune, more like twins in that respect – but she was always so much more . . . how can I say? Feminine, I suppose, for want of a better expression. Very dainty in the movement of her hands – always smelling sweetly of Lily of the Valley. She had a way with tweezers that made her eyebrows always just so. She even used eyeshadow, which I thought was very racy. Me, I could never really be bothered. I'm not saying I wasn't always very nicely turned out – my costumes were very becoming, and I could never abide a laddered nylon. But with Eunice, her grace and beauty seemed to come from within – all the cosmetics merely a perfectly natural extension of it, if that isn't contradictory. And when it became clear, early on in the war, that all we women were required to do our bit, I didn't at all mind being shunted off to Hayes every morning on the five o'clock train, there to inspect twenty-five-pound field guns, if you please!

And we were even sworn to secrecy as to the exact location. But Eunice, oh dear me no: she was having none of all that sort of very unladylike malarkey. She eventually secured a job in Marshall & Snelgrove for the duration, advising hard-put housewives on how best to eke out their precious clothing coupons – taught them how, in terms of dressmaking, making do and mending – to quite literally cut their coat according to their cloth. Often she'd bring home a few remnants and fashion them into the most extraordinary creations: flair, that's what she had. Me, I would just have consigned all those very unpromising scraps of material to the duster drawer.

And so we went along. I had more or less forgotten that I was a married woman: it didn't seem real to me. Often Eunice and I would go to a Lyons' Corner House or maybe a matinee at the pictures with a couple of lads – but they were very nice fellows: never a hint of monkey business, nothing of that sort. You could trust a boy in those days. Eunice, of course – she could have had any man she tipped her hat at, but she was never really very interested, much to all the soldiers' very visible disappointment. It would happen one day, she said. One day, Milly, when I'm not even looking, then the right man for me will come my way, and I'll know it – I'll just know it, the moment I look at him. And that, you know, is just exactly the way it happened.

David, his name was – a very nicely educated young man just two years her senior. He taught English and history at a boys' preparatory school in Fitzjohn's Avenue. I took to him immediately – and although the schooling that Eunice and I had had was nothing particularly special, nothing too out of the way, I have always upheld the supreme importance of a good education. Youngsters, they need to be led out of themselves – they need to be astounded by possibilities. I always did vow that if ever I were to be blessed with children (a thing I yearned for – and the only point of getting married in the first place, so far as I could see) then I would move heaven and earth to make sure that they got off to the very best start in life. David lived just a few streets away with a couple of bachelor pals, both of them teachers – and one of them, Thomas, made it perfectly clear that he regarded me as something rather out of the ordinary. We had picnics on Primrose Hill in the shadow of the guns, the four of us. Thomas would read us poems – Clare, Keats, that sort of thing. It was a happy time, in the midst of dangerous days. Then the war, it just came to an end. I don't know that we truly believed it ever would. And suddenly now it was VE Day – and oh that was a time, that was a time and no mistake. All the emotions you'd expect: the laughter, the happiness. And then the crying. Confusing – it confused me, and I suppose I could hardly be alone in that. It was then that I told Thomas that I was in fact married. It had not occurred to me to do so earlier, just as I am sure it had not so much as crossed his mind that I might be. He was very civil about it all, I must say. Such a very nice young man. Frightfully handsome. Still think of him sometimes. So anyway, that was the last I ever saw of

Thomas . . . and then I got a telegram from Jim. He was coming home the following Tuesday from Minehead. When he would reopen his ironmonger's in England's Lane and we both would live ('so very cosy', is the way he put it) in the flat above, as man and wife. I stared at the telegram for such a long time. It contained no fewer than three errors of spelling. When I saw him again, I realised I had not thought of him at all. He had very recently grown a sort of moustache, which was repellent. He wears it still. His demob suit, grey pepper-and-salt, was rather too small. He puts it on when people get married . . . he puts it on if someone should die.

David and Eunice were married in 1947, and one year later little Paul was born. David by this time was a deputy house-master at a small private school just outside of Reading, and they all lived in the dearest little cottage there. Eunice and I, we didn't see nearly so much of each other as I would have liked – but there: she had a husband, a home and a little boy to look after, so I quite understood. I never really had a chance to get at all close to little Paul, not at first – saw him only at Christmas and a few odd days over the summer holidays when I'd go down and stay with them. In a way that was maybe a good thing because by this time it had been made clear to us that Jim was not able for fatherhood. There had been tests. So that was that, really. No point crying about it. Many during the war had to overcome far worse things than that. So you just muck in and carry on, don't you? Nothing else for it.

David and Eunice had been out for a spin in the brand-new dark blue Humber that David was paying for on the hire purchase scheme. In her letters, Eunice told me how every Sunday morning he would be washing and then waxing it, buffing it up with a shammy to a bright and mirror shine. I was in the cottage taking care of Paul; Jim was back in London in the ironmonger's, doing whatever it is that Jim habitually does there; I never did ask him to accompany me, and he had never offered. I had not before been in the cottage all on my own, and I was admiring all of Eunice's little knick-knacks and the way she had made each of the rooms so very welcoming and gay. They had a gramophone and everything. Soon they were going to put a down payment on a refrigerator. I was nervous, I remember, about being in sole charge of an infant – because Paul, he could only have been eighteen months, not even eighteen months old in those days. But Eunice had told me not to worry – that once he was fed and changed, he was as good as gold. And he was, he really was – good as gold: no trouble at all.

When I answered the door, the policeman – he had tears in his eyes. He asked me to sit down, and he seemed himself upon the brink of collapse. In the days that followed, those terrible days and nights that followed, I was given a few more dribs and drabs of awful information. The car had veered off the road – some said to avoid an oncoming lorry, though other reports suggested defective steering on the Humber – and careered into the parapet of a bridge across a river. The car just hung there, literally in the balance, as the local police had tried to locate the necessary machinery and expertise to right and steady it so as to be able to cut the passengers from amid the twist of the thing. They both, dear souls, had sustained injuries: more than that I was not told. And then the balustrade just suddenly crumbled – buckled, gave way, the car pitching over the edge in the full sight of the despairing and helpless police and ambulancemen. After far too long, frogmen were sent into the water, but by that time, of course . . . but I pray, you know – I still do pray that Eunice, my dear dear sister Eunice, was no longer conscious as the car just teetered there. Her thoughts, otherwise, would have been far too terrible for me now to even contemplate. To know that Paul was to be left all alone . . . and that the child within her would now never be born; she had been hoping for a little girl, and she was going to call her Margaret. When the policeman had left the cottage . . . I decided to postpone the welter of tears, to close the door, if only for a short time, on all the racking agony to come . . . and I went to look at Paul, asleep in his cot. And although I neither touched him nor made even the slightest noise, he woke up immediately. He looked full at me, and smiled. It was Eunice's smile, and I had fallen in love with him.

Adoption in those days was a quick and relatively simple formality, particularly in the cases of relatives: so very many families had been recently rent asunder, one way or another. The reassembling of differing approximations had become an abiding process. And so Paul became my own. And now, well

. . . he is quite the young fellow. Eleven years old, not much away from eleven years old, and so very handsome and strong. The three of us still are living above the ironmonger's in England's Lane. Paul, when he was still an infant, he once looked up at me and called me Mummy. My heart was raw with the ring and then the tug of it. And Jim said 'No, Pauly – no. That ain't right, see? That's your Auntie Mill, that is. And I'm your Uncle Jim. See? That's how it is.' Another time, I had stooped to kiss his little head, and Jim, who had been eyeing me sidelong, he said this very slowly: 'You would, wouldn't you? I reckon you would. You'd give your life up for that little kid, wouldn't you Mill? Ay? Yeah, I reckon you would.' I just smiled, and turned away. That 'little kid', I was thinking . . . that 'little kid', Jim . . . he *is* my life. He is its beginning, its core, and he will carry me unto its end. The rest I merely tolerate. The rest I stoutly bear. I can do this. I can do this, yes. For I am a capable woman.

CHAPTER ONE

You Are Mad and I Am Right

My name is Paul. I'm eleven, nearly, and one day I'd really like to kill my Uncle Jim. I live with Auntie Milly who is lovely to me, and him, who smells of fags as well as some quite bad other things – don't know what, don't want to. He is a fool. Sometimes he asks me what I want to be, and although I don't say it, all I ever want to be is old. Older, anyway. Twenty-one would be really good, that would be the best . . . but that's ten whole years away, which means it'll be 1969, and that's just never ever going to come, is it? Stands to reason. But if I was twenty-one I'd have the key of the door and I'd be able to tell him, my stinking Uncle Jim – and I'll be so much taller than him, then – I'd be able to say to him: listen you, you are a fool and you'd better watch out, see, because now I'm going to kill you.

This is my favourite time of the day. It can sometimes be better than today is though, because today Uncle Jim, he's still here on the settee in the sitting room. Drinking his beer. Often he goes downstairs after our supper and sits on a giant pile of rags in the back of the ironmonger shop just talking to this budgie he's got there, called Cyril. Cyril's a lot unluckier than I am because whenever Uncle Jim starts talking to me and is maybe thinking I'm going to listen or something, I can just go up to my room and read or do a bit of prep, if I've got any. But Cyril, he can't. Just has to nibble on millet and blink at Uncle Jim, who sits there for hours, smoking fags, drinking beer, and going on and on and on.

We had Spam and sort of macaroni with tomato on, which I like, quite like, but not nearly so much as I like when Auntie Milly does chicken on Sundays. That's just the best food in the whole wide world – and you get crunchy potatoes and bread sauce and some sort of green muck which isn't actually very good, in fact it's really horrible, but Auntie Milly says if I eat it all up it will make me grow to be big and strong. After, we have jelly and Carnation, and it's best when the jelly is the red sort. In the week, though – like tonight – there's Jacob's Cream Crackers and Auntie Milly and Uncle Jim, they have Cheddar, but I get two portions of Dairylea because I really really like it. I'm sitting on the rug which Auntie Milly made in front of the gas fire which is blue, and keeps going pop-pop-pop. I've got my Matchbox toys and I'm making a road for them out of cardboard. Auntie Milly's knitting. She knits all the time – V-necks for me and Uncle Jim and also things like cushion covers and a tea cosy. She was humming a tune, but she's stopped now. She's looking at Uncle Jim. Because she can see – and I can see it too – that he's now going to open his great fat stupid mouth.

'Nice bit of Cheddar. You ever eaten human cheese, have you? I daresay not.'

Auntie Milly, she just looked at him, the way she always does. Like he's dead, or something. He went on, my Uncle Jim, like I knew he would. Always does. Pointing a finger at her now.

'They do make it, you know. Oh God yes. I ain't saying it's a common thing, because it ain't. Not by a long chalk. It's very out of the way. Very out of the way. Whole point. Why I'm asking, see? But oh yeah – they make it all right. No doubt on that score. Mongolia, round there, could very well be. I had it in Kilburn. Odd I never mentioned it before. Mind you – they only told me after, the devils. Now listen to me, Pauly – you might learn something. You want to know how they go about it? How it's, like – sort of done, do you? The whole great gubbins?'

Auntie Milly glanced across at me, and closed her eyes quickly. That was one of her warnings. A reminder to her dim and stinky husband that there's a young boy in the room. That whatever horrible thing he was about to say next, I was far too young to be hearing it. But I never feel that. Too young for anything. It's not what I feel inside. The only thing I really want to be now is old. No one else – nobody at school, anyway – wants this, but I do. And people say it's

19

not, um – don't know what they say, can't remember the word. But it means I shouldn't think it. Well so what? I do. Eleven's no good. It's no good to be eleven years old, no good at all. There's no point to it. Twenty-one is what I want. If I was old, older, then I could turn round and tell people what to do. Not in a bossy way, I don't mean – but just to explain to them. How stupid they are. Because they maybe don't know. How everything they do, they do it wrong. Like my idiotic Uncle Jim. His eyes, when he's going on like this, they're always so wide open. It's like he's egging you on into believing him. It is, you know – it really is like he expects you to listen.

'Whassamatter? What's wrong with you now, Mill? Boy you're worried about, is it? Well don't. Pauly – he can look after himself. Can't you, Pauly? Quite the young man about town now, aren't you Pauly? Hey? Yeh. That's right. Course you bloody are.'

'*Jim . . . !*'

'Sorry. Sorry sorry sorry. Bad word. Forget you heard that – hey Pauly? Pretend I never said it. And don't go telling on me down that la-di-da school of yours, Gawd's sake. Never hear the end of it. Now where was I? What was I on about?'

'I think you've had quite enough beer now, Jim. It's bedtime,' Auntie Milly said – and I knew she was going to. She'd put down her knitting. 'I'm tired. And I'm sure Paul is too. Aren't you, Paul? Early start in the morning, yes? I'm going up, anyway. Can hardly keep my eyes open. And there's nothing la-di-da about it. Just happens to be a very good school, that's all. A proper school is what it is.'

She wasn't tired. Not really. I knew when she was tired. It was just that she was trying to shut him up. For my sake.

'Weren't like my school, I can tell you that much for free. He went to my old school, he wouldn't hardly know what hit him. It was Charlie, the beggar, what give it me. That cheese. I've remembered now what I was . . . yeh. And it was only after, he tells me. Else I don't reckon I would've. Mind you – I'm not saying it weren't tasty. Because it were. Not a flavour you forget in a hurry. Weren't, like – mouldy nor nothing. What they do is – they get together all of these women, right? And then they're—'

'God's *sake*, Jim . . . !'

Auntie Milly, now – she's got me by the shoulders and up on to my feet. I was waiting for this. She knows he won't stop. Not after the beer. The only way – poor Auntie Milly – is to quickly get me out of the room. Leave him to it. And he'll open up another bottle of Bass. Put another Senior Service between his hard and orange fingers. One night, his fag caught the edge of the evening paper: lucky I was around to see to it – got it down on the floor and stamped it out. He didn't even know what he'd done. Offered me a beer. I think he must have thought he was still in the pub with Charlie, his horrible friend. He smells of sweat and old wet tweed and Christmas whisky and his moustache is the colour of the cat we used to have before he choked to death on a wishbone, and it's got all bits in it, usually. He's disgusting. Eric, the cat was called. I used to feed him, but I don't know why. He'd look at me, and then just walk away. Auntie Milly, she loved him a lot. Always had him on her lap. Talking to him like he was a person. Let him play about with her ball of wool. But I didn't. Love him. How could you? He was only a cat. A woman – a proper grown-up woman, that's the only thing worth loving. When you're married and you've got a big bed and everything. I'm trying hard to think of that now. Auntie Milly, she's just turned off my light (still makes me say my prayers out loud – God bless my Mummy and my Daddy who residest with Thou and Auntie Milly and Uncle Jim and please God make me a good boy). It's freezing in here, as per usual, but I'm really trying to think of the woman I'm one day going to marry. She'll be very beautiful, warm and kind to me. Like Auntie Milly says my mother was. Before she was killed. Don't know. Can't remember. But I expect it's true. I cut out a photo of Elizabeth Taylor who is a film actress but I've never actually seen her in a film from the *Evening News* and I've put it in my missal at the back with all the holy pictures, which I know is a sin. But she is very beautiful. And I'm trying to concentrate hard on her now, and how she would feel to me if I was ever to touch her. But all I can think of is cheese.

He knows nothing, Uncle Jim, and he always goes on as if he understands the lot. Some subjects I do at school he's never even heard of. He is an ignorant pig. If I say anything – and it's not even him I'm talking to – then it's wrong. Got to be.

All wrong. If I was twenty-one, I'd point my finger dead at him, like he does with Auntie Milly, and I'd say to him – Listen, ignorant pig: you are *mad*, and I am *right*. Got it? And then I'd biff him on the nose, just before I killed him.

Sleepy, now. And awfully cold. I'd really like it if Elizabeth Taylor was here – to be beautiful and warm, and kind to me. But all I can think of is cheese. And how it can be human.

I always wake up just a second before Auntie Milly turns the squeaky handle on my door and comes in to tell me that it's another lovely day, even if it's foggy or the rain's all streaming down the window – and she smells of what I think she says is Lilian Valley, which I like very much. Then she draws open the curtains and I pretend to sort of hide under the eiderdown and go all squinty when the light comes in, but it really doesn't bother me, the light or anything. I only don't want to get up when it's freezing like it is now because there's a rug just by my bed which is a half circle and Auntie Milly made that one too in front of the fire every single evening last winter with a great big hook and different coloured wool from a kit and there's a thatched cottage on it with flowers and this smoke coming out of the chimney – but otherwise it's all brown lino that's meant to look like wood but where it's cracked and coming up in the corners you can see it isn't really. So I get my slippers on really fast, but the bathroom's even worse. It always smells of Palmolive shaving soap when I go in there because of stupid Uncle Jim and there are sticky little bristles in the sink. He never shaves above his mouth though, so there's always this lump of fuzz there that looks and smells like hamster. I have to brush my teeth with a powder which is Gibbs but it's only a powder when we get a new tin because when you wet it it goes all sort of crumbly.

Auntie Milly lays out my uniform on my chair the night before. My school is a good school, a proper school, is what she keeps on telling me, but I can't see anything very special about it: it's just a school. Uncle Jim goes on about what it costs him and I say well I don't mind if I don't go and then you can save the money and spend it all on disgusting beer and disgusting fags you disgusting and ignorant pig, except I don't really say that. I don't like my uniform because it's got short trousers, and apart from looking stupid you get really freezing knees. They're very thick and they look like Spam, only grey. There are stockings which itch and you have to keep the little green tabs on the garters showing when you fold them over. The blazer's okay, though – I quite like the blazer because of the eagle on the badge and it's got heaps of pockets for your diary and biros and a Matchbox and sweets which you're not supposed to have because they're against the rules and I always take my newest free gift from the cereal packet with me as well as some others for swaps. It's Dogs of the World at the moment (I don't think I'll ever get the Dobermann Pinscher) and they're from Rice Krispies which I don't much like, or not as much as Frosted Flakes anyway which Tony the Tiger says are grrrreat, but Auntie Milly says they're bad for my teeth.

Breakfast is nice because it's just Auntie Milly and me and we have tea and cereal and boiled egg with soldiers because Uncle Jim is already in the shop downstairs which I don't know why he always opens so early when there's nobody about. It's called J. Stammer, the shop, because that's his name. It's not my name, it's his name. I'm Paul Thimbleby, because that's what my Mummy and Daddy were called. We live in this street called England's Lane and there's two rows of shops opposite each other and houses on the top. Our shop is the ironmonger and it's really dark and stinks of Pink Paraffin and varnish and dead animals or something. All these wonky drawers with nails and hooks and washers and hinges and stuff. Brooms and bins and mousetraps and candles. My friend Anthony's father is six doors up and he's got Miller's the sweet-shop, which is just typical. Sometimes I get a chew or a flying saucer for nothing, but Anthony, he just gets everything. If only we owned the sweetshop I'd never go up to my room at all – I'd just live all the time in the sweetshop and my tea would be Toffee Cups and Fry's 5 Centre and Picnics and maybe even the really expensive chocolates in the glass counter and piled up in these plates with a doily on. I get a quarter of sherbet lemons every Monday and they're supposed to last a whole week which is impossible. And the last one is never good anyway because you have to pick the bits of paper bag off it but you never get them all.

Another great shop is at the other end of the Lane and called Moore's but the people who own it are called Jenkins so they must have bought it from the Moores and never changed the name which is painted in big white loopy letters on shiny black I think it's glass. This is a stationer's which is run by an old lady called Miss Jenkins and an even older lady still called Mrs Jenkins, and they haven't got any children because although related they obviously aren't married. Auntie Milly says they're very sweet. Anyway, as well as all the paper and envelopes and birthday cards and things they've got Platignum biros in eight different colours and I've got five of them already and I can't wait to get the other three because then I'll have the set. I still need light green and orange and pink. Anthony says that the pink one is pathetic and I know what he means but I've still got to get it because otherwise I won't have the set. The yellow one you can hardly see when you write with it, but the brown one's lovely – it's really narrow and doesn't smudge, or anything. I don't know anyone else who's got the brown one. They're one-and-six each though, and Bics are only a shilling but Bics you can only get in four colours and masters have them so they're not nearly so good. You can't use the Platignums for proper writing at school though because it's against the rules. Old Colly, who is the Latin master, would go all purple and have a fit because he's stupid. You have to use your Osmiroid except for drawing margins which you've got to do in pencil. Anthony's got a Parker 51 in a box with silk in it. At school they glug out permanent blue-black Quink into the inkwells in the desks which are always clogged up with blotch and bits of bungee.

And they've also got Matchbox Toys in Moore's, which I really really like. If I was rich like the Queen I'd get every single Matchbox Toy in the whole wide world – two of each so that one could be all brand-new in the box, and then the others I could play with. I've got some really good ones – the dark-green Jaguar racing car is best and I've got a maroon and cream Austin A40 with a hook at the back which you attach this pale blue caravan on to. And a United Dairies milk float – and there's a real United Dairies in England's Lane nearly opposite us and you see them outside with the horses and everything and on our way to school Auntie Milly always gives them sugar lumps and apples sometimes and she tries to get me to but their teeth are a bit big and disgusting. Not so good Matchboxes are things like the cement mixer which my Uncle Jim brought back for me one time, which is just typical. He was drunk, I could tell. He stank even worse than usual and was staggering about the place. Broke a teacup which Auntie Milly said was one of her very best. He only ever buys me something when he's drunk, but it's never anything I want. That time he put the wireless on and was waving his arms around and he said Come on, Mill – let's you and me have a little bit of a dance, will we? What you say? She said to him not to be so stupid, which I really really liked and I wished I could say it too. He got hold of her anyway and she tried to laugh because of me, I think, and he dragged her about the room, barging into the sideboard and Auntie Milly getting her legs kicked to pieces. She hated the whole thing, I could tell. If I was twenty-one I could've got him by the scruff of the neck and chucked him down the stairs and said Let that be a lesson to you my man and dusted off my hands like I've seen at the pictures. But when you're eleven you've just got to sit there in your stupid short trousers and itchy stockings and pretend you don't mind that he's hurting Auntie Milly.

There's loads of other shops too. There's Barton's the butcher (he's really big, Mr Barton — his hands are huge and as red as all the meat he chops up with an axe thing. He's got a daughter called Amanda who's my age and I really like a lot and she says he puts Brylcreem on his eyebrows and moustache. And his hair as well, of course). She's very pretty, Amanda. Much more than all the other girls who live around here. Sometimes she has plaits with bows, but not always. And there's Dent's the fishmonger. Very pongy in there (I don't like fish except for yummy fish fingers made by Captain Birdseye) and Mrs Dent, Auntie Milly says, is a martyr to her bunions, which I don't know what it means, but that's why you never see her smiling. And a bread and cake shop called Lindy's and the woman in there who isn't called Lindy but she is called Sally is so very fat she can hardly move because she's always eating her own eclairs. And Lawrence's the newsagent where I get my *Beano* (Bash Street Kids is my favourite — wish I could go to school with them) and *Dandy* (Desperate Dan is great, miles better than Korky the Cat which isn't much good because cats aren't really like that) and sometimes if Auntie Milly's in a really good mood and feeling a bit what she says is flush, then the *Beezer* and *Topper* as well. She gets *Woman* and *Woman's Own* and the *Radio Times*. Uncle Jim gets the *Evening News* every day. But he doesn't actually read it or anything. He just goes over things like the racing results and the football pools and usually he says all bad words when he does it. And there's what is called Bona Delicatessen which I'm not quite sure how you spell it and they've got foreign food in there which must be quite delicate, but Uncle Jim says it's all muck. They've got open barrels of things which do look quite bad – and there's a man and a woman in there who wear white coats like in *Emergency Ward 10* who must be called Mr and Mrs Bona I suppose, but I don't really know for sure. Auntie Milly says they're Swiss and Uncle Jim says they're chancing it. I go in because they've got Pez, which Anthony's father's shop doesn't sell for some reason, and I really like the dispensers because they click open like a cigarette lighter and I've got a yellow-and-black one and I want a red-and-white one next. The little sweets come in tiny packets and they're twopence each which Auntie Milly says is a scandal and I like orange but my favourite one is wild cherry. Uncle Jim hasn't even got a cigarette lighter, of course – not even a cheap one. He uses Swan Vestas, and sometimes he scrapes them on the underneath of the dining table after his tea to light up a fag and Auntie Milly says You're not in the Washington now, Jim. Which is the pub on the corner where he goes all the time, and it's across the road from Barclays Bank. It would be really great to be Mr Barclay with a shop full of money, but I've never seen him because I think he might be one of those millionaire madmen who never cut their fingernails.

There's also a greengrocer called M. Levy who's missing the little finger of one hand and the thumb on the other which he goes and scares people with. I love to go there because of all the smells and heaps of fruit in coloured tissue and imitation grass. There's another shop called Marion's which sells all pink stuff for ladies like Auntie Milly's corsets and stockings which she keeps behind a cushion on the settee, but I don't know why. I sometimes go in there with her, but you do always feel a bit funny. What else is there . . . ? Oh yes – there's Amy's the hairdresser but that's just the name of the shop because the main lady who works there is called Gwendoline. I know that because she does Auntie Milly's perm which takes about a million years and Auntie Milly keeps it all yellow with this stuff called I think she says prockside which she puts on with an old toothbrush with cotton wool wrapped around the handle and she says don't come near when she's doing it, and it makes her cry. Gwendoline also gives me haircuts – she's not really supposed to because it's a hairdresser for ladies but Auntie Milly won't send me to the barber that Uncle Jim goes to because she says she doesn't want them using the clippers on the back of my neck, I don't know why. Maybe because the back of Uncle Jim's neck looks just like Fray Bentos corned beef. Which we get every Tuesday at school and I hate it. It's the second-worst lunch after Thursday cheese pie. Best is mincemeat on Fridays and chocolate splosh for afters.

Then of course there's the wood shop, wood yard, sort of carpenter's place which is quite new and that's the one that's run by the negroes, who I've only ever looked at but not talked to. I'd never seen one before because usually they're in Africa. One of them smiles a lot, but he still looks a bit frightening but I wouldn't say that or anything because it's rude. I can't believe they're really that colour all the time. It's so odd. Uncle Jim says they swing in trees and don't belong and they've all got filthy habits, which is very funny coming from Uncle Jim because everything about him is a filthy habit. And anyway he thinks the same things about pop singers, and especially Cliff Richard who he says is a cosh boy. Auntie Milly says about the negroes, who she calls coloured – like with my brown Platignum, except you'd need zillions of them – that she's sure they're very nice people, just different, that's all.

Another shop is Curios, which I'm not sure what it means – maybe it's the name of the man with a beard who sits in the window on a rocking chair and always seems to be doing a crossword and smoking a big curvy pipe with a funny little lid on it. Anyway it's all full of old furniture and vases and clocks and jumble sale things which Uncle Jim says just after the War everyone was chucking out or burning for firewood and now they're trying to flog it, what a hope. Everything he says is about Before the War, During the War or After the War. I once said to him I'm glad you remember it's over then, and he said I didn't know I was born. Another very stupid thing to say because obviously I do.

There's other shops too, and we know all the owners because everyone's been here since the Battle of Hastings 1066. Not the darkies, though. Nobody seems to know them. Uncle Jim, that's what he calls them: darkies. Also sambos and wogs. I don't know why he talks about them so much if he doesn't even like them. But all the other people we do know – and at Christmas everyone gets together in someone's sitting room or one of the shops (they take it in turns) and Victoria Wine – oh yes, that's another one: Victoria Wine on the corner opposite Allchin's the chemist which I also forgot – she always gives things like sherry and cherry brandy and gin and whisky. I've never met Victoria Wine though. She's maybe shy, like Auntie Milly says my mother was before she was killed. Don't know. Can't remember. And I always get Britvic pineapple juice which is my absolute favourite drink in the whole wide world, not counting Tizer and Lucozade when you're not well and in bed. Which can be good if it's only a cold or something, except for Beecham's Powders and thermometers, but not if it's mumps which I had last year and it hurts quite a lot and you don't even want any Lucozade. Chicken pox was worst though because you're not allowed to scratch yourself and Auntie Milly put this I think it's called calomine lotion on my face which goes all hard and feels like you can't move it and then when it's gone all scabby you can't pick them off because if you do you'll be scarred for life like a leper in the jungle and no one will ever want to marry you. The decent bit is that you don't have to go to school, but when I had mumps I got prep which Anthony had to bring over which I really really hated. I got Algebra, and I'm no good at that because I don't understand why if you've got all these numbers you go and use letters instead and Dismal Dawkins my maths master just goes mad and says 'I – I – I – Cor*wumph*' just like Mr Wilkins in the Jennings books which are the best books in the world and then he says If I've told you once I've told you a thousand times. Didn't say x and y times though, did he? No he didn't, QED.

This is what I mean about grown-ups, you see. I look at them, and I see some very strange things. They don't understand anything, you see. Most of what they say is just total rubbish, actually – that's what me and my friends think. I hate them. Particularly masters.

I'd just like to line them up, the grown-ups, and say to them Look – you are *mad* and I am *right*. Got it? And then I'd biff them all on the nose. Except for Auntie Milly. She's the only one. I can talk to my Auntie Milly. She's the only one who ever makes any sense. And I really do think that she loves me.

CHAPTER TWO

It's Truly Very Clean

They don't like it, of a morning – Mill and the boy. They don't take to it at all if ever I'm still just hanging about up there in the kitchen – after she done with rousing the lad, and me still sat there, having my tea and a slice. Oh no – they don't like that, not one iota. And don't they make you know it. Feel like I got something catching. Well – don't bother me. Don't touch me a bit. I'm best off down here in the back of my shop, way I see it – have a little natter with Cyril here, while he nibbling away at his millet, and me with my Thermos of Tetley's and a nice heel of Hovis with a real good slick of blackberry jelly on the top of it. Then I lights up a fag. And Cyril – he don't come the high and mighty with me, Cyril don't. Not like them two upstairs. The king and queen of wossname. He'll peck at my finger, Cyril will. I run the back of my thumbnail across the bars, coo at him a bit, and he get all perky, like – then I holds out a little bit of seed for him: come on, I says to him, I won't hurt you, will I? I loves ya, I does . . . and he'll be pecking away like billy-o, I can tell you – happy as Larry, he is. Mill, she says to me it's cruel, she says, cooping up a budgie down here with all the fumes, and all. *Fumes?* I goes to her. Dunno what you talking about. Fumes? What fumes? I don't smell no fumes. And I don't, neither – I'm being straight with her when I says it. I been down in this shop for so bleeding long, I don't smell nothing no more. Paraffin. Creosote. Bleach. Rat poison. Don't smell none of it. What I do do, though, is I senses things. Like if Cyril's poorly. Or like, see, I got this little bell way up the top of the door there. Jangly bugger it is – cracked some years back, blessed if I know how, no one never touched it. And yeh – it ain't melodic. Anyway – idea is, customer open the door, I'm out the back and I hears the bell and comes running. Only it ain't like that, on account of for years now – more bleeding years than I want to know about – I senses it before. Just before some cove's barging in here, right? I senses he's about to. Ain't never wrong. Why I says to Cyril: half a mo, son, back in a jiffy – some bod's about to jangle the bell. And he do, this bod, in he come, just like I always know he's going to. Turns out this time it's Barton, the butcher three doors down. Expect he'll be wanting the usual. Christ only knows what he do with the buggers. Every other week he's in for more of the bleeding things. Not complaining – charging him twice what I got to pay for them, ain't I? I tell you, though – I can't be

35

doing with him, God's honest truth. He ain't like no butcher I ever knowed. Always got a three-piece suit on him, rain or shine. Stiff bleeding collar and all, don't know how he stick it. Sunday best, and all he is is a bleeding butcher. Hair as shiny as a gramophone record – and that tache he got on him, looks like a photo in the bloody barber's. Now Mill, she reckon the sun shine out of his wossname – but then of course she would do that, wouldn't she, my Milly? Had an education, Jonny Barton has – plain as day to anyone with half an ear. And in Mill's book, well – puts him up there with royalty, an education do. Another way of getting at me too, course. Giving me a dig. Reminding me how bloody low I am. Reminding me she married into a bloody farm-yard. Goes without saying, all that. As if I need reminding. Most of the reason I act like I does – come out with all the muck I does. Feel I owes it her, somehow. Make her feel better about herself. Cos she a real good sort, Mill is. Better than me? I should bloody say so. Mill's in another class. I don't know I does it right by her, though. Whether it's like the right thing to be doing. But I can't go changing it now, can I? After all this time. Wouldn't hardly know how to begin. Yeh so I reckon she just stuck with me the piggish way I is, poor cow. Don't hear no complaints from her about the money what I'm taking, though, do I? Hey? No – don't hear no complaints about that. Enough to put food on the table, buy for Milly any little knick-knack, and send young Pauly to that bleeding school up the road. That bleeding la-di-da school of his, where they teaches him how to be a bloody little girl. All he's wanting is a ribbon in his hair. Yeh. And I don't know why I does – the school, I mean. Well – do really. It's Mill, ain't it? All she wants. And of course it's on account of we never had no kids of our own – think I don't know that? Think she never told me? Think my nose ain't been ground right into it? Well . . . weren't for the want of trying. Said I were sorry, didn't I? Thousand bleeding times. But she ain't never like forgiven me for, I dunno . . . all that sort of side of things. Like I wanted it, or something. Like I had a say in it. I could've done something, I would've, wouldn't I? What's a bloke to do, hey? It's hard, that is – dead hard. Women, they don't understand. And then when her sister Eunice pass on, well . . . Pauly, not much more than a baby, he weren't, not back then he weren't. Yeh so he suddenly come into her life and, well – he take it over, don't he? Lock, stock and wossname. I mean, she wanted it to be took over, I ain't saying she didn't. Took over mine and all, whether I liked it or not. Never said nothing. Can't, can you? And now me, she just don't see me no more. She don't look at me, she can help it. She don't listen. Why I got to shout. Why I got to get plastered. And so now, me, muggins, I just got to lump it, ain't I? Yeh well. But still it's her I does it all for. Right or wrong. Well you got to, ain't you really? And they're real good mates, the two of them now. Mill and the boy. Two peas in a . . . yeh. Snug as a bug in a wossname, sort of style, them two is. But

37

me . . . well me, I'm just out of it. Oh well. Attend to this bloody butcher bloke now then, will I?

'Good morning, Jim. How goes it? You're very well off in here, I do assure you, because it isn't a good morning at all, as it happens. The weather is exceedingly unkind.'

'Yeh? I ain't been out. Cold, is it?'

'Raw, Jim: raw. Soon there'll be rain, or worse, mark my words.'

'Don't never do nothing else, do it? Always bleeding raining . . .'

'Take heart, dear man – spring is just around the corner. Buckets, Jim – that's what I'm here for, as is my custom. I think I might take three upon this occasion, if you can run to it.'

'You're one of the few what still have the galvanised off of me. Women round here, they can't get enough of all the plastic doings. Even your dustpan and brush. It's all plastic now.'

'No use for my needs. Sturdy and durable, that's what I'm after.'

'Yeh but what I'm saying is it's the way of the world.'

So I'll rattle out a couple of metal buckets from the stack just by the door, here – and then I'll clank me up another for this stuck-up bleeding bastard butcher. Normally I got them hanging up on hooks outside, along with them bales of twine, a couple of washboards, me brooms, the same old tin bath and all the clothes pegs. But this Barton bugger, he so bleeding early I ain't even had a chance to get them out there. Ain't even finished me tea. Ain't yet had a proper word with Cyril. Like I says to the man, I ain't been out. And why my Pauly likes to play about with that daughter of his – well I'll never understand it. That Amanda. She's as bleeding stuck-up as her dad. But then Pauly, he's only the bleeding same. Well there's my answer, I suppose. Two stuck-up little girls together. Mill's all for it, but then she would be. It's only me – I'm the only pig about, up to his neck in shite.

'Good. So how much do I owe you? Don't suppose you *can* open up a window in here, can you really . . . ? Except for conceivably the fanlight, there. Mean one hell of a draught, I suppose . . . but still it might clear a bit of the . . . it's the paraffin largely, I think. Not sure I could tolerate it, for my part. Fiona, she's rather wanting one of those, um . . . what are they called, in fact, those heaters . . . Aladdin, is it . . . ? For the upper back room.'

'Aladdin, yeh. Nice line. Move a few of them, I does.'

'Mm. But I won't have it. I'm quite firm with her on that score. Rather freeze, quite frankly. Tend to render me drowsy, you know. Somewhat queasy. You're never queasy, then? No? Doesn't affect you?'

Jim just shrugged.

'I'd be the same in your place, I daresay. What with the blood. Horses for courses, ain't it really? Now then, so what are we now . . . three at eight-and-eleven . . . that'll be twenty-six-and-nine then sir, if you'll be so good. Call it twenty-six bob, hey?'

'Kind of you, Jim – thank you. But blood, you know – there's no smell to blood. It's more of a . . . chilling purity that rather sort of surrounds you. Is the best way I can put it. It's truly very . . . *clean*. Really it is.'

Jim nodded.

'If you say so. And four shillings in change, I thank you.'

'Right-o – extremely grateful. Well – back out into the elements, I suppose. Thank God I'm nearby. Anyway, Jim – let you get on. There's always so terribly much to see to, isn't there? First thing. I never understand quite why this should be so, but nevertheless – it's always the way.'

And nor do I understand, thought Jonathan Barton, clanging shut the shop door behind him and swinging from their handles the three new silver buckets as he hurried in a flurry of sleet to his butcher's shop just three doors along . . . quite why I ever bother frittering even the merest time of day with that thoroughly loathsome and boorish creature – crouched like an animal, uncouth and uncombed, in his dark and fetid lair. He never seems to manage to shave the whole of his face – it's as if he does it in the night, or something. There's often even the hard and rind-like traces of lather in the creases of his jowls. Sometimes a dab of lavatory paper, I can hardly believe it, adhering to a cut. And if one presumes to affect a moustache, well surely then one is duty bound, in the name of simple manners, to nurture, trim and shape it, no? Such a thing requires a degree of attention, as I can attest with a degree of authority. Below this oik's rudimentary nose, however, there lurks but a patch of scrubland, a treacherous fen of which he stays well clear. What we have here is not so much a moustache, as a flagrant oversight. Never wears a tie. Christ, he never wears a collar. Shows a lack of respect, I think. A distinct and blatant lack of respect for your customer. And of course I understand why he has to wear that tobacco-coloured work coat, but God Almighty it's always so utterly filthy! Doubt he's changed it in all the years I've been here. And biro markings all down the pocket. But then amid all that seemingly charred and umbrous wooden shelving, the dust and dim lighting, the rotting chalked-upon boxes, skimmed with grime and retching their mystifying contents . . . that man has surely found his place. *Le vrai milieu.* And the gut-crawling, head-spinning stench in there, it's amazing he isn't dead. Breathing it down, day in day out. I think one of the reasons, you know, I do still go in there is in order to demonstrate — to deliver unto me a salutary reminder — that things really could be much blacker. Blacker even than being reduced to no more than a common butcher, in so humdrum and faceless a street as this. That, and for the buckets, of course. Which I now shall fill with the blood of an illicitly murdered pig. It takes more than three, naturally, but sometimes the chum who comes to collect them in that rusted and derelict lorry of his — sometimes he remembers to return all the old ones (other times not, of course – which is why I keep having to line the foul Stammer's pockets by buying yet more of the things). And then in the fullness of time, said chum returns in said rusted and derelict lorry with great glistening truncheons of black pudding which I sell in the shop at a suitably indecent profit. There is still a surprisingly thriving market for it. Among the nostalgics, not to say the poor. The Irish, of course, to boil with their damned potatoes. As well as, rather intriguingly, our recent influx of coloureds over yonder in the timber yard. The niggers in the woodpile. Maybe reminds them of pot-roasted missionary, who is to say? Also avid buyers, of course, are those endless threadbare tribes of widowed old biddies who ask me for bones for their dog. They have no dog: the bones they scrape and mix what they can glean with the fatty detritus and scraps of gullet and genital which I also wrap up tidily and drop with a wink into their wicker baskets, so tight clenched in the crook of their arms. For their cat. Another creature they do not possess. And so the pig, he may not be said to have died in vain – while the chops and fillet, of course, are very much sought after by the better off around here (and I am rather partial myself – Fiona, she has a way of broiling them, you know, that seems to bring out all of the flavour). I have another good chum – a doctor who must now be so very careful, helping young ladies in the manner he is forced to, following on as I suppose an inevitability from that unfortunate run-in with the Medical Council. He must now be so very careful, you see. He remains a very good fellow, though – and so often useful to me. In this instance, he anaesthetises the pig – which is delivered to me under dead of night by yet one more good fellow, who has a smallholding in Middlesex. The pig knows no pain, then, when I slit its throat – such bloody silence denying the motley of my generally very vulgar neighbours the sanctimonious delight of summoning the constabulary, as surely they would do if the squealing of a pig mid-slaughter were ever to alert them to just this one single and pretty paltry element of all it is that I get up to.

I enjoy . . . yes, enjoy, I do enjoy it: I suppose I ought to be honest about this thing. I enjoy the order of the shop, during the hazy quiet and just before the hurly-burly of the day. The fresh drifts of white sawdust which I acquire from the blackies, softly surrounding my toecaps. The little mahogany stall in the corner, its big brass till, and next to it, those tight little coloured and stiff paper bags of coppers, threepenny bits and silver, weighed by the bank and slid across the counter, like so much chunky loot. The quarter carcasses hoisted up on to hooks by Billy, the boy here. Though never will I have them outside – oh dear me no. What? A row of unskinned rabbit? Half-plucked poultry, hanging by the neck? Irredeemably low, in my opinion. Not a cornucopia, not munificence this, as is the common perception, but merely a trite and showy display. In the manner of an ironmonger. My knives too, they give me pleasure, newly honed and laid out in order of diminishing size. The axe, the cleaver, and all of the saws. The vast and scrubbed wooden block, concave and cross-hatched with so much bladework and thudding, where I dismember and gut. And then the white marble slab, for more delicate work. A woman . . . I have always rather thought I should like to take a woman, brutishly, across that slab. When still it runs with blood, right into the gullies. And she, an apple-cheeked stranger, in a fresh spring frock. It is all about the pink, and wetness – a splay of thighs, but of course. Here is an English daydream – quite distinct from the deep dark velvet of the affair of my life, which still is to come. My love will be a black-eyed and voluptuous Italian . . . conceivably a contessa. We will squirrel ourselves away upon a houseboat – moored in Chelsea, but with the bobbing potential of anywhere at all in the whole wide world. And there we shall reinvent fire. Yes. Fire, though . . . what a word. Will it be kindled this evening, I wonder, when the full-throated intention is to insinuate myself upon this newest and I don't for one moment imagine unsuspecting docile, sweet and powdered fragrant woman of my choosing? Well we shall see. For my part I shall of course be assiduous in applying the spark to the tinder, as is the way, and so I think I can feel safe in presuming upon at the very minimum an eventual wisp of smoke, oh yes that – the coaxing of embers, and so to a degree of warming, surely? But still this will be as nothing, for of course what I actually at root very earnestly require is to find myself once more toppled over into love. It is, like the throb of blood, most necessary to me: I crave again that glamorous agony.

Dear God, though . . . reveries aside: how, actually, has it all come to this? How am I fallen? How can these two fine hands of mine be as red and raw as the meat I cleave? And seemingly growing – ever longer and broader, day by day: a veritable phenomenon, I swear it. How can it be that Fiona, my beautiful if distant, well-born and sensitive helpmeet, now resides above a butcher's shop along with our dearest and blameless daughter, Amanda? And why, further, must that child – given the spread of this mighty and eternal city – be so gallingly friendly with that bloody Paul child, the vacuous and chinless little *Stammer* boy . . . ? Or nephew, as I gather he is. We earnestly trust on the wife's side, poor long-suffering woman that she so evidently is, and has been now for how long . . . ? Maybe then the brat has none of that idiot Stammer's genes and inclinations. Yes . . . I ask myself these things constantly – but of course I do know. The answer why. Why we all of us are come to this. For here is the result of my sin, and I am in the midst of enacting an optimistic evasion. An elaborate deflection in the simple and pious hope that the past will leave me alone – that the swine who hounds me might get sick of the scent, lose it even, go off chasing someone else entirely. All it ever can be is hope, though – and one that is almost certainly forlorn. But for now, at least, still my luck is holding.

I did mean it, though — I really meant what I said about the blood. I do always find that there is about it this chilling purity that rather sort of surrounds me. Is the best way I can put it. It's truly very . . . *clean*. Really it is.

CHAPTER THREE

That's the Way it Goes

Stanley Miller the sweetshop owner was not looking forward to today – no sir I am not, he would easily confide in you: not at all looking forward to today, not at all, not one little bit. It's hardly as if, though, something very bad is slated to happen to me: no terrible storm is known to be breaking. It's only just the thought that it might do, that's all. Just the thought of it, you see . . . more than enough to lay me down low. An impending whatever they call that thing – cloud, if you like. Raincloud, sort of style. No – it's more than that, more than even the blackest raincloud. Maybe the Sword of whoever it was who had a bloody great sword dangling away above him, poor little bastard. In the legend. Not Tantalus, was it . . . ? No, don't reckon so. Not Sisyphus either. They were just another pair of unlucky old sods, saddled with other agonies. Sadistic swine though, weren't they really? The buggers who made them up, wrote them down, all these myths and legends. You don't seem to get many happy ones, do you? Labours of Hercules? Not too happy, is it? No laughs there, I wouldn't have said. Makes me sweat just thinking about it. Anyway — that's the way of it, the way it's always been. But it's what definitely *is* going to happen today, though — that, knowing that, that's what gets me down as well. Because what is definitely going to happen today, you see, is the same old thing. The same old thing that will just keep on coming around. What makes it the same old thing. And that's all my every day is now, really — coping with the same old thing, best way I can, and hoping to God that my terror of something else, something unspecific but truly bloody awful, doesn't actually crack open on the top of it all. Or not today, at least. Get past today, and then of course I'll still be dreading this thing, whatever it is, but not till tomorrow, you see? Whatever it might be. And that's how it works. That's the way it goes. With me, anyway. Eternal, is the word. Relentless. Never ending. Until, of course, it does end. Which it will. Sooner or later and one way or another, an end of course will come.

But for now it's a case of climbing the thirteen steps up to Janey's dark and fusty bedroom (she won't even let me draw the curtains, let alone open the window) and bringing her up her tea. Touching her shoulder when I set down the cup, and she just stirring and turning around to look at me. I know the face, the expression. It never alters. Isn't an expression, that's the point. Just blank is all she is. Just staring at me like I'm not even there at all. And she does look old, now. Much older than me, she looks, and she isn't, you know. Five months younger, point of fact. Sometimes in her face I'm aware of a bit of confusion – little pinpoints of worry at the back of her eyes. Sort of dancing up and down there. Time to time there's a little glimmering of fear – and I well know what that looks like because I see it in the mirror every bloody morning – but even then, only barely: the very tiniest glimmering, really. Won't talk, of course. Won't say anything to me about it, so you're just left to wonder. Hardly speaks at all, now. Days can pass without a single word. Wearing, after a while. Very. Then later, when I've seen to Anthony and all of his doings – and that's a day's work in itself, believe you me – and once young Paul comes to fetch him and they both go off to school (and I thank the Lord for him, young Paul, I bless his head) . . . well then I bring her up another cup of tea, don't I? Take away the old one, which she won't have touched because she never ever does, and put down the fresh one in its place. And yes I did try, didn't I? Of course I did. I did try not taking up the first of them – waste of money, waste of effort – but Christ Alive, you should've seen the state she got herself into. Agitation, that's the word. Fingers all stiff and trembling, and up to her lips. Head going this way and that. So I went back to taking her up her early morning tea, and she went back to staring right at me, like I wasn't even there at all.

It's just as well for Anthony that I've got this little confectioner's. If I had, I don't know – the ironmonger's instead, Stammer's say, then I don't honestly reckon anyone at

Anthony's school would talk to him at all. Apart from Paul, I mean. He's a good boy, Paul – really goes out of his way for our Anthony – and it's uncommon in a lad, that is. Healthy young lad. Thinking of others. Because my Anthony, well . . . he's got to slow him down, hasn't he? Clunking along behind him in those blessed metal callipers that every morning I have to strap him tight into. Like he's one of those poor little devils in a legend, or something – some young innocent, minding his own business, not doing any harm to a living soul, and here he is – trapped in a daily struggle, locked into a nightly torture. Not fair, is it? Not fair at all. And eternal. Relentless. Never ending. Until, of course, it does end. So no – it's hardly fair, hardly fair at all. But then who ever said it would be? Life isn't, is it? Famously. Ever fair. It's a cheat, that's what it is: a lying cheat. And being the sweetshop owner's boy, Anthony, he's heard all of the jokes: 'Ah – Polio. The mint with the hole'. Yeh. Not so funny after the first few hundred times. It's his life that's got the hole. Right through the bloody middle. It's his life that's got the hole. Jesus wept. Lovely lad, though. Doesn't complain. Love him so much. Asks me, time to time, when he'll be better. Don't know son, I say to him. Soon, I hope. I daresay soon. You keep up with all the exercises and what have you and you'll be breaking the four-minute mile. Once he came home from school and he said that all the boys were going to get vaccinated. So if I get vaccinated, Dad – will it all go away? Not sure son, I say to him. Not sure that's how it works. Not too sure that's the way it goes. And he's the only one in his year who's cursed with the damn thing, you know, and that's against all the odds. So why was it me then, Dad? Don't know son, I say to him. Just the way of it, I suppose. How it all falls out. Lovely lad, though. Doesn't complain. Love him so much . . . Anyway.

I think it was the first sight of him, though, with his little crutches and all – I think, looking back, that's what tipped my Janey over. Over the edge, sort of thing. I mean, she wasn't A1 even before. Always nervy. Delicate little thing. Spent half her own childhood in a bloody hospital. Then there was Freddie, our first. Nine months she carried him – sick as a dog, most days. All for nothing, though. And they say it, don't they? All about God, and his mysterious ways. Yes well. Don't go to church any more, not after that. Thing like that, some people they'll be kneeling down and blessing themselves, blathering on about this faith of theirs being tested to the limits – yeh and all the rest of the Jesus baloney, and praying like the dickens to what they still do seem to believe is the heaven above them. Lighting candles and bawling their bloody eyes out. And others, other sorts – well like me, for instance – they just turn away from the sight of it. No demonstration, none of the fist-waving . . . just a cold shoulder, sort of style. Yes. And so God now, he can go on working in any kind of ways he bloody well likes, but I'm damned if I'll be seen to encourage him. And then Janey, seeing our Anthony that way – all lopsided and a brave little face on him – well . . . couldn't handle it, see? Turned away from the sight of it. Can hardly blame her: pitiful to watch, it can be. But somebody had to, didn't they? Deal with it. Somebody had to. So now, well – it's what I do. I do the shop, yeh – but what I really do is Anthony. It's hardest in the holidays, when I've got him all day. Weren't for young Paul, I'd be in a bit of a spot. Yes I truly would. And talk of the devil . . . here he is now, look – bang on time, just like always. That'll be on account of his Auntie Milly, of course. She's a wonderful woman, she is. And I do feel mean, some-times, just slipping him a chew or a stick of liquorice from the penny tray. Piccaninnies and flying saucers he's partial to as well, so I let him have a couple of those, time to time. But see, if I were to run to a packet of Spangles, or something – tube of Smarties, sort of style . . . well word gets out at that school, and they'll all be down on me like a plague of flies. Bad enough as it is. And with Anthony there, well I'd have to, wouldn't I? Give it out to all of them. And I can't afford that – just can't afford to, simple as that. It's not a question of mean-ness, it's a question of money. Those school fees, they don't ever lower them, do they? Reduce them, bring them down. No they don't, sir. Most of the people round here, of course – they don't have that problem because they just won't put the effort in, my way of seeing it. Happy to send their kids to the ordinary schools. I'm not saying there's anything wrong with them, the council schools, not saying they're really bad, or anything . . . but I do think it's your duty as a parent to secure for your child the best that's on offer. That's it in a nutshell. And it's difficult. I wouldn't try telling you it's easy. But it's duty. It's duty. And love, of course. Dedication. Though what I've seen of Jim Stammer, I doubt he can be thinking like that. But Milly – it'll be Milly behind it. Such a nice woman. Handsome woman. Hard worker. He's a very lucky man, Jim is. To have such a woman as that. Very lucky man. I'll never forget: she was in the shop, one time – stocking up on her parma violets and getting in some Tizer for Paul, as I recall – and she said to me right out of the blue 'Just think, Stan – if I'd married you I'd be called Milly Miller. That would be funny, wouldn't it?' 'Oh yes,' I said to her – and we were both sort of laughing by this time – 'that would be funny: that would be rich.' Yes it would. Rich indeed. Odd though, isn't it? The things you remember, and the things you forget. So anyway I must, you see – I just must give him the very best start in life, the best I can. Except it isn't the start, of course. Aware of that. His start is buggered. His start is over. But his future, whatever it holds, and for however long . . . well: got to do my bit, haven't I? I'm his Dad, aren't I? Yes I am. So I've got to do my . . . no, not my bit. My utmost – that's what I've got to do.

'Now then, Paul – all right, are we?'

'Yes thank you, Mr Miller.'

'Still raining, is it?'

'Not quite so much now. Just spitting. Anthony ready?'

I jolly well hope he is ready because I'm only just on time today because my stupid Uncle Jim – he really is so completely stupid, Uncle Jim – he called me into the shop just as I'd got

53

my satchel all buckled up and my raincoat on and everything, which is just so typical. Come in here Pauly, he was going: it's my string. And honestly, it's quicker not to argue or ask questions or anything because then he only starts up and goes on and on for hours. So I went into his dirty old stinky shop and there was the string, unwound from the tin thing, the tin sort of dispenser thing, and all over the floor. Dropped it, he said: help me wind it all up again, hey? There's a good lad. Well honestly – how stupid can you be? To get the string into such an awful mess. Amanda, she says I'm always going on about Uncle Jim and he can't be that bad. Oh yes? Well you just try living with him Amanda, that's all, is what I said to her. It's all right for her, isn't it? She's got a proper father, and he's normal. Auntie Milly says that Mr Barton the butcher, he's a real gentleman. Uncle Jim isn't. Uncle Jim is a real idiot. I really do like Amanda, though. Talking to her, and everything. I wouldn't tell Anthony or anyone, but last summer in Regent's Park, she taught me how to make daisy chains and she put this buttercup under my chin and she said oh look, Paul – you don't like butter. I didn't actually know what on earth she was talking about or anything, but I didn't say so – and I do like butter, actually. It's margarine I don't like, and I said so to Auntie Milly and she doesn't get it any more. And then we lay on the grass and it was really hot and I went all squinty in the sun and I sort of just touched her on the knee once, and she didn't say anything. And a bit later I wanted to do it again, but I didn't.

'Where is he, Mr Miller . . . ?'

'He won't be a jiffy, Paul. Just going to the Gents. Spending a penny. And talking of pennies . . . what takes your fancy on the tray today, eh?'

'Oh gosh. Thanks a lot. Um . . . think I'll have a Black Jack if that's all right, Mr Miller.'

'Black Jack? That's a new one for you, Paul. Well Black Jacks – they're only a ha'penny, they are. So take a couple, eh? Three, say. Take three.'

'Oh thanks. Thanks a lot, Mr Miller.'

'They colour your teeth, mind.'

'That's what's good about them. Gobstoppers – they colour your tongue.'

'You boys. You boys. Ah! Here he comes – the man himself.'

Anthony, wearing his customary expression of anticipation, his bright blue eyes seemingly eager to be caught by anything at all, clumped his way through the shop from the stockroom at the back. His cap was crooked on his head, and what with grabbing at that and raising a grey metal crutch in greeting to Paul, he very nearly had himself over. Both Paul and his father moved instinctively towards him, but he batted them away.

'I'm okay. I'm fine, Has the rain stopped, Paul?'

'Pretty nearly. We'd better get a move on, though.'

Stanley Miller laid his hands on Anthony's shoulders and bent down to softly kiss the side of his head. And he would have embraced him – hugged him so very tight, squeezed the

55

very life out of the little mite, oh yes he would, such was the welling of love inside him. He got that. He got that all the time. Just looking at the boy, he got that.

'Have a good day at school, you two. Learn lots, eh? Wish I was coming with you. No, I mean it. I've got my work cut out for me today, I can tell you that much. It's Sally Day, Anthony.'

'Oh no!' laughed Anthony. 'Sally Day! Big fat Sally. She'll wreck the place again.'

'What – Sally from Lindy's, you mean?' said Paul.

Anthony nodded. 'Big fat Sally from Lindy's. Once she's finished shovelling down three million eclairs, she'll come over here and start on the Mars bars.'

'She does our window,' Mr Miller explained to Paul. 'Dresses it, sort of style. I can't honestly remember how it all started. I could just as easily do it myself, but . . . well anyway, she seems to enjoy it. Won't take any money.'

'Just Mars bars!' Anthony guffawed. 'And honestly, Paul – it's so funny. She's so huge that every time she turns round she knocks over what she's just put up!'

'You're right,' his father grinned. 'But she's a good soul – she means well. Now come on, you two. You'll be late. Here, Paul – just a sec. Here. That's for you. Tuck it away.'

'Oh gosh, Mr Miller. Spangles! Are you sure . . . ?'

'Course I'm sure. You're a very good boy. Now off with you. Can't have you getting a detention, can we? Or lines, or something.'

Paul pocketed the Spangles, thanked Mr Miller again, and the two of them went out into the drizzle. Tall for his age, Mr Miller was thinking as he watched them go. And a healthy-looking lad as well, Paul is. He could grow up to be a hero. A man among men. A leader, a strong man of principle. Like Nicholas Nickleby, as a for instance. And there's my Anthony, ever at his side. Little Smike, with nothing but hope. Oh dear God. The trouble with me is . . . I'm over-sentimental. Much too soft for my own good. That's what Janey always used to say. Back in the days when she said anything at all. It doesn't do. It really doesn't do. So . . . right, then . . . just give the shop a little check over, make sure everything's shipshape. Think we need some more Kensitas and Player's Cork Tipped from the stockroom, if memory serves . . . and I'll take my tin of St Bruno while I'm at it. Get out the new display stuff for when Sally comes round. Cadbury's have come up Trojan this month – some very nice material indeed: open boxes of Milk Tray with the most realistic chocolates you ever did see, and a big sort of fold-out stand-up affair with little compart-ments for all the dummy bars. Christ Alive – Sally'll make mincemeat of it. Last time, she even managed to bring the shelves down. Could hardly believe it. Rawlplugs ripped clean out of the wall. Had to get one of the negroes round to make good. Nice enough feller. Well that one is, anyway – can't remember his name. Odd sort of a name – well, you'd expect that, wouldn't you? Got lots of k's in it, fairly sure, though I could be wrong about that. But the other one, his partner, not too sure about him. Seems a bit shifty. Might not be, of course. But the one who came round to do up the shelves – couldn't have been nicer. Always wagging his head and smiling. Great big teeth. Or maybe it's just the way they seem. Did a good job. Charge was very reasonable. Cleared up all of his mess. We had a cup of tea and a bit of a chinwag. Where he comes from . . . Christ Alive, you wouldn't believe all he was telling me. Made it sound like heaven on earth. Used to put up houses, little wooden houses by the seaside, though I can't suppose for a minute that it'd be like any sort of seaside that we might have ever been to. Southend, Bognor, one of them. Bit of boatbuilding and all, he was saying. Sunshine, white sand . . . bananas. Coconuts, I shouldn't be surprised. Makes you wonder why he ever left there in the first place. He did say he feels the cold. And the people, he said – they're not very friendly. Not what he'd been told the English would be like. Before he managed to buy the woodyard (had a bit of money tucked away by then – been saving every single penny he earned since he was a nipper, is what he was saying to me: all he ever wanted since he was knee-high was to come and live in England, and you can hardly blame a man for thinking that) . . . yeh but before then, he and his mate had the very devil of a problem finding any digs, is what he said to me. Everywhere they looked it was 'No Coloureds. No Irish. No Dogs'. Ending up dossing down in Paddington Station for the better part of a week. Well you can sort of understand it with the Irish, but I reckon coloureds and dogs are all right. Then he starts talking about Geoff Lawrence, the newsagent's on the other side. Says he used to pop in there of a morning for his paper – *Telegraph* he reads, if you please. *Express* man, myself – all it is is what you're used to, isn't it really? Anyway, few days in, Geoff Lawrence, he says to him 'I tell you what – how about I get my lad to deliver it for you? How's that sound, eh?' And our negro chum (wish to God I could remember his name – I must make a point of it. Get him to write it down) he says to the man 'Deliver? But I'm only five doors down,' and Geoff, he says 'It's no trouble. Honestly. I insist.' He insisted, you see – wasn't any choice in the matter. Makes you think, doesn't it? How people can get. And Geoff, of course – he's got a very nice little sideline with all those postcards he bungs in the window: 'No Coloureds. No Irish. No Dogs'. And then he laughs, my negro pal, and he goes Oh but not *you*, Mr Miller, you're not like that at all – I didn't mean you, you understand, Mr Miller. Then he gives me that big and toothy grin of his, and he says 'You great fine English gentleman, Mr Miller. Like Winston Churchill.' Dear oh dear. You've got to laugh.

Check on Janey before I open. Bring her a bit of toast with her tea. Sometimes she'll eat it, most times she won't. Later, she'll go and sit in front of the telly. Whatever's on. Shipping forecast. Flowerpot Men. Football pool results. I say to her: we've got two channels, Janey. Remember? You don't like what's on, you can change the channel. See what's on the other side. Might be something better. I taught you how to do that, didn't I? Change the channel. Hear me? Do you hear what I'm saying to you, Janey? Janey . . . ? Janey, love . . . ? Yeh well. Like talking to a bloody wall.

Said she was coming round in her dinner hour, Sally. I wonder if I ought to say something? Say to her, look Sally – it's very kind of you and everything, coming round to help me out and all, and don't think I'm not grateful, but . . . well, I don't like to be a burden, specially in your dinner hour, and I could just as easily . . . no. No. Wouldn't wash. Couldn't do it. Couldn't put it across right. I'd only end up hurting her feelings. Just thinking it out now, I can see her little piggy eyes going all dull, that tiny mouth that still she manages to cram all those eclairs into – truly a cakehole, if ever there was one – I can see it turning down into a schoolgirly pout as her head drops forward and all of those chins start to tremble. No. It's just something I've got to live with. Something else I've just got to live with. Only every two to three weeks, after all. One day, though, she'll get stuck. She will. She'll be in that window bulldozing everything around her, and she'll get wedged. Jammed. Have to get the glazier round to take the whole pane out – even the Fire Brigade – or else she'll just die there. Jammed and starving. Surrounded by imitation chocolate. Christ Alive – she could become deranged. Poor little Sally. Well – not little, of course. But still just the one more helpless victim in a legend, isn't she really?

'All right are you, Janey my love . . . ? Got you a bit of toast with your tea, look. Eat it up while it's still nice and hot, eh? Help you sit up, can I . . . ? Janey? You awake? You are awake, aren't you? You're just not opening your eyes. I know when you're asleep. Well look . . . I'll just leave it here on the bedside table, all right? Just leave it here for you. And you can get to it in your own good time. It's not a very nice morning. Was raining quite heavily. Just spitting, now. Just a little bit of drizzle.'

Yes, well – that was about par for the course. She really ought to see someone. Clear to anybody. Some sort of psycho person, don't know much about it. Not going to happen, though, is it? Not the sort of thing we do. So she'll just go on sitting there for ever, I suppose. Or as long as she can bear it. Or me. Because there's my needs too, if anybody cares. Which, of course, nobody does. Who would? Janey? I hardly think so. And there isn't anybody else, is there? Sometimes, I can hardly care myself. Forget I've got them, needs. Sometimes can forget their very nature. Other times though, I can hardly think of anything else. Burns me right up. Oh well. Stick to burning my tobacco, ay? Yeh – much the best way. Have a pipe down in the shop now, I think. Unlock the door, put the Wall's sign and the litter bin outside on the pavement, get the lights on and smoke my pipe on the tatty old stool in the corner. Serve Mrs Goodrich with her quarter of caramel whirls same as every morning at nine o'clock on the dot, and then get back to hiding away from the day. Much too early to steam in on to dreading tomorrow, so just duck away from this round. Hope most of the shells go over my head. But bloody hell: the silence. The silence she gives me, it's terrible, it really is terrible. Don't know how much more of it I can take, if I'm frank with you. If it wasn't for Anthony . . . Mind you, when she does say something, it can be even worse. Like last time. Was it Friday? Might easily have been Friday. Don't think she's uttered so much as a syllable since. But last Friday, I take her a bit of toast with her tea as usual, and her eyes are wide open and just staring, like they do. And before I could open my mouth, she puts up her hand and she says to me 'Why don't you kill me . . . ?' Voice all hissy. Eyes open wider than ever. And this time, at the back of them, the light of something else. I just looked at her. Just looked. Couldn't think of anything to say. Not a damn thing. So I muttered something about leaving the toast on the bedside table, look . . . and then I got myself out of there. Dear God, though. She goes a week of silence, and then she comes out with that little lot: 'Why don't you kill me . . . ?' Dear God, though. What's a man to think? Hey? Why don't I *kill* her . . . ? Christ Alive.

CHAPTER FOUR

Anything Not Familiar

Milly could tell by the neat, still steaming, curlicue of dung – those stray bits of straw stirred up by the wind in the alleyway to the side of the United Dairies – that she'd fetched up just too late for her selection of treats to be eagerly crunched by the milkman's horse. She folded the sugar lumps back into her hanky, along with the chopped-up chunks of a withered pippin. She missed seeing the horse's big brown eyes grow larger with greed as she approached him. Not though, naturally, from love or affection – she wasn't a fool. Nor even recognition, not of herself; but even for one's bounty to engender just any sort of a desire in a single living soul . . . well that could be something too. Champion, his name is. Champion the Wonder Horse – so silly to call him that: he's sweet, but it's not as if he were a steeplechaser or anything. But they got it from an American programme on the television, Paul was telling me – a sort of a cowboy show, I can only imagine, but I really wouldn't know a thing about it. Don't really seem to get much time for the television these days, although I don't really know quite why that should be: other people seem to. I used to love it when Paul, of an afternoon, would cuddle up beside me on the sofa, happily waiting for *Watch With Mother*. Were we sitting comfortably? Yes we truly were. I'd have a nice cup of tea and a digestive, and Paul would be sucking on a chocolate finger until it threatened to play mayhem with his clean white shirt. Much too old for all that sort of thing now, of course, my little Paul – but sometimes if he's home from school on a Friday promptly, we'll still watch that cartoon show he so much adores. The sailorman. Popeye, that's it, that's the fellow. And his skinny girlfriend, Olive – she does makes me laugh. In the early days, Paul – he begged me to buy him lots of tins of spinach from the United Dairies, which I was more than happy to do because to get him to eat up any vegetable at all apart from peas and potatoes is little less than a miracle from heaven, quite frankly. And it seems so funny now, but golly – I wasn't best pleased at the time, I can assure you of that: well he refused to have anything to do with them, didn't he? Those three large tins I'd got for him – and Smedley's, so it wasn't as if they were cheap or anything. And why? Because he couldn't squeeze them open with the pressure of his hand. In the cartoon, he was wailing – just like a silly baby – Popeye does that and the spinach whooshes right up into the air and he catches it all in his mouth. Yes I know Paul, I said to him

– but that's a cartoon, isn't it? It's not real life, is it Paul? It's just a cartoon.

So that was me eating all the spinach for it seemed like years. I really didn't care for it. I tried it on Jim, but he just eyed the wet green mound of it on his plate as if it were about to reach up and throttle him. 'What's this muck?' he wanted to know. Anything not familiar – anything that isn't a pie or a roast or a fry-up – all of it's just 'muck', in his eyes. Once I bought some real Italian spaghetti from Bona, and my golly was that expensive. It was terribly long, in a bright-blue paper wrapper and a diamond-shaped label I couldn't make head or tail of. I've kept it in my drawer, the label, as a sort of souvenir. I only got the stuff because I'd seen this recipe in *Woman's Own*, and all it needed was tomatoes and a bit of mince. Make a nice change from cottage pie, I thought. Well you just should have heard the furore: 'We fought the b-word Eyeties all through the War! Those b-word Eyeties – they're all b-word fascists!' he was ranting away. Yes well, I said – not you personally, Jim. You were in Munitions in Minehead, if you remember: not too many Italians to fight in Minehead, I shouldn't have thought. Wrong thing to say, of course, but I was really very peeved with him, if you want to know the truth. I'd been to quite a lot of trouble over that supper – set the table nicely with the floral cloth and the proper cruets and even a cupful of marigolds from some pots I had in the backyard, at the time. Refused even to so much as try it. When I urged him, he threatened to throw his plate against the wall.

If Paul hadn't been at table (and he ate it all up like a good little boy) then I'd have dared him to do it, I was, ooh – that angry with the man. And he would have, you know – yes and then who do you think would have been up till all hours clearing away all of the mess? Exactly. Anyway, I thought it was actually very tasty – a lot of cutting up involved, of course: you wonder why they make it quite so long. The recipe said to put cheese on the top, but that would have made it more like a rarebit sort of affair, to my mind. And anyway, all I had in the house were some portions of Dairylea. I get it for Paul – he likes it on his toast.

And isn't it funny? I'm looking now into the window of the United Dairies, and what's the very first thing that catches my eye? A pyramid of tins of Smedley's spinach . . . ! Yes well you can keep them, thank you very much. But I do love this window – I sometimes think I could stand on the pavement and gaze at it for hours. And maybe in the past I have done – well, not for hours, obviously . . . but more than once some-body like that busybody Mrs Goodrich or the lady from Amy's the hairdresser – not Gwendoline, not the one who does me, but the other one – they've touched my arm and they've said to me something along the lines of Are you quite all right, my dear . . . ? And I've come right back to earth and laughed at myself for ever having drifted away. Oh yes quite all right, thank you, I eagerly assured them. But that Mrs Goodrich, she obviously thinks I'm touched. It's just that I love to look at the displays, that's all – why I don't really care for these supermarkets, as they call them; even the new food hall they've got in John Barnes – I've never been in. Before I go into any of the shops in the Lane, though, I always pause to look at the windows. In the Dairies, it's mostly these tapering piles of packets and tins – they look so very impressive, I always think, when they're all massed together like that. Ranked like soldiers. The red of the Heinz Tomato Soups always makes for a cheery sight – reminds you of winters by the fire: I always add the top of the milk – gold top though, it's got to be that. Stir it in – makes all the difference, I can tell you. And those great big boxes of Force, with Sunny Jim looking always so very posh and happy. Worlds away from my Jim, isn't he . . . ? My Jim, he never could be said to be sunny – perpetually overcast, rather more, with the threat of anything from showers to an out-and-out tornado. I don't think they can be real though, those enormous packets – there'd be more than enough cereal in there to feed a family of six for a year. The manufacturers must just make them for show, I suppose. Well if that's the case, their money isn't wasted. If it wasn't quite so nippy today, I'd linger longer – savour all these brand new Huntley & Palmers big square tins and the handsome jars of Marmite. But there's always the devil of a wind just on this corner, so I think I'll go in there now and get what I came for.

I always smile at the sign on the door: 'Yes! We are open for the sale of Lyons' Cakes'. When they shut the shop in the evening – and even when it's half-day closing on Thursdays

– I've seen Edie, the manageress (and she's always the last to leave) . . . I've seen her turn it around: she never forgets, she always turns it around before she locks up the shop. And then it says 'Sorry! We are closed – even for the sale of Lyons' Cakes'. I wonder if there's anyone else who even so much as notices? I hope so – because I think all these windows, they're really a bit of an art that we all just take for granted. And oh my goodness, the number of times I've said to Jim – God's sake, man: you've just got to do something about the state of your window. Well you can imagine his reaction: 'Window? My window? State of my window? What's b-word wrong with the state of my window? Looks all right to me. Nothing wrong with my b-word window.' On and on. Yes well – like so many men, he just doesn't see. I mean . . . even the glass itself, that hasn't been cleaned in a decade, and every day he hangs up the same old things outside – and that tin bath, I'm telling you: it must be a museum piece, by now. All dented and grey – not silvery and shiny like galvanised is when it's new. When it's not a museum piece. It's not even as if anyone's ever going to buy a tin bath in the first place. We may not all be living in Buckingham Palace, but I think we've at least progressed from that. And everything else out there is coated in grime, from the traffic and the flies. The idea of a window display, I say to the man, is to entice people into the shop – to tempt them to buy something they may not have thought of. People look at your window, they'd run a mile. He says I don't know what I'm talking about: they come in, they buy

68

their flypapers, their nuts and bolts, their paraffin, their brooms and their four ounces of tacks – and the b-word butcher buys his buckets. No doilies and pretty pink bows in the window are going to make the slightest bit of b-word difference. And I don't know – he might even be right. I still used to argue, though – and then I stopped. I used to do a lot of things where Jim is concerned. Yes I did. But now I've stopped.

It is true though that Mr Barton, Jonathan, he does seem to buy an awful lot of buckets. And in his line, you don't really care to enquire, do you? I did think of asking him one time, but I didn't like to in the end. Now *his* window – oh my goodness! That really is a work of art, and no mistaking it. All these neat little white porcelain trays divided up by what I think is supposed to resemble parsley, though I must say the green is very vivid. The sirloin steaks, all fanned out so very handsomely, their creamy fat and marbling part of nature's wonder, to my mind. The carcasses of pig, the neatly trussed-up chickens (for those who can afford them) with those sweet little chef's hats perched on the ends of the drumsticks – and that parade of pinkish lamb chops, curling like commas. Mr Barton, Jonathan himself – oh, he's just such a gentleman. So very beautifully spoken and courteous, and always just perfectly turned out. Immaculately groomed, his hair and moustache always just so. Sounds so silly now, but I used to be quite . . . well, not frightened of him, exactly, no – but never really wholly at ease in his presence. Awed, I think I was, maybe just a little. He is rather commanding. He does tend to dominate any given space – and particularly so when he's behind the counter of his own very brightly lit and nearly glittering shop. Which always smells so . . . I don't know . . . clean, really. Is the nearest I can get to it. But it's true that I still hear people talk of him as being really rather intimidating, but you just have to see beyond all that: that's only his manner – he's actually very kind. I find it all, all of it, quite a comfort. Big strong hands. Well you need that, I suppose. If you do what he does.

But just thinking about it all now, you know . . . nearly all of the windows in the Lane – they're really rather wonderful, in their funny little ways. The nighties and stockings and petticoats in Marion's all got up as if they're just about to fly away – Bona, of course, with all these very strange packets of things, covered in seals and foreign languages. Some of them aren't even written in a recognisable alphabet. They're mostly, apparently – or at least that's what the gentleman in there was telling me one time – Jewish sorts of things . . . what do they call it? Hebrew sort of writing, I think it is. There are quite a few Jewish people living around here now – Swiss Cottage mainly, some reason or other. Older people – all of them refugees from that blessed Hitler person. What a villain. There really does seem to be no end to the trouble that man continues to cause us all. Jim says he can't understand it: how can they bring themselves to go into Bona? It's run by a b-word Nazi. No Jim, I say to him, no – they're Swiss, I'm fairly sure. Austrian, conceivably – but definitely not Nazis, for heaven's sake: how can they be? They're not even German. They're all of them the same, is what he says then: they're all of them the b-word same: wouldn't trust a man jack of them. Oh dear dear. Well . . . that's my Jim for you, I'm afraid. More or less sums him up. And I hardly think he's alone. That's the trouble.

And then there's Dent's the fish shop, with its ranks of wet and glimmering shimmers of the sea. And in the summer – the colours of all those mountains of fruit on the pavement outside Levy's. And Miller's too, the sweetshop – that's always quite a fine show. But oh dear – poor Stan. I really don't know how he copes with it. With Anthony the way he is, and everything. I can't help wondering sometimes whether I'd be able to handle it all myself, if Paul were . . . well, you know. If he had that. God – I feel like I might be struck down dead for even thinking it. And Jane, his wife, I never ever see her. She's never in the shop, or anything. I don't think I've seen her for years. I do know she's not been well, but Stan . . . he never mentions it. Doesn't say anything. Well men – they don't ever, do they? I hope he knows though that if he ever does need help, he only has to ask. But I was proud, so very proud of Paul, when he took up with little Anthony a couple of terms ago. Like my shining knight. But I don't think that's it at all, now: the two of them genuinely seem to be the very best of friends, and that is truly a blessing. I know that Stan thinks so, anyway. And in his window – so many tempting sweets and chocolates (if only I didn't so very easily

71

put on weight!) and posters for cigarettes that are kind to your throat. I used sometimes to have a Craven "A" of an evening, but if I'm honest it was only really because I do think those wonderful women in the films always look so very poised and elegant when they lower their eyelids and slowly blow out that long blue plume of smoke ... Joan Fontaine, Rita Hayworth, Katherine Hepburn. Those. I can't say I like it, though – I never could inhale, I'd die of choking. And I always had to have a Trebor's mint, to take away the taste. Jim, of course – he never stops. If he isn't stubbing one out he's scraping a Vesta to light up another. I've told him repeatedly that it can't be good for him and he just puffs the smoke right into my face and he says to me 'So what? At my age, there's nothing that's good for me.' His attitude, that attitude of his, it really can't be helpful to Paul. It's all wrong. When there are young people about, I think you just have to be more positive and brave, to be seen to meet life's challenges head-on. Set an example, I suppose is what I mean.

Oh God – I'm suddenly frozen to the marrow. And it's not just me hanging about in the street, looking at tins of soup like a lemon – it's this thin and silly coat I'm wearing. November now, and it's not at all up to it. Much more of a spring coatee, this one is. My proper gaberdine with the quilted lining ... well that's seen better days. But I've bought this length of wonderful tweed – got it from John Barnes, oh, months ago now. Scottish it is, and very good quality. And what I think will be a very smart and toning lining with a stripe to it.

Quite fetching. I've had the pattern propped up on the sewing machine for Lord knows how long. If I don't get a move on, the winter will be over. I've got the thread – I've even got the buttons, so there's no excuse at all. Leather-covered, they are: look like little footballs.

And yes I suppose I can hardly be surprised that there is Mrs Goodrich, bold as brass as usual – standing four-square at the centre of the shop, and somehow managing almost to fill it. She always plants her wicker basket on top of the marble counter, just by the scales and the bacon slicer. As if she's establishing a kingdom – her very own sort of territory, or something. Marking out her area. I sometimes imagine, you know, that there somehow has to be a fleet of Mrs Goodriches, a marching army of them – for how else could she ensure that no conversation, nothing that ever goes on (or anyway is said to) can pass unheard or unwitnessed? For it really does seem, sometimes, as if the woman is just simply everywhere. It's only a small street, England's Lane, and there's a limit, you'd think, to the number of times in a day when you need to pop out to the shops . . . and yet I can hardly recall a time when I haven't encountered her somewhere. And although I don't for a moment believe it to be true, sometimes it can even appear as if she's actually following you from place to place. Keeping an eye on you. 'Ah,' she'll always say – her face so smug, and packed with secrets, real or imagined. 'Mrs Stammer. So we meet again.' And then some or other patronising comment concerning the shop.

'Ah – Mrs Stammer. So we meet again. And how fares the world of ironmongery? Continuing to prosper, I very much hope. Edie and I were just explaining to young Doreen here the necessity of a reliable laxative.'

Edie, behind the counter, smiled and slowly shook her head, while Doreen – the trainee at Amy's the hairdresser, Milly remembered now – rolled up her eyes before closing them tightly.

'So embarrassing . . .' she barely murmured. 'I only came in here for some Quaker Oats.'

'Nothing embarrassing about keeping regular,' said Mrs Goodrich, rather sternly. 'When you get to my age, you'll know all about it. Essential to inner cleanliness. Ex-Lax is next to useless. Won't shift anything. Senna pods – they'll see to you properly. And it's All-Bran you're wanting, not Quaker Oats. I swear by it. All-Bran is your man, believe you me.'

I think, thought Milly, that the hairstyle young Doreen is affecting – and young she very surely is, can only be seventeen at the outside – they are calling it a 'beehive'. I saw it in *Woman's Own*. I wonder if Gwendoline did it for her. Not her usual approach. Looks more like candyfloss than hair – a great deal of backcombing, I should have said . . . can't be good for your ends . . . ton of lacquer, looks like. And what a lot of make-up around her eyes. Like a panda.

'Never mind, Doreen,' Milly was laughing, as she leant on the counter, unknotting her scarf. 'We'll change the subject, shall we? What very smart slacks you're wearing. Quarter of Green Label when you're ready, Edie.'

'They're not "slacks",' muttered Doreen moodily, looking down at her legs and spreading her palms. 'They're ski pants. They're the latest.'

'Are they, dear?' said Milly brightly. 'And there was I thinking slacks were the latest. I thought they had taken over from jeans. Silly me. They certainly look like slacks. Why aren't they slacks, in fact, Doreen? And two pounds of granulated, Edie.'

'Slacks,' sighed Doreen, rapping the counter with an impatient red fingernail, 'don't have these little straps, see? The little straps that go under your feet.'

Mrs Goodrich was also sighing. 'Whatever next? Little straps that go under your feet! You'd never catch me in trousers.'

'They're not *trousers* . . . !' Doreen nearly was squawking.

'We know, Doreen,' said Milly placatingly. 'They're ski pants. And very nice they are too. And where do you ski, dear? Primrose Hill?'

'*Christ* . . .'

'Now now,' snapped Mrs Goodrich. 'Language. I won't have language.'

'Can I just buy my Quaker Oats?' Doreen pleaded with Edie. 'It's all I came in here for.'

'Here you are, Doreen love. On your Mum's slate, eh?'

Doreen nodded, grabbed the packet, and looking only at the floor, quickly made it to the door.

'Young *people* . . . !' spat Mrs Goodrich, with scorn.

'Mustard powder, please Edie,' said Milly, consulting her list. 'Small tin. You make them sound like a plague of vermin, Mrs Goodrich.'

'Not far short. The more I look around me, the gladder I am not to be encumbered. I made a conscious decision. I said to my Colin right at the outset – Colin, I said: I have not the slightest intention of spending the best years of my life up to my elbows in nappies and ordure and kowtowing to a bawling brat. Oh no. Not me. I made a conscious decision.'

'You don't know what you're missing, Mrs Goodrich. Packet of lard and the large drum of Cerebos, and I think that's all of it, Edie.'

'On the contrary. What I am missing, Mrs Stammer, is the likes of that Doreen strumpet who no doubt by now is already off gallivanting with yet another man. They may be terribly sweet when they're toddlers, oh yes maybe – but that's what they grow up into. There's what you are left to deal with. I pity that one's mother.'

'She's not so bad . . .' Edie said quietly – looking now nervously from Milly to Mrs Goodrich.

Milly wasn't really listening to anybody now because she had just caught sight of the cardboard box on the counter, crudely wrapped in a scrap of last year's rubbed and creased Christmas paper, alive with robins and snowballs, a slot gouged into its lid. The sight of it depressed her terribly because this year it was Milly's turn to be in charge of the festive party, and apart from the gathering together of all the food and drink donations, there was always a collection box stationed somewhere prominent for the inevitable extras – decorations, crackers, little token presents for the kiddies, on top of all the rest of the palaver. This year, though, it had been decided – and which idiot was it, Milly would dearly love to know, who came to so foolish a decision? – that there should be a separate box in every single shop the length of the Lane. She herself with reluctance had dressed up an old Price's candle carton and placed it on the counter at Stammer's, just by the string dispenser. Two weeks ago she did that, and still it was empty. This was the trouble – and why could they not have foreseen it? Everyone will ignore each of the boxes, claiming they have already given to another one. The net result will be zero: she felt it in her bones.

'Not so *bad* . . . !' hooted Mrs Goodrich. 'What – *Doreen*? She's one of the very worst, she is. No respect for her betters. Man-mad, of course.' And she puffed up the scarf at her throat, so as to make it clear that she meant what she said.

'How much do I owe you, Edie? I'm sure that can't be true, Mrs Goodrich.'

'Oh you're sure, are you? Well, Mrs Stammer, I am here to tell you that you are very wrong. Only just broken up with that teddy boy – what was his name? What was his name, Edie? You know the one. Works in the garage in Winchester Road. Anyway – name doesn't matter. And he was up to no good, you just had to look at him. Hair like a pop star, tight trousers. Those things on his face – what are they? Sideboards. Well that lasted no time – but now our Doreen has very much bigger fish to fry, from what I see and hear. Oh yes. Her current tastes seem to be running to rather the more mature sort of gentleman. The sort with a bit of money behind him.'

'Oh Mrs Goodrich . . . !' Milly couldn't help but giggle. 'Honestly – where do you get it all from? Do you make it up, I wonder? What do you think, Edie? Do you think she makes it all up?'

Edie now seemed almost to be cowering away from something to come.

'That'll be nine and tenpence ha'penny please, Mrs Stammer.'

Milly passed across to her a ten-shilling note and stowed away everything into her basket. Suddenly keen to be back at home now, cosy in the warmth of her kitchen and making herself a good strong cup of tea, she had already become careless of Mrs Goodrich beside her – happily unaware of the narrowing of her eyes, a new and purposeful tightness at the mouth. And then, with relish, a slip of wet tongue was darting in and out of it.

'Well you can think I'm making it up if you want to,' Mrs Goodrich was huffing, her voice growing steadily more threatening. 'That is your privilege, I'm sure. But if the gentleman Doreen was seen with coming out of an X-certificate and doubtless very bawdy screening at the Swiss Cottage Odeon just this last Friday evening and then getting into a taxi with him, if you please – if that gentleman wasn't the greatly esteemed husband and father Mr Barton, our family butcher . . . well then it was someone who very much looked like him, I can assure you of that. Might it conceivably be his twin brother, Mrs Stammer, do you imagine . . . ?'

A fleeting and malign twisting of triumph was swiped across the press of Mrs Goodrich's lips, her small eyes bright with satisfaction at the result of her goring (its surgical precision, its undoubted effect). Edie looked away as Milly, suddenly flushed, turned upon Mrs Goodrich a shocked and affronted face – and then she felt the heat in her cheeks quickly fade into pale. She had to go, quickly and immediately, and so she strode towards the door with unbending purpose, not at all aware of Edie calling out after her about a penny-ha'penny change. And then she just stopped. Her hand was frozen, reaching for the handle on the door, and then she just stopped abruptly. Milly was only sort of aware of Edie asking her now if she was quite all right, but still grimly she focused on the reverse of the sign hanging against the glass, not smiling at it this time, but reading it with care, over and over. 'Sorry! We are closed – even for the sale of Lyons' Cakes'. It was not the collection of her change, though, that was making her pause, but a pain – more than a throb – deep down and within her. Milly was hardly a one to give in to such things: an active person – hadn't she said this a thousand times? – an active person has to expect the odd little ache, the occasional twinge. It'll go away by morning – hadn't she said this a thousand times? – and always her comforting homily had proved to be true. But this one, this particular pain she had had before. Just yesterday, as a matter of fact. And now it was back. This gnawing then stab that is grabbing her, this sickly convulsion, well . . . it hadn't gone away by morning.

CHAPTER FIVE

A Day Unlike Others

It's true, you know: there really could be nothing better, nothing nicer . . . here is how Fiona Barton would idly be talking, how she would languidly confide in you . . . nothing at all she could think of, nothing whatever that swam into her mind – with just possibly the exception of a quarter or even a half pound, goodness, of violet creams from Miller's up the road – that was quite so very heavenly, so indulgent, as a deep hot bath at the end of yet another very ordinary day. Or so, anyway, is the way she remembered it. That was how she recalled it had been in the past. But in this rather beastly bathroom she now was forced to cope with, may the Lord have mercy upon her, we have an altogether different circumstance. The bath itself, well . . . cramped, very – and there is a curious, tawny and curling stain loosely meandering down from a big old tap which forever is seeping, and nearly to the plughole, so little chrome still flecking the brass beneath.

Sometimes the water is brownish, which yes I suppose might go some way to explaining it. The stain, I mean – not at all why the water should be brownish. There stands alongside it a large and squat black meter – no no, it's true, I am not joking, believe me. Would that I were. And therefore – rather in the manner of one having to make a series of telephone calls from an outside box – a great number of pennies has to be consciously assembled before a bath of any substance may even be contemplated. I crouch down – oh yes I do, just one more thing to which I am these days reduced – I crouch right down and insert the first of the pennies into the ugly gash there, and then I dutifully revolve a sort of key thing until the coin is heard to clang down into the box. I then must wind back this key thing, this twisty little handle sort of affair, and repeat once more the procedure. Five times if a puddle is all you require – a foot bath, no more, and charged with Radox – though easily a shilling if the water is to cover you. And when I think back to the house, the old house – that wonderful old house where we all were so terribly happy, the sunlight forever lighting up our faces . . . yes well. Best not to dwell, I think. Far better not. Just get on with it, really. What else is there? Except to dwell. And dwell I do . . .

So, the bathroom notwithstanding, I still do go through the business of pretending to enjoy what used to be – and, if Jonathan is to be believed (of course an unfeasible premise, at even the best of times) one day will be again . . . a luxurious soak at the end of every evening. I close my eyes. The green of the walls is hardly conducive. One finds oneself irresistibly tracing the descent of this or that little rivulet of condensation. I try so hard not to be aware of the clanking in the pipes, the plumbing's moan as it shudderingly recovers from the breathtaking exertion of having disgorged its bounty with seemingly pain and a deep reluctance – its only purpose, after all, but still there would appear to be harboured an abiding resentment within the rusty guts of it to ever be a party to the entire affair. But when Jonathan enters the room, as is generally usual – unless, of course, he is off again into the dark on yet one more of his unspoken and wholly probably unspeakable night excursions – well then when Jonathan comes in so very silently, I will snap open my eyes and look at him in fascination. For still he maintains this grip upon me – I can see him only in awe. Why, I can only suppose, I still am here with him. Why else would I be? Stranded in this measly little flatlet above a meat shop. Why else would I be? If not from love, and an ever deeper passion – one which neither of us could even come close to understanding, while needing very badly all of its warmth (and are dazzled by its edge, so stark). Except that he feels it to be his due, my patent adoration – that much always I have seen in him. Despite his behaviour, his extraordinary attitudes, nothing less than reverence could ever be acceptable to him . . . oh yes, I have always seen that in him. And much to my own surprise, sometimes anger, and always resignation . . . I am able to supply it, unequivocally. There is not even effort involved – a sort of wonderment exudes from my pores, and I know he must smell it.

He will nod to me, Jonathan, as he stands before the mirror to loosen his tie. His glance encompasses my breasts, which I never would seek to conceal, though alas the water is never so deep that they may float, buoyantly. He afterwards will take out the iron and press that tie where the tightness of the knot has been, then hang it on a rotating rack, and with care. His trousers he will place between two flat boards beneath the mattress. It is a knack and a habit, he told me so very many years ago. One more knack and habit, picked up along the way. And then he shaves. Unusual, one may think, to shave last thing in the evening – but he is so very meticulous, you see. His appearance is so terribly important to him. And to me, of course. Oh yes. And to me. For Jonathan, though, it need not at all be the end of the day, you see. Sometimes, yes – sometimes he will get into his bed, having put on his hairnet and the gauzy cover for his moustache, and sleep immediately. Other evenings, late, he will change his underthings, shirt, tie and suit, and off he will go. I used to enquire. At the beginning I did. And then I think I became wiser. Why invite a lie, an evasion, some very undignified subterfuge? Because he would always respond to my enquiry with elegance and a disarming plausibility – an apparently so very open agenda . . . though who knew? On occasion it might even have been the truth. And then he would smile the smile that soothed all things: even as I basked in it, he was gone.

Sometimes, at night, he is, I know, attending to business. I am aware of comings and goings, and always under the generous cowl of darkness. Business is a fine thing: I enjoy the fruits of this terrible trade to which he has so very deftly taken. I like to buy beautiful things. Apart from Amanda, my sweet Amanda, this is all that is left to me – though often my trinkets act as no more than a savage reminder of before. But mostly, of course, it's women. Always there have been women. Though I am not at all convinced that he has a 'type', you know. I have known him with all sorts, many ages and colourings, backgrounds and even nationalities, but I believe even he might draw the line at a negress – though of course one can never really know. A fine face and figure would appear to be mandatory, together with a modicum of intelligence. Not necessarily education . . . though I think he wouldn't tolerate even a hint of crudeness, a lack of manners or femininity . . . but other than that I think that no fleeting potential may be safely discounted. And I mind, do I . . . ? Well I don't, no. Not. I really ought to, I do quite see that – I should be burned by the white heat of outrage, I should feel betrayed, insulted, less of a woman, failing in my wifely duties – all these tedious and rather humdrum things which you read about in the magazines – but of course I don't. I have tried – I really did try in the early days to muster a smidgen of moral anger, even a touch of hatred. But it never really was coming – not to me; and he . . . I doubt whether even in passing he observed my muted attempt. But you see . . . he is a man, after all. A very fine and nearly greedy man, and I honestly do believe that in his place I would do the same. Were I a man too. Not through need, but simply because it was possible. Because there was fun and diversion to be had – something new and exciting. I cannot see for the life of me how pursuing such ideas could be wrong in any way. How much worse not even to sense them, to be quite unbound from lust and curiosity. Or to feel these things keenly, and then stamp them to death – but never quite to death, no, so that a mewling whimper of hopeless protestation always is dimly to be heard, a feeble just-alive gesture from a mangled and bleeding almost corpse. It is sex, after all – only sex. Do you see? A mere release. What is that, when compared to his love for me? The one thing I know to be true. There was just one occasion . . . only one – still we were in the house at Henley – when his abiding passion for another did cause me such very serious pain. For he had, you see, fallen very help-lessly in love with one whom he believed to be a goddess, and as a consequence, and for a good long time, my future and even that of Amanda did lie in considerable peril. I said not one word, extraordinary circumstances intervened, and now all that is passed. And so . . . as he walks into the bathroom, just as my water is cooling, do I feel love for this utterly tremendous man before me? I do. It pulsates. And it collides in the air with his love for me, the soft explosion and the balm from that, they engulf me.

'I trust you are well, my dear. All seems secure.'

Which is what he always says, when first he approaches me – stoops down then to kiss the top of my head. It makes me feel so safe, protected, while even as I sense his caress, I am alarmingly aware – inside and around me – of my retention of such tremulous screaming at this so spectacular a folly: to succumb if even for a moment to so rosy an illusion. A nebulous threat is never distant, of course I know that, and yet mercifully Jonathan is able to raise up a barricade so as to screen at least the looming prospect, to contain its swell, to muffle the very worst of its maniacal hammering.

'Just rested, thank you Jonathan. And your day . . . ?'

Jonathan gazed in seeming astonishment at his own reflection in the mottled mirror hung above the basin. As if genuinely amazed that it should be he who was in there, tired, wide-eyed and calmly staring back out at him.

'Ah . . . my day. Yes indeed, my day. Well it was quite a day, that may be said for certain. A day unlike others, I should regard it. But then, in their ways . . . each one is. No?'

'I suppose. In its detail. And after? Tonight, are you . . . ?'

'Indeed I am, I fear. Some things just must be attended to. Tiresome, but there it is.'

Yes: there it is. There it very much is, damn and blast it. There is mess to be cleared. And mess I dislike intensely. Because today, well . . . all had not gone according to plan. Well in truth, of course, there had been no plan – how could I have formulated a plan, when nothing remotely of the sort was even anticipated? All was to be straightforward, just as it has been for how many months? But there was something about the man, this time. Not just an air, but something he was clutching within him, with glee – people of this class, they are incapable of concealment. This bloody man whom I had assumed all along to be no more than a Middlesex smallholder and of little brain, eager to conduct a bit of brisk business by moonlight, while creaming the goodness away from the Revenue. The acceptance of the pig, it never took too long. And very soon I had a young lady to attend to, did I not? So I was hardly eager then for a pig to detain me, and nor its loathsome breeder, whatever the bloody man's name is. Here was not a friendship, God in heaven – why ever should I have known his name? Soon my benevolent doctor would arrive to administer sedation to this gross and gently squealing creature which – in a butcher's yard – scented something malign: its eyes were far from easy. And then two five-pound notes were in the man's hand – his signal, surely, to touch that greasy cap cocked so very comically upon a bony skull and be gone the way he came. But no: he then began to utter.

'Well then, Mr Barton – everything sweet, is it?'

I imagine I must have looked at him in open amazement.

'I beg your pardon? *Sweet*, did you say . . . ? I have no idea what you can be meaning. And now if that's everything, I really must be . . .'

'Ah no see – what I'm meaning, Mr Barton – what I'm actually sort of getting at, Mr Barton, is that I don't reckon it is. Sweet, see? Everything. In your life, if you get me.'

'What in God's name are you talking about? Now listen to me – I have neither the time nor inclination for conversation with a slack-jawed hooligan – whatever your name is. And what I certainly shall not tolerate is your own particular brand of impertinence. Now if you will please excuse me . . .'

'Well yeh – I will in a minute. And I apologise, I do, for myself, like. I can see that you're a man of breeding. A gentleman of quality. I know it can't be easy for you, talking to an uneducated man. A man such as myself. But there's no way round it, see? Point is, Mr Barton, if you pardon me, is that I know. I know. All about it.'

'I sincerely believe you to be deranged. Kindly leave my premises. We shall not be conducting business in the future, do you hear me? Plenty of grubby and dishonest little farmers about, I think . . .'

'Dishonest, yeh – that's something you would know about, isn't it Mr Barton? Your past – been a lot of that, far as I can tell. And much worse besides. I been digging a little, see? Little hobby of mine. Always quite fancied myself as a bit of a Sherlock Holmes.'

Jonathan Barton glared at the man, and took a step forward.

'You're a babbling idiot. Leave this instant. Do you hear me? If you refuse, then I'll—'

'What? You'll what? Call the police? I hardly think so.'

'It is not my slightest intention to call the police. I shall eject you forcibly. You are a miserable little weed, by the looks of you. I could break you in half with the fingers of just one hand.'

'Doubtless you could, sir. Doubtless you could. But consider this, if you will. I know about Somerset. See? John Somerset. Oh yes – that bit got to you, didn't it Mr Barton? Know what I'm talking about now, do you? You gone all pale.'

'I don't know anyone by the name of John Somerset. Now leave. I'm warning you for the very last time.'

'Oh yes you do, sir. Lost time. Wants to be accounted for. That's what I were told. Though even more than that, if I got it right, is to exact some sort of . . . I don't know . . . vengeance? Would that be too strong? Maybe not, in the light of the son, of course. What copped it. Now me – I don't give two hoots either way. About the boy. Why would I? None of it's no skin off of my nose. Don't mind, do I? But I reckon it matter a lot to you though, Mr Barton. As now you has taken to calling yourself. Am I wrong? And whether I keeps quiet, and whether I don't. See what I mean? I think you might do. So . . . now I laid the facts before you . . . what you say?'

'I say nothing.'

'You sure . . . ?'

Jonathan Barton looked at the man levelly. His eyes then relaxed into a sort of amusement, and he fingered his moustache.

'What is it that you want . . . ?'

The man gave a whoop, and jubilantly slapped Mr Barton on the arm – who recoiled with a gasp and within an instant as if assailed by some so very vile thing, both deadly and repellent.

'Now you're talking, Mr Barton sir! That's much more the thing. I knew you'd see reason, clever man such as yourself. Now I understand you're very busy – a thousand things to attend to, shouldn't wonder – and I know this is all very unexpected and very likely quite, well – upsetting, really, I suppose it must be. Yes. So let me come right out with it, if I may: one hundred pounds, and there's an end on it. Not much really, is it? When you think of all what's at stake. Not much at all, I shouldn't have said.'

Jonathan Barton inclined his head, eyeing his toecap reflectively.

'I would appear to have misjudged you, Mr um . . . what is your name, in fact?'

'Walton, sir. You call me Jackie like everyone does.'

'Misjudged you, Mr Walton. Quite a head on your shoulders. Now tell me . . . this, er – information, of which you imagine yourself to be in possession. Spoken to anyone about it . . . ?'

'I'm not stupid, Mr Barton – like now I think you realised. What would be the good in that? What I'm offering you is pure. No one knows but me. And I'm also the only one what knows that Mr Jonathan Frost now go under the name of Mr Jonathan Barton, family butcher, and currently resident in England's Lane, north London. A very long ways from where anyone last clapped eyes on you. You been bright, Mr Barton. I take my hat off.'

Jonathan Barton nodded – threw across a grin of complicity.

'One hundred, you say . . .'

'I was going to say guineas, but then I thought nah – who am I kidding? I'm not a guineas sort of a person.'

'Let me tether your pig in the yard – seems to be getting rather restless. Don't want the neighbours disturbed, do we? I'm assuming that the creature is still part of our transaction . . . ?'

'Took your tenner, ain't I? Business as usual.'

'Quite. Well . . . that sort of cash . . . I don't keep it lying about, you understand.'

'Understand perfectly, Mr B. But you got some of it, ain't you? Half, say. Rest tomorrow. How about that?'

'Half. Well yes I daresay I might be able to lay my hands on half of it. In the refrigerator, out at the back. Where I keep it. Shouldn't be telling you really, should I?'

'My lips is sealed, Mr Barton. You can rely on old Jackie.'

'Right – well come along then, Mr um . . . See what I can find. Galton, is it? Might only be forty . . .'

'Walton, yeh. Forty quid is a quite acceptable deposit, Mr Barton. I'm not grasping. Patient man. And then tomorrow you can hop across the bank, can't you?'

'Yes. I can't see that that should present a problem.'

Jonathan Barton had led the way out of the back door and into a small darkened yard, crates and sacking piled up haphazardly against the rough and crumbled walls. He tied the pig to a hook by the door, and it set to truffling its snout into the bits of bone, skin and sawdust that had drifted up into a corner. From the considerable fob on a chain that led from his trouser waistband into a pocket, Jonathan Barton selected the key to the large refrigerator, turned it and tugged down and forward sharply on the handle.

'Woo – you ain't never going to starve, is you Mr Barton? Look at it all! Cow, is it, that . . . ? Beef, so to say. Chickens – cor: how many chickens you got in there? Never seen the like. Lamb and all, if I'm not mistaken.'

Jonathan Barton was smiling, almost shyly. 'I like to keep a fair array. Shan't be a moment.'

He braced himself against the piercing lance and judder of cold as he entered the cold store, the shock of it already covering his fingers as he pulled out some wadding from the left-hand corner, down at the floor where the jugs of kidneys were.

'You're in luck,' he said quite easily, as he re-emerged shivering into the yard. 'Forty-five. More than I thought.'

'That'll be lovely, Mr B. That'll be just lovely.'

Jackie Walton's two large hands closed upon the rustle of five-pound notes. He licked a thumb and riffled them eagerly.

'And you rest assured, Mr Barton – I may be no gentleman when it come to clothes and speaking and that . . . but I does keep my word. You square me with the rest in the morning, and you won't never hear another dicky bird. You can stand on that.'

Jonathan Barton said he was sure that that was true, and then he brought down the axe swiftly and hard into the back of the man's neck, looking away briefly as the thud of it connected, wincing at the shot of hot blood that now splattered his cheek. As the man hit the ground, Jonathan Barton roared out briefly, caught up in a whip of fear at the shrieking that was tearing into the air around him. He just stared transfixed at the white of terror in the eyes of the pig, scrabbling on the cobbles and straining hard at the rope that still just held it firm. The squeal was insistent, hysterical and now quite out of control and it took him three and then a fourth quite wild and so very badly mismanaged swipe of the axe to end this noise that had so appalled him, and he gazed down now at the thick red blood that licked and then lapped at his shoes, invading the eyelets. And then from the shop he heard for the first time the woman who was calling him.

Stepping quickly out of the yard, he was careful to lock the door behind him. He only understood how he must have appeared when he saw the incredulity in the wideness of Milly's eyes as she just stood there before him.

'Jonathan . . . what was that unholy noise . . . ?' she was gasping. 'No, don't tell me. But look at you . . . you're all . . . you're all covered in blood. Are you all right? Have you . . . ?'

He did his best to raise a smile. Suddenly, he was utterly exhausted.

'I'm a butcher . . .' he said quite simply, and he heard the sighing behind the words. 'Of course I'm all right. Perfectly.'

'But your overall, your apron . . . you're not wearing your overall. You've ruined that beautiful suit.'

Jonathan Barton looked down at himself.

'Yes,' he said. 'I have. Why are you here, Milly? It is not, of course, that I am displeased to see you, but . . .'

'Well I'll tell you why, Jonathan . . . are you really sure you're quite all right?'

'I told you. I'm completely fine.'

'Well then I'll tell you why. Why I am here. Doreen. Say it isn't true.'

Jonathan touched his temple, and closed his eyes. The blood was dark and stiffening on his face and fingers.

'Doreen . . . ? Who now is Doreen?'

'You know perfectly well who Doreen is, and don't pretend you don't. The girl in the hairdresser. You know perfectly well.'

'Ah. Yes. Young Doreen. The child. How may I help you there?'

Milly was aware of the thump in her heart. She was ashamed by that. Even of being here.

'You can help me, Jonathan,' she said as plainly as her anxiety would allow, 'by assuring me that you did not escort her to the pictures and then leave with her in a taxicab afterwards.'

'Well . . . I'm rather afraid I did do those two things, but with the very best of intentions, I assure you.'

Milly was shocked by the hot flush of anger that now coloured her cheeks – was aware of her erratic and impatient tapping of a foot. Then came an aching deep in her heart.

'Very best of *intentions* . . .' she was hissing. 'I *see* . . .'

'She had not the fare. What do you call it? The price of a ticket. I was happy to oblige. And afterwards, well – it was dark, it was raining . . . I could hardly just leave her there, could I? Of course I had to see her safely home. Being the gentleman I am.'

Milly blinked, and looked up at him.

'Really . . . ? Is that really what happened?'

Jonathan smiled in the way that just made her dissolve. He walked towards her and stooped to kiss the top of her head.

'Milly, my darling. What a foolish thing you are . . .'

Her head was against his chest. She hugged him hard.

'Oh Jonathan . . . it's just that I get so . . .' And then her nose was twitching. 'You smell of blood . . . I'm covered in it . . .'

'No. I don't. Blood, actually, it has no smell. It is simply . . .'

'I know. Clean. Very pure. You've told me.'

'Well good. So you know, then . . .'

But, he thought, gazing over her shoulder as she gripped him close to her, focusing uneasily on the bright white tiles above the chopping block . . . but . . . if that man knew, then others too must surely be aware . . . ? Or no – he clearly was working alone. But how did he come to find me? Man was a moron, wasn't he? Was he? But anyway instructed to seek me out, that much is certain. And to whom has he spoken? Who did he tell? How much money did he seriously imagine that eventually he might have pumped out of me? And now . . . will someone else be coming for me? Yes . . . oh yes . . .

there is bound to be someone else. Soon . . . ? Will it be soon? That remains the only question: when will they be coming for me? When? And what then will they do . . . ? All I can do is wait, I suppose . . . that, and administer to young Doreen, the child, a thoroughgoing punishment.

CHAPTER SIX

He Knows Nothing

'Where you bin then? Ay? Tea gone cold . . .'

Milly glanced at Jim as she unknotted her scarf and let the coat shrug away from her shoulders. An uncharacteristic and jagged shudder of irritation had made her eyebrow momentarily flicker. Merely it was the sight of him – still sitting at the dining table in that curiously hunched-up position he habitually adopted, the wetness of the cigarette end between his hard and rust-coloured thumb and the pad of a finger that was flicking it, that other mitt pawing at a teacup. Paul was there too, sprawled across the hearthrug and playing with cardboard boxes. Milly had observed with amusement that lately he had abandoned even his very most favourite toys – the soldiers, those little cars – in favour of empty cigarette packets, Smartie tubes . . . and he even had one of my old Coty powder boxes down there, look. He'd stack them up, and then he'd knock them down.

'I had to . . . there was something I forgot to get at the Dairies.'

Jim was stubbing out the cigarette with ridiculous force – grinding hard. His fingers were scrabbling in the packet for another.

'Dairies is shut. Dairies been shut for, aw – good hour-and-a-half, I'd reckon.'

'She . . . Edie left it for me round the side. On the windowsill. Down the side of the shop. Sometimes she does that. Now young Master Paul – bedtime, I think. Say good-night to your Uncle Jim.'

Paul stood up, leaving the litter of boxes behind him. He looked at Jim as he might an iguana, when safely behind glass. Jim, unaware, was scratching at the back of his head.

'On the windowsill . . . ?'

'Ready, Paul? Done all your prep, yes?'

'Did it ages ago. We've got a test tomorrow. Double Maths.'

'Left it on the *window*sill . . . ? What you talking about? You saying she left it on the *window*sill . . . ?'

'Well let's go up then, shall we? Are you keeping the fire on, Jim? Only I won't be down again. Not this evening.'

'Left *what* on the bloody windowsill, Christ's sake . . . ?'

Milly just barely winced long enough for Paul to have looked up and seen it. Then she held him softly by the shoulders, revolved him in the direction of the door, and they both walked out of the room. Jim was just left there, blinking into an empty space. And not, he thought – with the usual wad of resentment hard in his stomach (wagging his head, hissing smoke through his two front teeth) – for the first bloody time, neither. You try to please people – you do your bleeding best. And what you get? Ay? What you get? I tell you what you get: you get a smack in the chops, that's what you bloody get. It's like I don't dare open me mouth no more. I mean to say – it's my house, ain't it? My little business what pays for all of the doings. So why I got to feel like I'm just some pile of dogshit what got trod in the carpet? Ay? Not right, is it? Not right, in your own bloody house. Englishman's *home* . . . ? Don't make me laugh. And what's all that about a bloody windowsill round the side of the Dairies? Ay? What's all that malarkey? Blimey – Mill, she in and out of that shop every hour of the bleeding day, far's I can see. So why can't she get whatever it is she's needing when the bloody shop's open like a normal sort of a woman? Ay? Why's she got to be creeping down an alleyway halfway through the night and picking up her bits off of a bleeding windowsill? And what she get, anyhow? Ay? Didn't have nothing with her, not when she come in. I dunno. What's a bloke supposed to think? Well me . . . don't suppose she reckons I'll be thinking at all, that's the worst of it. She know how to think, oh yeh, but not me. Pauly, he can think . . . blimey – you listen to Mill, you'd reckon little Pauly's like one of them, what are they, them geezers what you hear on *The Brains Trust*, and that. Bleeding Bertrand Russell. One of them. Like that Barton bastard down the road. Talks like he's King of England, he do, but all he is is a bloody butcher, Christ's sake. But Mill – oh dear me. On and on. And what it is – I don't know if I'm meant to get this or if I ain't . . . but Mill, when she start up on it, she ain't really saying what a swell he is, jumped-up cunt. Nah. What she saying is that I'm just a pile of dogshit what got trod in the carpet.

Yeh well. She married me, didn't she? It's her what said yeh. And I ain't been that bad. I ain't been too bad at all, way I look at it. Who else gonna shell out hundreds – hundreds it cost me – to stick someone else's kid in a la-di-da school then, ay? You show me the poor bloody sap what's gonna do that. And Mill – I give her all the things she says she's needing. Give her them lavender bath doings, don't I? Birthdays and of a Christmas time. Religious. And she got all of them . . . what you call them – appliances. Yeh. She got all the appliances. She got appliances coming out her bloody ears. Telly, twin washtub – fridge, she got. Hoover, you name it. Blimey – she wants to take a leaf out my old mum's book. When I think back what my old mum had to go through, fair makes me weep. It do. Never give it no mind at the time. Well you doesn't, does you? When you's a kid, you don't think about nothing nor nobody. It's only after, you get to seeing it – yeh, and then it's too bloody late, ain't it? Because the poor old mare's dead in the ground – worked herself to death. Don't reckon she ever got to bed of a night time, my old mum. Seven of us there was. And my bastard of a dad. He just come home to knock us all about a bit, then he fuck off back the

pub. How she got the food on the table, I will never know
. . . but she done it, she always done it: we was never hungry.
Mind you – what we was eating . . . dripping and a slice,
beans, bit of scrag end in a soup . . . you try putting that in
front of Pauly, Mister high-and-mighty Pauly, then sit back
and see what he do with it. Bleeding Bertrand Russell . . .

Yeh – and then she were heaving out the mats, beating the
filth out of them on the washing line, there. Boiling up water.
Dragging buckets up the stairs. Scrubbing the floor. Me, I left
school – help her out, like. Weren't too keen on the lessons,
yeh it's true – I weren't no scholar. Yeh but I couldn't just
watch it, could I? Ay? My old mum. Slogging her bleeding
guts out. So I get a job in a shoe mender's. Never paid much
– least though she never have to take in washing no more.
My dad, he buggered off by then. Spent all the money what
the ironmonger's took, left us all of the debts. Then my mum's
brother, he kick the bucket and leave her a few quid. That's
when I get the shop up and running again. Worked it all hours.
Fifteen, I were. My mum, she says to me – Jim, you're a good
lad, you are. I says to her – What you talking about? Yeh.
Good lad, that's what she said I were. Only one what ever
did. Yeh. And next thing you know, well . . . I just turn round
and she gone. Come up from the shop one night, and it all
dark and ever so quiet. I thought – funny. Come into the
room. Parlour, we called it. Don't no more. And there she
were, all keeled over. Half in the old tin bath what she been
filling out of kettles. Burned her arm something terrible. Red

and white it were. And all down the side of her face. Didn't matter. On account of she dead. Doctor said it were her heart. Just must've burst, I reckon. Yeh well.

After that, my brothers and my sisters, they was all fostered off. Adopted, one or two of them – formal, like. So then it were just me. I put my back into the shop. All I had. Started making a few bob. Then the war come along and, well – got to do your bit, ain't you? I didn't mind. I were one of the first to volunteer. Never saw no action, though. I got this Achilles problem, is what they says to me – don't know the ins and outs of it. But sometimes, my feet, they'll just buckle from under me, and I goes all useless. Bugger if I got a cup of tea in my hands. Anyway, the army – they bung me in a desk job down Minehead. Least I kept safe. And then I goes and meets Mill. That were a day. Won't never forget that day in a hurry, tell you that. Lovely-looking gel, she were. Still is, my eye. Ever so posh. That were a worry. But she never seemed to mind all of that – that I were common and don't know nothing. We had a laugh, Mill and me. Never were bothered. She never minded. She do now. Now she do. You can smell it. Wherever I am, there's the stink of it. I only asked her to marry me because that's what the lads were doing in them days. And Mill, she were the only gel what I knowed. You could've blown me down with a wossname when she turn round and go yeh to me. Blimey, I thought.

Reckon . . . I reckon I'll get myself upstairs. Turn off all the doings. Mill, she'll be in the box room tonight, if I know her. Like what she were last night. Don't know why. Couldn't tell you. Don't like to ask.

Milly heard the creak — saw the passing of Jim cutting the bar of white beneath the door, and then it winked back. She heard then the snap of the light switch, and it was gone again. All is quiet and darkness. So now and at last I can relax, and turn out the bedside lamp. Now that I know he's not going to come in here and start making an unholy fuss like he did last night. You could smell the Bass from the doorway. But this time, clearly, he's accepted it. Well good. Because it's getting harder and harder, you know — it really is so terribly difficult for me. Lying next to him in that so very narrow bed of ours. I have suggested we throw it out — get a nice pair of twins. Why, he says. Wholly predictably. What's wrong with it, he says. Good bed, this is. Served us Trojan. Got years of life in it, this bed has. Yes. Well, I couldn't tell him — could I really? Of course another man might have known. Might maybe have understood. But he doesn't understand. Jim, he knows nothing. About anything, really. And I suppose I ought to be grateful for his seemingly utter blindness where I am concerned. I mean to say — he did go on a bit about all that nonsense I was talking about the windowsill and the United Dairies . . . but of course he was taking it nowhere because he never really has anywhere to go with a thing. I'm not even sure that there is a window, never mind a sill. It just floated into my head — and I'm rather pleased it did, because I had to say something, didn't I? I couldn't very easily say Yes well I'll tell you where I've been Jim, since you come to ask me. I have in fact just been visiting Mister Jonathan Barton, family butcher, who was at the time covered in blood. Fresh blood: warm. All over that beautiful suit of his. And the reason I had been calling upon Mister Jonathan Barton, family butcher, is because I was consumed with a no doubt girlish and extremely idiotic panic and the burning red-hot poker of jealousy, but I can assure you they felt no less real to me for their lack of foundation. You could indeed say that I was in anguish. And all because that awful Mrs Goodrich had invoked the name of a silly little girl called Doreen. And of course there had been a perfectly rational explanation, as – had I stopped to think for just for a moment – I knew there must. Deep down. I just had to hear it from his own so very sweet lips, that's all. Because the thought of it otherwise . . . well I simply could not bear it, I do know that. This is the position in which I find myself, considerably to my surprise, and I am somewhat stranded, I admit it. Though still that desert, that place of abandonment from what used to be the comfort of my everyday life, has become the very place I long to be. So thrilling is my exile, that were it not for Paul, I should happily live there forever, on my secret island. Yes – it's not a desert, it's a paradisical island. I row there, back and forth.

Yes of course I would love to take Paul with me, if only I could. But impossible. Such a prospect would require all things to be equal, and when ever are they that? He does get on so very well with Amanda, though, my Paul. Which is just lovely – and so very in keeping, somehow. He only just has been telling me so, as I was putting him to bed. He's such a funny little boy – he hates it, absolutely hates it, if ever I mention her (he blushes so prettily it makes me want to hug him), and yet out of the blue he will suddenly start jabbering away about her thirteen to the dozen, and so very animatedly. She is such a lovely creature, and of course so very beautifully brought up. So beautifully spoken. I suppose there will have been some sort of contribution there from . . . from the mother, but I really wouldn't know. We rarely encounter. Fiona, I believe she is called. Paul says that Amanda never speaks of her.

'Well what does she talk about then?' I asked him. 'Lie down and let me tuck you in.'

'Nothing, really.'

'Well she must talk about something, Paul. What do you have to say to her, then? You're together an awful lot. Aren't you? Hm? Must talk about *something* . . .'

Paul was screwing up his nose and narrowing his eyes into a parody of concentration.

'Don't know. Just things.'

Milly smiled and nodded. Smoothed away the hair from his forehead.

'Does she . . . ever mention her father, at all?'

'Her father? Not really. She says he's pretty generous.'

'Mm. He is. I expect so, anyway. He does seem quite well-to-do. Is that all she says?'

'Think so.'

Actually, it now occurred to Paul, I don't think she has ever said that – about her father being generous. She's said that his moustache is quite prickly, but she likes it. I must have looked a bit sick or something when she said that but only because I was thinking of Uncle Jim's disgusting moustache. I wouldn't ever get close to that. To know if it prickled. It would just smell. That's all. I said all this to Anthony, once. We'd just come back from school and we were in the sweet-shop and Anthony's father had just finished selling cigarettes to Mr Bona from the delicatessen and he had given us both a liquorice pipe with all those little red dots on the end that I always save up till last and then he said he was just going to boil up the kettle and wouldn't be two ticks. And then I said to Anthony – who was sitting on his father's stool now behind the counter because he always gets tired if he stands too long: he says the metal of those things he has to wear starts pinching him; it must be horrible.

Anthony's dad came back in then with a cup of tea, and we went up to Anthony's room. It's quite nice in there actually because he's got posters for R.White's Cream Soda, Smarties and Rowntree's Fruit Gums on the wall. He said he rescued them from big fat Sally from Lindy's before she managed to tear them all to pieces. He calls her Hippo now.

'Is your dad okay?' I asked him.

'What do you mean?'

'Crumbs. Why is it, Anthony, whenever I ask you anything you ask me what I mean? I mean – your dad. Is he okay?'

'Think so. Sort of okay. He's just Dad. Don't know what you mean.'

'It's just that . . . I don't know. He looks a bit – sad, that's all.'

'Mm. I suppose he might be, a bit. There's me to look after. The shop. Mum, of course . . .'

'I've never seen your mum.'

'Oh I have.'

'You are a complete and utter twerp, Anthony! Do you know that? Of course you have! She's your mum, isn't she?'

'Yes. I know. But I don't see her often. She doesn't like people, really. Seeing people.'

'Yes but at teatime, and things. When she puts you to bed, and everything . . .'

'No. Dad does all that. He says she's not well. Says she's quite ill. Don't know what's wrong with her. She's been like that for ages.'

And I thought – gosh, that must be really awful. Like not having a mum at all. I mean – I don't, of course. I don't have a mum, not really. But Auntie Milly, she's even better. She's the best mum in the whole wide world. I'd hate it if she didn't tuck me into bed every evening. I wish she wouldn't make me say my prayers, though – but I do it really quickly. I don't like to ask God to bless Uncle Jim because I don't really think he deserves it. And when it's over she kisses my head and I smell all her Lilian Valley and she tells me that she loves me and that tomorrow is a lovely day.

'Nighty-night then, Paul. I love you. And tomorrow – tomorrow is a lovely day.'

'I love you too, Auntie Milly. Night-night.'

Yes – I love him so. Every night I say it to the little mite, and every night – every single night without exception – I walk over to the door and I have to switch off the light before I turn around to smile and then just flutter across to him my two-fingered wave, or otherwise surely he would catch the glinting of those tiny stinging pinpoints of tears in my eyes. The rush of just loving him, the sourness and twist in my stomach whenever I just must leave him, even for a single night . . . and when I wake in the morning, always exactly two minutes before the alarm is set to go off, my only thought is: Paul. Yes. But at night . . . at night, though . . . at night, in the still and dark, it is another I think of.

The moment when I first encountered him was on the morning of the reopening. The old butcher, Mr Blake, his nerves had eventually got the better of him: never really was the same since the end of the war. And now this Mr Barton had taken over the shop. It did look very spruce. There was bunting outside, and the rather odd cashier woman he has in there, mousy little thing, was handing out thimblefuls of Harveys Bristol Cream. Rather too early in the day, though – not that anyway I am a lover of sherry – so I marched up to the counter and I said to this very tall and handsome man there 'Good morning. Welcome to England's Lane. I hope you will be very happy and prosperous. I should like three pork chops and a pound of lard please, if it isn't too much trouble.' And his eyes, they creased into that smile of his that I have come to know so very well, and he said to me 'Quite the reverse, I do assure you, madam. It is both my honour and my privilege to be able to serve you.' Well. And the beautiful deep rich tone of his voice, the quite perfect accent . . . His large and capable hands as he wrapped the chops in a sheet of greaseproof. I think I blushed. I know! So terribly shamemaking. But I do think I must have. And looking back . . . looking back, you know – whether or not I admitted it to myself at the time (and I didn't, of course I didn't – I strove so hard to put it out of my mind for weeks and weeks, and then simply months) . . . I was, at that moment, completely smitten. A thing that never before had happened to me in my entire life on earth, and nor did I ever expect it. Here was the stuff of novelettes and serials on the wireless – hardly applicable to everyday life. Hardly applicable to mine, anyway. And yet . . . here it was within me.

There was, over time . . . what I suppose you might term banter. No more than that. And of a mild, quite casual and perfectly friendly nature, it ought to be understood: Jonathan was ever the gentleman. And then one day – the shop was empty, even the funny little cashier was absent from the box that he keeps her in – one day he said to me, across the counter:

'Mrs Stammer. Please do forgive me, if you can find it within your good heart, should I in any manner whatever come to cause you even the very slightest offence . . . but I am moved to be bold.'

Well I ask you! How on earth is a lady expected to respond to a speech such as that!

'Why Mr Barton. I cannot imagine what you mean to say to me . . .'

Which, due to my abiding love for Jane Austen, is the sort of thing that always I had rather longed to utter.

'Oh but surely, Milly . . . may I call you that? Would you permit me? It is simply that I feel that already I know you so very well . . .'

'I'm sure that cannot be, Mr Barton . . .'

'Jonathan. Please. I entreat you. I should regard it as a rare and signal honour should you feel able to bring yourself to call me Jonathan.'

'Well . . . Jonathan. Of course I shouldn't mind. Why on earth would I? And I should be delighted for you to call me Milly. Heavens – everyone else in the Lane does. Apart from such as Mrs Goodrich, of course. The Lord alone knows what it is that she might call me!'

'Ah indeed! Our own, our one and only Mrs Goodrich. Truly a force of nature. One may only stand back and behold, in awe. Well Milly . . . it occurs to me that possibly one lunchtime – Thursday, conceivably, when I close at twelve . . . you may care to partake of a little, what do they say . . . ?

Bite? Yes? A bite to eat? If only so that you may know me without an apron, and elsewhere than behind a counter.'

'Well, Mr Barton . . . Jonathan. I hardly think . . .'

'You would be doing me the most tremendous service, I do most earnestly assure you. I still do rather feel myself to be the new boy, you know. And you, Milly . . . well you are clearly locally so very admired, so highly respected, and there is so much knowledge, information, that you could . . . well, I really should be most awfully honoured if you would consider my invitation. Think of it, if you will, as a charitable gesture.'

Well you can't, can you? You simply can't. Refuse so gracious and really very flattering a request. And nor did I. And until that Thursday dawned, I thought of nothing else. I was shopping in the Dairies, and I thought of Jonathan. I was getting Paul all ready for school, and he looked at me strangely: I hadn't heard his question because I had been thinking of Jonathan. I shoved a plate of Welsh Rarebit in front of Jim, and all I could think of was Jonathan. And the following Thursday, we went out. To a little Italian place he knew, just behind Swiss Cottage. For a bite to eat. Rather jaunty awning, and inside was very cosy with red-checked tablecloths and all these wine bottles in raffia baskets. And goodness – I don't know where the time went. We talked, we laughed – oh, how we did laugh. The spaghetti was lovely – I hadn't had it before, not the proper thing. And wine! In the middle of the day! I think I might have been slightly tiddly. I even had ice cream. And then there was a little cup of coffee for him, and I had tea. When I glanced at my watch, I could hardly believe it.

'Oh heavens, Jonathan – just look at the time!'

'Time so very blissfully spent . . .' is what he said.

'Yes I know, but—'

'Milly – I have something for you. Little thing. But a trifle. Though I should dearly love you to have it.'

'Oh nonsense, Jonathan – you've given me quite enough as it is. This lunch must have cost an absolute fortune . . .'

'I have it back at the shop. Could I ask you to accompany me? We can enter via the rear, of course, in order to save you any . . . and then you can be away within the minute. I do so entreat you to indulge me, Milly . . .'

I carried on with one or two more token and muted protestations, but of course I knew that I was going to go there with him. Simply, I didn't want to be parted from this man. I was also, I confess, intrigued as to this 'trifle' he had for me: I could not remember the last time anyone had given me a present, not what I would call a proper present. At Christmas, Jim leaves for me under the tree a carton of Yardley lavender bath cubes. He doesn't ever wrap them: that, he says, would be stupid because I'll only tear off the paper, and I know what it is anyway. For my birthday I receive a further and identical supply, similarly unadorned. My wardrobe now is piled high with the blessed things: I don't at all care for lavender. Our anniversary he disregards altogether, and I too affect not to remember it. Eunice – dear Eunice, she used to: she used to give me presents all the time. Silly little things, often – a novelty pencil sharpener, or a card of pretty buttons. A length of ribbon. Or a book, which I always knew would be so well chosen. And it was Eunice now I was thinking of . . . now, as Jonathan paid the bill in the Italian restaurant and left on the table, I could not help but notice, a whole half-crown as a tip (this both thrilling and appalling me in equal and baffling measure) . . . because Eunice once had expounded to me her theory about the 'business', as she called it, between the genders: this whole mysterious 'business' of male and female relationships.

'It's the woman, you know, who always makes the decision.'

I was, to say the least, extremely sceptical about that.

'How on earth did you work that out, Eunice? It's pure nonsense. The man is in control. He always is. It's been like that for ever. Man's world – remember? It's a man's world. Ask any woman. Or man, come to that . . .'

'In one sense, it is of course. But for all their physical superiority . . . the money, nice cars, important jobs . . . despite all that, it's always still the woman who decides what is or isn't about to happen. The trick is, of course – because men, they really are such tragically fragile little things – the trick is to conceal that power. To make him truly believe that it is he who has caused all this to come about. Do you see? No . . . ? Well look – if a man . . . say there's this man, all right? Staring at a woman in a café, or something. Yes? Well if she doesn't catch his eye, if she doesn't hold it for no more than a second or two, and then just smilingly look away . . . well then he's sunk, finished, and he knows it. Pretends he wasn't even looking in the first place. But if the woman even fleetingly returns his interest, he simply has to believe that here is an ample demonstration of his complete and utter irresistibility, but of course it's nothing of the sort. The woman already has singled him out. The woman has decided that he'll do. And later on in a relationship, when you-know-what begins unfailingly to raise its perfectly beastly head . . . well if he does eventually have his wicked way with her, poor dear, then he thinks it's all down to his mastery, his prowess, his oh-so-manly powers of seduction. And the wise woman will encourage him to go on thinking just that, because a happy man is also a manageable one. The truth is that even when that woman was bathing and dressing in preparation for the evening, she had decided that tonight a permission would be granted. All that remained was how, effectively, to disguise it. But if she had thought No . . . well then no seduction on earth was going to change that resolution. See?'

I remember just gazing at her.

'Do you really think that's true . . . ?'

'Of course it's true. It's obviously true. Naturally, though, you have to watch out you don't have too many gin-and-Its. And there'll always be the odd bastard who'll just force himself on you . . . but if that happens, you simply get out fast. Kick him, if you have the time. Shouldn't have been there in the first place, of course . . .'

I laughed. I did see what she meant, I honestly did – but still I simply laughed, just as I did at all of her terribly bold and increasingly unsettling pronouncements. It was more her intensity as she expressed herself, I think, that provoked the laughter in me – it was that more than anything. But as I left the Italian restaurant and accompanied Jonathan to his car (the Chianti, it had gone straight to my head – the car, a Riley, it smelt of both leather and safety) I knew that he desired me. Desire . . . ! Just thinking the word had made me go shivery. I knew too that I could deflect any such suggestion with barely more than a glance – not even that, just the lack of a smile and the lowering of eyelids – and I further knew that I harboured within me no such intention. I saw then that Eunice was right: it was I who possessed the power (I was charged, and quite giddy) and it seemed so very certain that I was about to wield it. Simply by doing what he wanted . . . and not because he wanted it, but because I needed it now, and with a force so sudden and utterly strange that it nearly frightened me. I needed for the first time ever unquestionably to be *me*, to allow myself that – and it was Jonathan whom I had selected to affect this transformation.

We found ourselves in a little wedge-shaped room behind the shop that I had not even known existed. Not a room at all, not really – more a sort of partitioned section of what once had been a bit of the yard. There was a large oak roll-top desk, two glass-shaded brass lamps, a swivel chair on castors and covered in very dark green leather – almost black, deep in the well of it, faded and rubbed to bright apple on the arms. Grey mottled box files stacked very neatly, and the sort of chaise longue that your maiden aunt might well have been proud of – though this was a fairly caved-in sort of an affair, tufts of yellowed horsehair breeching the slack and blousy buttoned chintz. Jonathan Barton smiled his smile and made a gesture towards it – so very elaborate was the ushering supplication in his arms that he might have been gushingly presenting a debutante at court.

'Hardly much . . .' he said quite quietly, 'though possibly more comfortable than at first it might appear. May I offer you something in the way of a digestif, dear Milly? A liqueur of some sort, conceivably . . . ?'

Milly laughed quite shortly as she sat at the edge of the chaise longue, her fingers probing to the left and right of her.

'You have liqueurs . . . ? Oh dear, Jonathan . . .'

'I find it always rather assists one to know that a selection of life's little comforts is never too distant. A drop of Benedictine, possibly . . . ?'

'I don't know what it is. But yes – thank you, Jonathan. That would be lovely.'

'It is created by monks,' he said, pouring it steadily into two small cut-glass tumblers. 'The best liqueurs do seem to be. I expect it helps to keep the poor blighters warm – less cold, anyway – during all those black and solitary nights they have elected to endure.'

'An extraordinary existence . . .' said Milly, quite idly. 'Mm. It's strong, isn't it? Very strong. It doesn't burn you, though.

The warmth . . . it very gradually spreads. I like it. I like it very much indeed.'

'I myself,' said Jonathan – enquiring with his eyes whether he might join her on the chaise; when she smiled, he sat down gingerly. 'I myself, I feel . . . would not be perfectly suited to the life monastic.'

'Few are, I imagine.'

And yes, she was thinking – you least of all. And why, I wonder, am I not consumed by trepidation . . . ? Why do I feel so far from in pieces? Why do I not stutter, while stumbling clumsily towards the door and stammering out a tumble of such ridiculous excuses . . . ? Because I have not been lured here: I am not the innocent victim. On the contrary: I see myself as the happy volunteer who knows quite well that easily she can deal with whatever is to come. For am I not a capable woman . . . ?

'Lovely luncheon, Jonathan . . .'

'A humble repast. A bite. So glad you cared for it.' Something then seemed to occur to him. He turned around to face her. 'Milly, my dear . . .'

She set down her glass on to a gunmetal filing cabinet. Then she leaned across to him and as those eyes of his were glinting, eased his head down and towards her. The flood of heat from those full red lips that she had tried so hard, and all through the afternoon, not to ogle, nor even to glance at – the prick of his perfumed moustache – these were so exactly what she had imagined and then longed for them to be that she felt no flutter, no immediate convulsion, but merely a languid relaxation: this easing into, at last, contentment. Her clothes he dealt with as if he had been scrupulously rehearsing each so delicate a stage of the intricate procedure until his performance was both deft and immaculate. Milly was muted by the shock of barely remembered sensation, and then a series of small amazements at every new release from the constraint of her tightly elasticated and clipped together underthings, at each fresh deluge of touch from two so soft and yet insistent hands (and through closed eyelids, she saw their looming redness). She gasped only in the giving of a long-awaited welcome as she felt herself quite suddenly and completely full of him, her face tugged aside into an ever-widening smile that was happily and wildly beyond all control. She clutched his face. Slid fingers into his brilliantined hair and hugged him to her as he buried his face into the side of her neck – she gloried in his guttural and stunted roaring as they both quite briefly were quivering, and then so gorgeously subsided. And although no sound escaped her, she was singing within. Then there came a silent sigh.

Nothing, no part of her had been the same, following that charged though really very brief encounter. Immediately after, she had put herself together quite quickly . . . and as she looked at her face in the oval mirror of her enamelled compact, she giggled as she flicked her eyes sideways and said that she looked quite utterly ghastly. Though never had she been so thrilled by her colour, this wholly irrepressible sheen upon her bursting cheeks, the bright white points of dazzle in her eyes. Jonathan had given her the brooch – the gift he had had for her – as she continued to smile quite helplessly. A gleaming-faceted amethyst lozenge set in plain bevelled gold – and he pricked his finger as he attempted to release the pin. Milly kissed the rising globule of blood – would have sucked at it quite avidly. Despite his protestation, she blotted the blood from the pad of that finger on the stark white cuff of her frock, and eyed its careful seeping. The provocation of such passion did not astound her. That frock she now kept in her special box, her box of small and special things. She had new clothes quite regularly now – not from Jonathan: she bought them for herself, and more than ever she had in her life. She could not help but think that Eunice would approve – of every part of it, actually. A tallyman would call at the back of the iron-monger's at as discreet an hour as Milly could arrange, and she would choose from all sorts of very lovely things (he knew her size, he had her measure) – and of course all this on the never-never. How else could she have managed? This winking joker with his two big scuffed and brown fibreboard suitcases would tell her she had made a very wise choice indeed: in this she'd look a proper picture. And Up West, in the Bond Street fashion houses, they were selling this very article, madam – on my mother's life, I tell you no lie – for twenty guineas, not a penny less: to you, though – three-and-a-tanner down, thirty bob all told.

And Jonathan . . . every time she appeared in something

new, he behaved as if he were struck by a vision from on high: his compliments were ample and various, and she cherished every one. Jim . . . he did not notice. Ever. Whatever she had on. The amethyst brooch she now wore daily – Paul had said oh, what a beautiful colour. Jim had yet to spot it. And of course he knows nothing. Nor did he observe when just last evening, when she had been knitting, close to the fire, she had suddenly caught her breath and resisted the impulse to double right over, her stiffened fingers seeking out the source of the pain deep within her, needing to delve, and soothe it away. And now . . . alone in the box room, as the night crept on, it attacked her again. The spasm, it never lasted long, but the surprise and intensity were always quite shocking. And as once more it passed so slowly away, she blinked up at the shadows barely there on the ceiling, and she set to frankly wondering whether or not this was one of those stories that was destined to have a happy ending. In books they do, often they do. Though not, of course, always.

CHAPTER SEVEN

Best Interests

Stan Miller was carefully placing each of his feet quite flatly on the treads of the stepladder, having just fetched down from the topmost shelf the large glass jar of chocolate raisin fudge. Only last spring, it was – or was it the spring before? Do you know, time . . . it passes that quick, I can't even be sure in my own mind. But it was a bit before Easter time, that I do know, because I'd just been having the devil of a job storing all the eggs that my wholesaler had just dropped off on me. Yes – and he'd given me no sort of a warning, you know. Just turned up in his van without so much as a by your leave with all these hundreds of Easter eggs, and me with a stockroom packed to the rafters as it was: mainly down to the crates of Tizer returnables – they just take forever, these people, to come and pick them up. So what's all this, I says to him, my whole-saler: it's not Easter, is it? Not for weeks. Yeh, he says, but that's the way it is, see? People are wanting them earlier and earlier, don't ask me to explain it. Creme Eggs – them little Cadbury's numbers? Can't get out enough of them, I can promise you that: they're clamouring. That's what he said.

Anyway, I'd had a bit of a flap on that day, as I recall, what with all the eggs coming in on top of everything else. Some days, the shop, it's like that: busy from the off. Other mornings, I'm checking the door to see if I remembered to unlock it. How it is, in retail. My line it is, anyway. Sometimes the whole world and his brother is wanting his fags and his sweets for the kids – lollies, ices, fizzy drinks, gobstoppers, what have you – and the very next day no one so much as walks through the door for the better part of an afternoon. It's a mystery, really. So as I say, I was up the ladder later in the day, just like I am now, and ooh – I come a terrible cropper. I'm on my way back down, and the step, that last step on the ladder, it just wasn't there – can't understand it. Anyway – went flying. The fruit bonbon jar, that broke. Sticky sweets all over the place: everywhere, they went – so that was good money right down the drain. Christ Alive. And my ankle wasn't right, not right for weeks. Black and blue my leg was – all down the one side. So now I play it very safe. Come down nice and slowly, arm around the jar – and they're heavy when they're full, you know. You don't realise. They can be quite a weight, those big glass jars: people don't think of it. And that top shelf . . . covered in dust. I've really got to give the whole of the shop a real proper going over. Been putting it off for ages. There just doesn't seem to be the hours in the day, that's the trouble. I'm always saying I'll do it of an evening time, after I've listened to the wireless. But once I've seen to Anthony – got him his tea, sorted out his medicines, massaged his little legs for him and all the rest of the palaver . . . and then there's the wife, of course. Changing her sheets. That's become a daily occurrence, I won't go into it. Don't like to take them in to be done any more, not any more, so I have to see that Anthony's all nicely settled in with his homework and a Kit-Kat, and I nip round the corner to the Laundrette. Then I'm taking away all the plates of food she hasn't eaten . . . her favourite biscuits, the sausage rolls she always said she was so partial to. Cups of tea she's barely touched. Clearing it out, washing it up. Yes – and once I've done all of that, I'm fair fit for nothing, I'll be frank with you. Just watch the news and have a smoke of my pipe. While trying not to dread tomorrow. And that never works, of course. Never works at all. Clouds my evening, the thought of tomorrow.

Anyway, I've given the lady her quarter of chocolate raisin fudge – isn't a great seller, the chocolate raisin fudge, not these days it's not: a jar, it'll last me a good six months – whereas your sherbet lemons and your aniseed balls and your liquorice comfits, those I'm replenishing most every week or so. Yes, so done that, got her her change, and now it's Mr Barton who's rapping the edge of a florin on the counter. He's like that, Mr Barton – ever so mannerly, always a smile on him, I'm not saying that – but he's not the most patient of people. Always very eager to conduct his business and be off. Well –

businessman, you can hardly blame him. I'm very accommodating, of course, very eager to please, because there's no one
in the Lane who's such a good customer for my more higher-
class lines. No one comes close. Like today – his usual eight
ounces of violet creams for his wife ('violent', he calls them
– it's his little joke, says it every time). Fiona, I think she's
called, the wife. And twenty Sobranie Black Russian, which
he'll buy from time to time. Not on a regular basis. I only
get them in for him. And often of a weekend he'll take a box
of Terry's 1711, the two-pound box with the bow. I only get
those in for him, and all. Never sell one of them round here,
not unless it's Christmas time, maybe. There aren't that many
who are willing to spend a guinea and more on a box of
chocolates. But there – I daresay there's money in meat.

'Keeping well are we, Mr Barton? Everything shipshape, is
it?'

Jonathan glanced at him sharply, as if he had been stung.

'Shipshape . . . ? In what way are you meaning shipshape
. . . ?'

Stan was widening his eyes – rather taken aback by the
challenge in the man's voice, and eager to dissociate himself
from any intent whatever.

'Er . . . well truth to tell, Mr Barton, I wasn't meaning
anything. Just came out. I say these things, and I'm hardly
aware.'

Jonathan held his gaze before relaxing his face into an easy
smile.

'Of course. Yes yes – I maybe even am guilty of doing so myself. With the customers, you know. Becomes something of an automatic routine, doesn't it really?'

Stan was nodding. 'You're telling me. Yes indeedy.'

'Quite. And maybe some Black Magic, I'm thinking . . .'

'Certainly, Mr Barton. Pound box all right, is it? Largest I have, I'm afraid. Just at the moment.'

'A pound should do me very well, thank you Stan. How much do I owe you? Rain's kept off, anyway. Thus far. Something, I suppose . . .'

'That'll be, let me see . . . with the cigarettes, the chocolates there, that'll be thirteen and eleven, thank you Mr Barton. Quite a black time you'll be having, then . . .'

And he was immediately alarmed to see that the gleam of accusation was back in Mr Barton's eye. He babbled his explanation.

'I was just meaning, you know . . . what with the Black Russian, the Black Magic . . . yes. I think they said it might come on later. That's what it said on the wireless. And seven-and-a-penny change. Thanks very much. The rain, I mean.'

And Stan was thinking two things: that he wasn't sure whether it was just remembering about that old ankle injury of his a while back that had made it maybe somehow lodge in his mind . . . but either way it was suddenly giving him gyp. Aching terrible. And why is it . . . here's my other thought: why is it that I call him Mr Barton, and he calls me Stan? Seems to come quite naturally to the both of us, though.

I suppose it's just him being a gentleman, really, butcher or no.

'Well thank you so much, Stan. Until anon, I have no doubt. And now I must be gone.'

Indeed I must: so very much to see to. The, ah . . . incident, shall we call it? The incident, yes, with the unconscionable pig man, this has, you know, honed my mind into incisive concentration, as any impending peril will. The status quo is very evidently in the balance: the merest touch, even no more than the approaching warmth of a finger – an angel's breath, the kiss of a feather – will trigger the lurching of the scales, and then the clattered capsizing of all my equanimity, this followed closely by immediate, sprawling and unseemly collapse. There can no longer be any doubt upon the matter. And as a consequence, I have to take immediate and decisive steps in order to protect myself, in order to keep from harm those few who are dear to me, while flagrantly utilising as part of the essential process all those who are not. All those who are thoroughly expendable – and it is extraordinary, I long ago realised, how very many are. People at large, they seem not to see this. They maybe wish, I don't know – to love and be loved by all? Can such moon-eyed gullibility truly be so apparently universal? Though of course certainly one may, tight up to the razor's edge of one's own advantage, appear to embrace so nonsensical an illusion, but only for as long as so distractingly colourful a facade continues to conceal the true intent, while covertly furthering all one's best interests. I, but of course, have my own best interests at heart – well naturally I do – and at the moment it is clear to me that no one must be alienated – not now, not yet. An even keel – this is what at all costs must surely be maintained. No just palpable flutter of panic, no easy gesture of impetuosity – all must be serene. The circumference of my charm, indeed, must even be further extended – for I need now within my circle and close to my side a big and stupid man who will unquestioningly do my bidding. And this is why I made so singular an approach to the negro carpenter: Obi, his name is. Which, coincidentally, it glancingly occurs to me, sounds not unlike 'obey'. Sort of name, I suppose, one of these would have.

I had been observing the two of them while they were side by side and working in my yard. Though considerably prior to that . . . the clearing up, the making good – the appalling task of clearing up, of making good, following the demise of the loathsome pig man, that inept and importunate blackmailer whose cupidity was his downfall . . . this I confess to having found taxing to the utmost. It is fortunate that in a butcher's yard, the embedded grime of hardened blood is hardly out of keeping – for despite my constant swabbing, the interstices between the cobbles, still they are thick with it. The pig I had dismembered in the customary manner – alas, no buckets of blood for the black pudding man upon this occasion, for it was awash, and seeping into my shoes – hurtling away into the gullies, there to coagulate. Church's, I had been wearing at the time – half brogues, in a very fetching chestnut shade. Thoroughly destroyed, of course, as was my suit, shirt, tie . . . and the number of times dear Milly has since, like a magnet, cleaved to the topic: 'How on earth could you have forgotten to wear your apron? Hm? And oh – your suit, Jonathan! Your beautiful suit . . . !' Yes well, dear Milly, I had constantly to assure her, I do have other suits, yes? My wardrobe is reasonably extensive: it is hardly a calamity. And all this pursuant to that ludicrous outburst of petty-minded and so very bourgeois jealousy upon her part – for all the world as if, I don't know . . . as if she can somehow imagine that she has some sort of a claim upon me. As women, girlishly, so often seem to come to believe. And how very thoroughly stupid of her not to have perceived that I was lying. Could she not honestly have addressed the question as to why else a person of my stature should care to spend so much as even a moment of my time with so vacuous a child as Doreen, if not in order to ravish her rigorously? She is, after all, so very young. Firm, yes . . . and not inflexible. She is also in awe of me, and in common with seemingly just everyone, may be bought in exchange for so very pitifully little. A pound of Black Magic in her particular case – as I later shall be demonstrating. And even in my hot and fevered bloodied state, following an unforeseen and wholly impromptu murder, whatever abject nonsense I had come out with, Milly had accepted without question: was gaspingly grateful to me for having expressed so evident an absurdity, along with my lavish contrition for all the distress that so silly a misunderstanding had quite evidently occasioned her. Women, you see. Oh dear. Oh dear dear me.

Well I burned them, all of my clothes. Burned them in a brazier in the yard, along with those of the pig man. Had to cut them off him, with my boning knife: his body had so very quickly become unyielding. It came to my ears that one or two neighbours and passers-by with nothing else whatever to occupy the chasm of their echoingly vacant minds were grumbling and wondering at the rising smoke, and so I quickly spatchcocked a couple of chickens, threw them on to a grille over the flame: gave away the pieces in the shop. The peasants were predictably delighted and silenced: what a very fine idea Mr Barton, they chirruped and chorused – and how uncommonly generous of you, Mr Barton: this to be a regular thing, is it . . . ? Simple-minded to a fault. A scrap of griddled poultry . . . they seemed to value it above sovereigns.

I have hanging on the wall a series of tough jute sacks which I regularly fill with bone, gristle, skin and heads. In France, they would pay you for the heads, and handsomely, but in this benighted country we tend not to care for all that sort of thing. Each week, someone from I know not where with a gammy leg and just the one tooth in his skull – a nicotine fang, in tune with the horn of his fingernails – calls to collect them, the sacks, in exchange for hardly more than pennies. They boil it all down, he was telling me. Yes, he said: we boil it all down. I did not enquire further. I simply added this to my fund of redundant information: that all across the nation there are sick-seeming, angular and maimed individuals, malodorous in greasy leather aprons, who heave up on to their slight and bony shoulders large, weighty and bulging sacks of nearly putrid animal detritus, and this, at a later date and for some unspecified purpose, is all boiled down. The pig man I have had to eke out. Mingled with cow bone, trotter and chicken carcass. Dribs and drabs, you know. Piecemeal, so to say. Unrecognisable parts, chopped up small. There remains, however, still a fair deal of him within the refrigerator. I daresay by Christmas I shall see off the very last portions. In reasonable time to take stock of the turkeys.

I had called in the negroes to build for me a sort of a shed affair out there. Not really a shed, I suppose – more what you might call a large stout cupboard, in which I intend to have installed a sizeable butler's sink – in order to make for more convenient sluicing – as well as a safe. My money, that which still I have, all that is left to me, it is strewn about the building in a manner which now, in the light of these recent and more than somewhat unsettling events, I regard to be wholly unsat-isfactory. The money, it must be consolidated, easily acces-sible and neatly portable, should sudden and solitary flight one fearful moment become an awful necessity. And at first I had thought there was nothing to choose between them, the negro chappies – both rather tall, fit and able . . . well you see they really all do appear to me to look exactly the same, is the truth of the matter, and I hardly think I can be alone in that. Even the women, when occasionally you glimpse them

– if you take away those childish decorations in their unspeakable hair, ignore the gaudy garb, then they look not at all unlike the men . . . all of whom, of course, so very closely resemble one another. Must be so strange for them. Or maybe they don't quite see it like that. Who could know? And who, frankly, might even care? But then I observed that one of these black and glistening strapping young lads, while they both were toiling in the sunlight, was constantly smiling. Truly, all the time – great big beam, the size and whiteness of his teeth, the flash of gum and tongue, so very startling, in a lascivious if also faintly nauseating manner, within all the encompassing sweat-flecked black of him. Even was singing a bit, some or other rather irritating thing. The other, though – he moved with reluctance, like a sullen cat. His ugly hooded yellow eyes, hard and glowering at me with undiluted loathing. He was taut with bands of anger, his brow so rigid and heavy from resentment embedded darkly, and fathoms within him. Cheated by life, does he imagine himself to be? Dealt with harshly by God himself? A justifiable grievance, I should have said, though one clearly unshared by his lackadaisical, conceivably merely simple, companion. In my judgement though, here was a man both ready and waiting . . . though quite for what, I am sure he would be thoroughly at a loss to articulate. He is coiled, tightly coiled, quite prepared to pounce, seared by the age-old weals of barely deadened burning rage, soon to bubble back up into fury – and therefore most certainly of easy morals. In return for the proper remuneration, this man, I considered, would be most eminently biddable: there is nothing he would not be prepared to do for me. As so indeed it proved. For Obi – he now was my man.

I have, of course, to gamble upon the supposition that the pig person had neither the time nor motivation to pass on details of my whereabouts. After considerable reflection, I now am quite convinced that this distastefully oleaginous and slack-minded attempt at blackmail was a thing of his own creation. A hastily arrived at piece of personal business – a bonus, as it were, riding on the back of his doubtless bountiful recompense for having located me, which I am positive is all that he was charged with. For here was no louche and professional executioner – though that particular swift and silent ghost, he would soon enough have manifested himself in order to slickly deal with me. And so with regard to the pig man, I have deduced that a confrontation could hardly have figured within the remit of his instruction: for why would it be desirable for my senses to be pricked by such an odour? The swinish scent of imminent catastrophe. So one must, I suppose, come grudgingly to admire this pig person's spirit of enterprise: really too too sad that it couldn't have turned out more positively for him, one might even come to think – should ever one find oneself in so preposterously generous a frame of mind as to be teetering upon the cusp of losing it altogether. But you see, if one is to be a successful criminal, then brains and determination can never be permitted to flag, no not even for a moment: one must always be devotedly committed to seeing the thing through, no matter how appalling that thing might well turn out to be. As I was, in the case of John Somerset, all those many years ago . . . but for that one single and really very vital element: I should have quickly killed him. I must say that now, it really does appear quite terribly obvious to me. And yet I hesitated. I cannot even take succour in the milky protestation that I was done and gone, that all now was finished and over, before such an idea could even have begun to flower. For no. Always it was at the forefront of my mind. And yet I hesitated. A thing that I so extremely rarely have done in my life as to render it virtually without precedent. Such shilly-shally, this lack of action, that now could easily evolve into the weapon of my undoing. For two things now are very plain to me: Mr Somerset, following all those years of enforced absence from society, finds himself once again at large, while demonstrating – quite as I might have foretold – no sign whatever of eventually having succumbed to any state even approaching that of surrender. He has not seen fit to absorb all the happenings of the past into the core of his bones. On the contrary – he has been avidly feeding the avenging fire. And how, sanely, could ever I have imagined anything other? He remains quite wholly determined to find me, to deal with me . . . to deal with me, yes, and in a manner – aware as I am of his mighty resources, not to say the depth and solidity of his hatred – I hardly would care, or dare now, even to dwell upon.

Long ago though, we were friends. I think it axiomatic

that any bitter enemy will once have been a friend: for surely no one other could come to care so very deeply. Fiona and I had recently removed to Henley when first I encountered John Somerset. Amanda in those days was terribly young – the prettiest and sweetest little thing in my life by far, and so very tender. Henley was, and I am sure remains, a highly agreeable little town, though I found myself living there solely by way of happenstance. My father, who had always been a very keen boating man ever since his balmy and golden days at Cambridge, over which he seldom ceased to rhapsodise, had resided there for many years, and quite recently had become a widower. For some quite unfathomable reason, he had been, throughout his marriage, perfectly devoted to my mother. On one occasion, I recall, I even made a point of pleading with him to explain to me how this could possibly be – for he seemed on the face of it a sensible man, an educated man, and even something of an intellectual, in an admittedly minor sort of a way (he had published several papers on various arcane matters – uniformly abstruse and punishingly dull, though doubtless academically worthy). His discernment in such as literature, music, wine, epicureanism, art and tailoring were immediately and strikingly apparent to all, and commensurately admired. For prior to the barbarian age in which now we are each of us compelled to dwell, all such attributes bestowed upon a gentleman a notable distinction among his peers, and also the sort of well-intentioned though rather grimy and besotted uncomprehending affection that arose like steam from the heated flanks of the common herd. They would metaphorically clamber in jostling huddles in the winter snow to eagerly take turns in hoisting one another to scrabble at a windowsill, this in order to catch even so fleeting a glimpse through the lit-up mullion of the warmth, erudition and munificence within.

My mother, by contrast, I could not possibly love because she was the one thing for which I could never forgive anybody, and least of all her: she was, you see, irredeemably ordinary. There was nothing to openly despise – no single act of cruelty on her part had been perpetrated that would have justified any abiding resentment, let alone a lifelong grudge. Though equally nor was there anything that struck me as being even within the broadest vicinity of fine or laudable. My father had told me that in her youth she had been a considerable beauty, and despite how she seemed to me now, I had no reason to doubt his word (while noting in passing with a withered cynicism that never within my hearing had an old man recalled his boyhood bride in any other terms). But it was this one particular man who exercised me, and I found it so puzzling as a boy – it gnawed at me, I wrestled with it daily – for surely a man such as this, I earnestly reasoned, must so in his heart have needed to be with a woman who was quite thoroughly bedazzling: a woman whose smile and wisdom, whose style and demeanour (her laugh, her grace, her beauteous eyes filled with the sparkle of private amusement while very nearly veiling such maddeningly tantalising secrets) would have rendered her as a goddess to all who were fortunate enough to have basked within the sphere of her radiance: the one true shining star at any gathering, no matter how grand, the cause of heartbreak to legions of forlorn and listless suitors, all now quite bereft of hope. And then amid the hot thick velvet of the night, she would inspire and impel the scribbling by candle-light of all such breathless stuff in fevered diaries, their scribble quickly degenerating into a panicked and impassioned scrawl, and accompanied by a howl of longing for the thrill and glamour already now waving its final farewell, before seeping away into the encroaching dark – though desperately still clutched at like the very most gorgeous dream, on reluctant awakening.

But my mother, she was possessed of none of this. I might be able to go so far as to say she was 'kindly', while often she was not at all. On one morning only, I saw her but briefly before she had attended to her toilet (I believe the reason for this unprecedented state of déshabillé was that she had been taken unwell during the course of the night). The face was of the palest bisque, an unglazed white and stark Venetian mask, awaiting cosmetic decoration, a carefully drawn person-ality – spurious and daubed-on characteristics. But for now, there was nothing for me to see there, nothing at all. When she died, my father was inexplicably broken: all means of expression were quite lost to him. And in silence, he set to wandering among the catacombs, the corridors of death: you could observe and only wonder at his meandering progress day by day – all life leached out of him, a pained and insidiously gradual process that stole from his eyes their shine and alacrity, leaving just a blankness without enquiry; his skin translucent, his heavy limbs just simply hanging there. No blood, you see: there was no blood. Within less than a year, he was gone – guttered for so very long, and now snuffed out.

And this, I own, was sad, though timely – for I, as the only child, inherited the house at Henley. Fiona, Amanda and myself had hitherto been living in no style at all in an exceedingly nasty two-bedroomed flat in the Charing Cross Road. Her annuity had never been bounteous, and I was struggling ever harder in order to have published fewer and fewer poems. For this is what I did, this is who I was: I wrote verse. Elegiac. Romantic. Pastoral. Metaphysical. I was the poet. And yes, there still was then an abundance of little magazines, this is true, but you were seen to be prospering should you manage to secure for yourself half-a-guinea for a sonnet that had been quarried with a pick and bloodied senses from within a golden seam at the depths of your soul. Fiona on more than one occasion suggested I should try my hand at the novel, and of course I simply laughed at her, not to say the very idea. The novel, I did my utmost to explain to her, is no more than a baggy contrivance, a ramshackle edifice without foundation – alluring only as is a tawdry bauble, a bright-painted Jezebel jammed and caked with gimcrack coincidence so as to insult the intellect, while peopled by the flimsiest shades that defy all absorption or credulity. Poetry, however, is water and air: fire, as well. Pure, yes. It is clean, it has no smell – and yet it lingers within and around you for ever and ever.

It is difficult to project . . . quite what might have happened, had it not been for the fortuitousness of my father's legacy. I was feeling as caged as ever I have done in that perfectly wretched little flat in the Charing Cross Road – a dangerous sensation, if you happen to be me. But now, liberation had come.

'New around these parts, aren't you?'

I had been strolling on the towpath hard by the arch of Henley bridge, I recall it well, and doubtless grappling with the peculiar nuance of an elusive iambic pentameter – for such then was the extent of my inner contemplation. The man was sitting on a bench, the ferrule of his cane gently disturbing the earth at his feet.

'Name's Somerset,' he continued, with rather a beguiling and languid grace. 'John Somerset. Do please call me John.'

He was standing now, and extending a hand. A man rather older than myself – here was my initial observation – though devilish hard to put an age to him. The defiant and aristo-cratic curvature of a proudly prominent nose was dapplingly encrimsoned by crazed and hectic lattices of detonated veins. He still was strong and vital, while carrying easily the heft of experience. Educated, supremely confident, and not without an undertow of danger.

'Frost,' I told him – for this, I should say, is indeed my

name. Barton, well . . . such a coining . . . that, perforce, came after, really quite a good time after: initially in the form of a capricious and momentary improvisation, and then later as a means to my continued survival – a quickly rigged-up guise, an attempted baffle, tightly bound into the intention to temporarily elude, if never quite ultimately escape, the eternal tenacity of the very gentleman whom now, and for the very first time, I found myself to be so very casually addressing. 'Jonathan. Yes – quite new, I suppose. We've been here for, oh – no more than a couple of months now, I daresay.'

He looked at me narrowly, the smile on his lips considerably kinder than the light in his eyes.

'Frost . . .' he said with care, and very thoughtfully. 'Frost . . . Anything by any chance to do with, um . . . ?'

'Indeed. He was my father.'

'Ah. Your father, yes of course. My sincere condolences. He was much admired, your father. Fine man.'

I nodded and lowered my head. 'He was,' I said. 'He was.'

Later in the conversation – and by way of an unwontedly extravagant flourish of his arm, the gleam in his eyes now wholly determined – he invited Fiona and myself to dinner the following weekend, as I knew he was bound to. Not simply as a result of manners – the common courtesy extended to a newcomer with strong and respectable local connections: I just knew he was bound to. His house, The Grange, was well known in Henley, I soon was to discover: the grandest, the smartest – although, being early Georgian, by no means the oldest. During the interim before we dined there, I learned from several quarters that such an invitation was to be highly prized. For this is how people in a provincial town – no matter how ostensibly sophisticated – will habitually evaluate any given situation. Almost achingly parochial, but there it is – what can be done about it? A readily defined hierarchy is always required in England – others by whom to divine denominators, measure the necessary degree of distance and – quite paramount – make evident the wink of complicity, to subtly acknowledge the perception of parity, whether true or fantastical.

In addition to the house, my dear father also bequeathed to me a smallish though still unexpected amount of assets. His current account, something in a building society, a modest portfolio of shares made up of shrinking, cheaply acquired oddments and too few gilts. There is also the Constable oil sketch in the drawing room of which he was inordinately fond, but that is worth hardly more than a hundred pounds. He had earlier alerted me to the existence of a brass-bound strongbox behind the sprung secret panel in that venerable green leather-topped pedestal desk whose rich mahogany is partially faded to ginger, due to the early morning sunlight that comes in shafts through the study's big bay window: it would catch from the side his unlined forehead and the softness of his hair, rendering it then into a fine-spun and silvery floss. Within the box were my mother's wedding and engagement rings in addition to a bracelet or so, pearl studs, a locket she habitually wore on a thin gold chain (and within which I was surprised though unmoved to find the tiniest oval and sepia photograph of myself as an infant) together with the platinum choker that so ill became her. And two rolled-up bundles of five-pound notes, tied in pink ribbon. Of which, rather fortunately, I had, by the time of my initial encounter with John Somerset, already invested a rather large proportion in much-needed clothing for Fiona and myself – for oh dear me, I simply cannot tell you: the state of our attire hitherto had been very shamingly little short of threadbare (we sometimes laughed about it, though often we did not). And so we had taken the train up to London by way of something of a rather joyous spree, staying for just the one night at The Strand Palace Hotel, and dining at Gennaro's – an abiding ambition of Fiona's, and one I was pleased to at last be in a position to satisfy. She acquired some very fetching costumes, blouses, gowns and tea frocks from Liberty and Harrods, while I had repaired with quite boyish excitement, I freely admit it, to Hilditch & Key in Jermyn Street to stock up on a goodly selection of shirts, ties, cravats, nightwear, hosiery, underthings, and so forth. I commissioned Anderson & Sheppard in Savile Row to kit me out with three day suits, a couple of decent tweed sportscoats, a flannel blazer, various pairs of bags, and of course black tie. This last, very happily, having been delivered just the very week before Fiona and I were to attend this much-vaunted dinner at The Grange, courtesy of Mr John Somerset, and his lovely wife. Ah yes

– his lovely wife . . . Anna, by name. Who soon, but naturally, was to be conspiratorially instrumental in the weaving together of yet another coloured and intrinsic strand into what was destined to become – and really quite frighteningly quickly – a narrative tapestry of extraordinary scale, and very telling detail.

The dinner itself, I should say, was no more than a something and a nothing. Or so, certainly, I appear to view the thing from well behind the battlements of hindsight. Though due to one factor and one factor only, this is not at all how it struck me at the time. Other than this single jewelled and glowing highlight, the evening ran its course more or less as one might have expected: seeds were sown, depths experimentally plumbed – ideas, opinions, prejudices, quips and a plethora of half-truths, all were let loose freely as a sequence of child-blown bubbles, or the barely there feathering of a new-born chick to flutter idly on the air above us, some then mysteriously melding to rise up as a halo and into the ether, while others would dissolve, or fall to earth. The dining hall . . . well what, now, do I recall of the dining hall? Panelled in oak so very dark, I should imagine, as to be artificially tinted, and in the Tudor style, linenfold – though I cannot say that it carried very well in a room of quite patently Queen Anne proportion. The fare relied upon the expense of its ingredients for whatever impression it may have made upon us, though it was gracefully served by a civil, dignified and suitably silent man whose name I later discovered to be Anton:

clearly he knew his business well. Each of the wines – there must have been four – was, at that untried juncture of my life, the finest by far I had ever tasted. For still, you see, I was comparatively young – not maybe in terms of years on earth so much as the fact that I remained quite wholly inexperienced, as well as – yes, utterly innocent. How very odd to think it: that actually there existed a time when I was that. Fiona had been perfect, perfect of course. Always with exactly the correct gesture, a variety of scintillating bons mots, each dropped just so – the ideal degree of humorously arch coquetry, by way of flattering our host. Whereas the hostess, meanwhile . . . was regarding the scene with a degree of detachment, though also something approaching amusement. As if a floorshow such as this were a nightly occurrence (which, for all I then knew, it well might easily have been), though that this particular evening's cabaret was thus far markedly more entertaining than the general run of the mill of the thing. And have I also said that Anna . . . that she was, oh – quite ravishingly beautiful . . . ? I think I might have, without having had recourse to so stark and unpoetical an utterance – which now, prosaically, is out of my mouth. And would it be too foolishly fanciful to suggest that all those unearthly properties I had so zealously yearned to be thriving and vibrant within the body and soul of my mother (for her to be drenched in them) were present, and abundantly, in the form and being of Anna Somerset?

Although I was too naïve at the time to be even aware,

each of John's conversational gambits was as a skirmish into unknown territory: he was scouting – not in order to discover any detail of what it was I did, nor indeed what, if anything, I wished for . . . but, crucially, that of which ultimately I was to be judged capable. It was only when the ladies had withdrawn and the two of us were still seated at the dining table with sweetmeats, the ruins of walnuts, bijou glasses of Benedictine – a liqueur quite new to me – and smoking exceptionally fine Hoyo de Monterreys of the type that nowadays it is perfectly impossible to obtain . . . only then did John seem able to relax into that which, in his measured appraisal, he apparently felt sure now to be me. What coded signals, I still do wonder, can he possibly have received, when I was conscious of having tapped out none? Well of course it has to be said that his extreme and often alarming intelligence has never been in any doubt: his perception is a foil of the finest steel – it can impale you with a sigh before even you are aware of its unsheathing, let alone the quite silent coldness of its entry. And if what we now were sharing might indeed be termed intimacy, then I grant that it excited me to be a part of it.

The proprieties of course then were to be observed: we rejoined the ladies, and the talk was small. Fiona had been enjoying the port to a degree that had brought her just maybe to the very verge of over-refreshment, though still she remained quite properly decorous. And soon we were seen to the door, whereupon John had insisted that Anton should now drive us home, despite my protestations that we had strolled across here at a leisurely pace in little more than minutes. John then gently steered me by the elbow into a corner by a window heavily curtained in a gold brocade, where he lowered his voice:

'Jonathan . . . I cannot help but think that our meeting was a lucky one. Yes? I feel sure that we might be able to conduct a little business. Business, yes? Jointly, as it were. To our mutual advantage. Yes? And in the very near future, I do so hope. Yes?'

I confess I had no idea as to what brand of business he might be – and I thought rather fancifully – alluding. There was no sort of business to which I aspired, nor was I skilled in any of the disciplines – and although I therefore was very acutely aware of my own incapacity, it thrilled me still that he appeared not to be.

As yet I had not spoken. He added, while taking my hand:

'I shall, if I may, be in touch. I know where to find you. We have, I am positive, much to discuss.'

Then it was time for myself and Fiona to thank each of our hosts together and in turn no more than a dozen times in all, and for all sorts of aspects of the evening – though, as ever, not until the front door had been flung wide to the elements, and all of us there were shivering throughout. The cushioned ride home in the dark-blue Bentley I should like to have lasted forever. Fiona's chatter I refused to allow to distract me: I was striving to retain – hard and blinding bright, like a diamond – the memory of Anna Somerset's quite utterly startling face as then, in the doorway, she had for the very first time truly looked upon me . . . yes, and wholly into my eyes. The piercing that this had effected upon me rendered at once the rapier of her husband's perspicacity as no more than an abrasion. And I took up with immediacy John's subsequent offer of a working business partnership, the details of which I was barely even hearing, and was so far away from any comprehension . . . because how else? How else, yes? How else, I had reasoned – if reasoning may ever succeed in its struggle for breath within a man so very heated and wild-eyed – how else would I ever be able to maintain a proximity? To have liberty of access to his home and his life, and then be free and able to feast upon his wife . . . ?

Indeed, indeed . . . My, though: what a veritable deluge of memories. It affects you, you know: I am quite overwhelmed. But for now, while remaining ever aware of its predatory malice, its eternally lurking presence, I must for a time blind myself to threat. And so too, alas, must I wrenchingly relinquish the uplands, the sublimity of all that is Anna . . . in order to plummet, yes, to the inanity of one who is called Doreen. I go there now, so that she may quickly attend to me. Her mother is away from the flat, as I was chatteringly told is customary on a Thursday evening. At 'bingo', I gather, whatever more than detestable thing on earth this 'bingo' might be. No matter – the child, she is alone, and therefore mine. I shall smoke a Black Russian, idly blowing rings, and she will be this close to swooning merely at witnessing such appalling sophistication on the part of a perfectly splendid and older moneyed man. She will coyly ask whether she might try one, whereupon I shall ease a second into my mouth and flourish again the Dunhill lighter. Then I shall with the most infinite care place the cigarette between her two plump and sticky lips. This will both frighten and excite her, she knows not why. Then she might cough – an apologetic splutter, after the pantomime of which she will laugh with hesitation as she recovers herself. She then very easily could wrinkle her eyes: she will hold aloft the cigarette and say that it is strong. Then I shall instruct her to remove her clothing and bend very sweetly across that chair there in order to receive just punishment, and without any further delay, please. She will close and then reopen her gorgeously caked and over-made-up eyes in a manner which she may genuinely imagine to be suggestive. Then she touches my arm, giggles quite irritatingly and tells me not to be in such a hurry. I say it is impolite to keep a gentleman waiting, although then I shall have to, I'm afraid, kiss her – which, since she will have been smoking, can only be distasteful – and after that wet and tedious little necessity is over and done with, I shall elect to wear the smile that devastates while producing as if by the most dextrous sleight of hand a one-pound box of Black Magic. The intake of breath will be audible. Her eyes, they then will melt. After the melt, they all of them, women, are yours for the taking: after the melt, there is nothing they will not be quite avid to do for you: this is known. How very wonderfully ridiculous. And what a deliciously contemptible and vulgar little slattern we have here in our young Doreen, to be sure.

CHAPTER EIGHT

We All Need Help

It really is, you know, so terribly pleasant to be out in the air and walking briskly. This is the thought that was idling contentedly in Milly's happy mind as she girlishly was swinging to and fro a shopping basket in time with her purposeful steps, squinting up at the sun that alternately filtered softly, then suddenly was sparking silver through the overhanging lattice of thin and quivering quite black branches, so very high above her. On this cold and bright afternoon (and it really is freezing today – winter truly now is biting). But then on a Thursday, always on a Thursday, everything does seem to me so very . . . well what, actually? Heightened. My senses among them. It is the anticipation, I have long ago decided, that is so very largely a part of the thing. Seeing him, finally to be with him at the end of the day, that of course is quite wonderful . . . but the electric tingle that is just all over me throughout the afternoon – it makes me feel fizzy and it makes me smile irrepressibly: I imagine I appear like a perfect loony to any passer-by . . . but that terrific thrill, that I wouldn't be without, no no, not for worlds. This is what an illicit sexual relationship will do for a woman, I suppose. Though the thing itself, the actual act of intercourse . . . and yes I quite see that it is essential to Jonathan, to his very being . . . for me really is just perfectly ordinary. I'm not saying ordinary in the sense of its being particularly dull – I just mean that it comes so very naturally to me. Which was surprising, at first. I thought I should be most awfully shy and embarrassed, not to say consumed by nerves and the most terrible guilt about, well – the whole of the affair, really. So I steeled myself as best I could and placidly awaited to be bombarded by all of this . . . and so it was actually mildly shocking when not a thing arrived. The fact that I remained unassaulted by so much as even a jot of it. Something of a bonus, really. And although I have taken to it all with considerable ease, I do not experience a physical hunger, as Jonathan seems to (my own appetite would appear to be for something more, well . . . spiritual, in a way – sort of that, for want of a better word), though still I do most wholeheartedly welcome all of his attentions. I do not believe Jonathan to be in any way unusual in his very tangible need for this thing – I am sure it is simply a male characteristic. A vital release, so to speak – an inbuilt genetic necessity. He is even so terribly accommodating on those unfortunate occasions when it just happens to be that time of the month and the curse is upon me – gently schooling me in a couple of techniques requiring a certain amount of deftness: tricky to begin with, though I think now I am mistress of both (though one of them had been so far beyond the boundaries of my imagination that at first I had assumed him to be joking) . . . whereby he might, at last, be contented. And I am quite delighted to be able to be his means of expression, as it were – to be so integral a part of the intimacy, such fusion as that: because it does so seem to please him. Or gratify. Certainly there is about him – when, so to speak, the hurly-burly's done – an air of completion, of finality. Do I mean that . . . ? I'm not actually sure that it is what I mean, you know . . . because it's really so very hard, isn't it? Attempting to articulate all this sort of thing. What I mean is that he will grunt just once, and then there is a sigh, I must presume of satisfaction.

I think the part I truly most enjoy is just silently sitting there, and being undressed. He does it quite languorously – I like very much the feeling of being so very gradually taken apart. Each new release of just some of me, until finally the lady is laid bare, and then he may feast upon the whole. Which is really a reasonably lascivious observation, and I am surprised, though pleased, to have made it. I love then afterwards to be simply held by him . . . although it is true that often at this point he is eager to be up and away. And yes, I understand even that in a man, I think: certainly I don't resent it. And it's not, after all, as if we share the luxury of an actual bed, or anything – it's only the Turkish rug in his office – that, a couple of cushions, and the rather beastly bolster that lives on the chaise. Then there is the matter of time, of course – always one has to be aware of the constraints of time: we each have our various responsibilities, and always in a street such as this the proprieties must be so very carefully considered. Alas, we no longer visit the Italian restaurant in Swiss Cottage: Jonathan decreed that it was a risk, an unnecessary danger to our continuing future together. I agree, really – though I do rather miss the spaghetti. But we are happy enough in his little back office. We drink red wine and Benedictine, and always I bring along a selection of sandwiches. I thought, having some measure of the man, that it would be ham and English mustard that he particularly would favour, though it turns out instead that he is inordinately partial to Wensleydale, in a bap. I get it in the Dairies. Jim, he noticed the wedge in the fridge last week: amazing in itself. Well, you can imagine: 'What's this here?' he goes. 'Cheese, Jim. What does it look like? It's cheese.' 'I know it's cheese – I'm not bloody stupid. I can see it's bloody cheese, can't I? But it ain't Cheddar, is what I'm saying. It's Cheddar what I like, you know that.' 'Yes well it's not for you. It's not for you, Jim.' Rather brazen, I know. But I do seem to have become rather like that, just lately. If something is not pertinent, not relevant to all that I am now, and care about, then honestly I simply couldn't give two hoots.

And sexual relations with him, with Jim, all those many years ago . . . I can barely even remember. I tolerated his charm-less invasion of me simply because I yearned for a child. As soon as it was made clear to me that he was quite incapable even of that, I stopped the whole business. Well of course I did — what on earth would be the point of continuing? To endure such a mauling with no end in sight. I don't think he minds, or anything. Never said anything about it, anyway. One way or the other. The matter simply ceased to arise. I think that Jim, he's maybe not as other men are — though having said this, I am not at all sure precisely what I am meaning by it. It is possible that actually I'm quite wrong about it all: it could be that he minds very much. Well there — if he minds, he minds. I don't — that's all I know. Because with Jonathan, you see . . . each time is always something of an occasion. I love to know of the pretty underwear he trembles upon the verge of discovering: it excites me to wear it every Thursday, beneath so ordinary a skirt and cardigan. Just as I am now — marching the length of Eton Avenue, looking for all the world exactly like any other housewife in her coat, hat and scarf, her sensible shoes, a shopping list, compact and a packet of Polo neatly tucked into her handbag. But what other woman, I wonder . . . in Westminster Bank, where now I am headed, and then a bit later on in John Barnes department store . . . what other woman will be secretly hugged by satin, tugged by lace, and all in a very fetching shade of cerise? Last week it was turquoise. I also have black, of course, which always seems to me to be the very most wicked of all. I really am awful, aren't I . . . ? I sometimes truly astonish myself. I honestly never did think that I had it in me. Do you know,

I've even taken to wearing Cutex nail varnish, though only in a colour they call Damask Rose: even I am hardly ready for the bright and shiny red talons you see on all the film stars. Also now I am a regular user of a depilatory by the name of Veet-Odourless, which I had seen advertised in *Woman*. I bought it in Boots – and do you know, it really is quite as easy to apply as the little leaflet inside it suggests, and upon more than one occasion I have been pleased for Jonathan to feel and be enthralled by what I love to hear him term the 'sweet and so soft silkiness' of my ankle, calf and thigh.

But as to my undies, of course I don't buy all these lovely and frothy things in Marion's in the Lane, where I am used to getting everything else: you know, all the usual bits and pieces – the slips, the nighties, the corselettes. John Barnes, I get a good deal of it – partly why I'm going there now, as a matter of fact. Occasionally, I'll take the 13 bus down to Selfridge's – and there, the range, it's truly outstanding. The money I am spending – not just on this but also by way of the endless and blossoming debt to the tallyman … it is becoming rather alarming, I have to acknowledge that. My savings, such as they were … well, practically gone, of course. And yes he has, Jonathan, of course he has – he has on many occasions offered to buy me things, all sorts of things, but I don't really somehow quite care for the idea. And anyway – he pays for the wine and Benedictine. What I did accept from him just the other week, though, was an exquisite little crystal flacon of Chanel N°5: he said it was the only scent that was worthy of me. I dabbed it on immediately, and he truffled around in the nape of my neck: 'Ravishing!' he cried out. Ravishing, yes . . . that is what he thought me. Paul . . . that evening, little Paul, he piped up 'Have you got a new perfume on, Auntie Milly? It's lovely – I really really like it.' Jim looked up from his pools coupon, sniffed the air like a character in a pantomime who might with suspicion be smelling the blood of an Englishman. And then he said to me 'I thought there were some bloody funny pong going on in here.'

I do quite like it in the bank. The sheen of the marble floor – black-and-white chequerboard pattern, with the odd oily swirling of an iridescent green – that air of weighty silence, dust suspended in the sunlight, and a general impression of timelessness and certainty. It's all obviously very far from accidental, of course I do know that, the atmosphere they've created here – because people want to, they have to feel safe, don't they really? When depositing all of their hard-earned money. The gravitas, of course, also serves to terrify, should you be applying for a personal loan, as once, just briefly, Jim and I were forced to: like waiting to be summoned by a Victorian disciplinarian. But at other times, the dark deep panelling burnished by beeswax, the pendulum clock with its comfortable and sullen thump of each second's passing – all so terribly calming. And of course the tellers, they're always so very nicely turned out and endlessly polite to you – even if you've come in just to break a note because you're needing some shillings for the meter, or something. I do Jim's accounts for him, such as they are. Well of course I do – if I didn't take care of all that side of things there'd be no books to show to the Inland Revenue at the end of the financial year, and then where would we be? And no – I won't tell you what Jim has to say on the subject of income tax – I don't really think I need to, do I? All of his business is conducted in cash – it's almost unheard of for anyone to write a cheque: maybe for a heater or something, but it's terribly rare. Sometimes I'm quite surprised by the weekly figures in the lodgement book, once I've totted them up – it's only a small shop, after all, and really so very shamingly shabby that I'm often amazed that anyone would be moved to go in there at all. But it's the convenience, isn't it really? There's nowhere else around here that sells all that sort of thing. Even in John Barnes, you'll get your plastic buckets and dustpans and the rest of the kitchen side of things, but they wouldn't touch anything at all in the way of, oh I don't know – paraffin, say . . . or such very grisly and horrible things as mousetraps and flypapers. So at least we're fulfilling a local demand. And it's just as well really that Jim puts all God's hours into the place, having no outside interests whatever to his credit. Because my housekeeping, well that's modest enough, heaven knows, and the domestic bills – utilities, rates and so on – they're not really too significant. But it's Paul, of course, who's the main expense. Every other term that school of his will send you a letter saying they regret that the fees must rise yet again in line with, well – with something or other, some sort of waffle, but never in line with ordinary people's earnings, that's for sure. Jim says 'If they bloody regret it so bloody much, then why do they bloody well do it? Ay? Ay . . . ?!' And I have to say I'm at one with him on that score. The cost is terrible. Worth it in the long run, of course – I mean, I'd never skimp, not where Paul is concerned . . . but still, it has to be said: the cost is just terrible. And it's not only the fees, of course: there's the uniform – from Harrods, if you please. And no, they won't accept any cheaper substitutes, I thought of that, tried that: wouldn't have it, would they? Very sniffy indeed, they were, at the very suggestion. And then all the little extras that you just don't really think about, but golly do they soon mount up: a class trip to the theatre, all those books, Cash's Woven Name Tapes, sports things . . . although Paul, bless him, he's always so apologetic if ever he grows out of something. It was his cricket whites last time. 'It's all right, Auntie Milly,' he was going. 'We can just fold down the turn-ups!' So sweet. Not his fault he's a growing lad, is it? He's shooting up. My, what a masher he'll be one day. Do they still say that? Masher? Probably not. But how many young girls' hearts are destined to be broken? Or will he maybe stay with Amanda . . . ? Silly to say that, of course – they're both no more than children. But it would be rather nice. And you never know, do you? What the future holds. One day, who knows, it might be just the four of us – Paul and Amanda, Jonathan and myself. Fanciful – well yes, I suppose. But who's to say, actually?

Always on a Wednesday evening I count out all the notes

and then the coins, which I shovel into these differently coloured stiff little paper bags that they give you at the bank: they won't accept them, otherwise – quite strict. Five pounds in silver, a pound's-worth of coppers. Takes a good while, and even after giving your hands a jolly good scrub there still is always a dingy residue, a filmy sensation of soiling. Could be my imagination: I always feel that coins en masse – and particularly pennies – there's just something too earthy about them: can't explain. Weigh an absolute ton – and gosh, the way I was swinging about my basket earlier, I felt I had nearly dislocated my shoulder: but there – I just was so gay, feeling so carefree. Anyway – got rid of them all now and I've had the lodgement book stamped by that nice Mr Curtis – I always go to his booth if he's free, such a gentleman: he said to me 'Thank you again for your custom, Madam, and I do trust that you will pass a most pleasant afternoon, Madam' (Jim – and I think this every time – he could learn one or two lessons from that nice Mr Curtis). And now I've just crossed the road at the zebra and here I am in my beloved John Barnes – but we all adore it, of course: everyone in the Lane. Well it's we women I'm talking about, quite naturally: men, I don't know . . . they just seem quite wilfully blind to the joys of all this sort of thing. Never seem to go into a shop from one year's end to the other. Except their own, of course, the duskier recesses of which they inhabit like voles in a warren – if a warren, indeed, is the thing that is inhabited by voles. Not Jonathan. Of course not Jonathan: he is always the glorious exception to any given rule. He constantly is buying quite beautiful things in all sorts of lovely places, a lot of them I'm sure in the rather classier parts of the West End (I would put him out of my mind, you know – try rather harder to concentrate on the matters in hand, but I really don't want to). But we laugh about it, we girls, our infatuation with John Barnes – Edie in the Dairies, Gwendoline at Amy's, every one of us. Edie, I remember, she once was looking for a certain little something for her sister's birthday, and she said to us she'd searched and searched high and low but couldn't find one anywhere – which, as we all knew full well, meant simply that they hadn't got it in John Barnes. I wish I could remember what exactly it was she was wanting, actually – because it's really so very strange that they didn't have it, whatever thing it was: usually, and rather bewilderingly in so comparatively small a space, they appear to stock just absolutely everything. Anyway, enough of all that . . . let's get up the escalator to the lingerie department. I do think, you know, that it must really be the slowest escalator in the whole of the world. You are overtaken by people in no sort of a hurry walking up the adjacent staircase. If I'm honest, it had actually been my intention to take care of buying all the rather boring things first – darning needles, hankies for Paul, a few everyday serviettes, and some Basildon Bond notepaper and envelopes; I tried to get them in Moore's in the Lane, but they didn't have azure. But all that seems too dull, and I just can't help myself – I'm going straight upstairs: I need now to freely indulge myself.

I don't, though, actually think I'm going to find the main thing I came in for: much too racy, I should have said, for good old John Barnes. But you see Jonathan, just last Thursday, he had mentioned in passing – well I say in passing, but with men you're never quite sure, are you? Maybe his seemingly casual comments had actually been rather more considered – but what he said was that one of the spectacles he does enjoy, should ever he catch a sight of it on the television, is a performance of the cancan. You know – that terribly raucous French sort of dancing where there's this row of highly made-up young ladies in wigs and all manner of petticoats and so on, and they'll kick up their legs and all the rest of it before ultimately, by way of doing the splits while howling like Red Indians – all very faint-making – show off these very frilly and virginally white camiknickers of theirs. I once did actually see some of this – I think it might have been on *Sunday Night At The London Palladium* – and the knickers themselves, I actually remember thinking them quite chaste, if that isn't just too perverse of me. But voluminous, is what I mean. And thoroughly unrevealing. It's the frills themselves, I suppose, that are wholly the thing. Well so you do see what I mean – not quite the thing for John Barnes, are they really? Even Selfridge's might not run to them – but still I thought I owed it to the two of us, to Jonathan and myself, to at least try to look for them: both his reaction and the sensation of actually wearing the things, after all, could only be entertaining. I quickly passed by the children's shoe department (always on a Saturday there are queues of excitedly giggling kiddies repeatedly X-raying their feet in the Start-Rite machine they've got there up a little flight of steps – the sight of the thing rather uncomfortably reminding me that Paul was in sore need of not just wellingtons but more to the point those horribly expensive hard-soled indoor shoes that his school just absolutely insists upon . . . and here is his Auntie Milly on the hunt for a pair of Parisian camiknickers . . . oh dear me). And I had only just reached the department – had yet even to riffle through the racks – and goodness, heavens above, I was simply stopped dead in my tracks: I could barely believe my eyes. For there, no more than just yards in front of me, was Stan Miller, of all people on God's mellow earth, and holding out at arm's-length distance from him what looked like a sort of a very filmy gown affair, a sheerish thing that a lady of leisure might slip on over a nightdress, and in a pretty shade of coral with contrasting little satinet bows at the shoulder: he seemed quite lost in earnest contemplation – devoting to the thing a very thorough appraisal. Well my brain, I have to tell you, was urging me to turn around then and there and just walk away as rapidly as possible: my brain, it was quite insistent that I should instantly be gone, to quickly retrace my steps to the escalator before Stan could have the chance to look up and just register my utterly astonished presence, gaping now full at him. And although I can vouch for the fact that this brain of mine remained very stubbornly set upon so decisive a course of action, I can also tell you this: my body, well – that apparently was having no part of it. I just continued to stand there, as if both my feet were cemented into the flooring. And then of course he did, didn't he? Well of course he did, Stan – idly glanced over, and then he saw me. And blinked. I don't think that yet he had focused, quite established the connection – because it can be like that sometimes, as I know to my own cost, should you ever encounter somebody somewhere so bemusingly out of context. Then a smile, a kindly smile of recognition did begin slowly to play at the corners of his mouth – before suddenly, it froze there: his eyes now were those of a hunted creature, spotlit and exposed, the concern and simply quite boiling embarrassment dancing rather alarmingly all over his reddened and perspiring face as roughly he rammed back the gown on to the rack and started up babbling to me in a pitch rather higher than his usual one some or other gobbledegook, not a single word of which was remotely comprehensible. Though finally, a sort of sense began to filter through:

'. . . tea, really. Just on my way there – cafeteria, you know. It's just down the, um . . . well I expect you know where it, uh . . . Nice cup of tea, thought that would be nice. This thing, this nightgown thing, I just saw it hanging there, and er . . .'

'Hello, Stan. How lovely to see you. Not often we can escape from the Lane, is it? Only on the blessed and sacred half-day closing. Except for Jim, of course. He never closes. He'd stay open all through the night if he thought there'd be any customers. How are you?'

'Keeping nicely, I thank you Milly. Kind of you to enquire. And yourself? Seem to be blooming, as ever. Saw it just hanging there, you know – and then I thought that Jane, Janey – you know, Janey, my wife, you remember – always was partial to that particular colour. Wore it on our wedding day, matter of fact. Just struck me out of the blue, sort of style.'

'It seemed very elegant, from what little I could see of it. Are you going to buy it for her, then? How terribly sweet.'

He looked at her like a culprit in an orchard whose jersey was bulging with freshly scrumped pippins.

'Buy it . . . ? Well – hadn't really, um . . . I'm not really, um . . . versed, you know. Not very good at . . . all this sort of gubbins.'

Milly was smiling encouragingly, though closing her eyes and silently sighing: what is it about men, actually? Why always must they be so very actively hopeless? With, of course, the one great glorious exception (and just thinking this, she was pleased to feel that keenest little surge of excitement rippling right into her).

'Maybe I might be able to advise . . . ? Perfectly happy to, Stan – if you think I could be of any . . . I mean to say, we all of us need a little bit of help, don't we? Time to time. If something is beyond our ken. Now are you aware of her size? That's the prime thing. Listen – speaking as a member of the fairer sex, I'll let you into a little secret, shall I Stan?'

He gazed at her half-expectantly.

'Secret . . . ?'

'Mm. I just can't tell you how terribly important it is in such delicate matters as these to make sure that the sizing's bang on. Too large, and a woman will be quite convinced that you see her as being fat. Too small, and she'll believe that she must be fatter than ideally you would like her to be. And nothing you can say, I'm afraid, will persuade her otherwise. Awful, isn't it? Neuroses, you see. It affects every single one of us, silly ninnies that we are. It really is rather a minefield. You poor things. I do quite sympathise.'

'Twenty-six, I think . . . Can't be sure.'

Milly regarded him.

'Twenty-six what, Stan? I mean to say – although I haven't actually seen Jane for quite a long while, I hardly think she can be a size 26 – that would put her on a par with Tessie O'Shea and Bessie Bunter. Both of them bundled up together.'

'No no – that's her waist, I think. Used to be, anyway. Might be wrong. But I couldn't tell you all the other bits, not for the life of me. Look – I'm not sure I'll bother, you know. Like I say – I was just really on my way to have a nice cup of tea, and very possibly a portion of fruitcake. I just saw it hanging there, that's all. And Milly – you wouldn't, I don't suppose, um . . . I mean, thousand things to see to, I expect, but er . . . you wouldn't by any chance care for, maybe, a um . . . ?'

'If you are inviting me to take tea with you, Stan, then I can think of absolutely nothing more divine on earth. I'm completely parched. But honestly, though – I really do mean it. If you'd like me to . . . I mean it's no bother Stan, you know, no bother at all. I can put it on, if you like, and then you can sort of see how it might look on her. Yes? I'm a size 12. Could that be more or less right, do you think? Is she my sort of size and shape, Jane . . . ? I honestly can't remember, it's been that long . . .'

Stan now was openly staring at her.

'Your size, yeh more or less, I suppose. Not really your, er – shape though, I wouldn't have said. She's more sort of . . . don't know. Hard to say. Can't remember. Straight up, maybe . . .'

'I see . . . Well I'll just slip it on for you, shall I? Can you just hold my coat for me for a minute? Thanks, Stan. Oh it is nice, isn't it . . . ? Beautiful fabric. And such a pretty shade. There! What do you think? I'm your very own model. You'll have to ignore the shoes and everything, though. Not quite designed for the boudoir. Shall I twirl . . . ?'

Stan still was openly staring at her. And then he just about managed to say:

'Lovely . . .'

'It is, isn't it? It really is. Oh gosh – eighty-nine and eleven, though . . . ! Still, it is a quality garment. You can certainly see that. What do you think . . . ?'

'I think . . . no, I don't really think so. Thanks, Milly, for all the, er . . . looks lovely on you, it really does, but I think I'll leave it, you know. Now I come to look at it – now I come to see the thing, I don't think she'd . . . well I just don't really think it's her, somehow.'

'All right then, Stan. You know best. I'll just slip it back. Anyway – you can always get it later, if you change your mind. They don't shut till five-thirty, so you've got heaps of time. Now then – is your offer of a cup of tea still open? It is? Oh splendid. Well then lead me to it – I can't tell you how that will so hit the spot.'

They walked the short distance through ladies' coats and nursery things to the broad and handsome entrance to the cafeteria – very lovely, to Milly's eyes, the walls and reception counter still clad in the original 1930s rosewood veneer and gleaming streamlined chromium fittings – not unlike, it has just occurred to me, a smaller version of the Odeon just down the road. How awful if either had been bombed in the war. Can you honestly imagine a life without John Barnes or the local fleapit? Dreadful. Now on the left, well – cafeteria is really too humble a word for the section on the left: proper and crisp white napery, and a single pink carnation with a sprig of fern in a silver flute on every single table: terribly smart. Waitresses quite like the old wartime nippies, all in black, with snowy pinnies and token mob-caps Kirbigripped to their nets and perms. Some of them I remember from so long ago: must be perfectly ancient by now – and yet still they're all scooting about the place, smiling and scowling according to temperament and the state of their feet, the make-up never less than caked – orangey powder and thin and puckered mouths smarmed over with bright red lipstick painted into an optimistic bow that far exceeds the contours of their nearly vanished lips: maybe the use of cosmetics is as strictly regulated as the code for uniform. Anyway – this is much more of a restaurant than anything (and many's the time I've enjoyed a more than adequate plaice, chips and peas here: very fresh, beautifully breadcrumbed, and not at all bad value at five-and-six, all things considered; Paul adores it, whenever I take him). The section to the right, however – well this is a far more modern and casual sort of a thing altogether: lemon and sky Formica tables, pale-green and cream linoleum tiles – and it's all this new 'self service' idea where you slide a tray along a shelf sort of thing – not a shelf, not really, but I don't know what else you'd call it – and select whatever it is you want from all these see-through plastic boxes: all so very contemporary. That's quite the word at the moment, contemporary. Normally it's applied to that rather funny new furniture and so on – a chair that looks more like a raffia dog basket on these very thin and spindly black metal legs: far from cosy-looking. Or a side table, coffee table they call it, in the shape of an artist's palette; coat hooks and magazine racks with all differently coloured balls on the ends of them, don't ask me why. The things they think of. It's all very gay, I've no doubt of it, but not honestly to my taste – I much prefer the traditional and altogether more comfortable sort of thing.

Anyway – Stan is ahead of me in the queue, and whether I like it or not I'm looking for the first time at the back of his neck. I think he must go to the same awful barber as Jim

– that dark and cheap little place just opposite Chalk Farm tube station, an area I wouldn't ever choose to visit, not if I could help it; certainly that neck is clippered, and it does seem rather raw. Nor, now I come to think of it, have I ever before seen him in a coat and hat and out and about. I think in everyone's minds, you know, the people in the Lane over time have gradually evolved into essentially no more than the most visible component of the shops they are running: one is unthinkable without the other, and it is strangeness itself to see them apart. Oh dear . . . there seems to be a blockage in the queue: we're not even budging, and I'm very sick of looking at a pyramid of Lyons' Individual Fruit Pies and this largish glass tank of perfectly ordinary milk, though churned up constantly by some or other sort of a device in order to make it appear so very temptingly bubbly, in the manner of a milkshake, I suppose – which, I see from the tariff, would cost you a whole shilling more, which does seem to me to be slightly excessive. So anyway . . . I think I handled the whole business of the negligee, or whatever you would like to call the thing, really fairly satisfactorily – not too badly, I'd consider. Well I was so completely thrown – didn't know what to say, really. Thank the Lord, though, that it hadn't been the other way around – because just imagine if Stan had happened along at the very moment I had been standing before a full-length mirror and holding in front of me a pair of white and frilly vaudeville knickers . . . ! And was he really thinking of buying that perfectly hideous thing

for Jane? It was horrid, when it actually came to the feel –
clung to my clothes very clammily: clearly synthetic, and
not nice at all – not to say daylight robbery at even half the
price, I should have said. Mind you, from what I've heard –
admittedly at third hand from someone who had been talking
to the beastly Mrs Goodrich (and I know I shouldn't listen)
– Jane, his wife, poor man, she doesn't even trouble to get
dressed at all, these days. Doesn't even take the pins out of
her hair – and that it's Stan who has to see to poor little
Anthony. Cooking, cleaning, shopping – and all this on top
of the sweetshop. Can that really be true? I think I'm going
to have to find out, if ever we can pay for our teas and get
settled at a table. But if it is true, if she really is, Jane, just
lounging about the house all day in her nightclothes . . . well
possibly buying that gown thing was a genuine intention
after all. Well of course it was – what am I thinking? It had
to be. Why else would Mr Miller the confectioner be in the
middle of John Barnes' lingerie department and staring at a
pink nylon ladies' nightgown? An impetuous gift for his
vampish fancy woman whom he keeps in some considerable
style in a St John's Wood villa? I hardly think so, do you?
Not our Stan.

'Gosh – *finally* . . . !' Milly was laughing, as she placed on
a table quite close to the window her cup of tea and two
McVitie's digestive biscuits, wrapped in printed cellophane.
And then she glanced about her in a vague sort of a way for
somewhere to put this mottled brown Bakelite tray, eventu-

ally leaning it against the table leg. 'What on earth was the hold-up, Stan? I was imagining I'd die of old age before I even got to drinking my tea. I thought it was supposed to be quick, all this "self service" business. I thought that was meant to be the idea.'

Stan was sitting opposite her and unwrapping his briquette of fruitcake.

'Some woman. Forgot her purse. Wanted to write them a cheque.'

'What – for a cup of tea? I don't believe it.'

'And a packet of Ryvita . . .'

'Oh but still! A cheque! How was it resolved? Silly woman.'

'Well . . . I paid for her, in the end. Wasn't much. Nearly in tears she was, poor old thing.'

Milly had been stirring her tea, but she stopped that now.

'Did you really do that, Stan? Oh I think that's just so sweet.'

Stan looked down and wagged his head.

'Nothing. Only a bob or so. She did offer to put back the Ryvita, but I said I wouldn't hear of it . . .'

'Do you know, I wasn't aware of any of this. Must have been miles away. Well anyway, Stan, I'm sure she must have been terribly grateful to you. Is that her over there . . . ? Oh gosh – she's waving, I think . . . how ghastly . . .'

'That's her, yes. Don't look over. Wanted my address. Pay me back. I said to her, listen dear, it's hardly worth the stamp and the envelope.'

'Well maybe she'll come into your shop one day. Tea's divine . . .'

'I think we both of us needed a cuppa, didn't we Milly? Yes, you never know. Maybe she will . . .'

'So tell me, Stan — golly it's just simply ages since we had a chat, isn't it really? You're always so busy in the shop, I never like to detain you.'

'Never too busy for you, Milly. You detain me as long as you wish. No, well — I'm not too bad. You know. Anthony — he can be a bit of a handful, of course, but Lord knows it's not his fault. Good-natured lad. Don't begrudge him, not at all. Sometimes it gets a bit on top of you. Can't think what I'd do without your Paul, though. What a boy he is, ay? Lovely boy, Paul. Should be proud.'

Milly was smiling widely at the mention of his name.

'They're very good friends aren't they, the two of them? And I'm so pleased they are. And, um . . . how is Anthony, Stan? I mean — is he . . . ?'

'Well as can be expected. That's all the doctors give you. That's all you get. So you don't know, do you? You just don't know. Not getting any worse, fairly sure of that. But whether he'll ever, well . . . how it all turns out in the long run — anyone's guess. They say that medically they're making progress all the time, but . . . Strides, is what they say. Making great strides. That's what I'm always being told. Yes well . . . but you don't ever really see the benefit . . .'

'Must be so difficult for you. For you both. As parents, I

mean. And Jane . . . how's she keeping? Not been well, I hear . . .'

Even Stan couldn't resist a stifled sort of a laugh at that: he hoped it hadn't emerged as smirking.

'Not well, no. I think it would be fair to say that she hasn't been at all well, Janey, for quite some time now. But it's . . . well it's all very hard to talk about, Milly, you want me to be frank. Never mentioned it to anyone. You're the first one who's even so much as . . . but it's not like . . . it isn't as though she's got an illness – disease, sort of style – anything you can put your finger on, if you know what I'm driving at. A lot of it's in her mind, seems to me. But I'm no expert. Not by a long chalk. Don't know what she's thinking, half the time . . . haven't a clue. Christ Alive though, ay? What a business. Life.'

'Well . . . what does she say, Stan? What does she say to you is wrong?'

'Yes well that's it, isn't it? She doesn't say anything. Doesn't talk. Not really. Oh look, Milly – I don't want to go on to you about all my little troubles. Let's just enjoy our tea, ay? What about yourself? You all right, are you? And Jim? And Paul?'

'No – never mind about us, Stan. We're all fine. Let's talk a bit more about this problem of yours. I'd like to – honestly. Maybe I can – I don't know . . . help a bit. Look – I don't want to butt in where I'm not wanted, all right? I'm not prying or anything, I do hope you know that, Stan. But I mean – would you like me to . . . I don't know – come round and see her, maybe? Drop in for a chat, sort of thing.'

Stan looked up to the ceiling, his eyes now midway to closing, as a wistful little smile crept across his mouth.

'Can't honestly think it would help, if I'm honest, Milly. I mean – it's ever so kind of you to offer, and everything . . . but I wouldn't want to inflict it on you. And anyway – if she doesn't talk to me, I don't really think she's going to . . .'

'Ah but that's just the point, Stan. People do, you see. Often, people will talk to a comparative stranger. Say things they wouldn't dream of to someone who is close to them. Why don't you let me try? At least I could try. Nothing to lose, is there? Hm? When you think about it. If she doesn't speak, well then she doesn't speak. No worse off, are you?'

Stan sat in silence, simply gazing at her. He said it before he knew he was going to:

'You're a wonderful woman, Milly . . .' And then in an effort to recover himself, he quickly tacked on: 'Sorry. Sorry, Milly – I didn't mean . . .'

'Not wonderful, Stan, believe me. Very far from it, I do assure you. Capable, is all I am. I can do things. Simple things. So let me try. Yes? I mean – who knows? It might make your life just so much easier if at least you could learn what the problem is. And then later on, maybe I could persuade her to see someone, you know – professional, as it were.'

Stan was nodding slowly.

'It could well be . . . yeh, I must admit it's crossed my mind that it could well be that what she's wanting. Well . . . I wouldn't know where to go. How to, you know – set about it. What I was really asking for. And it's not a thing you like to – well, talk to anyone about, is it? Strangers. Not really. And then again, Milly – look at all the guff I'm always getting from Anthony's doctors. All that stuff they give me. All I told you about. Lost track of the number of doctors who've seen him. It doesn't change anything, does it? Nothing changes. Shall I tell you the only thing that's changed? Shall I? Well Anthony – he's growing, isn't he? Yes he is – and I'm grateful for that, I thank God for that, because they don't, you know – not always. And last time they had him in – Hampstead General, that's where I take him – the doctor, he says to me, these callipers, Mr Miller, he says: these callipers – we're going to remove them. And little Anthony – he looks at me, see. He looks at me, and those big eyes of his – they're that bright, I'm telling you. And I'm going well yes, doctor – that would be marvellous, doctor. Three bags full, doctor. Because I can't really believe my ears. Yes and then he says to me: Mr Miller, I don't think you quite understand. No well I didn't, did I? And nor did the boy. Damned doctor, he said to me they're going to take away the perishing things, so what else am I supposed to think? What would you think? Hey? Turns out what he's meaning, all he meant was, they're getting a bit tight on him. Well we know that, don't we? Anthony, he's been saying for ages they're pinching something terrible. Told them that the last time. So anyway, they measure him up and blow me if they don't just bung the poor little blighter into bigger ones. Same blessed thing, only bigger. So that's all that's changed – now he's got bigger ones. And Anthony – still just looking at me, he is. Doesn't say anything, though. And then he does. He's smiling. I'm telling you the God's honest truth, Milly. He's smiling, and then he says to me "It's all right, Dad." That's what he says. Can you credit it? Believe that? Boy of his age? Trying to make me feel better, see? Christ Alive. I don't know. Fair breaks your bloody heart . . . excuse language.'

Milly's eyes were creased into sympathy. She reached out a hand to him.

'Oh Stan . . . I'm so, so sorry.'

'Well. Way it is. But all I'm saying is, Milly – we go to a doctor about Janey, some other sort of quack, and . . . well, same old story, isn't it? One person sees her and says one thing, someone else sees her, and he says another thing. You don't know where you stand. Pills is all they'll give her. That's all you'll get. Already got thousands of them, hasn't she? Pills. Prescriptions . . . that GP we've got, Fellows Road, completely hopeless, he doesn't come and see her any more. Says there's no point. So the prescriptions, he just pops them in the post. Spend half my time in Allchin's, getting them filled. And what'll they do to her? New pills, different pills that she gets from somebody else? You don't know, do you? And they don't know either. It's all hit and miss. They haven't a clue. And if

176

she goes and gets worse, which is highly likely – do you know what they'll do then? Do you?'

'Stan. Try not to upset yourself. Please, Stan . . .'

'You'd be upset, Milly. If it were your Paul, your Jim – you'd be upset, I can tell you. Look. All I'm saying is – they'd just go and give her some other pills. Wouldn't they? Hey? What they do. Another colour. Different shape. It's the same thing, though. It's just the same old thing.'

'Stan . . .'

He shrugged. Looked at the floor, and then sharply back at her. His face then began to relax as he slowly released the grip he had taken on her hand.

'Forget it, Milly. Forget I even spoke. Don't know what came over me – going on like that. Forgive me, please. Here – let me get you another cup of tea, hey? How about that? We could do with another cup after all of that malarkey, yeh?'

Milly smiled, very fondly.

'That would be quite lovely, Stan – but I shall get it. No no – I insist. You paid for the last one. Indeed, you seem to have paid for tea for everyone in the whole of the cafeteria . . . !'

And he laughed, thank heavens. Oh thank heavens, Milly was thinking: he laughed, he laughed. And now he was up on his feet.

'Don't be silly, Milly dear. I'm halfway there, aren't I? Just tea, is it? All right for biscuits, are you? Sure? Only I might go another slice of this fruitcake. It's really very tasty. Always had a soft spot for it. Dundee, that's my favourite.'

Stan was sliding another tray the length of the sleek chrome ridges of the narrow counter, his wide eyes now at last and at least averted from Milly – now they may finally be freed from the terrible constraint of such enforced and mendacious neutrality: able to express just a very small part of all this so unaccustomed and really quite agitated energy, the spike of animation now alive in his mind. He'd never spoken, not before. About anything at all, really. Not Anthony. And certainly not Janey. Good grief – was I really? Talking like that? About all those things I bottle up? Did I just come out with it all? And to Milly. To Milly, of all people. Milly, who, in the past – in the shop, in the street – I never really dared speak to before, not properly. Not even think about – not in any, you know . . . proper, sort of a way. Yes – and I'm not too comfy about it. Airing it all. Makes it real, makes it much too real. And I mean – she's right, of course. I can't go on like this. Stands to reason. Amazing I've put up with it all as long as I have. Janey. Not natural, is it? Way she goes on. She can't be right in the head. Got to be faced. Yes, Milly's right – she has to talk to someone. We've got to get to the bottom of it. Can't go on burying our heads in the . . . and it's for my sake as well – oh yes, I'm very aware of that. Else I'll be the next one in line for the asylum. And Milly, yes – she might not be a bad place to start. Really. She could maybe, I don't know

. . . well, like she said – what was it she said . . . ? Kind of feel her way, sort of style. See how the land lies. That's more or less the gist of what she was on about. Can't do any harm. And she said that too, didn't she? Can't do any harm, can it? What's to lose? She's right: what's to lose? And she seems to mean it. She's a very sincere sort of a woman, Milly is, if I'm any judge at all. As well as, ooh – a whole lot else, I'd say. Oh but look: just seeing her standing there . . . just looking at her, wearing that nightdress thing. Christ Alive. A picture, she was – proper picture. Never forget it. I won't. Not as long as I live: never forget it, no not that. What a woman, hey? Nicely turned out. Talks sense. Trim little figure. Not like Janey at all. Why I decided not to buy the blessed thing. Not once I'd seen it on Milly. How could I look at it again? On Janey, all hunched up in a corner, not drinking her soup, not watching the telly, not saying to me a single bloody word . . .

Why is it? Hey? How does it come about? That I get Janey. Because I'm not a bad sort of a bloke. I mean to say – I'm nothing much to look at, granted. I'm no matinee idol, God knows. No great brain either. But I work hard – love my kid. Honest everyday Englishman, really. Was a time when there wasn't much seen to be wrong with that. And then there's Jim . . . Well I'm not saying he isn't all of that too. I'm not saying that. But how is it that he gets to have Milly? As his wife. I mean – look at him. And look at her. See what I mean? Why is it? Hey? How does it come about? And now

I'm stuck with it, aren't I? That picture of Milly, forever in my mind, standing in the middle of John Barnes in her walking shoes, that brown plaid skirt of hers and a greenish sort of cardigan, and then this pink sort of nightgown over the top of it all. Won't ever forget. Don't want to, of course: don't ever want to – but I couldn't, even if I did. That, and the touch of her hand. I held it – I held it, yes . . . and she never pulled away. Soft, it was. Soft, and ever so small. Christ Alive. If only I had a woman like that . . . well . . . I wouldn't be the man I am. Beaten down. Exhausted. Just going through the motions for the sake of my boy. I had Milly, I wouldn't ever again be dreading tomorrow. She'd look after me, she would. Smile. Do the house. See to my supper. And loyal – she'd be loyal to me, that one: written all over her. Oh dear God . . . my mind, it's just all over the place. Haven't ever known it. Oh dear me. Anyway . . . what I've got to do now is really very simple. Just mustn't mess it up, that's all. I've got to stop my face looking like I've gone a bit mental – because that's how it feels to me: as if it's gone all a funny shape. So make it normal. Make it like Stan: all normal again. Then I'll turn around with my tray, walk across to that table, put down the two cups of tea . . . and try not to make that thing I get in my stomach whenever I even so much as look at her, try not to let it show. Christ Alive and the devil's thunder . . .! I'd battle my way through the very fires of hell if a woman like that was waiting there at the end of it for me.

Milly quite eagerly grasped her teacup, and smiled at him.

'Lovely . . .' she said.

Stan nodded briefly as he sat down in front of her.

'They'd run out of fruitcake,' is all he had to say.

CHAPTER NINE

More the Merrier

'What's going on, then? Ay? What you getting the boy all dolled up for?'

Milly had been beaming at Paul, his eyes ablaze with the excitement of all that was to come, the bright light of it reflected in her own.

'Nothing that need concern you, Jim. Paul is going off for a very special treat – aren't you, Paul? Hm?'

Paul simply couldn't stop grinning.

'Just can't *wait* . . . !' he sizzled.

'Where you off to then, Pauly? Sunday, ain't it? Nothing doing on a Sunday.'

'Zoo . . . !' blurted out Paul. 'Going to the Zoo with Anthony and Amanda.'

Milly smiled – kissed his flushed and shiny cheek.

'Stan, Anthony's father – Mr Miller is taking them. So terribly kind of him, don't you think so?'

Jim was thoughtfully lighting up a cigarette.

'Zoo, ay . . . ? Well – I could've done that. I could've done that.'

'Yes but you don't ever, do you Jim? Take anyone anywhere. When was the last time you offered to take any of us out? I honestly can't remember. Can you? Because I can't. Sunday is the only day of the week you're not down in the shop, and all you ever want to do is just lie there on the sofa and snore in front of the fire.'

'Yeh but . . . Zoo, that's a different kettle of wossname, ain't it? Like the Zoo. I do. Always did. Animals. Only animal I ever get to clap eyes on is little Cyril.'

'Cyril is a bird,' said Paul, quite primly.

'Still an animal though, ain't it?' snapped Jim. 'Mister Cleverclogs. Budgie – not a human, is it? Ay? Not a vegetable or a watchamacallit, is it? Ay? Mineral. No it ain't. So it's a animal. See? Bertrand Russell . . . Yeh. So anyhow, tell you what – I'll take them. Yeh. Why not? Ain't been to the Zoo since I don't know when. Be good to get out a bit. Stretch my legs. And what you mean "snore"? Ay? I don't never snore . . .'

Milly watched the light die down in little Paul's eyes. Then they were bright again, but with a silent pleading to his Auntie Milly. She had winced when Paul had let the cat out of the bag: she had told him not to mention it while they were having their lunch, although she knew he would simply be dying to. And nor was she sure quite what it was she had been dreading . . . though possibly something along the lines of this.

'Well you can't, Jim. It's all arranged. Stan is taking them. And anyway – you're not even dressed.'

'What you mean I'm not dressed? I'm dressed. Not sitting here like Lady bloody Godiva, am I? What you on about?'

'I mean you're not *properly* dressed. When ever are you? And don't use language, please – I'm tired of telling you. Of course you snore – you snore like an absolute foghorn.'

'Blimey, Mill – it's the Zoo we's going to, not Buckingham Palace. I don't reckon the chimps and the elephants is going to care too much about what I got on. And I got it, I understand what you said: Stan's taking them. Well that's all right. I'll go with him. I don't mind old Stan. Just nip upstairs and get my shoes . . .'

Milly despairingly watched him as he gruntingly heaved himself out of the hammocky slump that a very long time ago had been a perfectly respectable sofa, and then followed with her eyes his effortful shambling towards the door, careless of ash dropping away from his cigarette and on to the carpet. Oh dear . . . Paul, now – he looks positively panicked, poor boy. Whatever can I say to him . . . ?

'It'll be all right, Paul. Don't worry. Once you're inside the gates, you just run on ahead with Anthony and Amanda. Leave your Uncle Jim with Mr Miller. Yes? And Mr Miller, he'll, I don't know – talk to him, or something. Two grown-ups. Men together. You don't have to worry. It won't affect your day. Promise. But heavens – I really don't know what's got into your Uncle Jim, though. Hardly believe it, really. Going out! And on a Sunday afternoon! Gracious . . . Now here, Paul – here's some money for ice creams. All right? Although it really is so beastly cold today, I think you might want to buy something else. I went out to the bins this morning and I'm telling you: like the North Pole. Now this money – keep this money separate, because this is for your tickets to get in. All right? There's enough there for the three of you. So you will remember not to let Mr Miller go paying for everything, won't you? Yes? Good boy. And keep it safe. Here – let me tuck it into this little pocket, all right? You'll remember it's there, won't you? Right, then. Now is your coat in the hall? Well let's get you all bundled into your scarf and cap and everything, shall we? Ooh . . . you're going to have such a lovely day . . . ! And it looks like the rain is keeping off, so that's a good thing, isn't it?'

Oh God I do so hope everything's going to be all right. What I mean to say is, I simply couldn't bear it if Jim were to spoil this. Because there are so many ways, you see, he could quite easily achieve this end, and he would be perfectly oblivious to each and every one of them. Whenever he says or does something utterly appalling – which is a good deal of the time, let us face facts – he is constantly amazed by other people's reactions. He demands to know what's *wrong* with them. Because he doesn't see it: he simply doesn't see it. Well . . . at least he hasn't had too much beer, anyway – not yet, at any rate. I'm not sure whether they sell it at the Zoo. If they do, he'll find it, of course. But maybe because it's Sunday, they won't. I think there's a law, not sure. But Jim, though . . . I truly cannot imagine what has possessed the man. I mean – he does like animals, it's true . . . but only in the rather floppy and endearingly English way that we all do. Though for him to volunteer to actually pay to see them – and in the company of children . . . ! I would, you know, for Paul's sake, go up and try to put him off . . . but that would only be the proverbial red rag to a bull: make him even more determined than ever. Because he really is so very stubborn and juvenile whenever he is quite set upon getting his way – and particularly so when any sort of a treat is in the offing – that I am afraid the only way I might just possibly be able to deter him is to dangle enticingly some or other alluring alternative . . . though naturally enough, I have nothing to offer.

Oh well. None of this affects anyway what I have to do. Because I'm committed, of course, after all my promises to Stan, to not now letting him down. It was just before I left him in John Barnes' cafeteria that I had rapidly formulated and then put forward to him a sort of scheme: I ran through it fairly speedily, and not just for the reason that I'd felt that his attention had been steadily eroding – suddenly he had become really quite intent and serious, seemingly completely preoccupied with something else entirely, the Lord knows what – but also because this anyway wholly unexpected little tea party was now becoming somewhat protracted (two further cups he'd bought for himself by this time, this making four, or was it five, in total: I can't think where he puts it) and I was terribly aware of the remains of the precious day now quickly trickling away: I had been so very eager to abscond into my secret and velvet existence. A vision had suddenly come to me: the cosiness, the intimacy, of our little back office ... the Turkish rug warm in the smouldering glow of the woodstove, my skirt and cardigan not at all neatly folded over the back of the chair, but rumpled and roughly discarded in a corner – and then the chink of our two little crystal glasses, brimful of Benedictine. But before I could go, before I could escape into the wonder of all that, I had to get things straight with Stan. So I had said to him: Listen, Stan – are you listening? Are you sure? Right. Well on Sunday, after lunch, if you can take the two boys off out somewhere for a couple of hours ... although I don't think I'll really be needing that long, nothing like it, probably – but then I can come over when you've gone, you see, and have that little chat with Jane we talked about. Just remember to leave the back door open, that's all. Because from all you've said, she's never going to get up and answer the bell, is she? And don't tell her I'm coming, obviously, or else she'll almost certainly say no, and then you're in a spot. It's better the house is empty, I think. That you and Anthony aren't there. Don't you think? Yes – I do too. So – good idea? Yes, Stan? Good idea ... ? Well he looked quite startled at the very prospect, of course. Instead of agreeing with alacrity, thanking me for my forethought, the brilliance of the wheeze, my keenness to strike while the iron is hot and so forth, and then eagerly coming up with a variety of suitable destinations for the projected jaunt . . . he just sat there, blank-eyed, as men so often will. He looked as if I had just suggested he take an impromptu rocket trip to the moon. So I fed him with one or two ideas of my own – which were hardly dazzling, I grant you: cinema, Stan. Pictures, yes? Must be a U on somewhere – if not at the Odeon, then the Classic, or maybe the Ionic . . . ? Look it up in the *Ham & High*. But it turns out, oh dear, that Stan isn't at all keen on picture houses because he always feels uncomfortably enclosed – and the second the lights begin to dim, he suffers an irrepressible urge to bolt right back up the aisle and fight his way through the series of curtains and out into the freedom of sunlight. Right, I said: okay – pictures no good. Well what about the Hill, then? Primrose Hill, Stan . . . ? He shook his head. Can't be in the park for a length of time, he said, not in this weather – and of course he had a point there: don't want Paul getting chilblains. So then I hit upon it: of course – the Zoo. A proper treat for the children, and a warm cafeteria to hand, so very necessary for all the tea that seems to take the place of Stan's very life blood (and who knows? They might even run to a wedge of fruitcake). Anyway he seemed to like that option – or, at least, he didn't openly object to it.

And so the thing was settled: you should have seen Paul's face when I told him! It did make me think, though – he really doesn't get out much, poor little fellow. In the holidays it's marginally better – in the holidays I do make the effort – but during term time, he really is rather cooped up in here. And it's not as if we've even got a garden – only a patch of yard at the back, and that's piled high with scrap iron, along with a motley of other rubbish all so utterly unspeakable that I don't really care even to think of it. The number of times I've told Jim to for God's sake get the rag and bone man round to clear out the lot, but of course he won't ever hear of it. He says that one day it will all come in useful. Whether he's so simple as to actually believe that or not, I really couldn't tell you, and nor can I spend any more of my time even wondering about it. Anyway, Paul then asked if Amanda could come too – and I said yes of course she can, Paul: what a perfectly sweet idea. If it's all right with her father. If it's all right with her parents. And now, quite wholly out of the blue, Jim has added himself to the party as well, a thing I could never have foreseen in a month of Sundays. Well, I suppose it makes no difference. His absence or presence, it never does make a difference – or not, at least, as I think I've made plain, in any manner one would actually wish for. So in fact I'm rather contradicting myself – aren't I, actually? Yes – so let's be clear: while Jim's absence is a thing to be actively cherished, his presence, alas, can make all the difference in the world.

When I waved the two of them away, I literally had my fingers crossed behind my back. Awful, really – but it's hardly my fault, is it? It's Jim's. Paul, though – he looked quite the

handsome young gentleman in his navy gaberdine raincoat —
double-breasted in the military fashion, very becoming, and
the only item of school uniform that is anything close to being
worth the very high price they have the gall to charge for it:
it's a quality garment — and yes made to last, though still
within under a year it'll be far too small for him. I bought
him a pair of flannels just over a month ago — his very first
pair of long trousers! Can't tell you how thrilled he is. He
yearns to wear them at school, but it's strictly forbidden until
you are in the sixth form. I had to take them in a fair bit at
the waist and buy him a pair of braces to hoick them up: well
you see I just had to allow for an enormous amount of growing
room. They're actually so tremendously huge that they do,
in all honesty, look the teeniest bit daft, but obviously I'd
never say so; still, though, he's delighted with them. He didn't
want to put his school cap on today, but it's freezing, I had
to insist — and the whole ensemble is quite nicely rounded off
with a scarf and gloves, both of which I knitted for him in a
very soft angora in RAF blue — there were just the three balls
left of it in John Barnes' clearance sale, and they were gener-
ously reduced: the angora, it doesn't irritate his skin, because
his neck and wrists, you know, they can be rather sensitive.
Jim, by contrast . . . oh dear God, where to begin? Whenever
he goes out now — and it's a rare enough occasion — he will
wear this sort of three-quarter-length jacket-coat affair that
he bought — yes he did, actually paid good money for it — in
some sort of a ghastly surplus store in, oh Lord, Camden

Town. It's very dark blue, as stiff as wood, and there are these terribly shaming two great black plastic patches to either shoulder. I tried explaining it to him as gently as I could, the day he had borne it home in quite foolish triumph, that these coats, they are standard issue to workmen. People who dig up the road, Jim. People who see to the drains, yes? It is, I believe, called a 'donkey jacket', I can only assume because the people who are compelled to wear it are doomed then for the duration of their lives to no more than donkey work, do you see? And so to voluntarily wear one, not to say buy one, is surely the action of an ass. Needless to say my intemperance on the subject guaranteed that he is wedded to the thing, I suppose for simply ever. And prior to the acquisition of this abomination, he used to wear his old army greatcoat which was made out of horse blankets, so far as I could tell (while smelling like it too), and was of course the familiar wartime colour of dung. And here is a thing I shall never forget: Jonathan, just the other day, was wearing a perfectly cut camel cashmere covert coat with contrasting velvet collar, which might be termed 'chic', you know, as the French will have it. And wearing that coat, he stood before me, opened wide the wings of it, and then I was enveloped. That coat, as he held me within, it became a cocoon, and I happily could have lived inside there, fused to the man, until the day I died. I have no doubt that during my life on earth as a woman, this might so very easily be the single most wonderful thing that has ever happened to me.

But . . . it is Jim's 'attire', for want of a more credible term, that currently I am forced to contemplate . . . and what therefore cannot possibly be ignored then is his wretched flat cap. Simply the very sight of this will always occasion in me a correspondent stirring of queasiness: he will not throw it out – he will not have it cleaned (although now it is long beyond that). Well – there it is. So where Jim is concerned, please do erase from your mind any images of such as David Niven, James Mason, Charles Boyer – or, indeed, Jonathan Barton: for what we have in Jim, as he waddles away with my Paul at his side, is rather more akin to a jobbing dustman.

'So then Pauly – looking forward, ay?'

Paul nodded eagerly. 'I am,' he said. And he did not say that it would though be a whole lot better if it wasn't for *you* . . .

'Bet you are. Me too. So what – we cross over to Stan's then, do we? That the set-up?'

'Yes. Amanda said she'd meet us there. We're actually a couple of minutes late . . . oh look. There they are. They're all outside.'

'Yeh well, couple of minutes. Blimey – Zoo ain't going nowhere, is it? Wotcha, Stan – all right?'

Stan had been eyeing their approach with a degree of unease, though quickly he assembled a smile of greeting.

'Hallo, Paul – all ready? Fighting fit? Good of you to bring him, Jim – but I'm sure young Paul is more than capable of crossing the road on his own, aren't you Paul?'

Paul though was already in quite animated conversation with Anthony and Amanda ... and there was another girl there too, who was slightly holding back. Amanda then said Paul, this is Susan – from my school: we're both best friends. And Paul then shyly had said hello.

'Four kids! Blimey, Stan – that ought to be enough for us, ay? No no – thing is is, I coming along, that all right. Quite fancied the idea.'

Stan's face was set.

'I see. Well yes of course, Jim. More the merrier.'

A pale and sickly sun did seem to be straining with reasonable might to break through the weak and silvered sky that bound it. There was brightness enough, however, at the summit of Primrose Hill, and the six of them stood there, despite the bite of the cold. Jim had shouted to them all 'There it is! See it Pauly? See it everyone, do you? St Paul's that is. Named after you, Pauly. St Paul's Chapel ... no. Church. No – ain't a church neither, is it? What's it called? Cathedral, that's it. St Paul's Cathedral. Yeh, that's it. With the dome, look.' Stan stared straight ahead while the children glanced around at one another, Amanda and Susan struggling not to laugh as Paul glared down at the ground, his ears now throbbing with a crimson heat. Stan then checked that the fair old climb up to the top of the Hill had not affected Anthony too badly – who smilingly swung up a crutch in happy dismissal of the very idea. Paul was used to helping him a bit on the descent into Regent's Park, because it really was rather steep – and in the past, Anthony had skittered along rather more quickly than he intended and more than once had managed to pitch himself over. Stan had been expecting the usual queue at the entrance to the Zoo, but there seems to be no one, which is all to the good: quite do with a cup of tea, now I think of it. Paul then was eagerly pressing into his hands the amount of money that his Auntie Milly had given him for the entrance fees – he was pleased to have remembered, and remembered too what pocket it was in – while Stan was saying No no no, wouldn't hear of it, my treat Paul, of course it is: my idea, wasn't it? And then he paid the sleepy man in the little glass cubicle for all six of them (well the children, they're halves at least, so not too bad, but still rather pricier than I thought it would be) and as they filed through the turnstile Jim said boomingly Blimey O'Reilly – they sure do know how to charge in these places, and no mistake: last time I come here, it were pennies. Here, Stan – fancy a quick one, do you? Kids'll be all right. What you say? Little snort, ay? But Stan wasn't listening – Stan was saying this: Now listen boys and girls, before you all run off – mind you read all the signs and behave your-selves, yes? No mischief. And stay together – don't get lost. We'll meet you in the cafeteria in, what – hour, say? See how everyone's doing. All right? Got your watch on, haven't you Anthony? Yes – and Paul, he's got a watch too, so that's all right. Off you go then, all of you – have a good time . . . !

'Nice move, Stan. That's the boy. Got shot of them. So how about it, then? Fast one, yeh?'

'Don't you think we ought to, well – look at the animals or something . . . ?'

'Well there's a bloody great elephant, look, stood right in front of you. Can't have missed it, Stan. No but yeh – we'll get to all of that, course we will. Gorillas is what I like. Lions. Penguins – they're a right laugh and a half. They got a pub here, or what . . . ? Nah – outside licensing hours, bloody country. Maybe in the caff you can just get a bottle of Double Diamond or something, what you reckon? It's legal if you get some scoff in, ain't it?'

'Don't think so, Jim. Sunday, you know. Wouldn't mind a cup of tea, though.'

Jim's whole face was stopped, his enthusiasm frozen.

'Oh blimey yeh. Bloody Sunday. Never thought of that. Oh well we're buggered for the whole of the day, then. What they want to pass a law like that for? Bloody country. But the Lord God, you know – I can't see him minding, you want a tickle of something you fancy of a Sabbath afternoon. No harm I can see . . . oh well, never mind ay? Let's go and have that cuppa you was on about. Cos look what I got, Stan: wouldn't let you down, would I . . . ?' And he drew out from inside his donkey jacket a flat half-bottle of Haig. 'Give your char a little bit of oomph, ay . . . ?'

Stan now tightened his smile because he knew it had come loose.

'Let's just find the café, will we?' he said quite flatly. 'Round this sort of direction, if memory serves . . . And Milly, Jim. Milly keeping well, is she?'

Jim now clapped him across the shoulders, chucking away a fag stub.

'Or we can muscle in with the chimps at the old tea party, ay? Reckon we'd fit in prime. Yeh – she Trojan, ta.'

Stan just looked at him.

'Pleased to hear it. They don't have it in the winter. It's a summer thing, the chimps' tea party. They don't have it in the winter.'

'That right? I think that's the caff over there, look. Blimey – all brand spanking new since I were here last. Used to be more like a bloody Nissen hut. Looks like one of Billy Butlin's now: very bleeding posh, I must say.'

As he queued behind Jim for his tea, Stan was thinking he wouldn't have fruitcake on account of he'd not that long ago had his dinner. He'd fried up some chicken thighs and wings he'd got from Mr Barton's. He chops up the birds into portions: only place I know that does. It's handy: you don't have to go the whole hog. Anthony and me, we'd tucked into the thighs with a few peas and a jacket potato: it was nice enough. The wings I'd brought up to Janey: not much meat on them, but then that's ideal, isn't it really? For someone who's not going to touch them. I don't want to think about how Milly's going to get on with her: just can't visualise – can't imagine the scene. Janey, to my way of thinking, she's either just going to sit there and stare at her like she does with me, or else she'll start screaming the place down at the sight of a human being in the room. Either way, daresay Milly will be able to handle it: like she says – she's a capable woman. And it was only a couple of days back I was sharing a cup of tea with her . . . just after she caught me. Well she did, didn't she? Red-handed, I was really – holding out that blessed stupid nightie thing: didn't know where to look. Yes and what can she have thought of me, that's what I'd like to know. And then I go and tell her all about Janey. Dear oh dear . . . Funny, though, that that was just a couple of days back, when I was sharing a cup of tea with her . . . and now it looks like I'm just about to do the very same thing with Jim. Her husband. Can hardly believe it. What's he doing here anyhow? Why did Milly send him? She didn't say anything about it, I'm pretty sure. I wasn't really listening all that closely though, God's honest truth, towards the end: I was just watching her. Watching her, and thinking. But I am fairly sure there was nothing about Jim in that little scheme of hers: can't remember that he had featured at all. And what on earth are we going to talk about? Nothing in common. Except for the Lane, of course. And, well . . . Milly, I suppose. His wife.

'Nice big cup, at least,' said Jim, putting it down on a table by the door. 'Oh bugger – I gone and slopped it in the woss-name. Wonder if they got a rag . . . ? Saucer, look – gone and slopped it in the bleeding saucer . . .'

'I've got a tissue,' said Stan. 'I always have them for Anthony . . .'

'Yeh? Well give us it over, there's good lad. Clumsy sod, I am . . . you want to ask Mill. She tell you. Wanna fag? Oh right – you got your pipe.'

'I don't see very much of her,' Stan said, quite tentatively. 'Milly . . .'

'No well you wouldn't, would you? Stuck in your shop, same as me. But she do go in, don't she? Time to time. For the boy, and that. My smokes, of course. Blimey, Stan – the money you had off of me down the years! Sixty a bleeding day. I'm a fool to myself. Here, mate – give us your cup. Get a slug of this down you . . .'

'I won't actually, Jim. If it's all the same to you. But yes – Milly. She's quite a regular customer.'

'Please yourself, Stan. Your loss.'

'Seems a nice girl, that Susan,' said Stan, quite wistfully. 'I've not met her before. I do hope the children are enjoying themselves . . .'

'Don't you worry about them. When did kids not have a good time at the Zoo, ay? I never got no treats like that, not when I were a lad. Zoo? I lived in a bloody zoo, never mind go to one. Nowadays . . . well nowadays they don't know they're born. That's what I says to Pauly. Pauly, I says to him – here, come over here, tell you something: you, my son, you don't even know you're born. He just sort of look at me, the way kids does. You know. But it's right what I says. Look at that la-di-da school what you and me is slaving our bleeding guts out to send them boys to. You go to a school like that, did you? No, didn't think so. No you did not. Nor me neither, mate. Me – I never gone to no school at all, not for more than two minutes, any road. You blink, son, and I were gone. Ain't done me no harm. But it's all different now. Whole world. It's a different world from before the war – well you knows it yourself, Stan. What ain't changed though is the way what they look at you if you ain't talking all hi-falutin. You ain't got a red-hot spud stuck up your arse like Jonathan fucking Barton, pardon language – well then they reckon you got to be stupid, or something. But I ain't. I may not be, you know what I'm saying – I may not be posh, yeh well I knows that, don't I? But stupid I ain't. Bastards. Oh anyway. Way it bloody is. Here – you sure you don't want none of this, Stan? Beautiful smooth. You want to get in quick, son – down to the label. Don't know how that gone and happened so fast . . .'

Stan was eyeing him dully.

'Yeh. All right. I will have just a tot. Thanks, Jim.'

Yeh I will. Maybe, please God, it will make me numb.

'Right you are, son – there you go. That'll keep the chill out. Here . . . Gordon Bennett . . . ! Look over there, Stan! See them? Just walking past. See them? It's them Sambos out of the woodyard. Blimey. Come to visit their mum and dad, shouldn't wonder. Bleeding King Kong, or something . . . !'

Stan was looking in the direction.

'Yes – that's them. One of them – the one on the right, see him? With the stripey jacket, he's really very nice. Still can't remember his name. It's a funny name. I had him in the shop one time to repair some shelves. A happy bloke, he seems, Good at his job, anyway.'

'Yeh well – give them enough bananas and they won't never stop smiling, will they? Easy pleased, see? Law of the jungle. Other one looks a right bleeding bastard, to my eye. Wouldn't want to bump into him in an alley of a night time. Couldn't bloody see him, for starters. No – me, I wouldn't want nothing to do with them. Not like us, is they? Different. I mean – I ain't saying they's all bad people. They don't have to be bad people. Ain't saying that. Don't belong though, do they? Stick out like a sore wossname. Better off back where they come from, my way of thinking. England for the English. Nothing wrong with that. What we fought a bleeding war for. That's right, ain't it Stan?'

Stan was slumped in his chair, and slowly wagging his head.

'Don't know, Jim. Couldn't tell you. Sometimes I feel, these days . . . I just know nothing. Got any more of that Scotch, have you . . . ?'

'That's the way, Stan. But you drunk all your tea, look. Get in another cup, will we?'

'No, Jim. Don't bother. Sick of tea. Sick of it. Just pour it in, will you?'

Yeh, he thought. Just pour it in. Please God it will make me numb.

Milly was actually feeling quite foolish, even as she tapped with her fingertips the frosted-glass panel of the back door to the shop. I mean to say – I know it's unlocked, so why am I knocking? Stan has already assured me that he wouldn't draw the bolt – and even if Jane were to be fleetingly aware of any distant rapping, then still she is hardly likely, from what I have been told of her general demeanour, to cast aside her bedclothes with a cry of girlish joy and then come bounding down the stairs happily sporting the smile that speaks of enormous welcome, her bright eyes brimming with an inner tinkling laughter and the eager need to lavish upon her unexpected visitor this much unstinting hospitality. Therefore it is, yes, extremely silly to be knocking on the door, I do understand, but it's just that . . . I don't know . . . it seems, so very wrong to just walk into someone else's house.

And now that I find myself on the other side of the door – having eased it to as softly as if here there are babies sleeping – now that I am standing quite still in this chill and dank, rather shadowy corridor, I begin in a rush to sincerely question the wisdom of just any of this. What actually do I imagine I am doing here? When you have a moment, Milly, I should like an explanation, please. Why had I made such an offer to Stan? And look – it was quite a bit more than just an offer, wasn't it really? I had been quite insistent on the matter, as now I recall it. I did not quite go so far as to cajole, I very much hope. No, I don't think it ever exactly came to that, but still I did my utmost to overcome his initial very shocked dismissal of the entire idea, and then – following the greyness of his indecision – so very determined to tip over the pivot of what by then was really no more than a residual hesi-tancy. Why did I do all that? How suddenly had I come to care so terribly much about the state of Jane? A woman to whom, in the past, I have barely even spoken. We would encounter in the Dairies from time to time, sometimes in Amy's, beneath the dryers . . . but all that was back in the days when the unfortunate woman would actually bring herself to, well – leave the house. Do the shopping, have her hair done like any other normal sort of a person. Good heavens – unless Stan has been grossly overstating the case, it appears now as if she never even strays from the upper floors. Which is now, I suppose . . . where next I must venture. Oh dear. I do feel most unwilling to do this. And for the first time, it now just occurs to me, I have very good reason for my new reluctance. And I do feel so abominably stupid: how could I not have thought of it before? It's Jane: what of Jane herself, for goodness sake? My impulse to help, of course it had stemmed from compassion for Stan in his silent, unspeakable plight – that, and maybe the bewilderment of little Anthony, should he even be remotely aware of the singularity of his circumstance (because children, they are so very heartbreak-ingly accepting of whatever bitter spoonfuls are urged beyond their innocent lips). But Jane . . . how on earth – always assuming that I do manage finally to summon up the back-bone to go ahead with all of this rather appalling nonsense, as now I see it plainly to be – how on earth do I expect her to react to the sight of me? Just suddenly standing there in front of her, and within a space I suppose she now has come to think of as perfectly inviolate . . . ? It is Sunday, the shop is closed, and the house is as quiet as if it were night. Stan will almost certainly have told her that he is taking the children off to the Zoo, whether or not she will consciously have absorbed the information. Whether or not she actually minds at all whatever he does. And therefore, in the knowledge that on this afternoon she truly is quite utterly alone, then possibly in the light of that, she might be . . . she might be . . . well I don't know, I just don't know. She might be doing anything. Absolutely anything. How on earth am I supposed to guess at such a thing? I simply can't imagine . . . and the whole idea, this entire and very idiotic escapade, it does now more than slightly horrify me. And specifically, I think, because this particular confinement, if Stan is to be believed . . . and what now am I saying, actually? I hardly think that the poor man can be making it all up . . . is quite wholly voluntary on Jane's part in that her limbs are apparently functional, and nor is she suffering from any strictly definable organic disability. So . . . what does a person in so unthinkable a situation actually, you know . . . do, then? Well possibly she is watching television. That's fairly likely. Is there television on a Sunday afternoon? Do you know, I have not the slightest idea. Maybe they put on something religious, or an ancient film or something. The wireless, conceivably: maybe she's a music lover, or she could follow the serials. She might well be reading. She reads, presumably. Or asleep: she could be asleep. Alternatively – and here is the vision that chills me most – just simply sitting there. Motionless, in a high-backed chair. Staring at nothing, though almost certainly the wall.

I touch the newel post at the base of the stairs, smiling at myself for registering the sticky edge of neglect that has over a very long time bonded the dust into the very heavy dullness of the thing . . . smiling at that, yes, though not in any sense at all out of happiness at being here. The situation into which I argued myself so terribly eloquently, not to say volubly, almost evangelically . . . well I have it now, don't I? Here it is: the thing is mine. So how about it, Milly? What to do? Well get on with it, I suppose. No sense in hanging around. Just get it done and over with, for either good or ill: nothing else for it. So a sort of resolve is upon me, then – the partial allaying, anyway, of incipient panic – though I am newly unnerved that the very first tread on the staircase has just now emitted a woeful and deeply dispiriting groan. I slide the palm of my hand up and along the banister rail as I very slowly ascend, the cracked and brittle loose linoleum snagging insinuatingly upon the soles of my shoes: this, I think grimly, is a lurking deathtrap for any young child in a headlong hurry, but how it must be for poor young Anthony, well it hardly bears thinking about. He just must have, I suppose – as in so many other ways, little mite – learned to adapt: to be aware of the intrinsic treachery in this or that tread, and then to somehow negotiate it appropriately. And yes I do know that Stan has a great deal to see to, to think about – I am aware that his responsibilities, his daily duties are a considerable burden, an ongoing trial, though still I am surprised that he has allowed things to deteriorate quite to this extent: the patterned flock of the wallpaper, it is rubbed clean away and is shinily flush where it has been constantly buffeted by the traffic of countless elbows and shoulders, all down the years. On the landing, there is a rustic chair with its canework burst, an oval rug of indeterminate colour and a pair of wall sconces – one with a scorched and skewed tasselated shade, the other with nothing, not even a light bulb.

And now, of course, I come to a halt. For had I thought myself foolish before, I now feel quite as thoroughly imbecilic as they come – because hadn't I omitted altogether to ensure that Stan make it quite plain to me which room is Jane's (and nor, silly man, did he think to tell me). Well I have to assume that she is on this floor somewhere, because the layout, you know, in all these buildings in the Lane, it's very markedly similar: they all do rather conform. And so going by my own place then, I'd say that certainly she wouldn't be on the floor above because the rooms up there, they're really rather small, the dormer windows hardly more than a token thing. So now let's think about this . . . well, I am guessing that the front room here, that will be the lounge, the sitting room, whatever people like to call it. And next to that the dining room – that's the way we have it, anyway, and it does seem to make sense. Kitchen beyond that . . . then here there's the boxroom. And right next to that . . . what I think must surely be the main bedroom, the large one to the rear. Which Stan, I expect, will long ago have given over to her (maybe, who can say, it is the unhappy lot of doleful and uncomprehending husbands the length and breadth of the nation to be consigned to boxrooms on either the idle whim, strenuous disgust or serious instability of their wives).

I pause outside. Silence. Total and utter silence. Oh dear heavens. No television or wireless certainly, nothing of that sort – not even so much as the squirm of movement, or a single exhalation. So what to do . . . ? Well knock, of course – of course knock, yes. In this case, knocking is quite obviously essential. Yes I know but will that startle her . . . ? I don't want to startle her. That is the last thing in the world I should ever want, to startle her. And yet considerably less alarming, we think, than swinging wide the door and then striding right in with a hearty cry of greeting. So I'll tap, then. Yes – I'll very softly tap . . . And what if, as does now seem likely, what if she's asleep? Should I wake her? Or run away quickly, with glee in my heart. I think, you know, this is one of these predicaments where planning, really, is just no good. I am clearly going to have to react to whatever I might find at the very point of confrontation. Well that's all right – I came through the war, didn't I? One learned then to live on one's wits: no choice in the matter. One never knew from one day's end to the other quite how one's life would be, or even when and if it might suddenly end. So here – here is nothing. Nothing at all. Right, then. So here we go . . .

And now I'll tap again, I suppose. If only for the sake of politeness, really. Though it must be quite clear that she's asleep. She has to be. No other earthly explanation. For I don't really think – or at least I fervently hope and pray not – that Jane, dear Jane, has selected this day of all days to give up the ghost and just go and, well – die, or something. Oh Lord. Don't know what to do now . . . Should I go, I wonder? Just turn around and creep like a felon down the umbrous staircase and swiftly and silently leave the way I came? It really is so very tempting a prospect. But silly. Because I'm here now, aren't I? Won't get another opportunity will I? Shouldn't imagine so. Oh blow it – I'll just go in. And if she's asleep, then I'll decide on the spot what to do. Because whether I wake her or not, it really wholly depends upon exactly *how* she is asleep: the manner of it. If she appears to have gently nodded off in the middle of . . . I don't know – knitting, say. A crossword, or somesuch . . . then I'll softly touch her shoulder and then make utterly sure that the very first thing that she sees upon opening her eyes is the broadest and most reassuring smile imaginable from a friend who is only there to help. Though if she's actually all tucked up in bed and thoroughly dead to the world, then I'll certainly leave her to it: make my apologies later to Stan, and there's an end to the whole affair – a wasted afternoon, despite my best intentions.

It is rather dark in here, I must say . . . but then the whole of the house is: terribly lowering, actually. I couldn't myself bear it, not for a single day. And it cannot at all be conducive to Anthony, living always within a shadowy twilight. But my eyes, they're beginning now to slightly adjust. I look to the bed . . . single bed . . . a great upheaval of jumbled blankets and a faded floral eiderdown, though no one actually amongst it all. There is an armchair, wing chair, averted from the window, where the slightest slits of light are slicing where the brownish curtains almost are meeting. Nowhere else then that Jane can be – unless at the very first tap on the door she took it into her head to make a bolt for safety, and now is crouching at the base of the wardrobe amid a rubble of shoes. So I very gradually approach the tall and upright back of the chair with, I admit, a fair amount of trepidation – because I don't at all know – do I? – what I shall find there . . .

Well nothing. Is what I find there. No one. The room is empty. What has apparently happened this afternoon is the very thing, according to Stan, which is simply without precedent: Jane has left her room. And this puts me into another quandary now. One further dilemma. But before I decide quite what to do next, I can't really resist just the merest look around. I shan't be too nosy – I'm not going to be peeking into the drawers – but after all, I am only a woman, and therefore heir to all those things that women are prey to: for there is not one of us alive, let us be honest here, who really could bring herself to immediately walk out of a bedroom in a circumstance such as this. And I am sure that I am able to persuade myself that once I have witnessed at close quarters the, um . . . how can I put it? The way Jane lives, the little things she keeps about her

. . . then I shall be gaining a rare and valuable insight into quite what it is that I find myself up against. On this dressing table, for example: there is no scent. No make-up. Not even a lipstick. Though there is the largest jar of Pond's Cold Cream I have ever set eyes upon. Which, Miss Marple, tells me what exactly? Precisely nothing, I'm afraid – except that maybe she suffers from exceedingly chapped hands, or that the skin of her cheeks is as moist and soft as that of a baby. There is also here a rectangular cream porcelain tray with twelve pennies very carefully aligned, each of the reign of George VI, and all with that great man's profile to the fore. A fountain pen – Conway Stuart, I happen to know, because I had one just like it: Eunice gave it me one birthday, and I was inconsolable, so very terribly distraught when many years later I managed to lose it somewhere. Jane's is mottled green, mine was a sort of a burgundy colour. And hanging askew on one of the dressing table mirror's finials is a bonnet – a very flowery sort of, well . . . it's a veritable Easter bonnet, really: yellow gingham, basted on daisies and lacy ties dangling a good way down from it. Well. And books – there are some books on a side table, look: one about the Queen, *Ten Little Niggers* (very well spotted, Miss Marple!), Marguerite Patten's wartime recipes, the *Concise Oxford Dictionary* and a London *A–Z*. Not much else here. Over the bed, a sepia print of a waterfall, white plaster chips on the dull gold frame. On the bedside table, a pair of stockings, unopened – Ballito, size 10, sand gold. Alongside a brimful cup of cold tea, together with a sideplate bearing I think a sausage roll, quite intact. And suddenly, you know – I have to be out of here. I am very uncomfortable. My skin is creeping, and I wish I'd never come. I am leaving immediately. It is quite clear now that she must be in the bathroom, poor Jane, and I am certainly not intruding any farther. I am leaving immediately.

The door to the front room, I notice as I am about to pass it, is not quite to. Would it be too awful of me just to ease it open a fraction further? Because I have no idea, you know, how Stan . . . well – lives, really. It would be so very interesting just to glimpse the three-piece suite, to see which corner he has the television. So I do that, I do that – I slowly push open the door, and then of a sudden my heart is stopped by shock and I let out a short, shrill scream, which I am quite amazed to hear. A quiet voice from the corner – though it had annihilated the silence as if it had been thunder:

'You took a very long while to find me . . .'

I simply stand there, and I know that I am quivering.

'Jane . . .' is all I can stupidly say.

In this room too the light is very dim: the curtains are closed, though a shaded lamp is glowing on the table where Jane I can now see is sitting. She holds between her fingers a blue Bic biro, and laid flat open in front of her is an exercise book with narrow feint ruled pages. She looks surprisingly healthy: Miss Havisham briefly flares up in my mind's eye, and then falls to the very floor of my hot imagination, there to crumble into ash and cinders.

'Jane . . .' I say again, and so terribly feebly.

'Won't you sit down? Or must you rush . . . ?'

I walk just two steps into the room. I think I shall take up the offer of a seat – my legs are decidedly wobbly, and I can't seem to control that. And then I think I shan't.

'Jane – you must think me very . . . well I cannot imagine what you must be thinking, actually, but all it is, well – I just thought I'd come and see you. You know – pop in, sort of thing. Because, um . . .'

'It's Mrs Stammer, isn't it . . . ?'

'Yes. It is. Milly. I'm Milly. Look, Jane – all I wanted, well . . . I just wanted to see that you're all right, and everything.'

Her hair, greyish, it is hard in a bun. She is wrapped quite tightly into a quilted housecoat – not at all similar to the diaphanous and rather raggy thing that Stan had been considering. Her eyes – so very chillingly bright, though set into the slump of a face that has decided to be aged. She is setting down the biro into the gutter of the exercise book.

'Why should I not be? All right. What have you heard?'

'Heard? Well nothing. Well actually – Stan, he um . . .'

She is making a funny sort of a noise, now. I think she is almost chuckling, though it does sound very gravelly.

'Ah. Stan. Yes, of course. My husband. That Stan, yes? You do mean Stan, my deeply concerned husband?'

'Well he is, quite frankly Jane. Concerned. About you. He cares. Of course he does.'

'Are you really quite sure you won't sit down? Yes? Very

well. And what little tales, I wonder, has Stan, my husband, been spreading about me . . . ?'

'Oh no – no sort of tales. It's not like that at all, Jane. Please do believe me. It's just that he's worried – naturally he's worried because, well – for one thing, you never go out, do you? Like you used to. You never leave your room.'

'Ah but as you can see, that is not the case. Is it?'

'No. Right. Of course . . .'

'I come in here when Stan, my husband, is in the shop. Or elsewhere. As today. Then I come in here. I write, you see. I write.'

'Really? You write? Well that's very, um. What is it you are writing, Jane? Is it a thriller? Agatha Christie? Romance? Something of that sort?'

'No, Mrs Stammer. Nothing of that sort at all. It is simply a journal. No more.'

'Aha. I see. A diary sort of thing, then. And Milly – do please call me Milly. I used to do that when I was at school. Every night, quite religiously. Wish I'd kept it up now. I often wish that, actually. Jane, um – can I possibly get you anything . . . ? Cup of tea, perhaps? Some little thing to eat, maybe . . . ?'

'I expect you have been told that I don't. Eat. But I do. I do.'

'What do you eat, Jane? Because Stan says . . .'

'Stan, my husband, says that he brings me food, and I ignore it. That's what Stan says: my husband. Scorn it. Let him take it all away again. This is true. I do that. I do that daily. I eat chocolate. Chocolate, yes. Nothing else whatever. It is remarkably nutritious. Not good for the complexion, this is true. I have to use a great deal of cold cream. Though it does not seem to make me fat. Do I look fat to you? I don't think so. I am not fat, as you may see. Here is the evidence before you. I take it from the shop, sometimes the storeroom, the chocolate. Often at night. Stan, my husband – his book-keeping, I can only think, must be very loose. He never appears to miss it. And I do take rather a lot. Fry's Peppermint Cream I very much favour. Mackintosh's Toffee Cup – I don't know if you know it at all? A delightful mouthful. Mars, when I feel I need the energy. And water. I drink water. I do love water. It's very pure, Mrs Stammer. So very pure.'

'Well . . . why don't you . . . ? I mean . . . look, Jane – I know all this is none of my business. I am terribly aware of that. Even my being here. I feel so . . . Look, you just say the word, and I'll be gone. All right? But you see Jane, I'm, well – intrigued, if I'm being honest. Really I am. Intrigued. I mean – why don't you tell Stan that you eat all this chocolate? That it's all you ever want to eat. Then he could bring it to you. Then you wouldn't have to . . . and why do you let him believe that you don't eat anything at all? And why won't you talk to him? You're talking to me. Aren't you? So why won't you ever talk to Stan? He's very worried, you know. Concerned about you.'

'Yes. You have said. And I do believe he is. Sometimes, in turn, I feel quite sorry for him. Other times not. And now, Mrs Stammer – if you will forgive me. I yet have today's entry in my journal to complete. An entry in which, rather I think to the surprise of both of us, you are now destined to feature. And then I must snaffle a good deal more chocolate and repair to my room in advance of Stan's, my husband's return. Did you care for my room, by the way? A trifle drab for your tastes, I imagine. Fruit & Nut. I suddenly do have a fancy for . . . I think this evening, you know, it's rather looking as if it might well be Fruit & Nut. Will you leave me?'

'Yes, of course. Of course, Jane. But – will you let me come again? May I? Visit you again? Talk a bit more . . . ?'

The light in her eyes is really quite impaling.

'I do not know, Mrs Stammer. I am undecided.'

'Well – please do tell me. Somehow. Get word to me. I'm in the book, if ever you want to . . . Whenever you make up your mind. I really would like to. And Jane – won't you please call me Milly . . . ?'

The sourest smile now comes to her lips.

'No, Mrs Stammer. I rather think I shan't.'

And later, when eventually I could bring myself to reflect upon this day which yet was set to develop into something so very much worse – oh yes, really quite utterly intolerable – I do see that here was the moment I should immediately have left. For had I not just been the butt of a gratuitous insult, a haughty dismissal? Who then other than I would still have lingered? In apparently her customarily forthright and even wilfully rather cruel sort of a manner, Jane had indicated so very plainly the point of termination – yet I was dissatisfied: here was no sort of an ending at all, no, not to me. So what did I do . . . ? I said something. Something. Nothing of consequence – pure and utter waffle I imagine it must have been: I might even have once again offered to make her some tea. Which, yes, even to me seems beyond credibility, but there – that is what I did. And then she said this:

'Zoo, isn't it . . . ?'

'I'm sorry, Jane . . . ?'

'Where they have gone.'

'Oh yes. I see. Yes. Zoo, that's it. I'm sure they'll all be having the most wonderful time.'

'No doubt. But of course they won't take him, you know.'

The whole of this afternoon . . . it is beginning now to affect me quite badly. The dimness in the room. The twin assaults of challenge and directness from this very strange woman that yet are leading me further into all sorts of bewilderment. I feel to be the victim of erosion. And her gaze – still it is so quite frighteningly intense.

'Take him, Jane? Who? Who won't? Take who . . . ?'

'Anthony. My son. Oh and by the way – was not the very first thing you were intending to report to Stan, my husband, when he comes to quiz you over my general demeanour, the fact that during the entire course of our stilted and rather

215

singular conversation, not once had I so much as mentioned him? Anthony? My son?'

I might have stuttered out something. More likely I just continued to stare at her.

'All I mean to say, Mrs Stammer, is that they are extremely particular. The zoological authorities. I am not altogether sure that a human being is quite within their remit, but should they feel the urgent need of a young example, then I hardly think that it is to Anthony, my son, that they will turn. He is marred, you see. Defective. They know nothing of my first-born, Frederick, perfectly obviously. For he is dead, do you see? Though Anthony, my current son . . . no no. Never would they accept him, even as a gift – for never could they care, could they, for anything so very apparently detestable as a cripple.'

My heart, just then, it simply cracked. I do not remember the landing, my tumbled flight down the darkened staircase, the murk of the corridor – only that now they were behind me. I fumbled with the snib on the back-door lock and was ablaze in my craving for God's sweet air, and the kiss of sunlight. Outside in the yard, I simply stood there, trembling. I held out my arm, regarding it as a thing apart from me, as I witnessed its tremor. I was at that moment so terribly in need: and at once and of course my thoughts were of Jonathan. He could maybe just hold me, could he? My head against the warm and big deep throb of his heart, that would surely calm me. And so I skittered away down the alley, careless of who should see me, and prayed that the gate to his own yard had been left unlocked. Sometimes, he had told me, Sunday afternoon would find him in the office, attending to accounts. Maybe this was such a day . . . ?

Yes . . . it did seem so: oh thank you, thank you, gracious Lord. For as I stood just alongside that mighty and purring refrigerator he has there, I saw with relief through the tiny window of the office that one of his green-shaded lamps was lit, and so I rushed up to the door and would have hurled it wide . . . ! But for the merest murmur within that stayed my hand. It was a voice. Quite low, the words indistinguishable. Though here was not Jonathan's voice. No no – it was the voice of another. A woman's voice. And then there was laughter, which Jonathan now was indulgently sharing. For one appalling instant, everything inside of me was knotted into ropes, rigid and twisted, my eyes as hard as glass. Then I fled.

By the time I reached home, I had made up my mind to be numb. There would later be time – yes, and rather too much of it – to steel myself against just the very first and horribly corrosive seepage of the full and coming anguish that would rush in a welter and cover me over. But for now, in deferral of all such subsequent agony, I shall attend to Paul, my Paul, who is excitedly calling to me. They are back, then. The outing is over. I cannot comprehend where the time has gone, and no less how I have spent it. He is beckoning me up the stairs and into his room – and the light of excitement in his dear little eyes maybe will serve to urge me to inject if only a shard of animation into the lifelessness of my own. The reason the sweet boy is taking me away from the living room very soon becomes quite brassily evident: Jim, of course – jigging to some or other jazz tune on the wireless, his jacket with its pulled-through and inverted sleeves cast upon the floor, his loosened tie beneath an ear, his slackened face as red as blood. He is brandishing the neck of a bottle of Bass, the foam now coursing across his whitened knuckles.

'Oh it was just wonderful, Auntie Milly – I do so wish you'd been there. As soon as you go in there's this enormous elephant and you can get rides on him but Uncle Jim said it was too expensive but it didn't matter because Anthony and Amanda and Susan and me – Susan is Amanda's friend, she's quite nice and not too girly for a girl, not sort of girly like some girls are – and we ran off to see the lions who didn't roar or anything and they were just lying there because the man there said they'd only just been given their dinners and were having forty winks because it was Sunday afternoon but they probably do that every day, don't they Auntie Milly? And Amanda and Susan, they really didn't like the snakes but I did and Anthony did and I'd really like to have one, actually, a snake, one of the long black and green ones we saw, because you could keep it in a box under your bed and just feed it things and watch it when it goes all slithery around the floor. Amanda said she liked the giraffes the best but I told her you couldn't keep one of those in a box unless you had a really cracking great box, which she thought was funny and she was laughing. And then we went to the cafeteria and Mr Miller, he bought us all milkshakes and mine was banana and so was Anthony's and Amanda and Susan, they had chocolate and strawberry, actually I think it was raspberry but it doesn't matter. And I said to the grown-ups we'd just seen the apes and Uncle Jim said we've just seen them too walking past the window but I don't think that's true, well it's obviously not true because they're all in cages so that was just Uncle Jim talking like he does. I really didn't want to come home but they were closing. I'd really like to go back – it's really great there. Maybe next time you could come instead of Uncle Jim. Do you think you could, Auntie Milly? And we got some toffees in the gift shop with a picture of the chimps' tea party on the box. Do you want to see it? Here – it's great, isn't it? I've eaten nearly all of the toffees, but I did dish them out to everybody. Some had nuts in which isn't quite so good. We didn't actually see the chimps in real life because I think they were all asleep. And we got a hot dog which I'd never had before. Do you know what they are, Auntie Milly? It's not a dog, or anything – it's a sort of orange sausage which tastes a bit funny actually but the bread was nice with ketchup which you squirt in it. And an ice cream from a van like they've got on the Heath but it's not like Wall's Family Bricks or wafers or anything because it comes out of a tap all swirly and it's really really good and they put a Flake in it which are yummy. Mr Miller said they must make a lot of profit, which I don't really know what it means. Would you like a toffee, Auntie Milly? I've just got three left. What did you do today? Did you have a nice time?'

And as he continued to babble on delightedly, Milly beamed as hard as she could, and continually stroked his hair. His pleasure was tugging her only gently, while normally it would long ago have overwhelmed her, and she would be hugging him tightly. Now, though, she could for not an instant longer barricade her mind from the invasion of the women: she had today been slapped so viciously until she was stunned by these two women, neither of whom even was known to her. But it was not the apparent derangement of Jane that most now disturbed her, profoundly shocking though it was. No — because of course it was the voice, the voice and the laughter, which soon then was chiming with his own. That of my man, as I have come to think of him: my man, yes. For the voice, it had been that of Fiona. Fiona, yes. His wife. With whom he gets along, oh . . . very well indeed then, it would surely appear. I am not sure I have before ever properly thought about this. Of Fiona. His wife. Her existence, of course — of that I am forever aware. That is a constant, a simple truth to be borne. Though I feel that it is not somehow . . . right, that they both should be so apparently friendly. That it is not altogether . . . decent. And then there was that other noise that had reached my ears before I could act upon the spur and rush away swiftly, my head bowed down like a villain, my insides so madly alive, just boiling in the turmoil. For there had been a chink. A chink of little crystal glasses. And I think that they were drinking Benedictine.

CHAPTER TEN

Merely a Matter of Convenience

I've got a little bit of a head, to be honest. Not used to it, you see. But after just those few little nips of Haig I had off Jim in the cafeteria, I sort of got a taste for it. Which surprised me I can tell you, because in the normal sort of run of things, well – barely touch it at all, really: can't even remember the last time I was in a public house. Don't at all care for them. The smell and the men. But after we got back home, Anthony and me, all I was remembering was that I was fairly sure there could be a bottle of something or other at the back of the sideboard, just on the shelf over where we keep the photo albums – bottle of something left over from Christmas time. Buy it every year, I'll never know why: bottle of Scotch, one of gin, tawny port, another of Bristol Cream. Nobody drinks it. Never have anyone round, or anything. Well of course I don't. So come Easter, I give it away to be raffled, most times. Tombola, sort of style. Good causes. Red Cross. Lifeboats.

And those blind dogs you see about the place with some poor old sod there tapping away with his stick. Not the Polio people though, some reason; they wanted me to have one of those little plaster model boys in his callipers outside the shop, with a slot in his head for coins: soon sent them packing. Anyway . . . when I got back from the Zoo . . . oh, I was in all sorts of a state, I can tell you. All over the place, I was. In my mind, I mean: I wasn't like Jim, reeling about like an idiot. He had nearly the whole of the bottle.

I was very careful when Anthony and me got back to the shop. Jim, he'd already tottered off to his ironmonger's – talking to his budgie Cyril, if you can believe it, and him still three doors away – and there was Paul, head down, walking slowly, and on the opposite pavement. Amanda had already gone home with that other one – what was she called again? Dear oh dear: my mind – I'm telling you. Gets worse and worse. And she's a good girl, that Amanda – ever so grateful for all the tuck I'd treated them to: thought I'd never hear the end of it. The price of those toffees and that ice cream, though – how they've got the nerve. But you've got to, haven't you really? Kids out on a treat – got to make it as nice as you can for them. Yes well – didn't see Jim dipping into his pocket, though. Apart from a cup of tea and his whisky, it was all down to me. Christ Alive – it's not as if I can afford it, or anything. Susan – yes of course: that's the name of the other one: nice girl too, nice and polite. Not from the Lane I don't think, though: else I would've seen her about. Anyway . . .

when we came in, Anthony and me, I said to him – here, Anthony: have a nice day out, did you? There's a good lad. Well you go off up to your room now, eh? I'll call you down when your tea's on the table – but after that hot dog, was it, and ice cream and I don't know what else, I expect you're fit to bursting, aren't you? But I just want a little word with your mother, see? All right? Let her know we're all back safe and sound. Maybe bring her up a cup of tea.

But what I really wanted, of course . . . well I didn't know. I didn't know, did I, what I was wanting. Because I didn't know what had been happening. All that had been going on while we'd been out. And Milly, for all I knew – well, she could be dead on the floor. Janey, she might've jumped out the window. And I know I shouldn't even be thinking any of all that sort of thing. Or possibly, I don't know . . . they're both still up there, do you think? Chatting away, normal as you like. Or Milly – here's a possibility – Milly, maybe at the very last minute she thought better of it and left well alone. I know I would've. That's what I would've done if I'd been in her shoes, no question about it. But then she's ever so determined, isn't she? Strong. Very determined woman, Milly is. So, then . . . whatever the truth of the matter, well I had to now, didn't I? Find out. What had been occurring. And so that's when I was rummaging around in the sideboard. Black & White – barely an inch out of it: I maybe poured it over the old Mrs Peek's Christmas pudding, that tot, did I? Tried and failed to set fire to it, who's to say? Anyway, it was just that one little nip out of it that saved it, I suppose, from being donated along with the gin and the port and the Bristol Cream to the Servicemen's Widows and Orphans or whoever else had come rattling their tins in my face, last springtime. So I had a little dram – and it's funny how it helps you out. Get a grip, sort of style. Makes you numb, just like I wanted it to. My ears, though – they were straining, I can tell you. Any little noise, I would've heard it. Moaning, breakages, anything of that order. Seemed normal. All seemed quiet. So I quickly knocked back just one more little noggin, and then I braced myself: right then, I was thinking: no more messing about – time to go and see.

I stopped on the landing like I always do. Had another little listen. A creak up above me from Anthony's room – and he'd got his little transistor on, sounded like. Ever so pleased he was, when I got it for him. Says he likes to listen to Radio Luxembourg or Radio Lichtenstein or whatever he said it was. Why he can't be happy with the BBC like the rest of us I couldn't tell you. Kids, isn't it? But it's only the size of a packet of twenty Player's, and so there's no sort of a speaker on the little thing – for all that it cost me the best part of six quid, I am not joking. John Barnes. Five pound nineteen-and-eleven, and it sounds more like a bit of fish you've got frying in the pan than any sort of music, if you want me to be honest. But Anthony, well – more than content, he seems to be. Everyone at school's got one – that's what he went on telling me, one of these tinny little transistors. Well, that's all of it really, isn't it? Wanting what all the other lads have got. And anything I can do to make the poor little blighter feel like he's more a part of things – you know, not to be out of it at all – well, more than happy. You owe it, don't you? You owe it, you do. So anyway, that was little Anthony upstairs, but on this floor . . . and I was standing ever so still . . . nothing at all. No sort of movement. So I open her door – easy, like I do – and I'm not really knowing what it is I'm expecting . . . but I can tell you this: I was ever so relieved when I see her just sitting up in her bed, like she does. Arms out all stiff across the counterpane. Staring at something. Staring at nothing. I don't know.

'All right are you, Janey love? Oh dear – you never touched your tea, look. And the sausage roll – go off the idea in the end, did you? Fancy trying a little bit now, maybe . . . ? I can cut it up small. No? Well let me get you a nice fresh cup, anyway. Anthony . . . Anthony, yes? He had a lovely day. Zoo. Remember I told you, Janey? This morning, before we went off? Yeh. Zoo. That's where we were. Lovely day. Back now. Cushions all right, are they? Your pillows? Plump them up a bit? No? Sure? No trouble . . . All right then, Janey. I'll just pop off and make that tea. Shan't be a jiff. And when I come back, if you've changed your mind about wanting a little bite of something to eat, well you can tell me then. All right? All right, Janey? Hear me, can you? Well – like I say, I'll be back in no time.'

And then I shut the door behind me. And I just closed my eyes. The fizzing of Anthony's transistor, that was the only noise, the only noise in the whole of the world. So there it was, then. She was in exactly the same position as I'd left her in the morning. Hadn't so much as shifted. So if Milly did come, that's what she'd had to cope with. Just like I do – day in, day out. So now she maybe knows what it's like. What I was on about. If she did come. Don't suppose I'll know now, will I? Not till the morning.

So I got Anthony his tea: fish finger, few peas, bit of bread and a Kit-Kat. Nice big glass of gold top. Brought it up to him. Thought I would. And I didn't trouble with a brew, no I didn't. I didn't fancy any – which is odd for me, I can tell you that. So I had a Scotch. And Janey? Make a cup for Janey, should I? No point. Is there? Bring her a cup of tea, she's just not going to drink it. More than half . . . it's true, you know: more than half the PG Tips I buy, I'm pouring down the sink. Criminal. So I just sat there in the front room. With my Black & White. And it was the light that woke me up. Gave me ever such a start. Couldn't work it out, not at first. And then I twigged: it was daylight, coming through the gap in the curtains. Been on the settee for the whole of the night, then. My heart was in my throat till I looked at my watch: no, it's all right – still got plenty of time to get Anthony all ready for school: only just gone six. So I thought I'd have a bit of a wash and a brush-up – but when I went to get up, though . . . ooh, I did feel it. Right above my temple, there. Heck of a throb. And the bottle of Black & White – wasn't that much left in it, so it's hardly a surprise.

It's just after twelve now, and I'm down in the shop. Of course I'm down in the shop: where else am I going to be? Milly, she telephoned me earlier. Asked her a hundred questions before she could even get a word in: What went on? Did you come? What did she say? Did she say anything? Did you come? What went on? She just said she'd pop in at dinnertime, have a bit of a chat. Not sure I'm looking forward to it, really. Yeh and then I remembered who else was due to pop in at dinnertime: Sally from Lindy's, to do the window. Hippo is what Anthony's taken to calling her now. Ever so cheeky, but it did make me laugh. I'd laugh right now if I was in the mood. Phoned her, Sally. Tried to put her off. Not a great time if I'm honest, I said to her – maybe another day Sally, eh? Wouldn't hear of it: couldn't let you down Mr Miller, is what she said to me, what with Christmas just around the corner and everything: don't forget, Mr Miller, this is the season when we've got to display all the Cadbury's and Fry's selection boxes and the chocolate snowmen and all those little bags of gold coins and the really big gift boxes of All Gold and Terry's and Black Magic with all the ribbons! Then there's the special Christmas packs of cigarettes and cigars. Jingle Bells, Mr Miller! See you soon! Yeh . . . and never mind jingle bells – my head now, it was going like a pair of bongos. Christ Alive.

It's what I call patchy in the shop – just cigarettes and tobacco, very largely. Saturday mornings the smokers will stock up fairly heavily because they know I'm closed on

Sundays – and then on a Monday morning, bright and early, back they all come, poor devils. Kiddies are at school, of course, so I won't see them till soon after four. And me, my mind, it's not really on the job. That Mr Hoskins, he gave me ever such a look when I slid across to him twenty Woodbine. Can't imagine what I was thinking: he's been a Weights man ever since I can remember. And so now that she comes in the door – Milly, she's coming in the door – it's that much of a relief, I can hardly tell you. My head, it's not too bad, but the old stomach now – that's in the middle of giving me a bout of merry hell.

'Milly. Hallo. Good to see you. All right, are you . . . ?'

And Milly, despite just everything, she had to smile at the question, as well as the sight of him. He seemed to her at that moment to be the very embodiment of helplessness – eager yet defeated: his beaten face and questioning eyes vying for the upper hand in a hopeless, forgotten and eternal war: an abandoned Jap in the jungle, with everyone else gone home. And now he wants to know, Stan, whether or not I'm all right. Well – quite a question. Shall I tell him? Shall I say to him well actually no, Stan, since you come to ask me – I'm not. All right. Not at all all right: all right is very far from the way I am feeling. Of course he doesn't really mind either way – but even supposing he did, where on earth to begin? Stan, all he wants to hear about is Jane, of course. Well naturally – Jane makes up his entire concern. While for my part . . . well – is there anyone I have not been thinking of, all the terrible way through a thoroughly sleepless night? Because everyone I come into contact with begins straight away to affect me. They seep in under the skin and quickly become a part of my centre. I do not know why this should be so, but it is. I wish it were not, but it is. And then there are the abstractions to consider − the nebulous concepts. Such as marriage, to take just the most insistent of them. I was, as three o'clock this morning edged towards four, confronting quite squarely what it is all of it meant to mean. Is it, at base, merely a matter of convenience? Why do people do it? Pledge themselves to just this one person for the duration of their natural lives. Custom. For it is not natural. Can't be. Not . . . how can I say . . . ? Humanly natural. It is custom − society's need for apparent conformity. The need for children as well, of course. In most cases. But all this nonsense you see at the pictures and read in these romances and so on about meeting Mr Right . . . the love of your life. And it is nonsense, of course it is. Because by definition, the people you know are the people you have met. The others . . . you simply haven't. And from that pool, this motley selection of drifting souls into whose shoulders you have glancingly collided, you plump for the least noxious; or, in my own particular case, you quite cavalierly discard every hope for the sort of future that any girl dreams of on perfectly literally the very first man who comes along. And if there truly is a Mr Right, the colossal thing, your one great dazzling destiny, the key to all the love in your heart . . . well then he could easily be living in Borneo or somewhere, and you'd simply never know. And so to the realities of what now we are faced with: Jim and myself. Stan and Jane. Jonathan . . . and Fiona. Three very different situations, I think that's totally plain, though ostensibly identical: married couples, each with an only child. All of us living in the same little street, England's Lane, and all busy running our respective families and businesses. Though I think I am the only one of us who has insight into the lives of all the others, whether or not I want it. Jim and I . . . well we exist in a state of just about suspended toleration. He would be aware of all I do for him only were it ever to cease. He pays the bills. An arrangement, you see? I hold him in contempt, while he, I often imagine, believes me to be insane. Or at the very least irrational. But then of course I am but merely a woman, am I not? And so it is hardly to be wondered at.

Clearly, I have needed more. And what thinking person wouldn't? Which has led me to Jonathan. A man who should not really be here at all. He is not the butcher. Is he? He is an enigma – and yes I know that I find that, oh . . . infinitely more alluring than any plain and simple logicality. But however this gentleman came to be chopping meat, for whatever reason he finds himself here (and no I haven't asked him, because whatever it was, I couldn't bear the answer), he has seen fit to consort with me. Why, though? I never before questioned it, and now I can't stop. For his wife, Fiona . . . is, I have grudgingly to admit, a fine-looking woman. Beautifully dressed. She speaks very nicely – although I know this only from having overheard her in various shops in the Lane from time to time: I have never addressed her. And it would seem that they still have union. They share a room. They share a joke. And they happily will share a glass of Benedictine. And so in Jonathan's eyes . . . I am what, now? Merely a matter of convenience? Solely that? To an outsider, of course I can see that that is how it might appear. No — more than that: this would be the sole and quite patent conclusion. And I can smell and practically taste on my lips that outsider's disdain. For me. Yet when I am with him, Jonathan, I know that it is so much more. I am not delusional. The outsiders, they do not know. The outsiders, they have not even the slightest idea. For they have never seen a couple alone. No one, ever, has seen a couple alone: your very presence annihilates the possibility. And with Jonathan, you see, I am the only one there. I am half of that couple. I know it to be real, and I feel it very deeply.

And all these truths are hardly confined to just this little handful of marriages, you know. It seems . . . well it sometimes seems to me that every single one of them in the world is a separate kind of gated estate from which casual ramblers are strictly barred unless by prearranged invitation — though they may, over years, glimpse the occasional treetop or pasture through a chink in the towering wall, a gap in the thick and encircling hedges. For the facade is all: 'Business As Usual' is what the hastily erected notices are reading, though behind the shattered shopfronts there is nothing remotely usual occurring: every sort of unconsidered drama is being played out in the presence of no audience whatsoever: a two-handed play of a thousand acts, existing solely to generate for its unwitting cast an unstoppable invasion of agonies and rapture, rapidly supplanted by the simmering stew of an ugly complacency – yearning then, and wistfulness, or else a darkly secret and utter disintegration. Unthinkable examples are frighteningly everywhere: this very morning on my way here to see about Stan, I went into Dent's. Everyone says that you should never buy fish on a Monday, but Mrs Dent had told me ages ago that she receives a special delivery each Sunday afternoon from Lowestoft because it's the only day of the week the fisherman is not working and can make the journey to London. And it breaks her heart because for the whole of Monday his entire catch will be sitting there on ice in her window as passers-by do just that very thing and pointedly ignore it. Then just before she closes she tries to sell it off cheaply. By Tuesday she is thinking of it as catfood and she more or less gives it away – and that is when all the elderly women living alone will swoop upon it and have it for their tea. Since she told me, I make a point of going in early on a Monday morning – for I wouldn't want her to think I was in any way exploiting her confidence, nor seeking to profit from her misfortune. This morning I bought from her three good-sized trout – glistening, eyes bright and smelling of the sea: I love that, and the coldness in there – so very clean and bracing. She has terrible problems with her feet, Mrs Dent – bunions: and her shoes, she says, have to be specially made, this is what she was telling me, in some little cobbler near Chancery Lane. She said I wouldn't believe the prices they charge. But her feet – and this is when she lowered her voice, even though it was just the two of us there – they got much worse, so very much worse, she said, after her husband died. They had no children because Mr Dent, and I've known this of old, hadn't been at all well since the day she'd met him – something to do with his lungs, and then, she said, it was other things too. And please don't ask me why she chose to tell me all this – I never invite any such intimacies, nor particularly do I relish them – but it had been his pleasure to massage her feet every single evening, just after he had bathed and then anointed them with a peppermint balm. I miss that, she said – deftly wrapping up the trout in yesterday's *News of the World*: yes I know it might be selfish of me, Mrs Stammer, but of all the things Mr Dent and I used to do together, it's that I miss the most of all.

And in Bona, there he was as usual – Mr Bona we all call him – in his clean white coat and his hair of the very same shade. Looks more like an eminent surgeon than a seller of exotic specialities. I was buying a long blue packet of spaghetti. I like it so much – and he also has these tins of real Italian tomatoes, actually from Italy, which, I have discovered, if you stir into them a quarter of Jonathan's mince, makes for a very rich and highly satisfying sauce – a few flakes of Cheddar and a spot of pepper. I make it just for myself – Jim won't touch it, and I don't actually want him to. I said to Mr Bona – and gosh, you know, I've wanted to so many times, but I've never found the moment – I said to him: it isn't, is it? Bona? Your name? He smiled, quite fondly – he has a very kind face, quite pink and unlined, although I suppose he must be getting on now. No no, he said. *Bona* – it's Latin (which I should have known, really). Good things, was the general idea. Well, I said to him – it makes you quite unique in the Lane, then: everyone else has their name above the door. And then he became quite reflective. When he bought the shop in 1943 . . . and I remember that, you know, I remember when he came here: it had been a laundry up till then. Anyway, he said, when he bought the shop, that had been precisely his intention: to paint their name on the fascia. He and his wife had fled from the Nazis – I had no idea, though I might I suppose have surmised it. Austrian, it turns out they are – from Vienna. I used to think Swiss – although either way you'd never take them to be Jewish: bright-blue eyes, really quite Aryan. My father by then had died, he said, and my mother was taking care of our son. They were to follow as soon as something had been established in England. But they never did. They were, he said, 'caught up' in the Nazi advance, their where-abouts and fate not ever discovered. My name, Mrs Stammer, is Schmidt. The solicitor who contracted the sale of this shop, he said to me: Mr Schmidt – think of this as a piece of free and friendly advice. Put your name on the shop, and within hours your window will be smashed to smithereens. Since the Blitz, feelings are running very high. The distinction between

Austrian and German will not be appreciated. Your business will be boycotted: worse, your very lives could be in danger. And anything you can do, Mr Schmidt, Mrs Schmidt, to moderate your accent would all be to the good. So sad, Mrs Stammer: so sad. The breaking of glass, the destruction of legitimate trade, the need to conceal our origins, the threat to our continued existence . . . it is everything from which we had been so terribly desperate to escape. And our son, our dearest son, he never did. Mrs Schmidt: she thinks of these things: sixteen years have passed, and every day I must comfort her.

Yes. Well that was just this morning . . . so I'm still rather spinning. I am also quite suddenly rather fellingly tired, and my mind, well . . . it's just too full. But now I must speak to Stan on the subject of his own very singular marriage. Just look at his face, though: he seems so very far beyond what I would say to be emotion, true feeling, that I could weep for him, I honestly could. I think by now he has shied away from sensation of any description. But the Jane I watched and listened to yesterday, the Jane who shocked me so very profoundly, this is evidently not the Jane he imagines he knows. It is difficult to say quite what she is doing, but whatever it is, she knows it: she knows it well. So what, I wonder, do I say to him . . . ? And how much do I not . . . ?

'Yes I'm all right, Stan, thank you. Oh my goodness – what was that noise? There was a bang – is it upstairs, Stan? Should you go and look?'

'Just behind the screen there, Milly. Window. Sally from Lindy's. She's doing my Christmas window. Christ Alive.'

'Window? Really? Are you sure? Sounded like a bomb . . .'

'Yes well she's a little bit . . . here, Milly – never mind that. Come behind the counter, won't you? Just let me shift this box out the road and I'll lift the flap up, look. Have a little word in the stockroom, will we?'

'But what if someone comes in, Stan? A customer.'

'Daresay they'll call out, or something. It's a slack day. Think we'll be fine.'

'Oh my *God*, Stan . . . ! Did you hear that? Sounded as if the whole wall was coming down . . .'

'I know. I know. She gets there in the end. But it's always a bit of a worry. Listen, Milly – come on through, won't you? I'll keep an eye out for anyone coming in.'

'Well all right then, Stan. Don't suppose we'll get another opportunity, will we? Oh my word . . . look at this! A true Aladdin's cave if ever there was! I've never been back here before. Has Paul ever come in here, Stan? He'd adore it. Absolute heaven for a child. All these boxes and jars . . . ! Anthony – he must think he's in dreamland. And you – do you feel like Santa Claus, Stan? Oh heavens . . . I do wish I hadn't said that. It's reminded me how terribly close we are. I don't know where all the time goes. It's muggins here who's in charge of the party this year – did you know? Yes – my turn, worse luck. And I'm not sure I can face it. Stan . . . was that something breaking . . . ? Glass? I'm sure I heard something breaking . . .'

'Never mind all of that, Milly. You'll get used to it. Just tell me. You came, then? You did come? See what I'm up against, don't you? Doesn't say a blessed word. Beyond help, far as I can see. Wits' end . . .'

'Well, Stan . . . she did talk, actually. Speak to me. She did.'

'She did? She did? Janey? She *spoke* to you . . . ? What did she say?'

'Well, um . . . not, you know – much, or anything. She was in the front room at the time. Sitting at the table. Are you, er . . . quite all right, Stan . . . ? You do look rather . . . do you want to sit down, or something?'

'Eh? No . . . no . . . I'm all right, thanks for asking Milly. In the front room, you say . . . ? Are you sure? Yes? So she, what . . . moved, then. Must have got up and moved. Christ Alive. I've never seen it. Not in years. What was it she was up to in there, then?'

'Writing a diary, actually. Journal sort of a thing. She does it every day, apparently. It's quite likely she's in there right now, if you want to go and . . . no, maybe better not, actually Stan. Something you might possibly have to lead up to, I think. Stan – don't you think you should maybe go and see to Sally, though . . . ? These noises, they're becoming really quite frightening. That last one – sounded like, I don't know . . . a pearl necklace or something just exploding . . .'

'That'll be the aniseed balls. They're a devil to round up, they are. Death trap, if you're not ever so careful. But Milly, listen, just listen . . . I've got to be sure I've got this straight in my mind. A diary, you say . . . ? Writing a *diary*? Well strike me down. But what did she say, though? What did she say to you?'

'She said . . . well she said she eats chocolate. Is what she said. Stan . . . you don't look at all well, you know . . .'

'Chocolate . . . ? What – you mean, chocolate as in . . . ?'

'Mm. She takes it from this very room, I gather. At night, largely. And she's rather surprised you've never noticed. Fry's Peppermint Cream, I recall, she said she was rather partial to.'

'Fry's Peppermint Cream . . . ?'

'Yes, Stan. And Toffee something, I think.'

'Cup. That'd be the Mackintosh's Toffee Cup. Nice line. Quite a good seller. But Milly – why hasn't she . . . I mean, why did she never . . . ?'

'Yes well quite, Stan. But that's rather for you to find out, isn't it really? Don't you think? You really are going to have to make her talk to you, you know. It's the only way.'

'Right. Right. Yes I suppose so. It's a worry. It's all a real worry. Because I've never noticed any of the Fry's Peppermint Cream going missing. And yes but . . . what about that other thing, Milly? That we talked about. You know – seeing someone. Someone professional, sort of style . . . ?'

'Well yes, Stan . . . yes. I really do think that that is quite essential.'

'Yes. Right. I see. But I don't know what to . . . I mean, all this sort of thing, well . . . I wouldn't know where to turn, Milly. Over my head.'

'Well the first thing, Stan, is just to talk to her. Yes? You just have to talk to her. Try to get her to explain things to you. Got to be a man about it. Show some gumption.'

'You're right, Milly. You're right. Well course you're right – you're right about everything, far as I can see. Explain things to me, yes – that's what she's got to do. Like those Toffee Cups for starters – never noticed them going either.'

'That's not quite the point though, is it Stan . . . ?'

'No no – course not. I do know that, Milly. Just saying, that's all . . .'

'All right, Stan. Well look – I really do have to be off now. Million things, as per usual. Oh and Stan, I meant to say – thank you so very much for all your generosity yesterday. Really too much. Paul told me you wouldn't take his money for the tickets and the ice creams and so on and that was really very naughty of you. Look – must go. Oh my golly, Stan . . . what was *that* now? Do you think she's fallen over? Off the ladder, or something . . . ?'

'Quite likely. She's done it before on more than one occasion. After she's gone, I'll get in there and tidy things up a bit. Sweep out the worst of it. Call an ambulance, if needs be. But really, Milly – I mean what I say. You're a wonderful woman – no no, hear me out. I will be heard. Because I'm thankful. I really am. You're a truly, very wonderful woman, Milly . . .'

Milly had been knotting the scarf around her neck, tucking it into the collar of her coat, and now she glanced across to

Stan and beamed to him a farewell. She did think afterwards that she must actually have gasped, let out a sort of a gasp, just as she saw his head, his whole white face quite suddenly looming towards her: that gasp of quite total amazement must then have been smothered by the wet and fleshy softness of the kiss from a mouth that was shocking on her lips. She pulled away as if from the threat of an approaching blade and she was sure for an instant that the light of pure astonishment in both his wide and fearful eyes was briefly refracted in her own. She turned around without another word and was only very peripherally aware of the whining and leisurely spin of the circular lid from a large tin of Quality Street as it rolled its way elliptically from the window and wheeled across the floor of the shop, until it was clatteringly halted by just the outstretched toe of Mrs Goodrich's brogue. Milly was aware only then of the demonstrative raising of that woman's left eyebrow as Milly heard herself calling out laughingly some or other platitudinous nonsense as she edged her way slowly, hurriedly, and then really quite rudely around the unmoving mass of the woman. Back out into the chill of the Lane, she would have paused for just a moment in order to collect herself, but felt then immediately that she had now to be away from there, and so she walked quite quickly the opposite way to the very place that she had been intending to go, because always she quite unfailingly completed her daily round of shopping in a strictly clockwise direction, and so in a state of agitation and some confusion she was startled to now be discerning quite some way ahead of her the unmistakable outline of Jonathan Barton, striding quite purposefully onward – and she called out to him on impulse, a thing she never would even have dreamed of doing in any sort of a normal circumstance – and maybe then she sensed or imagined a momentary check in his step before his pace appeared to quicken, and within a blink he was lost around a corner. Milly stopped abruptly, surprised to find herself just outside Levy's the greengrocer's – and there he was, old Mr Levy, wearing as ever just his sleeveless and battered leather jerkin, and never mind the bitter coldness of the day. He gave out a bark of his harsh and phlegmy cough and then he said to her quite trillingly Well *morning* Milly, how are *you* today? Got some lovely Kent red apples, you're interested at all. And Milly was smiling at him now, a good and familiar face, and he was not to know, was he, Mr Levy, that when she would have completed her shopping expedition and approached him from quite the other direction, it was apples she had been intending to buy. And then she noticed that her shopping basket was not on the crook of her arm: she had left it on the floor of the stockroom in the sweetshop, and inside that basket was a long blue packet of spaghetti and a tin of real Italian tomatoes, actually from Italy, along with three good-sized trout wrapped up in yesterday's *News of the World* . . . and she just didn't know . . . what to do about that, now.

I feel sure that if I concentrate upon maintaining the briskness of my unbreakable pace for just a little while longer, then it will be perfectly safe to assume that she will not be able to – cannot, dear Milly – catch up to me. And it was exceedingly unlike her, you know – to call out in the street in so very brazen a fashion. In the manner of a raggedy hoyden, or else some low sort of costermonger. I did of course, though, discern the reverberation – the edge, shall we call it, which immediately made that voice of hers so very brittle at its rim while still it was hanging in the air, and rather shockingly. It was, of course, a uniquely female edge, and therefore to be avoided. I have heard it before. Within the just barely controlled and staccato stab of it, there loiters the palpable undertone of crazing – it is overwrought, it is insistent, it is less than rational and it verges upon the shrill. Worse, it augurs an agenda which I have not the slightest inclination to even so much as acknowledge, and certainly not in any way to indulge. And naturally I am aware of precisely its trigger: that single jagged and racing glimpse that she had of me just yesterday afternoon, snug in my den and enjoying a series of cheering libations with my enchanting wife, shortly prior to that good lady attending to one of my more unpredictable needs, which she alone has the instinct to understand. So despite the gnawing jaws of the green-eyed monster that no doubt Milly still winces away from, she is not to know that her arbitrary timing rescued her by merely minutes from a spectacle that would have left her emotions quite thoroughly eviscerated – ripped into bloody ribbons.

For all that these women, at the very outset of a liaison,

will with an ill-worn and starkly artificial aplomb and suavity protest their complete indifference to the existence of one's married state (this being particularly true should they too happen to be, if only in name, bound by the bonds), each eventually will come to rue it. Or else at that threshold they might easily begin by being notably and conspiratorially silent on the matter of their willing duplicity (though never could they dream of couching it in any such terms: their projection of all their spurious clarity is always so very tiresomely opaque). But something then will happen to them, do you see. One never quite knows when – but very surely, something will happen to them. At some indeterminate moment along this convivial and carnal path, they will of a sudden be speared by a latterday conscience. Then – redly flustered, choked by a guilt that is newly aroused from the hitherto convenience of the deadness of its torpor, together with who knows what other entirely useless, petty and smothering emotions – they will shamefacedly retire from the cut and thrust of so much joyous jousting. Or else, conceivably, they might grow tired of the intimacy, as generally I do myself – when the hot surge of blood, the frisson of anticipation cools to the weary expectancy of no more than the usual. On rare occasions, such ennui will be felt simultaneously, which makes the severance both sweet and immediate. While then others still, and much more dangerously, will fall in love. This, of course – although they are blind to it, for rose petals now are covering their eyelids – is not the kiss of balm but a virulent form of corrosive that will bubblingly nibble, eat at avidly and then burningly devour the very warm and lustrously golden thing that had given it life. For suddenly, in the seething crimson cauldron of their newly boiling minds, all else one does, thinks, plans or enjoys when not in the company of this newly wide-eyed and stricken inamorata becomes of quite paramount and pointed concern. Questions that are barbed and tumble too quickly come to be the awful replacement for not just mere idle conversation but also the erotic tattle of sexual affection, the giggled and whispered litany of innuendo, ever present in a prolonged and titillating dalliance. These women are flushed of countenance – though no longer from the impact of union, the heat of the hurly-burly. Now they are, is what they will say, 'at one with you'. But what they truly are is a damned bloody nuisance, to put it most plainly. Because I have seen it – oh yes, I have seen it all before. First a woman will fall in love, and then very soon after she will fall apart.

It is my current intention to speak to the man Obi in the woodyard, whose body and soul, should such people run to the latter, are now my exclusive property – I feel I might sooner than anticipated have need of the fruits of his thuggish demeanour – and so it is irritating and tedious that now I have been compelled to swiftly turn a corner that has taken me along this particular road whose name I can never recall, and then in a sweeping arc well away from the Lane. For next I shall have to effect a further circuit in order to engineer a return, though not before I judge it to be perfectly safe to do so. Tiresome, yes it is – but very necessary, you see: for I heard it, in just that single calling out of my name. A warning siren of bombing to come. I could before its note had faded foretell her fevered questing, to which I would find myself thoroughly disinclined to render any response whatever, even were it to be slow, and condescending. For why, please, should I justify the pleasure, even delight, which I continue to take in my spouse's company? Is this now to be a criminal thing? Am I again expected to stand trial in the face of yet one more so feeble a prosecutor? I think not. For Fiona, she is a quite splendid woman. I have always thought it. I know it to be true. This requires neither apology nor explanation. Did I not select her above all others to be my very own? To mother my little Amanda? Indeed – indeed I did. She cares for me, you know. I go further: she loves me very deeply, and still she continues to maintain that love on so pure, so very clean and elevated a level. She has never been mired by my peccadilloes: more, she embraces them as just another part of me. For would I be the man I am, were I without them? Of course not. And the man who stands before her is he whom she adores. Any woman . . . any woman who ever has so very foolishly attempted to curb me, to mould me, to tame me, to change me, to lure me away from my beloved Fiona . . . well that woman should have been possessed of at least the base intelligence to realise that within no time at all, she would be out in the cold. And after the warmth, the smoulder, the radiance of all of me . . . that is cold indeed. Milly, then –

dear though she remains to me – will, I observe with quite earnest regret, have to be watched, yes, and really quite closely. And at the very first odour of anything approaching censure, possessiveness or interrogation, I shall have to act decisively: one simply cannot tolerate any of all that sort of thing – and she, in common with all the others, must be made instantly aware. One sometimes has to ask oneself, you know: what, actually, do these women imagine themselves to be . . . ?

There was one. Just one other. During the course of my entire life on earth there has for me existed just this one other woman, and I had seen in an apalling instant that she alone possessed the power to quite utterly devastate me: Mrs John Somerset, yes of course it was. So well do I recall the midnight banquet that was Anna, where I so very greedily feasted. Although recollection . . . no, that's really not it at all: far too small a word – completely ridiculous in context of the might of this, for here is no mere miscellany of misted and unreliable memory, erratically spliced into rapidly jerked out and semi-lost imagery. For I carry Anna within me always – it is as if she were an organ, one of the most vital, which must never be diseased. And the lancing of my eyes at that almost quite literally shattering first encounter left me with penetrating wounds that I welcomed, that I prayed would never heal over: the loss of blood in passion is quite the perfect paradox, for it is as the most invigorating transfusion. And much later . . . when it had become our easy pleasure to entwine so hotly in the swamp of all we had, to feel its familiar sticky warmth ooze just tenderly between us . . . I had asked her whether she had known a mutuality – whether she too had been irrevocably licked by the scorching of the devil's own torch: set alight by so contrarily white a flame at just that same and sizzling fraction of a moment. She smiled like a leopard, touched my lips with the softness of that one so cool and elegant finger, shook loose from its ribbons the deluge, the waves of her lustrous and sweet-smelling hair . . . and then she said to me, simply, 'Jonty'. For this is what she called me: Jonty. I asked not why. Though I knew that no one before had ever done so, or else I should not have cared for it.

'That is hardly an answer, Anna my darling.'

'It is answer enough.'

'It is none at all.'

'It is all I have.'

'I cannot believe you.'

'Then . . . you cannot.'

'It is all you are willing to give.'

'It is all I am willing to give.'

'Why so covetous?'

'It is only you I covet, Jonty.'

'I you have. I am yours.'

'And I.'

'And you . . . ?'

'And I.'

'I love you, Anna. I love you, my darling.'

'You do. You do, Jonty. Oh, you do.'

'Anna . . . who are you?'

'I am me. Though only when I am with you.'

'You touch my heart. You are my heart.'

'I can feel us, Jonty. Beating.'

The bliss of all that, it continues to overwhelm me. Though prior to such sacred wonder, of course there had to be established the business arrangement – the enabler – with my goddess's husband, John Somerset. Who, true to his word, had contacted me so very soon, following that singular and ineradicable dinner at Henley: it might even, you know, have been the very next morning when the telephone rang. Would I care, he wondered, to accompany him upriver on his boat? On so fine a day? The very briefest of trips? An opportunity to be alone, did I see. I told him that of course I should be delighted. Little of the journey was immediately remarkable. John, I recall, seemed at enormous pains to make it quite perfectly clear to me that currently we were on board the smaller of his boats: his other craft, he explained at unnecessary length, required a reasonably sizeable crew, and on this occasion he did so want to have me all to himself. The sun was glancing through the lowered boughs of trees, and danced in spangles quite prettily on the water: I rather feel that we were drinking champagne.

'You might have to consider acquiring one of your own, you know Jonathan.'

'A boat, do you mean? I don't really think so, John. I struggle really to see myself as a sailor. My father, he was very keen, of course. Lifelong passion, you might say. Kindled at Cambridge. I'm ashamed to say that I sold it, you know. His old boat. Quite soon after we came to live here.'

'Oh yes well of course he was quite a feature on the river. A very familiar sight, your father, of course he was. What a shame that you got rid of his boat – trim little thing, might even have been in the market for her myself. Not that I'm any sort of a sailor, believe me. Not in, well – any proper sort of a sense. But in this town, you know, it's rather the thing. Almost like running a motor car, many ways. Gets you about. And then there's the Regatta, of course. Quite an event. Bit out of it, if you haven't got a boat. Always welcome aboard one of mine, of course. But there's nothing to it really, as regards actually steering the thing. I mean to say – look at me now: barely a finger at the wheel, and happily chatting away to you. It's not actually akin to being the skipper of an ocean-going liner, you know. Quite funny that, now I think of it. That's what I was going to christen this old tub, when I got her: *Queen Mary*. Might have been amusing. Didn't in the end.'

'I see. So what is she called? So sorry – I failed to observe. Do forgive me.'

'No forgiveness required, Jonathan old man. You are, after all, an irredeemable landlubber, it pains me to say. *Anna*. She's called *Anna*. Obvious reasons. Oh yes and talking of Anna, she did so greatly enjoy meeting you, by the way. Said to pass on her regards whenever next I saw you. So do kindly consider them duly passed on, would you?'

I smiled. I almost certainly did smile. But from the very first mention of her name, my mind had been alive with the giddy possibilities.

'So anyway, John . . . what do you, um . . . ? I mean to say – quite what sort of thing is it that you have in mind?'

'Ah yes – directly to the point. Good, Jonathan – very good. I like that in a fellow. Decisiveness. Determination. No time-wasting. Jolly good.'

'I am pleased you approve. And so . . . ?'

'Yes well – when I said "business" – it's actually been on my mind, this – I can quite see now that I might have instilled in your mind, oh . . . quite the wrong impression. It's not at all, my line, the sort of business whereby one, I don't know – goes in to the office, sort of thing. It's not all about attaché cases and boardroom meetings, if you see what I'm saying. We do however dress like businessmen – that's quite vital. Gives off the right sort of air, you know. When I say "we" – I am referring to my son and myself. Adam, whom you've not yet met, of course. But soon you will, I very much hope. Useful lad. Knows the ropes. These days, better than I do, I have to say. So if you do feel inclined to join us in our little enterprise – and I needn't say, I hope Jonathan, how fervently I wish it – then it is he who will, um – fill you in, I think they say. Explain the finer points, as it were.'

'These being the finer points of . . . ?'

'Oh dear – you really must forgive me, Jonathan. I rather seem to be waffling on and on, while not actually conveying to you so much as an atom of information. Well you see, in a nutshell – what we do is we . . . evaluate. Things. Objets d'art. Paintings. Jewellery. Curios. This sort of thing. And then we . . . acquire them.'

'Then I really do think you have quite the wrong man, John. I know nothing of this.'

'No no – well I didn't expect you would, of course. Few do. Whole point, actually. You see – in Berkshire, Oxfordshire . . . Home Counties generally, I suppose . . . there are quite a lot of elderly people, you know. Living alone. Well not even elderly, some of them. War, you know: scars of war. And often they find themselves, due to various unfortunate circumstances, temporarily embarrassed, so to speak. Financially, you see. So we do perform rather a valuable service, on the whole. Adam, he gets delivered all over the counties these handbills, and the interested parties, well . . . they'll get in touch with us, you see. He has a very good eye. Not really too sure how he gathered all of his knowledge. Bit of a mystery. Didn't get it from me, anyway. Nor Anna, I have to say.'

He went on talking. I missed a good deal of whatever came next because once again he had uttered the word: Anna. And so I bulged with the swollen vastness of so very lustful an imagination. By the end of this little voyage, however, all was reasonably clear to me. Two fine-looking, perfectly attired and well-spoken gentlemen would, by appointment, come calling. One – and that would be me – affects to appraise whatever item is being optimistically touted for sale (almost invariably, according to John, a gewgaw, some little gaudy trinket of neither interest nor value) while Adam on some or other pretext quickly and quietly investigates all the other rooms in the house. And I was told that it is a rare occasion when some or other treasure fails to be unearthed. Sometimes, the entire house contents are as an undiscovered museum. And so a deliberately exaggerated price will be offered and delightedly accepted for the initial piece of dross, while far smaller sums are then tantalisingly dangled over this or that picture or item of furniture – simply because, it would be explained to the householder (whose taste for cash by now has been thoroughly aroused) – it would be a shame, you see, what with the price of petrol being what it is, to motor all the way back with an empty van when the shop can always do with the ballast of ordinariness such as this just in order to fill in the gaps, so to say. There is no shop, of course. Each piece upon which Adam's expert eye would alight will always be a spectacular gem, which then is sold on to the appropriate West End dealer who, in turn, will be asking no questions. The profits – and John was rather surprisingly frank about this – are quite beyond credence. He recalled with particular glee the Hepplewhite commode bought for thirty shillings and sold in Bond Street for fourteen hundred guineas; all examples pale, however, before the drawing that was not actually paid for at all because it was found in the drawer of a Regency keyhole desk. The desk sold on for a hundred pounds – reasonable, John explained, for an item that had cost him just twenty-five shillings, this to include a black japanned davenport with original brasses. The drawing though – this went on to realise more than four thousand pounds, for it was a Raphael.

So. I was being asked to be a confidence trickster. John Somerset's insight into the human condition seemed to be as sound as his son Adam's appreciation of fine antiques. For in me, he had a natural.

'But it seems, John, that between the two of you, you rather have the ground quite adequately covered. Why would you want me . . . ?'

'Yes. I can see how you might think that. But the truth is, Jonathan, that more and more I am in London actually placing the items. The personal touch – so terribly important. Spot of lunch in the right sort of restaurant, drop of decent wine – works miracles, I assure you. My contacts are not insignificant, of course. So I am away these days rather a good deal. And two gentlemen, as you now understand, are quite essential to the working of the thing. How very serendipitous, then, that you should literally have ambled into my ken. Also . . . I could hardly help but observe, my dear chap, that you are a tall and finely built sort of a fellow, if you'll forgive my pointing it out. And often, so physical an appearance – bearing, as it were – can hold us in very good stead. Because there are some, you know, who can at the very sticking point – the nub, if you follow me – become of a sudden really quite mawkish and over-sentimental about, I don't know – granny's necklace, say, or the portrait of some old chap above the fireplace. And on such occasions, well . . . just the teensiest little scrap of persuasion can work absolute wonders, we've found in the past. Just to, you know . . . tip the balance, as it were. Well, Jonathan. There you have it. The bones of it, anyway. I could guarantee you an initial, shall we say . . . what? One hundred pounds per week? Cash, naturally. Later, though, there will be much much more, I can assure you of that.'

So. I was now being asked to be a confidence trickster who is not above coercion, intimidation and very probably bodily violence in exchange for something approaching five thousand pounds a year (and then later, much much more, he assures me). I confess to finding the gall of the man quite utterly breathtaking.

'Well, dear Jonathan – what do you say? I have laid my cards upon the table, fairly and squarely, I hope you'll agree. Now . . . this really might well be quite overly presumptuous of me, but ideally I was rather hoping you might care to try an inaugural sally this coming Monday morning. Too soon? Have a stab at it. See how you feel. Too soon? Adam you can meet this evening, should you be inclined. He is coming to the house. Where – and I do hope by now that you are aware of this, Jonathan – Anna and I will always be most delighted to welcome you.'

Yes . . . we had been drinking champagne: I remember it now. For it was of course at this juncture that he recharged my glass. The sun was warm, and I drank it quickly. I stood up to face him, and smiled.

'Monday would be quite convenient. And I very much look forward to meeting you and your son this evening. And Anna, of course.'

Anna. Yes, of course – oh my God, yes of course. For could you imagine I had missed or forgotten that glimmering detail? It lit up his monologue like a fiery beacon. That he is away, yes, and rather a good deal. More and more he is in London, actually placing the items. His blandishments were already beguiling, but here had resided the absolute decider. And so then, it was done. Though of course it very quickly became plain to me that he hadn't at all, John, laid his cards upon the table – not by any means all of them, at least. And as for fairness and squareness, well – such plain and noble concepts as those, they simply never once intruded. Soon the venture grew. I was decidedly instrumental in that – the driving force, in point of fact: expanding considerably the initial admittedly brilliant but severely limited idea. Within considerably less than a year, I was rather rich. John, of course, was already rather rich, though as a result of my efforts he now had become much more so. Fiona, but naturally, was quite girlishly delighted: always she had a taste for the finer things in life, which now I was very pleased to be able to furnish. And I had Anna. Of course I did. And as long as I walk this earth, never shall I forget what she told me when later that evening I walked across to The Grange. Over cocktails in the orangery I had been briefly introduced to Adam, and quite soon after she drew me through the French windows and on to the parterre (I was hardly unwilling) and then we were in the shadow of a rhododendron bush. As she spoke, I thought I must, I just have to, haul my eyes away from the radiance of hers: if I continue to fall so very deeply into them, I could come close to passing out.

'So then Jonathan. It seems you are to join us. That comes as no surprise to me. Though tell me – did you like him? What was your impression?'

'Of Adam, you mean? Oh – nice young man, he seems.'

'You're lying to me, Jonathan.'

'Lying . . . ? No no. He appears to be, as I say . . .'

'He is odious. Of course he is. It is plain for all to see. You think his own mother could be unaware? He is perfectly despicable – and if you are sincere in what you say and you genuinely have failed to perceive this in him, which I cannot for a moment believe . . . then very soon you will, I do assure you. I simply want to tell you just two things. We will not again ever be speaking of any of this, so allow me to tell you, please . . . just these two things: the first, of course, you already know. We are to be lovers.'

I gasped from the shock of the jolt in my heart. I moved on instinct quickly towards her: I was cupping her two bare shoulders under the palms of my hands – had barely been electrified by such sensation before she was shrugging me away.

'Not here. Not now. I think that soon you must return to the orangery, or else John, he will come to find you. So I shall be brief. The other thing I have to tell you is simply this: I know what Adam is. I know you will think him vile. He will rile you, very possibly disgust you. You will be provoked, though it must never be beyond endurance. I know too that in this line of business, strong temptations will be coming your way. Spurn them, for your own sake. Adhere to the principle of partnership – do not surrender to your maverick instinct. And should any harm ever come to my boy – if ever I even suspect you of doing him down in any way at all . . . should any apparently inexplicable accident ever befall my boy . . . then that is the very last you will ever see of me. Do you understand? I do so hope that you know I am sincere. Detestable though he undoubtedly is, no harm must ever come to Adam.'

Yes well. It did, of course. Harm. Come to Adam. And there was the undoing of us all.

CHAPTER ELEVEN

Flesh and Blood

Blimey – can't hardly recall the last time I were out the shop on a bleeding Tuesday. Nor no other day of the week, come to that. Saving Sundays, course. But I had to. It come upon me, like. Couldn't see to it Sunday, could I? Tried to put it out my mind for all of yesterday, I did. But now I got to. Sundays is when I usually sees to it because Mill, normal way of things, she be taking the boy out of a Sunday afternoon, and that's when I can slip off out, see? Partly why I cuts my losses and gone to the bloody Zoo. If Mill were going to be in the house, I couldn't just up and say to her well see you later alligator, could I? Smell a rat, she would. Never go nowhere on a Sunday. That's what she reckons, any road. Except for after my tea, when I'll walk down the Washington, couple of jars. Yeh well she wrong about that, ain't she? Me never going out of a Sunday. Just because I never take them nowhere. And she give me that, Mill – she give me that all the bleeding time:

her and Paul, I don't never take them nowhere. Yeh but look – they don't want it, do they? Course they bloody don't. Don't never want to be seen with me. Rather go out with Dr Crippen than they would with me. It's wrote all across their faces. Hitler – them two, they'd sooner go out with Adolf bleeding Hitler than they would with me. So I goes on my own. My little secret. Yeh because what I do is, I makes it look like I snoring my bloody head off on the settee there, look . . . and then when she nip off out with the boy – up the Hill, down the pictures, whatever it is they's always doing, them two – I gets my coat on sharpish and I'm off round Adelaide Road, see my Daisy. Don't never take too long. Then Mill, when she come back in, there I is again – back on the settee, large as you like, fag in my fingers, and then I hears her going Oh look, Paul – there's your Uncle Jim. Still fast asleep. Still snoring like a . . . what is it she say? Hog. Something like that. Not nice anyway, whatever it is she say.

Dead set on it Sunday, I were. That urge. And then I get all this palaver about bloody Stan and his bloody day out at the Zoo. And Mill saying it give her a chance to get on with her knitting and all the rest of the caper . . . bloody hell, I were that let down, I don't know . . . so I just ups and says I'll go along with the buggers to the Zoo. Never planned it, nor nothing: it just come out. Least I got a bit of air in my lungs. Because if I weren't going to nip round Adelaide Road, see my Daisy . . . well . . . couldn't stay cooped up in here, could I? Proper give me the hump, that would. So there I am in the bleeding Zoo. And that Stan – there ain't no life in that boy. Telling you. Like you's out with your teacher, or something. Vicar, or something. Got a bit better once he'd had a belt or two down him, I'm not saying – but still he's a dry old bastard and no mistake. Yeh and just before we come back home, just before I goes and lights a fag down the shop with Cyril – see how he doing, stick him a bit of millet, have a little natter – I says to Pauly: here, Pauly . . . let's you and me have a chat like, ay? Little word. Before we goes in to see your Auntie Mill, ay?

'What about . . . ?'

'What about? Well – this and that. Nothing in particular. Like – what we done today. Had a good time, didn't you? Got your toffees, look. And that elephant, ay? What about that elephant? Big, ay? That elephant? Yeh. Some of them animals – proper make you laugh, don't they? Chimps, and that . . .'

'You had a lot of whisky. May I go now, please?'

'Yeh yeh – in a minute, Pauly. It's just that, well – your Auntie Mill, right? She maybe don't want to know about all of that, ay? You just tell her about your ice cream and all them animals. Best way. She'll like that, she will. You telling her all about the animals what you seen. And your mates. Anthony. Amanda. That other one. Nice, she were. Didn't you think? What was her name? Nice, she were. Make a good little girlfriend for you, ay? What you reckon? Not so stuck up as that Amanda, didn't seem to me. Laughed a lot.'

'May I go now, please?'

'Yeh just hold your horses, can't you? What's all the hurry? So listen, Pauly – you'll remember what I said to you then, ay? About your Auntie Mill. And here – here, Pauly. Two bob. How's about that? Two-bob bit. What a day you's having! Ay? You can get one of them Matchbox cars, can't you? Like them, don't you? Bit left over for a Mars bar.'

'I don't eat Mars bars.'

'Crunchie, then.'

'I don't eat Crunchies.'

'No well – tube of Rolos, if you want. Smarties – you like them.'

'I don't eat Rolos. I don't eat Smarties.'

'Yeh you do – I seen you.'

'No I don't.'

'Yeh well get whatever you bleeding well want, you little sod . . .! Oh buzz off – get out my sight. Bleeding Bertrand Russell . . . you don't know you're born, you don't! That's your trouble! Bleeding Bertrand Russell . . . !'

So yeh, I thought: that gone like it always do. And then I gets a few bottles of Bass inside of me and Mill's put out a warmed-up slice of that steak and kidney with gravy and all of the doings, so come the evening I weren't feeling too bad. Still go down the Washington, though: got to do the thing proper. Got through Monday somehow, but it were on my mind. Yeh and this morning, I'm up early like usual – cup of tea, bit of toast – but I ain't feeling settled within

262

myself. Urge, see? Still got it. Ain't gone away. So I reckon I got to see to it. Tried it before, not seeing to it, and it don't do you no good. No, son – believe me it don't. Makes you all out of sorts. And it's for Mill I does it, really – she don't know the half of all what I does for her, Mill don't. Else I'm only going to take it out on her. I know she don't deserve it, but you got to face it – it's all I'm going to do. So now I'm needing to cobble up some great load of codswallop, and it got to be done now before I goes and opens up the shop.

'Busy are you, Mill? Next hour or so? Don't have to be now. Later, you like.'

'I'm always busy, Jim. You maybe haven't noticed.'

'Yeh no but I only ask on account of I'm wondering if you want to sit in the shop, like. Like I say, hour'll do it easy. It's just I got to go dentist.'

'Dentist, Jim? Why?'

'Why? Why? Why you bloody think? Because I got a bleeding wossname, that's why. Ain't I? Wossname. Got a – what the bleeding hell you call it . . . ?'

'Toothache . . . ?'

'Yeh. Toothache. Course I got a bloody toothache. Why else I want to go up the dentist?'

'Does it hurt?'

'Yeh it hurt. Course it bloody hurt. It's a toothache, ain't it? It's what they do, hurt . . .'

'Which tooth?'

'Which . . . ? How the hell do I know which bleeding tooth? One of them. Up the back.'

'I see. And it's bleeding, you say?'

'Hey? I never said nothing about that.'

'Oh but you did, Jim. And I quote: which bleeding tooth . . . ?'

'Here . . . you being funny, or what?'

'It would seem not, no Jim. Well now let me see . . . am I busy? Mm. I must think. Well this morning I have to do the shopping, clean the bathroom, scour the lavatory, polish the floors, hoover the rugs, rake out the grate, reline the kitchen shelves, sew that button on to your shirt, change the bed linen, attend to the laundry, the washing, the ironing . . . but apart from that, no Jim – I don't seem to be busy at all.'

'Right, then. Good. So – about an hour suit you?'

Look – I know she were being wotsit – sarky. I do know that – I ain't a bloody idiot. But sometimes you just got to let it go by. Else I would've been up there half the morning arguing the toss, wouldn't I? So I bung her the keys to the shop – and yeh I could just be sticking a 'Back in Half an Hour' sort of a notice in the window, yeh I could do that, but nah – I don't like to. Never done it, see? Not in all the time I been here. And I'm known for it, ain't I? Opening up bright and early. Famous, you could say. Always the first of a morning to be open for business in the whole of England's Lane: it's a bit of a tradition. Yeh but about Mill – don't get me wrong: it's me what's going to go down and put out all of the gubbins on to the pavement, I ain't asking her to do none of that. Hang up the bath – the brushes and the brooms. Pile up them galvanised buckets before that toffee-nosed Barton bastard can come and have the bleeding lot off of me. Yeh because I wouldn't want no one to turn round and catch a butcher's of my wife humping stuff about like that. I'm the man, after all. Ain't I? Got to be. Can't have your missus doing nothing like that. Wouldn't do. That's the way it go in England, and quite bloody right too. Island Race, that's us. Just ask Churchill, you won't take my word for it. They maybe do it different in Frogland, I'm not saying – and yeh I wouldn't put nothing past them Wops and the bloody Krauts . . . blimey, in bongo-bongo land they maybe get their wife to, I don't know – build their bleeding houses for them, and then when they finished cook her up on the fire there and have her for their tea, what do I know? You want to know all about that, you be best asking them sambos down the woodyard. Anyway – bugger all that: I's off now. Yeh and just before I does that, Mill, she says to me: still hurt . . . ? And just for a mo there, I don't know what she on about. Then I gets it. Yeh it do, I goes to her: it hurt something terrible. And it do, it do – yeh but it won't for much longer. Daisy – she soon sort me out. Yeh – she a good girl, Daisy is.

It were Charlie in the Washington that one time, the bugger – it were him what put me on to her. I were just off, pretty much had it, but Charlie, he get hold of me by the arm and he go to me – here, what's your game? Your round, ain't it?

And I says to him listen to me, Charlie mate – we had so many pints tonight I couldn't tell you my bleeding name let alone whose round it is. But here – never let it be said, son: you want another, that's all right by me. So I gets them in – can't have been much off closing, but Reg, he's a good lad: always give Charlie and me a little bit of leeway. And so he bloody should: what I ain't spending on hoity-toity Pauly's bleeding la-di-da girls' school, it all go to the Reverend Stan Miller of this parish for me ton of bleeding fags – and the rest end up with Reg here. But be fair – he do keep a good drop, Reg. A very fair pint. Bass, course. There's a Charrington's house down Haverstock Hill, but nah – bloke there, he don't know how to keep his ale: watered down with piss, is what it taste like. One place up Hampstead Village way, Charlie were telling me, they gone over to all of that fizzy sort of keg muck. Watney's Red bloody Barrel? Do me a favour: must be joking. Young people, he were saying – it's them what go for it. Yeh well they would wouldn't they, stupid little bastards.

So anyway, there we was in the Washington that time, Charlie and me, propping up the bar over in our usual little corner, having a fag, enjoying a jar. I like it in there. Dead lucky really, having it right on my doorstep. They still got all that fancy woodwork and all them big mirrors and that. Sort of boozer Sherlock Holmes is going to go in – and he have a glass of whatever it were he were drinking, nice big glass of opium, something like that, and then he can go to his mate Cheers, ay? Elementary my dear wossname! Yeh. It all old-fashioned, is what I getting at, and Charlie and me, that's the way we likes it. And there ain't never no kids nor women in to bugger it up.

'You off after this lot then, or what?'

'Yeh Charlie. Course. What else I going to do, eleven of an evening?'

'I know what I'm going to do.'

'Yeh? What? Fill in your pools coupon?'

'Nah. Here – talking of that, how you get on last week?'

'Nothing. Not a bleeding dicky bird. Why? You got lucky, did you?'

'Were looking like I got eight draws . . .'

'Yeh?'

'Yeh.'

'But you didn't, did you?'

'Nah.'

'Nah. So what you up to then, Charlie?'

'Aggie. That's what I'm up to. She's a bit of all right, Aggie is.'

'Who the bleeding hell's Aggie? Christine, your missus, ain't it? What – you got something going, have you? Dirty old bastard.'

'Nothing dirty about it, Jim. Here – got a fag?'

'Blimey. Why you always run out? Ay? Always of an evening round about closing time, you go and run out of fags. Reckon by now you owe me about a hundred bleeding packets.'

'Pay you Friday, chum. No listen – Aggie, she's a very accommodating woman. Classy lady, Jim, I ain't kidding you. Adelaide Road. She got a friend. Nice girl. They're in the basement there, right opposite the bus stop. Made it all real cosy. They got a orange bulb in the wossname.'

'A orange bulb . . . ?'

'Yeh. Real cosy. So what you say? Aggie, she don't fleece you nor nothing. She got reasonable rates. Daresay her mate's the same.'

I would've gone. I would've. Because comfort I do need. Always I'm wanting that. And like everything else what I does for myself, I shouldn't be too surprised if it end up costing me. Got to pay for the lot in this life, ain't you? The bleeding lot. Learn that early on. But I'm telling you, I'd had a right bleeding skinful that night and no mistake. I weren't even fit company for Cyril, never mind no floozy. But I do remember next morning down in the shop, and I were thinking to myself: Adelaide Road, ay? Nice and handy. Right opposite the bus stop. And Aggie, she got a friend. Nice girl, according to Charlie. And so the following Sunday once Mill gone out with the boy, I got myself down there, didn't I? And that's when I first come to meet her. Daisy. My Daisy. And floozy she ain't, let's be getting that straight right at the off. She got lovely manners. She a big girl, I'm not saying – but ever so dainty with it. Yeh and so it's her little side door what I'm knocking on now. I already give her a ring. She know I'm coming. And okay – only early in the morning, but still she going to get herself all done up nice for me. Only one what ever did, my Daisy. Because Mill, well . . . when we was first married, I got to say, it weren't too bad at all. Never forget that first time. Well, weren't actually my first time: there was a couple of fat old scrubbers up Minehead who was popular with all of the lads. But the first time with Mill, I mean. A proper lady. Wedding night. On leave, I were. Still a war on. Didn't have much time. That were the feeling then. Whatever you was up to, there were always this feeling at the back of your head that you better get a move on son, because you didn't have a lot of time. She were lovely-looking in them days. Still is, I suppose. Yeh – suppose she is, but I don't never look at her like that no more on account of I ain't meant to. Well – made that pretty clear early on, didn't she? She were keen on it, first off. And I were grateful. Tried to be nice. Never took up too much of her time, because I knowed how she were always so busy. Couple of minutes is all – can't have been a hardship for her. Anyway, she didn't never complain. One time I remember – well, couldn't hardly forget it, could I? Only time we never done it in a bed. She were rolling out pastry on the kitchen table. Just had her hair done – smelling lovely, she were. Little pinny on her. And yeh all right – I were just in from the Washington, granted . . . but I come up behind her bold as brass, I did . . . and, well . . . just done it. It were lovely. I think we was both surprised. She never said nothing. Didn't even stop rolling out the pastry.

What happened then though was them tests. Them tests

what I had down the hospital. She done them before, some other sort of women tests. And then I had to. Weren't too happy about it. Who would be? Anyway – turns out I ain't no good. Can't do it. Bloody useless. So no kids for Mill then, and it all she were ever wanting. Wasn't for young Pauly coming along, I reckon she would've . . . well, don't know what she would've done. Anyway – she didn't want it no more after that. So I got to cope with it myself. Years I done it. Art photographs I got. That's what they calls them – art photographs. Black and white. Some bird with her tits out and holding up a vase or something and there's this sort of curtain or a Roman ruin behind her. Between her legs though, it's a bit of a puzzle: she got no doings. It's all just white and painted over. Not really what you're after, is it? But they help you out a bit, them pictures. Bleeding daylight robbery what they're charging – don't get me on to it. Little shop down New Oxford Street it is, where they got rubbers and trusses and that. Years I done it. So when I met my Daisy – yeh, I were well pleased, I can tell you that. She ain't no art photograph, not my Daisy. Real, she is. Flesh and blood.

'Coo – we're up with the lark today, aren't we Jimmy boy? Come in quick, will you dear? All the cold's getting in.'

'Hallo Daisy, love. Keeping well, are you?'

'All the better for seeing you, my Jimmy. Been a little while, hasn't it? Come on through, that's it. That's the way. Let's all be as quiet as a mouse though, will we? Aggie – you remember Aggie, don't you dear? Course you do. Well she's still in her room, dead to the world. Had quite a night of it, poor love. Exhausted, she was – should've seen her. Now I've only just put the fire on so it's still a bit parky. Got your milk on the stove, though – I didn't forget. Ready in a tick. Haven't ever seen you of a morning before, have I Jimmy? Let alone a Tuesday. Could have knocked me down with a feather when I twigged it was your voice on the telephone. Only just had my Corn Flakes. Everything all right, is it?'

'Right as ninepence, Daisy. Now it is, any road. Don't reckon them, you know. Corn Flakes. My missus, she started getting them for the boy on account of they got submarines in. You bung in this . . . what is it? Baking powder or some-thing, she were saying, and they goes up and down. What they think of next, ay?'

'I know. I got a blue one today. Your boy got a blue one? You can have it for him, if you like. I haven't got any baking powder else I'd give it a go.'

'Couldn't tell you. He got a red one, that I do know. Yellow I think I seen knocking about. Might not be baking powder . . . could be flour, or something. But I'll leave it, Daisy, that all right with you. They're only going to want to know where it come from. Blimey – you're right though, ain't you? Bleeding perishing in here. I can always fetch you down one of them Aladdin heaters, you fancy it. Two gallons of Pink Paraffin, last you a week easy. Make it ever so snug. Do pong, but after a bit you won't hardly notice. Here – that remind me: got you a nice big bottle this time, see? You looking proper lovely

Daisy, I got to say. I go for that red on your mouth. Favourite, that is.'

'Done special for you, Jimmy my love. Now let's have a look . . . what bottle you got . . . ? Ooh – Parozone, lovely. Ta Jimmy ever so much. I'll bung some more on that bloody wall of mine right this minute, if you don't mind, dear. It's got ever so bad with all this rain. Creeping right up to the pelmet, now it is.'

'Yeh but bleach, it only get rid of the marks, Daisy. It ain't going to stop the damp coming in, is it? You want to get it looked at.'

'Yeh well you try telling my buggering landlord that, the swine that he is. Lost track of the number of times I been on at him. Once they got your rent, they just don't want to know. Bastards. Every landlord I ever had has been a right bloody bastard. Yeh but if you kick up a fuss, you're out on your ear without so much as a by your leave. Place I had before, up Belsize Park – I come home one evening and all my things is on the pavement. Said I hadn't paid the rent. Bastards the lot of them. Here, Jimmy – you sit beside the fire nice and cosy and get yourself all sorted, all right? Back in a just a jiff. Lovely to see you, dear. Sight for sore eyes, you are.'

'You could've had him for that, couldn't you? Landlord?'

'Well not really dear, no. Because I hadn't, you see – paid him his bloody rent. Not for near on three weeks. Bit of a lean time, it was – going through a bad patch. People wouldn't think it, but it's up and down, this business. Ooh – listen to me . . . ! Kept my deposit though, didn't he, the sodding bastard. So that was a fiver gone west. Towel's on the tallboy, look. Shan't be a mo, Jimmy.'

Lovely, ain't she? Ay? Just what I like. See how you can talk to her nice and easy? Always up for a little bit of a natter, Daisy is. Make me feel right at home. Which – you got to face it – is more than I ever does at home. Only other time I talking is with little Cyril. Apart from going on about the weather all the bleeding time with every Tom, Dick and woss-name what's coming in the shop. 'Raining, Mr Stammer,' they're going. Yeh well I can bleeding see that, can't I, you berk? I ain't blind am I, you stupid old sod. 'My it's a scorcher today, Mr Stammer!' Oh yeh well I'm right glad you telling me that mate, else I'd be putting on my mink bloody coat, wouldn't I? Blimey, I don't know. If it weren't for the dosh, I'd be happiest in my little shop if no one ever come through the bloody door again. Just me with my fags, a nice bottle of Bass and chatting away with little Cyril: do me perfect.

It only a little basement, this – but she got it real cosy. A orange bulb. And she got red on the wall both sides of the fireplace, what you don't see often. We got magnolia. I says to Mill one time – here, I says: how about we slaps up a bit of red distemper either side of the fireplace there? She says to me 'I don't really think so Jim, unless of course you are contemplating the conversion of this building into a fire station – or conceivably a jazz club . . . ?' See? Not nice, is it? Always that little dig she got for me. Always got to make me know I'm a pig in the shite and I ain't got no class. Ain't got no taste. Yeh and about that – another time she says to me in that voice she got 'Oh no on the contrary, Jim – you have plenty of taste, I do assure you. It's just that none of it is good, do you see.' Snide. Ain't it really? Putting me down, that's all she ever do. Up go Pauly and that Barton butcher bastard, and down go Jim. Happen all the bleeding time. Not nice, is it? Ay? Yeh but my Daisy, she don't do none of that. Care for me, Daisy do. Like this big white towel she got for me, look – all clean and fluffy it is. She done that for me. So I put the thirty bob under the candlestick there, and what I'm going to do now is, I'm just going to get my duds off and slip the towel on to me. Tuck it in neat around my doings. Then when she done bleaching that back wall of hers, she come along with this great big safety pin she got and make me all tidy. Then she bring my milk, nice and warm the way I likes it. And she don't mind it when I sits on her lap nor nothing – because like I say, she a big girl, Daisy. Take it in her stride, don't she? And the bosom what she got on her, it's a right lovely thing – proper homely, it is: something a bloke can proper get to grips with. Come to mummy, is what she say. Yeh. Come to mummy. And when I got the rubber thing on the bottle in my gob, she go and stick her tongue right down my lughole – and that . . . can't kind of like explain it really . . . anyway, it make me go all sort of funny. She sing me a little bit of a song, then. She got different songs, quite a lot. Baa Baa Black Sheep I like – always do like that one. Incy-Wincy Spider, that's a good one and all – because then she go all tickly on me. Always have a right laugh, the both of us does, if she go and do the Incy-Wincy Spider on me. And she stroking my hair, see – and then she get to stroking my other bits, like . . . and it's prime, that is. Prime. And she say Do you like that little Jimmy? And I goes yeh. And then she do her tongue thing again and I get all shivery with it and she say Do you like that little Jimmy? And I goes yeh. Then she go all serious and she say have you been a naughty boy little Jimmy and I goes yeh and she say Well let's have just a little bit of a look then, shall we? And I goes yeh. And I gets up off of her and I lies on the settee there and she undo the pin and the towel and she patting me all dry with another towel she got there and she do it real nice and slow and soft, like – and she say Do you like that Little Jimmy? And I goes yeh. And then I gets that lovely feeling all sort of bubbling up and right inside of me and I looks at her, see, and she smiling down at me ever so kind, and she kiss my brow and then she bring over this bowl of warm water and a little bit of soap what smell of lavender and she make me all clean again and then she put on all of this powder and she go There now, my boy – thanks to Mummy you're all nice and clean again, aren't you? Did you like that little Jimmy? And I goes yeh. Oh yeh, Daisy – I did. I did. Yeh I bleeding did.

Milly was flustered, there was no point in denying it – though neither, she knew, must she ever let it show. Everything this evening must appear to be perfectly normal: already I've blithely explained away to him, I think, the essential core of the thing with a light and easy touch, yes I feel sure I have accomplished that – for it is, after all, only Jim we are talking about here, whose instinct at the best of times may hardly be said to be acute: he is quite devoid of nuance or suspicion – he sees only that which is plainly before him. But treading with care and treating the man – a womanly approach that is bred in the bone and will make it certain, I am sure, that all now is well. But I have little excuse – none at all. It was perfectly stupid of me to do what I did, and ultimately so very terribly demeaning: the work of a madwoman, really – but passion, you see: this is what passion will do to you.

At first I simply was sitting in the shop, and feeling rather ridiculous. Here is not my place: everything here is utterly alien. This is Jim's domain, and the Lord knows he is welcome to it. It smells of him – or he smells of it: I think by now the two are thoroughly interchangeable. This so old and flattened frayed chintz cushion on his stool appears over the passing of centuries to have moulded itself into the inverse form of his buttocks. And beneath it is a mottled and dusty collection of old and creased thick paper carrier bags with knotted string handles from an assortment of places in the Lane, one or two of them long closed down. Why would you keep such uselessness beneath the cushion of a stool? And how many years had they resided there? The jagged teeth on the tin of string are wholly corroded: they would never cut the twine, which is why so very often in his efforts the whole thing would be upset on to the floor, the string unravelling, and Jim there cursing; Paul complaining later on that it was he, once more, who had been charged with balling it all up again. Next to the tin on the counter lay half a pair of scissors: not an operative and complete pair of scissors, no, for this would of course function immediately and efficiently, no no – just this one blade of a pair, the bent-over rivet still rattling at its centre. And so he would wield this blunted piece of uselessness, would he, as a cumbersome alternative to a straightforward knife, and all because the jagged teeth of the string dispenser are wholly corroded. Such a method, in Jim's world, I can see would pass muster: in this, he imagines, he has come up with a canny and coping system, a more than ingenious solution. All of this I instinctively know, while still remaining, oh . . . simply miles away from any sort of understanding. And then there are the odours – this mingled sweetness of distant rot, the veil of mustiness – the throat-tightening tang of paraffin, the rasp of choking bleach: all these fumes which he professes not to notice. And then on the perch in his rusted cage . . . there is Cyril, the light of my husband's life – and look: his tiny black eyes are seemingly angry: he is cocking his head as if eager to shout out at me 'Here! Here! What's going on? You're not Jim! You're not Jim! You're not Jim!' Well no – thankfully I am not.

And I was hoping that no one would come in. Not least because aside from all these piles of the more obvious commodities, I have not a clue where anything is. So if anyone wants something even vaguely obscure, I shall just have to ask them politely to call again when once more the king sees fit to resume the throne at the heart of his castle; or anyway this stool, with its old and flattened frayed chintz cushion, its substratum of carrier bags. Another reason I was hoping for no sort of disturbance was that I now had so much thinking to do. I'd closed my mind to a good deal of what has been happening lately by convincing myself that I had simply not a jot of time to dwell . . . yes but here now is time, hanging thick in the dead air of this dank and silent, fossilised cavern. I should love to first be able to deal with what I suppose I have to think of as the minor things – to evaluate their impact, and then to judge how best to handle the inevitable conse-quence. Yes, that would indeed be a rewarding luxury . . . but of course it is the black and gigantic shadow of Jonathan that swoopingly obliterates every trace of that, as it threatens to engulf me. Because I am now quite totally persuaded that that so very brief but telling hesitation in Jonathan's stride could mean only that he had indeed heard the calling out of his name – further, that he had registered its source, and yet was immediately determined to affect a total unawareness, and press on with purpose. Why? Why would he do that? A reluc-tance, fear even, to be seen to address me in the street? Hardly. Such a thing, after all, would be perfectly in keeping – we were in England's Lane, for heaven's sake, where both of us live and conduct our business. Not that, then. So what . . . ?

A disinclination to speak to me for some other reason. Yes. And of course I do know what that is: what else, after all, could it possibly be? For I can no longer blind myself so very wilfully . . . because that is surely what up until now I have been doing. Though still . . . even at this very moment, just to think of, to see again, that so brief vignette – to simply recall it, that just-glimpsed and easy conviviality that he was sharing with Fiona in his office, when I had so much needed to talk to him, to be with him . . . still I am astounded by how very powerfully that has wounded me. That, and the drinking of what I am now quite decided simply had to be Benedictine. Though I chastise myself for it, for my vain and girlish naïvety. I mean to say – what on earth did I imagine? That because he and I will occasionally encounter, that all manner of relations with his wife would immediately cease? It simply isn't logical. Yes but logic, of course, now is the po-faced, so starchy and irrelevant intruder – that so cold would-be annihilator of all that throbs inside of me. Logic, it is bloodless – and what I am feeling is raw and dripping, consuming me from without, while still so very hard and deep within me. Even now my gullet is tight, my stomach bunched and my pink-rimmed eyes are smarting. I can, though, justify without guilt or question my own behaviour, solely by means of regarding Jim. I can look at Jim quite wholly dispassionately, knowing that then my mind will be gorgeously flooded by wave after wave – a hot and unstoppable deluge of Jonathan: so of course then I must rush to him. How could I not? But

. . . for him, clearly, all is much different. His . . . wife . . . is a lady. An educated and handsome woman, and together, it would certainly appear, they still share a great deal in common. So what, then, am I? What does this make me? Am I just that so terribly casual a thing, then? Merely a matter of convenience? Painful, horrifyingly painful though it is to acknowledge . . . this recently, quite gradually and so very reluctantly arrived-at deduction is cruelly emerging as the one distinct and very lowering likelihood. Oh dear. Oh dear, oh dear, oh dear. What, then, shall I do . . . ? About it. Well, this is hardly the moment for irresolution of any sort at all: end it, Milly. Yes. If I have to my name even one tattered streamer of honour intact, I must end it. Yes. But then . . . were I to do that . . . I should be without him. Would I not? And I do not want to be without him. You see. I cannot bear the possibility of being without him. You see. The very thought of even one more tomorrow, and Jonathan quite excised from my existence . . . is simply intolerable.

I must defer my decision. Clearly, I am far too tender – I am in no sort of proper condition to go hurtling into the casting of so irrevocable a die, whose outcome would effectively paralyse my entire state of being. And why is it, I wonder . . . ? Why is it that unions, liaisons, dalliances, relationships and marriages . . . why must each of them be tinged with an always secret kind of dull and muted agony? I mean – just look at Stan . . . as now, and eventually, I rather fear I must. Whatever now can Stan be thinking? And at the very moment when he did that to me – when, so utterly out of the blue, that kiss, it fell upon me . . . what great tangle can have been alive in his mind? Or alternatively, was it maybe just wiped clean? I actually do think that that is quite entirely possible, you know – because recalling now the wide-eyed blankness of his expression, he could so very easily have been quite as astonished as I was. Nevertheless, though – it has got to be said that here was no fleeting and neighbourly gesture of affection, no simple peck of amicable gratitude. There was both spirit and intention behind it – that much, I think, was rather horribly and immediately clear to the two of us. Well to me it was, anyway. But then . . . oh, poor Stan: just look at all he has to cope with. Bad enough, you would think, having a boy so sorely afflicted – but a wife like that who treats him in such a way . . . yes, and over how many years . . . ? Poor Stan. Poor Stan. But Jane, though – can one utterly blame her? Is she any more a responsible person? Well I think it would truly take a professional to tell you for sure – but one thing I will say with conviction: whatever she is, it is not insane. Troubled, clearly – and with highly disturbed, not to say highly disturbing, outlooks and attitudes towards . . . well, her very own son, to begin with. How could she possibly have said such awful things? And to a perfect stranger. Is she even aware that Anthony is so very friendly with my Paul? I don't really see how she can be. And that diary – that curious journal she said she was writing. What can be in it? Didn't she tell me she attends to it daily? And she never leaving the house. Eating only all those chocolate bars purloined from her husband who is visibly at the end of his wits in his consistent and perfectly tragic determination to persuade her to swallow just anything at all. Well. Poor Stan. Well. Maybe we must all of us snatch at even the most slender possibility of comfort when and where we come to sense its tentative touch, no matter how unlikely or unpromising the source.

And then . . . there is Mrs Goodrich. Always there seems to be Mrs Goodrich. Oh . . . it was already so thoroughly confusing a moment. The noise – oh yes of course, I remember now: all those terrible noises that Sally was making from behind the window screen. Then, yes, there was the kiss itself . . . and following that, something, something else, now what could it have been . . . ? There was I am sure this further distraction of some sort – something rolling about on the floor, could that have been it? Well whatever it was, immediately after, and so very suddenly, there she was: looming. But at what precise point in all of this had she actually entered, Mrs Goodrich? What exactly had she seen? Yes well, there is the question – but whatever she had witnessed, it would most certainly be more than enough for her to have gleefully fabricated the most fantastic tale, and one that even now and with each successive retelling would be gathering close to it, like a clutch of gripping burrs, such increasingly gaudy decoration and lurid embellishment. And just imagine her joyous amazement were she ever to come into possession of the one and true big story: an intensely sexual relationship between the happily married and gallantly handsome butcher of England's Lane, and the low and salacious wife of the grubby little iron-monger.

So I continued to sit in the shop. After a very tedious while, I extremely half-heartedly began to jot down on a scrap of paper some names and skeletal ideas for the dread Christmas party. To be held the Sunday before the actual day, that's what we've all agreed upon. Possibly in our little local library, just around the corner in Antrim Grove. It used to be the custom to just have it in one of our front rooms or shops, but there really isn't enough space, you know. It can become really quite boisterous, once the children start playing with balloons and the men get a drink inside of them – Jim especially. And this year there will also be the two negroes to contend with, of course – and nobody is at all sure how they will behave, quite what they might get up to: different customs, you see – not even convinced that they know what Christmas is. And by no means everyone was in favour of their being included, wholly predictably, but I'm pleased to say they were after quite a lot of argument firmly voted down by the more level-headed and equable among us: no colour bar in England's Lane, I very much hope. Mr Lawrence in particular, I remember – he was most vehemently against them, and Jim would have been too, if ever he could stir himself and actually turn up to one of our meetings. Last year we had the party at Mr Lawrence's, actually in his newsagent's shop – he had very kindly pushed back the counters for us and so on – though he made it perfectly clear that he wasn't intending to do that again. I don't at all mind because the whole thing, it didn't really strike me as being over-merry: the lighting was so terribly gloomy, and somebody quite early on knocked over the tree. It was only artificial and ridiculously small: more akin to a lavatory brush than any sort of a Norwegian pine, to my eyes. So this year the library has been mooted – I forget who came up with the idea, but it's really not a bad one. The ceiling, though, is so terribly lofty – I simply can't imagine how we'd get the paper chains up there. And another thing – so very little money has been raised: I've just been rattling our box here on the counter: sounded like no more than a couple of pennies. Awful, really. Can't think how I'll manage. It'll be like the rationing during the war: how to make do with very little indeed. And there's no question at all of my being able to supplement whatever we eventually do manage to gather – this ever-increasing debt of mine to that blasted tallyman, whom I rather wish now I had never set eyes upon, is, I admit, becoming something of a worry. And I shan't for a very long while be able to buy any more little fripperies in John Barnes or Selfridge's, that's for certain. Oh dear – I so don't want to be part of any of all of this, you know. Christmas – it's the very last thing on my mind. I wish I could just escape to some warm and magical island. Yes well – precious little chance of that happening: you can Milly, I think, safely put all thoughts of that sort quite out of your mind. Yes but how at this party, please will someone tell me, am I expected to conduct myself?

And how will Jonathan be behaving? Oh . . . wonderfully well, I suppose: chinking glasses with his wife. Oh . . . it's really all just too too awful even to contemplate. Yes and right at that miserable moment in my very downcast ruminations, there came a sudden interruption – I had such a shock I just can't tell you, when that cracked little bell above the door was emitting its discordant clanking, and here now was someone coming in to the shop. Quite hauled me back down to earth, I can tell you that. And who should it be but Edie from the Dairies: she was so very surprised to see me there, that was more than clear. Because I never am, you see: I never am.

'Oh hello Edie – how nice to see you. Jim, my husband, Mr Stammer, he's gone to the dentist.'

'Oh I see. Yes well that would explain it, then. Well I can't stop even for a second Mrs Stammer because I've left the shop, see? Put a notice up in the door. Head Office, though – they really don't like you to do that. Come down hard. I've had a letter from them before about it. So could I just have a window wedge please Mrs Stammer, and then I'll nip off back. I'm sorry if I'm seeming rude . . .'

'No no, Edie – quite understand, of course I do. Now then . . . window wedge. Window wedge. Yes. I do know what you mean. What they are. We've got one in the kitchen. They're made of sort of rubber, aren't they?'

'Green, yes.'

'Green, are they? Ours is brown, fairly sure . . .'

'The last one I had was green. But yes they do come in brown as well. Think I've had a brown one in the past. I don't really mind what colour it is though, Mrs Stammer. It's just for the back door, you see. For when we get all the milk delivered.'

'Right. I see. So it's a door wedge you're really wanting then, is it Edie? Not a window wedge.'

'Are they different then? I'd no idea. I just always call them window wedges, that's all.'

'Yes. Well I've no idea either, to be perfectly frank. And I have to admit to you, Edie, I'm not at all sure where they're actually, um . . . kept. I mean – we will have them, obviously. Just a question of where . . .'

'I think the last time Mr Stammer got it out of a drawer.'

'Yes, that seems reasonable. Rather a lot of drawers though, aren't there? That's the trouble. Well let's just try a few, shall we . . . ?'

'I'll maybe come back later, will I? I'm just worried about the shop. Oh look – you've dropped your piece of paper, Mrs Stammer. Here you are.'

'Oh thank you, Edie. Nothing important. Just my little jottings – preparatory list for the Christmas party. Very early days, of course. I was just wondering if the library ceiling isn't rather too high to be able to get the paper chains up. Maybe we don't need them, paper chains. Well they're not in here, window wedges . . . this is just bath plugs and some sort of springs for something or other . . .'

'Got to have paper chains . . .'

'Really? You think they're essential, do you? Not in this

one either . . . fuse wire. This could take rather a while, you know . . .'

'I'd have thought so, yes. Quite essential, paper chains. Got to have paper chains up, I'd say. Not really proper and Christmassy, is it? If you don't have any paper chains up. Look – I really think I'd better get back, you know. It's not that urgent, or anything. Been using an old phone book for ages – daresay it'll be all right for a little bit longer. I'll call again when . . . you know, when um . . .'

'Well if you're really sure, I do think that might be best. I really am so awfully sorry, Edie. I just can't think where to look. Could be anywhere.'

'No no. Well bye, then. Not to worry.'

'Bye, Edie. And I will bear in mind what you said.'

'What? What do you mean, Mrs Stammer? What did I say?'

'You know. About the paper chains.'

'Oh that. Yes. Yes, I do think we've got to have those. Like I say, wouldn't be Christmas, really – not without paper chains. Well see you again soon, I expect.'

'Oh yes. I was meaning to pop in later on today, actually. I need some more Corn Flakes. Paul, he's just wolfing them down. It's the submarines, you know.'

'I know. They're selling ever so well. Haven't sold so many packets of Corn Flakes since they had blow darts in. Well bye then. Mrs Stammer.'

'Bye, Edie. Goodbye. And sorry again about the window wedge.'

'Door wedge, yes. No trouble, Mrs Stammer. Bye bye for now.'

'All right then, Edie. Bye. Goodbye.'

Yes well I just knew it would be like that, didn't I? Feel such a fool. Why doesn't he, Jim . . . I don't know . . . label all the drawers, or something? Well because he knows where everything is, obviously Milly: no need to, is there? Oh well. It would certainly appear though that Edie for now still is unsullied by any frothing and embittered effusion from the mouth of Mrs Goodrich – otherwise I'm sure I would have known it. And while this is quite surprising in itself, her state of happy innocence can not, of course, be expected to endure for very much longer: maybe, when later I go in to buy my Corn Flakes, her expression will be telling indeed. And I'd had no further time at all to gather my remaining thoughts when that blessed little bell was clanking away again and I was closing my eyes and thinking oh no, here we go – what's it going to be this time? Someone wanting a cement mixer, maybe, and here am I not knowing what drawer it's in.

But it was Jonathan.

Both his step and his eyes were frozen as he momentarily beheld me. I gasped out my delight – though had I not immediately crossed the floor and taken him very firmly by the arm, he would, I am convinced, have turned at once on his heel, and fled.

'Jonathan! Oh Jonathan – I am so pleased to see you!'

'Milly, my dear. Well this is quite a surprise, I must say.

Never before have I seen you in surroundings less becoming. So a considerable surprise, as I say. Though naturally a thoroughly pleasant one nonetheless.'

Mm, yes – well not too very pleasant, if I am compelled to be honest. Damn me for coming in here – I very nearly walked on by, and so now wish that I had done so. The thing I am needing, it could so easily have waited until tomorrow. And now I have confrontation, and I am wholly unprepared. Well – no escape this time. I rather do seem to be caught. So let us just calmly observe then, shall we? Gauge both her attitude and her persona. Possibly my instinct is errant. Maybe all is well. Maybe the enactment of one of these grindingly dull and awful female scenes is not after all an inevitability. For I do remain perfectly contented to continue to sail on an untroubled sea, well of course I do. But if there are to be signs of turbulence, any hint of choppiness, then I think it might be time for the captain to raise anchor and abandon this harbour – cast off, as I do, into yet uncharted waters.

'What are you, um – doing exactly, Milly? Scribbling away there . . .'

'Won't take a second. I'm just quickly writing a notice. Back in half an hour. I'll put it in the door. I really do have to talk to you, Jonathan.'

'Fearful rush, you know . . .'

'Won't keep you. We can go in the back.'

'Oh I hardly think that that is . . . the fumes in here, you know. Unsavoury, very. Don't you find? I should have thought that a lady of your very evident refinement . . .'

'It's better in the back. In the back it's fine. Not nearly so bad. I've put the notice up now, so you've got to. Oh come on, Jonathan – don't be frightened. I shan't bite you. Promise.'

'Gratified to hear it, my dear. But honestly, you know – truly not at all a good moment. The boy in the shop, I don't like to leave him for any length of time.'

'Oh nonsense, Jonathan – Billy's perfectly all right in there and you know it. Just come in to the back, won't you? Come on. People can see through the window.'

'I doubt they can see much. The window has the air of having been constructed not out of glass but of galvanised iron.'

'I know. It's terribly dirty and vile in here. So come into the back, yes?'

Jonathan sighed, and not untheatrically. He had his gold cigarette case in his hand, and he slid from it now a Black Russian. This he lit slowly.

'Very well, dear lady. Lead on, Macduff. But soon, I fear, I must be away.'

I really do not care for this: I do not like its odour. Both literally and figuratively. For it is I who decides when and where we meet. This is always the way with my ladies. And so I am not ready for this – I am disadvantaged. And nor do I at all care to be hustled into the doubtless no less noxious rear to this perfectly rank and disgusting sty.

In the cluttered and dark back room, Milly was eagerly bustling, and really quite energetically – hurling just anywhere rags, papers and unidentifiable pieces of metal and chunks of wood from the one good chair.

'Sorry. Bit of a mess. Never mind. Can I, um – get you anything, Jonathan? Something? Only I don't actually think there is anything here to, um . . . Haven't got any – you know – Benedictine, or anything. Cigarette smells nice . . .'

'Fear not – I am replete, my dear. Would you care to smoke? No? Very well. So what, um . . . ?'

And Milly was struck by the unspoken question, simply lingering. For yes – what, um – was it that she wanted to say to him, actually? What, now that it had come to it, could she possibly ask? How could she lend structure to no more than a feeling of profound unsettlement at the memory of the sight of just this man in a room with his wife? It seemed, rather suddenly, quite totally absurd. And then she looked up at him, at his magnificent face. His eyes, so intent – the fine moustache above a perfect mouth . . . and those blue curls of smoke seeping through his lips, and mingling with the air. And before she had been wholly aware of the strength of the impulse to do so, she was holding him so terribly tightly. Her arms were thrown about him, and she strained to hug him hard: her eyes were shut as she concentrated devotedly upon the beating of his heart. She whimpered and resisted wildly and then hopelessly when he straight away stepped backwards – detached her arms from him with silent determination and held them firmly to her sides.

'Please, Jonathan . . .' she heard herself just hoarsely whisper.

'What on earth do you imagine you are doing, Milly? Never before have I seen you like this . . .'

'Please, Jonathan . . . here: look. I can clear a space on the floor. We can put all these newspapers down . . .'

'God Almighty. I think you have taken all leave of your senses. Do you seriously imagine that I . . . that we should . . . ?!'

'But Jonathan – you don't understand. I *love* you! You see . . . that's what it is. I *love* you . . . !'

Milly was aware of his eyes full upon her. She stood there quaking, awaiting whatever was to come. Had not the banging on the shop door – the clamour, the terrible clattering – brought back her shattered mind into a new though confusingly distorted sort of focus, she might indeed have again and with renewed desperation flung herself at Jonathan . . . or else simply wilted to the floor, and there she would have wept.

'Oh my God!' she exclaimed – and her eyes as she gazed up at him now were quite fearful.

'Where is the door out of here?' asked Jonathan calmly. 'The back door – where is it? Can't seem to see . . .'

'Oh – behind the curtain. No, not there – that way. Yes – you go. Best that you go now.'

She batted aside the old and filthy curtain, wrenched open the door, stood well back as he quickly and without so much as a single word walked right past her, and then, with a sigh, she slid back the bolt. Still she could hear all of this ceaseless rapping coming from beyond the shop – and oh good heavens, just take a look at Cyril: hopping about and twittering in his cage in possibly terror, or else maybe high amusement. And Jim's face, by the time she had patted her hair, smoothed down her frock and got to the door – it was boiling red. She smiled at him very stupidly through the only scrap of dusty glass not obscured by browned and ancient advertisements. His eyes were bulbous, as sometimes, she knew, they can become. She turned the key in the lock and the bell was clanking quite frantically as he roughly barged open the door.

'What the bleeding hell is this then? Ay? Back in bleeding half a bleeding hour! I don't never do that. Why you think I leave you here? Ay? I could've done that, couldn't I? Ay? Put a bloody sign up. But I never. What the bleeding hell you reckon you up to, woman?!'

'Well I do think, Jim, that you might actually show me just a little compassion. It's this ghastly shop. I was quite over-come. Felt so terribly ill. These awful fumes – I thought I was going to faint. I had to go and splash some water on my face. And don't ever, please, call me "woman".'

'It don't take half a bleeding hour to splash some water on your face! Do it? Half hour! Could've gone up the bleeding swimming baths, done hundred sodding lengths in a half a bleeding hour! And I'll call you whatever I bloody well want, see?'

'Oh look, Jim – there's no harm done is there? Hm? You're back – and I'm all right. So it's fine now, isn't it? Oh and Edie

– Edie from the Dairies, yes? She's going to come back later for a window wedge. Door wedge. I didn't know where you kept them. Are they different actually, Jim? Window wedges and door wedges?'

'Window wedges is in the drawer by the till there, look . . .'

'Yes well she said they were in a drawer, but I wasn't to know which drawer, was I?'

'Yeh well window wedges is there. See where I pointing? With the three-pin plugs and the cable connectors, window wedges is. Door wedges – door wedges, they's under the counter with the candles and the washing lines.'

'Right. Jolly good. Well I'll know for next time then, won't I? So they are, then. Different. Door and window wedges.'

'Door wedges, they biggen them up, that's all. Who else come in?'

'No one. It's been awfully quiet. You didn't miss anything. Apart from Edie, like I said. But she will be back – she said so. Look, Jim – I have an awful lot to do upstairs. All right? Still a touch of headache. So if you're quite finished shouting at me, I'll go. And how is it?'

'What you on about now? How is it? What sort of a bleeding question is that then? Bleeding riddle. How what, Christ's sake?'

'Tooth, Jim. Your tooth. Dentist, yes . . . ?'

'Oh. Yeh. That. Good. Yeh. Good. Much, er . . .'

'Better?'

'Yeh. Better.'

'Doesn't hurt any more, then?'

'No. It don't. All right now.'

' . . . thank you for asking, Milly . . .'

'Yeh. Right. Ta, then. Right.'

So that, I am very much afraid, is all that happened to me this afternoon. Life really is, you know, becoming rather over-fraught, and I hardly even know now what is uppermost in my mind. A fearful inner agony, and the rumble of foreboding . . . these, certainly, are vying for position. But as usual, I can't really yet be dealing with just any of it – and anyway it is evening now: I have attended to Paul – pretended to listen attentively to all of his schoolboy chatter, when in the normal way of things I would hang upon his every word: couldn't tell you whatever it was he was talking about. Earlier, I went to Dent's to get some kippers for our tea. And no, not solely because I was disinclined to buy meat at the butcher's. Paul, he's always complaining about all the little bones in a kipper, but I did it mainly for Jim, if I'm completely honest: he does so enjoy them, and it is important that the household remain harmonious. It really is a mercy that it is so very pitifully easy to ensure the complicity, the easy cooperation of men. Some men. The biddable. But we need peace here because there is more than sufficient discordance elsewhere, I feel – and not least within me. I do have to idly wonder, though, quite where Jim went off to this morning. It was so perfectly obviously not the dentist. He hasn't been to a dentist since the day he was demobbed – and if a tooth of his was genuinely giving him trouble, oh well my goodness: wouldn't we all be so terribly aware of that! There would be no other subject on the agenda. So not the dentist – but where then, so early in the morning? I actually do find it rather encouraging: that he should have anything at all to attend to that seems not to be centred upon the shop, the Washington and Cyril. So I hope he liked it, whatever it was: because I do think he deserves it, really – any sort of pleasure he can get: I wish him no ill. One other thing though that also is rather troubling me . . . is the pain. I've got that pain back, the stab, and I actually think it's rather worse. Trying not to let it show. Just hope I'm making a good job of it.

'Nah, Pauly – it ain't no good you trying to pick the bones out of no kipper. Just stick it in your gob. Crunch it down. Learned that in the army.'

Milly recognised the look of mingled revulsion and dazed incomprehension passing across Paul's face before he turned it up to face her, in mute supplication.

'Here, Paul – I'll help you with the bones. And for dessert I've got steamed jam sponge pudding. You like that, don't you Jim?'

'Yeh. Partial to that.'

Yeh – partial to that, and partial to all this special treatment what all of a sudden she doling out to me. Couldn't work it out – not at first I couldn't. In the dark, I were. Because I ain't often let her have it like that – really give her an earful, like I done. But I were that narked, I can't tell you.

Back in half an hour! I'll give her back in bleeding half an hour, I were thinking. Because I ain't never done that, bung up a sign. Have I? In all the years I been here. So yeh, I give it her good – but blimey, when I cools down, weren't I expecting to cop for it after. Thought I'd get the right cold shoulder. Keep it up for weeks, that what I were reckoning. And now it like I's a film star or something. I don't know. Kippers. Steamed jam sponge pudding. What's all that about, ay? Well . . . reckon I got a clue. I ain't saying nothing – not yet I ain't, nah. But in the back of my shop, there weren't half a funny pong. Not like a normal pong what I always got – nah, this were something funny, see? And I goes to Cyril: here Cyril, my lad – smell that, does you? What been going on in here then, ay? You tells your Uncle Jim. Yeh – and him tweeting away there. Shame I doesn't speak budgie though, ain't it? But then on the floor just under his cage, there – I seen it. Yeh. So where's that come from then, ay? Mill? Don't reckon so, no. So what sort of a person is going to be smoking a fag what's black, with a bloody gold-coloured tip on it? Yeh well. You got to ask yourself.

CHAPTER TWELVE

Got to be a Man About It

Oh dearie me – feeling a little dicky, if I'm honest. Anthony, he's all over the floor and playing with his little motor cars after his tea – making all those sort of vroom-vrooming noises and shouting at me to look look look, and it was all I could do not to tell him to pack in all of his racket. Well – not to blame, is he? Young boy with his toys – only natural. Not to blame, is he? For his dad having had too much whisky, and now the man's under the weather as a result of it. Not his fault that his dad's a right and proper bloody idiot, and no mistake. Yes I know but look – I needed it, I did. Little snifter. Because tonight, once I've got Anthony off – see he's done his teeth, tuck him up nicely – well then tonight, I really am going to. Got to. Can't put it off. Talk to her. Get her to talk to me. Got to. She's got to. Because well we can't, can we? Go on like this. Not for a moment longer, I'd say. Milly was right: got to be a man about it. Show some gumption. And oh . . . just that one thought of Milly, now. She probably hates me. Must do. Can't blame her, really. What was I thinking of . . . ? I mean — what in blazes did I imagine I was playing at . . . ? Dear oh me — I still go red when I remember it: feel my neck and then my cheeks, feel them turning all red whenever it comes back into my mind. Hadn't planned it, or anything. Well of course I hadn't. Wouldn't have dared. Just happened. That's all. One minute I was chatting away to her — next minute I was kissing her. Kissing her . . . ! Christ Alive! Can't believe it. Hadn't planned it, or anything. Just happened. And she — she pulled out of it pretty sharpish, well naturally she did. Lady, isn't she? Real lady. And with a friend, with a neighbour in his sweetshop in the middle of the day — hardly expecting it, was she? No — nor me, either. Well of course she wasn't expecting it. Another woman, well — would've had the police on me. Oh dear. She probably hates me. Must do.

'Look at this one, Daddy! My favourite. See it? Ferrari, this one is. Racing car. Swapped it with Paul.'

'Ferrari, is it . . . ?'

'Yes. Ferrari. Think that's how you say it. It's a foreign car. Not sure where it's from.'

'Could be French. Could be German . . .'

'Could be. But I didn't believe it when Paul said he'd swap it because I think it's really really great and if it had been mine I never ever would have swapped it, not in a million years. And I really like the red. Do you like the red, Daddy? You don't ever see red cars, do you? In the street. They're all black and blue, aren't they?'

'Maroon. Sometimes you see a maroon one.'

'Yes. Old Patten – our headmaster. He's got a maroon one. Rover.'

'Nice car, Rover. Quality.'

'I gave him a Pickfords removal van and a cow. Paul. That's what he wanted for the Ferrari.'

'Cow . . . ?'

'Mm. From my farm. I had two anyway, so I didn't mind. The Pickfords removal van I did rather like because the door at the back opened up and you could put things in it but that's what he asked for and I really really wanted the Ferrari.'

'Well I'm pleased for you, Anthony. Very pleased that you got what you wanted. Now young man – time to get you off to bed, I think.'

'Oh Daddy – can't I stay up a bit longer?'

'Not tonight, my boy. Not tonight. Tonight Daddy's got to have a little word with your mother, you see.'

'Why? She won't talk back, or anything.'

'Well maybe she will. It's not her fault. She's not well.'

'I know. You keep saying it. When will she be better?'

'Don't know, son. Couldn't tell you. Maybe soon.'

'That's what you say about me always, isn't it Daddy? That maybe I'll be better soon.'

'And maybe you will. Who's to say?'

'Actually . . . one of my legs, left one – it did feel better today. I could move it a bit more easily. Wasn't so achy. Do you think it's going to go away, Daddy? In my left leg? And then maybe the other one after?'

Oh dear Lord . . . just look at him, won't you? His eyes, those two big innocent eyes of his staring right up at me, and full of hope. So trusting in his dad. Wanting me to make it all go away. Breaks my heart. It bloody well breaks my heart. I'm sitting here, sozzled on the whisky, trying to get up the strength I'll be needing just to talk to my own bloody wife . . . and my little boy, my own baby boy, is asking me when everything's going to be normal. It does. It does. It breaks my bloody heart.

'You never know, do you? Could be, Anthony. Could be.'

'Oh and I meant to ask you – what does it taste like?'

'Eh? What does what taste like? Talk in riddles, you do.'

'Black and White. Funny name. I saw you pouring some before tea. It's a lovely colour, isn't it? Not black and white at all. What does it taste like?'

'It's not for little boys.'

'I know that – but what does it taste like? Is it nice?'

'It's . . . nice, yes. Quite, um – strong. But yes. Nice enough.'

Because I can't just tell him, can I? That it burns my throat and sits so sour and heavy on the stomach. That it's not the taste I drink it for. That I drink it because it blunts the sharp edges. Of my life. And gives me a bit of courage to carry on with it. And the more of it you take, the more you seem to need. Which is odd, really. If you stop and think about it.

All I know is, a bottle these days . . . it just goes nowhere. And it's two pound two-and-six – that's what they're charging for it in Victoria Wine. Criminal, really.

'What are you going to say?'

'What are you talking about now, Anthony? And it's bedtime, my lad – I've told you.'

'To Mummy. What are you going to say to her?'

'I'm . . . well, I'm just going to have a little chat, you know? Maybe bring her up a little bite. Sandwich, or something.'

'But she won't eat it, will she?'

'Well you never know, do you? She might.'

'She won't. She never does.'

'Well she might, is all I'm saying. You don't know, do you? She might. Now come along, young lad – get up those stairs. I'll be in to see you very soon.'

'All right, Daddy. Can I read? When I'm in bed, can I read?'

'For a little while.'

'Oh goody. I'm reading such a good book at the moment. Really funny. It's called *According to Jennings*. It's Paul's. He didn't give it to me or anything – he wants it back. Just lent it, that's all. It's about these boys who are our age and they're in a prep school but it's not like my prep school because they stay there all the time. That must be quite nice, I think. And guess what? The author is called Anthony, just like me.'

'Really? Boarding school? You're saying you like that idea, are you?'

'Think so.'

'What – not to be here any more, you mean?'

'Well . . . maybe you could come too, Daddy . . .'

'I don't think they're wanting fathers and mothers there, Anthony. These places. Whole point, isn't it?'

'I didn't say mothers. I said you.'

Everything he utters – every single word that comes out of his mouth . . . goes right through me like a jagged bloody sword. And another thing – he's dead right about the sandwich. I've decided now I'm not going to make one. Well it's silly, isn't it? Because he's right, of course he's right: she won't eat it, or anything. There's no 'might' about it. She won't eat it, and that's that, plain as day. Will she? Because she never ever does.

'Come on now, Anthony. No more prattle out of you tonight, my lad. Up you get – chop-chop. See how quickly you can clean your teeth and get your jimjams on. I'll be timing you.'

'Oh you always say that, Daddy – you always say you're going to time me and you never really do. When I ask how long I took, you just go and make something up.'

'That's thirty seconds gone already . . .'

'Oh gosh – I didn't know you'd already *started* . . . !'

And he's up now, look at him. Got hold of his crutches. Off he goes, my brave young soldier. He tucks them under his arm, the crutches, once he's got a footing on the stairs. Holds on tight to the banister. Pulls himself up sideways, sort of style. One step at a time. Got his own little system. Takes a while, but he gets there in the end. Won't let you help him. Doesn't like it one little bit if you ever try to help him. So . . . I've just popped next door now to get myself a little nip, and soon I'm following him up the stairs. Ah . . . just take one look at him, will you? Sitting up in bed, he is. Smelling of minty toothpaste. Transistor on the bedside table there, fizzing out some awful tune or other. And he's got his book out.

'Oh yes, Anthony – I see what you mean. Anthony . . . what is it? Buckeridge. Well there it is – it must be that all the cleverest people are called Anthony, then. Maybe you'll be a famous author when you grow up. Like writing essays, don't you? Always get good marks for your English essays.'

'Must be nice to have your name on a book. Maybe I will. Anthony Miller. Yes – I will. I've decided. That's what I'm going to do. I'm going to be a famous author and have my name on a book. Anthony Miller.'

'That's the spirit. I'll be wanting your autograph next.'

'Are there lots of famous authors called Anthony then, Daddy?'

'Oh yes. Scores.'

'Who? What other ones are called Anthony?'

'Um . . . well there's loads of them, aren't there?'

'Yes I know but who? What are they called?'

'Well, er . . . let's have a think, now. Not Shakespeare, no – William, he was. Charles Dickens, that's no good . . . and then there's . . . who's that other one . . . what's the name of that other author? Oh dear oh dear. My mind. No – gone. Complete blank. Gets worse and worse. But there's bound to be lots of them, name like that. Fine name, Anthony is. Now you just read for ten minutes, all right? Ten minutes, and then you put the light out. All right? And turn off that terrible racket – don't know how you can listen to it.'

'Not terrible. Elvis the Pelvis. How long did I take? To get ready. Did you time me?'

'I did. I most certainly did. Four minutes and thirty-two seconds.'

'Really? Honestly?'

'Cross my heart.'

'Really? Gosh. That's quite fast, isn't it?'

'Lightning, I'd say. You'll be the quickest famous author in the whole wide world. Nighty-night then, Anthony. Give us a kiss. There's a good lad.'

'Night, Daddy. Good night. I hope your, you know – talk goes all right, and everything.'

Yes. Well so do I, I suppose. Dreading it, if I'm being frank with myself. Very tempted just to sit in the front room and knock back the Scotch until I'm just completely out of it. But no – I won't duck it. I can't. In fact, what I'm going to do is . . . I'm going straight in to talk to her now. Right this minute. I am. Just march in and have it out with her. No, hang on . . . what I'll do is, what I'm going to do now is, I'll have just the one more little nip, and then I'm going straight back up to see her. Talk to her. Got to be a man about it.

Milly was right. And oh . . . just that one thought of Milly, now . . . ! She probably hates me. Must do.

Well . . . this is it. Just had a little listen outside of Anthony's door: seems to be all quiet. Good little lad, isn't he? Did just as he was told. And now I'm having a little listen outside of another door. So silent. Feel like a thief. Used to be my bedroom, once upon a time. Our bedroom, I should say. Funny to think it, now. That that's where we both were, where we both of us slept of a night time, Janey and me. Husband and wife, both in the same bedroom, normal as you like. Not the same bed, mind – you don't want to go overboard. But still, back in those days, we were always quite chummy. Funny to think it, now. Anyway . . . so . . . what do I do? What will I do next? Knock? No – silly to do that. Going in anyway, aren't I? No point knocking. So I'll just turn the handle, and see what I see. Yes well . . . I've done that: I'm in now – and I got quite a jolt. Bed's empty. And no – she's not over by the window, sitting in her chair. In the bathroom, then. Of all the times I could have chosen to come up and talk to her properly for the first time I can remember, and she has to go and pick that very blessed moment to go off to the bathroom. Oh well – she won't be too long, I expect. Unless she's got a dose of what she had last year around Christmas time. That was pretty bad, I can tell you. In Allchin's with her prescriptions all the blooming time, I was – pills, some sort of pink stuff in a bottle. And she in and out of the bathroom – never seen her move so fast. Green, she was: looking ever so puny.

You wonder really that she had it in her – what with her never eating, and all.

I haven't been in this room for a good long while now when Janey's not been around. Even when I'm doing her sheets or giving the place a little bit of a dust, still she's always here, always the silent witness. Like a crow in the corner. I'll be chattering on about the weather – it's cold, it's not cold, keeping fair (crossed fingers), looks like a spot of rain – or maybe Anthony's school report or else I've got to remember to get another tin of Pledge on Thursday from Stammer's . . . and she just sitting there, lying there, eyeing me. It's got her smell about it now, this room. Not unpleasant – I wouldn't say it's nasty. It's all just somehow her – the sum of her bits: powder, smear of Vaseline, cold cream, touch of mouthwash you get off her winceyette nightie when you take it down to the laundrette. Airless, of course. Nothing I'd like better than to throw open that window there and give the whole place a right and proper airing – but Janey, she won't hear of it. I say to her Listen to me, Janey – it's only fresh air, isn't it? Hey? It's God's clean air – not going to hurt you, is it? No harm in it, fresh air, is there? Hey? Hey? Yes well – might as well be talking to a cardboard box. Once I did. Once I heaved up the sash and just let the net curtains be blowing all over the place: oh dear oh Lord – you should've seen her face. Two minutes later I'm downstairs and I hear the window go back down again with such a hell of a thump – I tell you, I expected the glass to be broken when I ran back up there. The amazing thing – this is what always amazes me about Janey – when I went in to her room again, there she was just sitting up in her bed, quite the thing – the counterpane smooth, her arms out in front of her, just like a photograph of the way it was when I left her. And yet I know that as soon as I was out of the door, she'd got up, gone straight over to the window and hauled it back down. And it's a heavy thing, I'm telling you: unwieldy it is, because one of the sashcords, it's been broken for years. So what I'm getting at is that there's a fair deal more brawn there than you'd think from just looking at her.

Daresay she'll be back any minute. Two cups of stone-cold tea on the bedside table there. That's unlike me, that is. Normally, I always take away a cup before I dump another one down in its place. Yes – that's the customary method, my little way of doing it. Always throw away one cupful of tea at a time: golden rule. And now there's two. Well well. Dereliction of duty, as they say in the army: drunk in charge, I wouldn't be at all surprised. And what's this, now . . . ? Not sure I've seen this before. Some sort of ledger, looks like. Bit like the one in the shop, where I jot down all the takings. Let's just have a little look then, will we . . . ? What have we got here . . . ? Oh . . . ! Oh, I see . . . this must be that thing that Milly was talking to me about – this, what did she say? Journal thing she said she was keeping. But hang on . . . there's nothing here . . . it's all more or less blank, far as I can see. Oh wait – what's this say . . . ? 'Monday 29th November . . . Another Day.' 'Tuesday 30th November . . .

Another Day.' 'Wednesday 1st December . . .' Blimey O'Reilly . . . I'm just flicking through the whole of it now . . . and that's the only thing she's ever written in it: Another Day. Well. I don't know. I don't know . . . I just don't know what to make of that . . .

'Ah! I see you've discovered my most intimate secrets . . .'

Oh my God in heaven – I did jump, I can tell you! I was that startled, I dropped the bloody book thing on to the floor. It wasn't the noise so much as the fact that she's spoken to me at all.

'Janey. Janey, love. Didn't hear you come back in. Gave me a bit of a start, you did. Help you back into bed, will I? Or do you want to sit in your chair, maybe? Ah – you do. Right then, Janey – all right, settle yourself down, nice and comfy. Blanket? Would you like? For your knees? And how about a nice fresh cup of tea? Yes? Like that, would you?'

I didn't really think she was going to answer, or anything. And then she said:

'Why is it, Stanley, that always you must prattle?'

I blinked. I'm still doing it. I'm blinking away like the merry clappers. She's asked me a question. She never asks me questions. She's speaking to me. She is. I didn't even have to try. What it is, is – we're talking. I'm saying something, and she's saying something back. Admittedly at this stage it's still not very much, not what you might call a proper conversation – but early days, eh? Just got to ease into the thing.

'Nice to see you up and about, Janey. Nice to see it.'

'God's sake, Stanley – I have been to the lavatory. It is hardly as if I am competing in the Olympics.'

'No no. I'm just saying, that's all. Um – would you like one of these maybe, Janey? Keep your strength up. I didn't know which you'd prefer, so I brought you one of each, look. Both, if you like, of course . . .'

'What are those? What on earth are you offering me?'

'Well . . . Fry's Peppermint Cream, yes? And this is the Mackintosh's Toffee Cup. What . . . ? What is it . . . ? I mean – good to see you laughing again, Janey, course it is. Can't remember the last time. But what, er – what's so funny? Did I get it wrong? Are these not the ones you like, then? Because I can easily pop down to the shop and fetch you something else. Picnic, maybe – nice and chewy. Or how about a good old Fruit & Nut?'

'Oh Stanley. Oh Stanley. I can see that your woman has been a good and faithful messenger. Oh Stanley. Honestly . . .'

'What? What do you mean? What "woman"? Don't know what you're talking about.'

'You really are quite perfectly hopeless. You do know that?'

'Just don't know what you mean, that's all . . .'

'Of course you do. You know exactly what I mean. That woman you sent here. Mary. She has dutifully reported to you our entire and very arid exchange, which I naturally sought to spice with a litany of fiction. Were you anxious about the diary, Stanley? Well as you can see, you really needn't have been. Poor lamb – did you think it might be all chock-full of extraordinary revelation and insight into my broken and twisted mind? Lots of fruit, ripe for the plucking by a psychiatrist who doubtless would have been the next step in this really very tedious charade. No no – none of all that, I'm afraid. So sorry to disappoint. I simply record the advent and passing of each successive long and lonely day. And then I sleep. Fitfully. And in the morning I wordlessly repeat the process. As we do. All God's creatures . . .'

'But . . . Janey . . . it doesn't have to be like that, does it? Lonely – you don't have to be lonely. Do you? Hey? I'm here, aren't I? And little Anthony. He's your son, Janey – your little boy. Misses you. He does. He'd love it, to be able to talk to you again. And so would I. What happened, Janey? Can you tell me? Why aren't we together as a family any more? Is it my fault? I expect it's my fault, isn't it? You can tell me if it is. I wouldn't be surprised, or anything. Offended. Nothing like that. Is it because you had a proper education, Janey? Is that it? And I bore you? That you think I'm boring? Is that it? Or you don't want to be seen with me? Well I could understand that. Course I could.'

'You don't want me, Stanley. Neither of you does. I am no good to you any longer. Especially now that you have Mary . . .'

'It's not Mary. It's Milly. And I don't. Have her. Don't know what you mean. Of course I don't. Have her. Christ Alive . . .'

'Well no I do know that you don't, actually. Have her.

Only teasing. But you really would love it, wouldn't you? If you had. Oh don't worry – I don't particularly mind, you know. I find it all rather amusing, in point of fact. That you could even cherish so impossible a fantasy.'

'Don't have any . . . what are you talking about? Don't have any *fantasies* . . . ! Listen, Janey . . . you're my wife. Aren't you? Hey? Better or worse – remember? And look – how come we're talking now? All of a sudden. What's going on? Hey? When you haven't – you haven't so much as opened your mouth to me for just . . . look: what can I do for you, Janey? Just tell me. Explain it to me, yes? And I'll do it.'

'Well for a start, dear husband, you can remove from my sight those perfectly revolting-looking bars of chocolate. I hate chocolate of any description, and particularly the cheaper varieties. I know I used not to, but now I do. And the reason, Stanley, you will not have observed the absence of hundreds of bars is of course because I have taken none. I detest it.'

'Well . . . why did you go and . . . ? I'm sorry, I'm afraid I just don't understand you, Janey.'

'No well. Maybe Mary will explain it all to you. She appears to be not unintelligent. Although of course I do know that she belongs to another.'

'Yes well I know that too. I am very aware of that fact, actually Janey. And it's Milly, her name. She's called Milly. Milly Stammer – married to Jim, yes? The ironmonger.'

'Married, conceivably. Though he, of course, is not the one to whom she belongs. Although I believe he remains in ignorance of this. It's extraordinary how men do. Though quite for how much longer the dalliance of his wife will endure is very much moot, I should say.'

'What are you . . . on about, Janey? My head, I tell you – it's spinning . . .'

'Yes well that would be the whisky, Stanley. I am surprised by your overindulgence only in that you haven't taken to it sooner. If I am not sufficient to drive you in despair and desperation to the demon drink, then what on this earth would be, I ask you? No no – the relevant person is one Mr Barton, of course. Jonathan Barton, family butcher. Yes? He and Mary are, shall we say . . . intimate. Did you really not know? I'm surprised. Even in you, this surprises me. Everyone else appears to be thoroughly aware. She sweetly imagines it is still her little secret, but I am afraid that in this and maybe much else, our Mary is deluded. What is wrong, Stanley . . . ? You are very quiet. And your eyes are protruding rather horribly.'

'You . . . you don't know what you're talking about! Who told you all that? How do you know that? That's the biggest load of codswallop I have ever heard in all my life. And it's *Milly*, God damn you – it's not a difficult name to remember, is it? Milly?'

'I daresay that each night you drift into dreamland with it touching your lips. Sweet. But alas, dear Stanley – she is not for you. But then we do have to remember . . . she is a woman, isn't she? So of course not for you. And how did you ever imagine she might be . . . ? Ah – silent once more. What could be wrong? I haven't inadvertently touched upon a nerve, have I Stanley . . . ?'

'You said . . . you promised me, Janey. You swore to me at the time that all of that was over and done with. Said you'd never ever say it to me again. You swore you'd never go and rub . . .'

'. . . your nose in it again. Yes. I remember. An image which ever since I uttered it I have found to be lastingly distasteful. But it can hardly be brushed aside though, can it? Under the carpet. Or maybe you think it can? Well I do not. You were my husband – you cannot honestly expect to do things such as that and then just get away with it, can you? It is unnatural, Stanley. Not to say illegal. And thoroughly repellent to any right-thinking person. You were very lucky, you know, not to find yourself in prison. If it hadn't been for Daddy's money, charges would most certainly have been pressed. For that young man, he very clearly meant business. Would have created all sorts of trouble. Yes and if your wife hadn't been volubly and, I now see, very stupidly so very supportive . . .'

'Look. It wasn't . . . much. Well it wasn't! Not really! It was only the once, just that one time, you know that Janey. Don't know what came over me. Still can't understand it. Some sort of brainstorm, or something. And anyway – I don't want to talk about it now. Why are you doing this to me, Janey? Hey? I mean – we haven't talked . . . you've hardly spoken in years. And now you're doing all of this . . .'

'Does it seem cruel? I don't particularly intend it to be –

though nor do I mind if indeed you are suffering. The reason, I suppose, I have decided to speak is that after Mrs Stammer and I had our ridiculous little chat, I saw then that all sorts of unsavoury things would be bound to emerge. And they are, aren't they? Emerging in rather a rush. My source for much of this, in case you were wondering, is someone who is probably unknown to you. Young Doreen . . . ? Do you know . . . ? No – well hardly surprising, really. She is the junior in Amy's. You wouldn't have encountered her. She comes across to see me every day. Oh – you are shocked. Good good. Oh yes – every single day. Dear dear – you don't seem to think things through, do you Stanley? She does my hair. That's how it started, anyway. Have you not noticed how it is always neat? My hair? Always clean?'

'Your hair . . . no . . . I never really paid it any mind . . .'

'No well. And not eating – why wasn't I dead? You just don't think, do you? Well I owe my continued existence, such as it is, to little Doreen, really. She soon started bringing me a selection of rather tasty delicacies from Bona. And it recently transpires that she is really a very fair little cook, for one so young. Oh yes – I do eat, Stanley. And rather well. I have to pay her, of course. Just as well I still have a little bit of Daddy's money left, isn't it really? It would be awful if I had to depend upon you. She spends it all on clothes, as youngsters will. Mrs Stammer does this too, although she is no – what do they say? – spring chicken. And nor does she have the money to do it, but there is yet another tale of coming woe, patiently waiting in the wings. Just lately though, little Doreen has become a veritable mine of information. Mr Barton I happen to know about because the silly little thing was foolish enough to have her head turned. Flattery, gifts and blandishments. A sophisticated gentleman, by all accounts – I really wouldn't know – who takes his pleasures where he may. And one afternoon just weeks ago – who should she see with him, arm in arm . . . ? Well – none other than your beloved Mrs Stammer. Doreen was left in no doubt as to the depth of the relationship: it was, she said, all in the eyes. Well well. And rather acute for a virtual child, don't you think? Anyway, the Lane is alive with it, apparently. The real joke – and I do confess to finding this rather intensely amusing – is that she, Mrs Stammer, while remaining clueless about the transparency of her actual infidelity, remains under the wildly idiotic impression that Mrs Goodrich is spreading her usual malicious rumours about herself and another. You, actually, Stanley. Does that, I wonder, make you feel most terribly manly? Does it, Stanley? Is that what you are, then? Terribly, terribly manly? And all this nonsense has stemmed from the fact that you were so very gauche and foolhardy as to kiss her, I gather. Our heroine, Mrs Stammer. Downstairs. In the shop. But of course no one in their right mind could possibly believe that a woman such as that, whom even I can perceive as to be not wholly without certain qualities – certainly she would appear to be capable – that she might entertain even the remotest interest in one such as yourself. Well obviously. Laughable, no? And this she would have in common, I imagine, with every other woman on God's green earth. Because this is not an area, is it Stanley, in which you particularly excel . . . ? So there, I am rather afraid, we have it. Mrs Stammer might even as we speak be contemplating abandoning Mr Stammer in order to pursue the course of true love. Oh bless. How terribly torrid. Though she really needn't bother, you know – because gentlemen who rove, such as Mr Barton . . . they will always return to the nest. For Mrs Barton, I am told, is quite the cultured beauty. And wise. Oh yes – very evidently wise. So how will the carnival end, I wonder . . . ? Where shall we all find ourselves, once the carousel has ceased its turning . . . ? Well let's see . . . if Mrs Stammer does indeed continue on her horribly misguided and really very wanton course, well then it clearly seems as if poor Mr Stammer might be finding himself at something of a loose end. Doesn't it, really? Though he is, I hear, not over-discerning . . . so I'm just really wondering aloud, I suppose, but possibly there might be, shall we say, some sort of opening for you there, Stanley . . . ? Maybe the two of you – who knows? – could find yourselves very happy together . . . ? Ah! Ah! Finally, you contemptible donkey – finally you rise to it! At last you are up on your feet. Any other man would have struck me long ago. That's right – come at me – that's right. Look at your eyes – there's hatred in your eyes now, Stanley, and that's how it should be. Can't you see it? And your hands – they're flexing, aren't they? Bunching up into fists. Are you intending to do me harm? I so much yearn for it. Do you boil with rage, with murderous desire? I see that you do. Well what are you waiting for . . . ? Show some gumption! Do it! Do it! *Kill* me, Stanley . . . ! Why don't you? Why are you waiting? Why don't you just kill me now . . . ? Do it! Do it! No – don't go . . . ! Don't you dare go and leave me like this, Stanley . . . ! Come back! Come back right this minute, you miserable imitation of a man, you! Come back! Come back now, you damn bloody bastard, and *kill* me . . . ! Please . . . oh please. Just come back now . . . and kill me. Please . . . oh please . . . Do this for me, Stanley . . . Please. Oh please . . . I am begging you for help . . . can you not see it? Please just do this one last thing for me . . . That's it – that's right. Come back. That's it – and now a little bit closer, Stanley, so that you can just reach down and finish me. That's it, that's it – good, Stanley: good. Ah . . . you have come back to me. Thank you, Stanley. Now and at last, you can truly be a man. A real man, Stanley – don't you long for it as much as I do? And now . . . and now . . . just this one last thing that together we both can achieve. Do it! Do it! Do it, Stanley – if not out of hatred, then as a pure and final act of devotion. Come on, Stanley. Be . . . gigantic . . . ! Kill me. Kill me. God's sake kill me *now* . . . !'

Even as he fell out of the back door of his shop, Stan was thinking quite feverishly: the boy, the boy – I can't, I shouldn't, I can't just be leaving the boy! Have to, though – got to get out of there now. Such a scene . . . ! Christ Alive – what an unholy scene that now I've just got to run away from. My face ... the whole of my face is stuck with sweat, and yet when I go to wipe it, I'm feeling so cold. Shivering, I think – but it could be still just the tremble in my hands. I'm holding them both out in front of me now as I'm scuttling down the Lane – my heels on the pavement, it's sounding like pistols – and useless, they're looking: plain useless, they are, the both of my hands. And the night – couldn't tell you if it's an icy one: got no coat on and I'm boiling inside of me. Even hotter now that I'm barging my way to the bar of the Washington. Haven't been in here for just so many years, and already now I'm remembering why. The beery hot breath of it, that gets you in the neck. This sweltering crush of men in their big grey belted gaberdines with an *Evening Standard* poking out of the pockets – folded to the racing, folded to the pools. The clatter and the stink of it. Smoke gets in your eyes. Doesn't matter, though – it's the drink I'm wanting. Once I get a couple of Scotches inside of me, I'll maybe be calming down a bit.

'Mr Miller, isn't it? Sweetshop, yeh?'

'Yeh. Whisky please. Scotch. Large one.'

'Don't see you in here very much, do we?'

'No. Whisky, yes? Large one?'

'Quite a stranger.'

'Mm.'

'Haig all right?'

'Black & White . . . ?'

'Don't do Black & White, mate. White Horse? Vat 69? Bell's, we got.'

'Fine. Doesn't matter. Haig. Fine.'

'Oh so now you do want Haig. You want to make your mind up.'

'Haig. Large one. Now.'

'Yeh all right – you just hold your horses, will you? Some people. Want soda? Water with it? Something else?'

'No. Just. That. Christ *Alive* . . . !'

And it's so bloody small even once you manage to get hold of it. And I'm ordering another from this red-faced man with his big raw hands who is eyeing me now with this open contempt which I've seen on people's faces before – I don't know why that's all I ever seem to get from anyone. And now I've got that one down me as well – so I'll get in just the one more, and then I've got to pull myself together, haven't I? Work out what it is I'm going to do next. Be a man about it. Show some gumption. There's nowhere to sit, though . . . couple of benches over the far side with a few old biddies sprawling all over them – cackling like witches, they are. Knocking back the port and lemon, grey little curls falling out of the hairpins: what an example to set, I ask you. What sort of mothers can they be? You just hope their children never get to see it. Yes so anyway . . . I suppose I'll just stay standing where I am, then. Might as well. No real point in moving. Jammed all over. Handy by the bar anyway, for when I'm needing another.

'Well blimey – this is a right bleeding turn-up and no mistake
. . . ! What you doing in here then, Stan? Ay? Ain't never
clapped eyes on you in here before, have I? Ay? No, not never.
Here, Charlie – knows old Stan, does you?'

'Yeh – wotcha, Stan. Gets my fags off of you, don't I? Forty
Capstan, regular as clockwork.'

'Yeh – me and all. That's how he affording the Scotches,
ay? Nice for some. Look at us, Stan – two poor miserable
bleeding bastards, ay? Both of us only got the leavings of a
pint of Bass.'

'Hello . . . Jim.'

'Yeh. So what's up with you then, Stan? Letting rip, is you?
Having a bit of a night out? Bit of a knees-up? Painting the
town wossname, is you? That's the sort of style, is it?'

'No I . . . not really. Just, you know – fancied a drink, that's
all. Think I'll maybe have another one, actually. Lot on my
mind. Oh, um – can I get you a, um . . . ?'

'Very handsome of you, Stan. That's dead handsome of
him, ain't it Charlie? Ta very much – don't mind if I do, you
twisting my arm. Well we'll join you on the Scotches then,
ay? Keep you company. Funny old world, really – I were only
just saying to Charlie, weren't I Charlie? How it always the
same old faces what you get in here. Weren't I just saying that
to you, Charlie?'

'You was, Jim. You was. He were, Stan.'

'Yeh and then who go and pop up but good old Stan here.
Funny old world, ay? Ooh – lovely, that is. Liquid gold. Keep

the chill out, ay Charlie? Just what the doctor ordered. Better than any hot-water bottle, that is. Here Stan – Charlie and me, we just been thinking we might sort of, er – go on some place else, kind of thing. Bit later on. Ay, Charlie?'

'Yeh, Jim. Some place else. One way of putting it . . .'

'Just wondering whether my dear old mate Stan here might quite like the idea . . . What you reckon, Stan? Up for a bit of that, might you be?'

'Um . . . sorry, Jim – I don't quite, um . . . what are you talking about? I don't know what you're saying. I feel a bit, um . . . I want to buy one more of these, if I can just get that man's attention . . .'

'Here, Reg! Hoi! Reg! Over here, mate! Good lad. This is Reg, Stan. You met? Yeh? Reg – Stan. There we go. Who would like three more Scotches off of you – and maybe one for Reg and all, ay Stan? What you say? Yeh? That's the style. You're a real good bloke, you are. Diamond. Ain't he, Charlie? Don't you reckon? Yeh – see? That's what Charlie think and all. Diamond. Now see, Stan . . . about that other thing. I mean. I don't know how you fixed, like. At home, sort of style . . . Missus, and that. But from what I heard, well . . .'

'What? What have you heard?'

'Here here – keep your hair on, Stan . . . ! What wrong with you?'

'You can't possibly have heard. What have you heard? Unless it was Milly. But she wouldn't. Not Milly. She wouldn't ever.

Was it Milly? Was it? Has Milly been talking to you, Jim? She hasn't been talking to you, has she?'

'Mill? Nah. Don't know what you saying. And she don't much, if I'm honest. Talk to me. Not much. Nor do nothing else, if you gets my drift. Not for me, any road. Nah – not for me. Something I got to look into, matter of fact. Yeh well – never mind all that. But it's all that what I'm sort of like ... kind of on about, see? Not to beat about the wossname. See what it is, Stan – there's these two gels. That right, Charlie?'

'Yeh. Lovely, they is. Aggie – that's the one for me. Do anything for you, Aggie will. And ever so pleasant with it.'

'Yeh. Reckon she'd suit our Stan here right down to the ground, Aggie would. What you say, Charlie? Here – don't mind, does you?'

'Nah. Can't get down there tonight anyway. Skint, aren't I? Cheers, Stan – your very good health, sah! Scholar and a gentleman. Ooh yeh lovely – hit the spot, that do.'

'What ... you mean – women who ... ?'

'Yeh. You got it. Ain't he, Charlie? He twigged now, ain't he? Women what does. Nutshell. And I ain't talking charring neither. Think about it. All right? Take you down there, you fancy it. And they better than a hot-water bottle, and all – tell you that. Put hairs on your chest. Have a couple more, maybe, and then we's can have ourselves a little wander down there, you like the idea. Ever so near. Adelaide Road. Just over from the bus stop, there. Telling you, Stan – make a man of you, Aggie will.'

'Let's go. Let's do it. Let's go now. Show some gumption. Do it! Do it! What are we waiting for? Let's just do it now . . . !'

'Ay . . . ? Blimey! Listen to it, Charlie! You hearing all of this, is you? We got a right keen one here, ain't we? Dear oh me. So all right then, Stan – listen: we'll have us just the one more for the road then, ay? And I'll slip round the back – give them a quick ring. Don't want to be walking in on nothing. Got any pennies on you, Stan? For the phone, like? Then you can get us in a last one, and we's off. It thirty bob they're wanting, you wondering. Each, like. Got thirty bob on you, Stan? Yeh? Good lad. Only you ain't got, say – three quid, has you? It's just I'm a bit short. Yeh? You does? Right then, Stan – Trojan. What a time we's going to have, ay? So what about you then, Charlie?'

'Me – nah. I'm buggering off home, aren't I? Had a right skinful, I have. Them Scotches just about done me in. Get my head down. Be out like a light. So yeh look – I'll see you then, Jim. All right? Tomorrow night, shouldn't wonder. See you Stan, yeh? Ta for the Scotches. Be in in the morning for my Capstans, ay? Here – that reminds me, Jim . . . ain't got a fag, has you? Just smoked my last one, haven't I?'

'You don't get no better, does you Charlie? Ay? Telling you, Stan – Charlie, he don't get no better. No matter how many Senior bleeding Service he have off of you, still I got to be giving him another one. Reckon he owe me about a million quidsworth.'

'Write you a cheque, Jim.'

'Yeh – bugger off Charlie, can't you? Here – take it: that's your last, you bleeder, I'm telling you. Here Stan – talking of fags, something you can maybe tell me, ay? You ever seen black ones, have you? Don't mean whiffs nor nothing – fags, proper fags, yeh? But with all black paper on them and a tip what's gold, if you can believe it.'

'Gold? Nah – never, Jim! Having us on . . .'

'Telling you, Charlie – I seen it. Yeh so what about it, Stan?'

'Let's go. Now, Jim. Do it! Do it! Let's just do it. What are we waiting for?'

'Right you are then, Stan – right you are. Blimey – never seen a bloke so keen. So look, what I'll do – I'll go and give them a little ring then, yeh? And you get us in a last one, ay? Good lad. Oh yeh, and Stan – you got some pennies then, yeh . . . ?'

I don't really remember it, you know. No, not really – the journey down there to Adelaide Road. I think we might have had a few more, Jim and me. In that pub. In that horrible pub. He only put the brakes on me when he thought I might not have enough money left for what was to come after: read him like an open book. No . . . I'm really straining now, and I can't – can't at all remember it, the journey down there. Not even certain I could take you to the right door. Down a few steps, that I am fairly sure of. Cosy little place. They'd made it very cosy, the two girls who live there. Not sure then what happened to Jim, exactly – he seemed to have just sort of drifted off, and I wasn't too sorry to be seeing the back of him, that much I do recall. He's friendly enough, Jim – I'm not saying he's unfriendly. It's just that he grates on you, after a while. And especially then, after all I'd been through. And then the drink. No . . . I wasn't at my best, it's fair to say. One thing that really did begin to irritate me, though . . . I might even have let fly at him about it, I'm not too sure. But the way he talks, the way he's putting things – he always ends up asking you all these stupid questions. Like 'hear me, do you Stan?' Well of course I bloody well hear him: not deaf, am I? And he'll ask you if you know what he's saying, what he's meaning, what it is he's on about – and then of course you have to keep on saying to him Yes Jim, Yes Jim – like you're, I don't know – some sort of a parrot, or something. Or his bloody budgie, Cyril. You just find yourself doing it. Reflex – is that what they call it? I suppose that's what it is. And you hear yourself going Yes Jim, Yes Jim and you think you could lose your bloody mind. 'You got a fair old drink there, ain't you Stan?' Yes Jim. 'Go in the door now, will we?' Yes Jim. 'Here, Stan – you're a right one, ain't you?' Yes Jim. Yes bloody Jim. Christ Alive – fair gets on your wick.

Anyway – it was lovely, really, just to be shot of him. And then there was Aggie . . . Aggie, she did seem to be ever such a kind person. Brought me a nice big cup of Cadbury's Drinking Chocolate, a thing I'm always rather partial to. Settled the stomach a bit. Lost track of how many Scotches I had in

326

the end. And then she was sort of stroking my brow. Which was nice. I was in an armchair by the little gas fire, and she was sitting . . . I don't know – on the back of it? On the arm? Well wherever she was, I couldn't quite see her, not all of her I couldn't, and she was stroking my brow. And it made me think. How long is it? Since a woman so much as touched me? How many years? How many years? The only touch I had is when I went and kissed Milly, like the damned fool I am. And where did that get me, I'd like to know. She probably hates me now. Must do. And if she doesn't . . . well then soon she will. That's for sure. Because I didn't, did I? Do what she said. No. I'm not at all sure I've been a man about it.

'Fancy a bit of a lie down, do you Bert? Nice relaxing lie down – how's that sound . . . ?'

'Wonderful. Sounds wonderful, Aggie. It's Stan, my name. Not Bert, no. I'm Stan.'

'Course you are, Stan. Course you are. Let's just go into the other room then, shall we . . . ?'

'Not sure I can stand . . .'

'Your Aggie'll help you. Won't she, dear? You lean on me, eh? Have you there in no time.'

And I suppose, then, that's what must have happened. Though how she took my weight I'll never know, because she was only a little slip of a thing. And then I was on this bed, divan sort of a bed, and Aggie – lovely pink cheeks, she had, bright and shiny eyes – she was smiling at me. Perfume – I liked the perfume she had on. Like a garden, full of flowers.

'Right then, dear. Comfy, are we? Nice and comfy? That's the way. Now let's just see what we have here then, shall we . . . ? There, my love . . . like that, do you? Nice, is it . . . ?'

'Yes Jim.'

'Ay . . . ?'

'Nothing. Nothing.'

'Bit tired – that it, dear?'

'Am tired, yes. Had quite an evening of it, really . . .'

'Couple of drinks with your mates, eh?'

'Couple, yes. Something like that.'

'Well I expect that's it then, lovey. Don't you worry about it. Quite normal, you know. Oh yes. See it all the time.'

'Normal? Is it? It's not really though, is it? Normal. Not really.'

'Course it is, dear. Don't you worry.'

'I think you are very . . . attractive . . .'

'Well aren't you the perfect gentleman.'

'So why can't I . . . ? I want to. Do it. Just do it . . . !'

'Blame it on the distillery, dear. Not your fault – course it's not.'

'I think, Aggie . . . I'll go now, then. Things to see to.'

'All right then, dear. If you're sure. Well now . . . why don't we just call it fifteen bob, then? All right? Under the circumstances.'

And then . . . well then I found myself fumbling about with the lock on the back door of my shop. Heaven knows how I got there. I remember her waving me off, waving me away. Holding that shiny red gown around her, and standing in the doorway. 'Bye, Bert . . . !' she went — and she kissed me on the cheek. Well look — it's the thought that counts. And I do wonder, though — I have to — if it was the drink. Or if it was something else. You sometimes just have to wonder about yourself, really. So anyway . . . somehow got myself up the stairs. Didn't make a noise. Crept into Anthony's room — had a little look. Peaceful. All quite peaceful. And then I went in to see Janey. Quiet as the grave in there. Oh yes. Peaceful as you like.

CHAPTER THIRTEEN

The Art of Persuasion

Have you ever, I wonder, heard the tale of the shadowy and unspeakable creatures who happily will compensate the more lowly and gullible, the needy people, in easy exchange for attending to – as it is customarily termed – their 'dirty work' ... ? The moneyed and well-suited gentleman bruisers ... ? If not, you will surely have heard tell of them. And I am delighted and irremediably relieved to be able to announce that from this very bright and icy morning, now I am firmly of their number: yes indeed – I have joined their despicable ranks. Although it is true that in the past, my past – and in Henley, most certainly – I had not the least hesitation, no qualm whatever, over personally seeing to any little necessity, taking a certain measure, the immediate need for which might unforeseeably have arisen during the day-to-day running of what, by this stage of the proceedings, I had come to regard as being my business, and my business solely (this headstrong attitude of mine being the source, I suppose, the fountain-head, of the subsequent . . . well now – shall we call it a rift? Rift, yes – which very rapidly yawned and deepened into a fathomless chasm of mutual sin, then ultimate depravity). No . . . I did not at all mind taking care of any such things – indeed, one might even say with not inconsiderable justifica-tion that positively I relished it. While always remaining rather tediously aware, of course, that intimidation, even physical harm – the threat of it, or its execution – if it is to be inflicted upon so very evidently inferior a victim . . . then it all and always was so very effortlessly accomplished: elderly ladies bound by correctness, embarrassment, the necessity for manners . . . inarticulate and greedy legatees, a legion of casually igno-rant and slaveringly avaricious idiots . . . ? Barely challenging, I think we can agree.

This time, however, the situation that confronts me could hardly be more different. For it is no less a personage than my old friend and subsequent foe whom, albeit involuntarily, I now find myself up against: John Somerset himself – the founder of both our feasts, long before all such gorging turned to sickness. And never must one forget that Somerset, he is not just utterly ruthless and extremely determined, but clever so very far beyond the regular intention and understanding of that word. My initial assault, therefore – for perfectly possibly, one more successive attempt might well be required – this must be mounted by a disposable and unthinking spear-head: the decoy, the bluff, the first and expendable wave –

cut, if needs be, to bloody and shrieking tatters, solely in order for the generals to better assess both the extent and ferocity of the enemy's firepower . . . so usual, in war. And this, in a word, is my man Obi. For I have decided, you see, to wait not a moment longer. The state of limbo, I have come uncomfortably to realise, is not one in which I any longer care to dwell. This impending threat of the glinting sword must dazzle and teasingly prick me no more. I shall now assume the great and gaudy mantle of the swaggering aggressor: I am firmly convinced that it is wholly essential to seek out now this one single person who already has come so very unsettlingly close to finding me, and must remain quite desperate to do so. The coming battle – and it will be, please make no mistake about this, very much one to the death – this looming attack, it must now be taken to the other side. Then, and at last, can there be elimination. This to put right the wrong of my unthinkable omission of all those years ago. Why did I not strike? At a time when I could have done so with such demonstrable ease, and decisive velocity. Was I merely distracted and hesitant? Was I fearful? Surely amid my inexcusable inaction there could not possibly have loitered even the merest suspicion of anything approaching mercy . . . ? I cannot imagine so . . . but well, let us see. Let us look at it: investigate the circumstance.

The time I am remembering – the pertinent moment – is so very far along and down the briskly straightforward route that initially John Somerset had charted for me. Over this, at first, I had no more than added merely a splatter of colour – rendered the rolling road but a touch more scenic – before abandoning utterly so circuitous a course in favour of something new. My way now was direct, you see: it got you to the desired destination so very much more quickly. They were oddly reluctant, John and Adam, when first I had put it to them; the money, though, soon made them recognise the folly of their ways. As, so often, money will. At the beginning, though – before all of that – I was happy enough to be obedient: to accompany John's boy Adam to each of our appointments, I there to engage the witless householder in always elegant and redly gushing banter (the thrown-up and roughcast walls of which, and purely for the purposes of my own quiet amusement, I would thickly plaster over, and ever more lavishly – though never, not on a single occasion, did even one member of this bland and self-satisfied battalion of proles, parvenus, withered aristocrats and money-grubbing derelicts appear to suspect that even so much as a smidgen of my so very orotund and full-barrelled praise for their home – my lusty laudations over their exquisite taste, personal charm, physical beauty, the very vast and limitless depths of their soul . . . that none of this could be in any way inordinate).

Adam's eye did indeed prove to be fine – this much was immediately evident to me. If he did not possess a positive knowledge of any particular piece, then surely his instinct was always more than sound. And of course we very gaily and gallantly took away from all these cold and crumbling piles every manner of unspeakable bric-a-brac, and solely in order to conceal the one and true intent. I sometimes did wonder about the eventual destination of all those sulking collections of vilely glimmering lustreware vases, the Edwardian bachelor wardrobes with always a cubbyhole devoted to 'sundries', utilitarian vanity tables in the Japanese taste, more than detestable elaborately spindled mahogany whatnots, bisque and friable Parian busts of forgotten dilettantes – those insolent, glossy and muscular blackamoors brandishing eternally their lances and flambeaux, murky conversation pieces in chipped gilt plaster frames depicting some whiskery and melancholy old fool in gaiters and fingering a churchwarden, or else a surprised and rouge-cheeked young milkmaid secreting a letter into the pocket of her pinny – these in twine-tied bundles together with the limitless depression of all those endless oils of cows, ruminating in a brown and waterlogged field . . . the beastly little bits of Sèvres and Limoges, stuffed and mounted rodents, the consoles and commodes – not to say the perfectly extraordinary quantities of mutely offensive Staffordshire dogs. It transpired that Adam would weekly transport this whole very terrible caboodle to some sort of junk shop on the outskirts of Oxford – which, I thought highly comically, traded under the soubriquet 'Oxonian Antiquities' – where in lieu of cash payment, he accepted first the hospitality of the proprietor's wife – by all accounts a first-rate cook in possession of a starred Cordon Bleu qualification – and then, following a digestif, the rather more carnal delights of both the man's twin daughters (though whether in turn or simultaneously, I have not an idea). How aware and willing a party was this trampled trader in pennies' worth of debris to so broad and encompassing an arrangement, I did not discover. Rather because I had no interest whatever in so tawdry a matter. Though I cannot but think this entire household quite purposefully mercenary to the exclusion of any of the finer senses – because to have suffered any time whatever in the company of Adam when not most absolutely necessary was surely more than any right-thinking person of taste, refinement or even good humour could remotely have contemplated, let alone endured. For Anna, it almost immediately became clear to me, had been perfectly correct in her summation of his character: it would be difficult to imagine any other young man on earth who could be less engaging. Anna, yes . . . Adam's mother, John's wife. For of course it was she, by now, who consumed me wholly.

I should like to coolly recall our genesis, that initial and inevitable fusion prior to so heavenly a collision – but all is too tumultuous. It comes at me in a rush, a desperate tumble of hot and haphazard memory that yet can provoke in me a gasp – the very same gasp that always was expelled from me when stirred from my wallowing in the loving bouillon of just knowing that I had her – yes, at the rippling thought of a coming union. As to her touch . . . her touch would send me wild. The skin, her skin – just downy – was like none I have ever encountered: so shocking in its feathered softness, and then engulfing warmth. Her eyes, in bliss – so inkily black with a slash of whiteness, and yet they were the colour of fire. Her hair, those great and heavy shimmering handfuls, I would inhale until my chest came close to bursting. I wrote her poems, though none I could present to her. My poems, they could not reach, could not come close to approaching all inside of me and about her that was clamorous and pleading for expression. She was a greater woman than I an artist, that much was so very humblingly clear – but more than that . . . she was, in herself, the very highest art. For only a woman – the woman – can be the one true mark of the power of the work of God that screamingly surpasses, and with such unnerving and laughable ease, all and any merely earthly endeavour. A woman – the woman – abandons the insignificant artist to vaporous distance.

Fiona . . . I had all but forgotten. She was, however, by no means neglected: at this time I was a reasonably wealthy man, and so naturally I provided her with everything. Everything, yes . . . bar myself, of course. Oh I was there, to be sure – sharing a luncheon, idly listening to the wireless, the two of us taking a spin in my new and still very much missed Bentley . . . but all that I carried within me alas was no longer for her. Here was the only period in my life when knowingly I was wounding her, and I so very deeply regretted it – yet it remained quite utterly beyond me even to for a moment contemplate smothering, annihilating, the source of her pain: this, I am afraid, was just wholly unimaginable. And so she remained in silence, for which I was grateful, while all I could do then in parallel muteness was to witness the commensurate suffering which always and famously must accompany any such selfless restraint. In the past, Fiona had adored me unquestioningly, and always she chose to strike a forgiving and unusually modern and enlightened attitude towards my philandering – I sometimes even imagined, maybe somewhat fancifully, that rather to her own surprise, she might even quite approve of it . . . although here, she knew, was something other. The unspoken concern was whether Anna could ever have taken me from her. For the sake of Anna, would I have reneged upon my wedding vows – turned my back upon my beloved wife and little Amanda? Well . . . there now lies so very large and ponderous a question. A question, however, that never did come to any sort of resolution . . . no, in the end, that looming dilemma, it never did have to be faced . . . because then came the moment when each of the characters in this ultimately and I suppose quite predictably very woeful tale – at turns malevolent, grasping, cruel and salacious – each of us, yes, was immediately confronted by so very rapid and violent an implosion.

For some long time past, John and Adam had accepted my modus operandi. For John, here was little more than a formality: a grunting nod of acquiescence. His interest lay solely in our constant acquisition of valuable objects, his task to place them for the optimum price: he had no role to play at the forefront of the theatre. And should he one chill evening come to suffer from the sourness of guilt, fall under a grey and sweeping shadow of shame, or else experience no more than a bilious bout of queasiness as a result of the glancing and intrusive thought of all that now was occurring . . . well could he not simply elect to no longer dwell upon it? To place a long-playing record of some or other jolly waltz by Strauss on his mirror-polished gramophone, light up a Cuban cigar and pour a further cognac? Adam, however, was daily at my side. He had become, did he but know it, my right-hand man, though hardly so vital as that might suggest. Whereas before I had been content to be the simplest of foils, now I had become the sole and central figure – the pivot, as well as the aggressive lance – and he no more than an attentive acolyte. His artistic discernment, our need for obfuscation, these were so much less important than formerly, for now the tendency was simply to take whatever it was that we wanted. Quick, you see? Saves such a great deal of nonsense. Initially, the boy was stubborn. Here, though, was nothing to do with conscience: in Adam, demurral, open and ill-informed argument were simply built into his nature – he would have contended any given premise as a matter of utter principle: agreeability had no part to play in his really extremely moronic existence. He had no friends – well perfectly obviously he had no friends – and he was loved by his parents as only parents can: each of them scaldingly aware of his base and intrinsic loathsomeness, though tugged by the tie that binds. His indulgences seemed to be confined solely to the sexual and the gastronomic, these obtained weekly in a suburban junkyard, and quite handsomely paid for with a dismal succession of dusty trinkets prised from the blue and gnarled arthritic fingers of tremulous and uncomprehending widows – from very old and badly shaven men, jowls rendered angry from whisky, and whose eyes were made milky by inoperable cataracts.

'Ah Adam, hello. Glad to have caught you. Won't you come in and take a glass of wine with me? There's something I'd quite like to discuss with you, if you've got a moment. I was having a word with John, with your father, earlier this morning – I don't know whether he mentioned it to you at all . . . ?'

He scowled at me: here was his habitual manner. It was as if I had suggested that possibly he might care to lick clean the soles of my boots.

'Haven't spoken to him today. I'm busy.'

'But maybe time for just a glass . . . ? Few minutes . . . ?'

'Two. I'll give you two minutes. No more. Right?'

'Perfect – very gracious of you, Adam. Two minutes. Excellent. Do sit down, won't you? A glass of Chablis . . . ? It's perfectly chilled.'

'No.'

'No? I see. Something else then, conceivably? I have a reasonably decent Beaujolais Villages? Glass of sherry, perhaps? There might be a bottle of beer in the refrigerator . . .'

'No. Don't drink. Well not all your rubbish, anyway. I'm quite particular what I drink. Who I drink with.'

'Well I must say it is exceedingly good of you to indulge me, Adam. I shall be brief.'

'Do. One minute up already . . .'

'Quite . . . Well here are the bones of what I have been thinking. When we go to all of these houses, Adam – why do we actually bother any more with my doing all of this chit-chat, when often these people can barely even hear me, let alone understand what it is I'm trying to say to them?'

His two dull eyes were bulging, as might those of an infuriated bloater.

'Why? *Why?* Well that's pretty stupid, even for you! You know why. What's wrong with you? So I can go upstairs and—'

'Yes I do understand that, Adam. But wouldn't it be more convenient, more – you know – easy for all concerned were we simply to march right into the house and tell them what it is we want, and then just take it . . . ?'

'God! You're even dopier than you look, aren't you? Wouldn't have thought it possible. Haven't you learned anything, all the time you've been with us? Because, dimwit – that's telling them, isn't it? What's valuable and what's not. That's the whole point, stupid! And what do we do if they say no, I'm not selling? Messes up everything. God, I can't believe how stupid you are . . .'

'Well I rather fancy a good many of them may well say that. In which case, well – as I say: we just take what we want.'

'What do you mean . . . ? And you've had your two minutes, by the way.'

'Please do indulge me just a moment longer. And I apologise if still I am behaving so perfectly stupidly. I shall endeavour to phrase this more comprehensibly for you. We. Just. Take. It. Yes . . . ?'

'What – *steal* it, do you mean . . . ? Joking, aren't you?'

'We virtually steal it anyway. Don't we? What about last week. The house in Goring. Yes? Gainsborough, wasn't it?'

'Reynolds. You know nothing . . .'

'Reynolds – forgive my ignorance. And we gave for it . . . ?'

'Can't remember. Couple of pounds . . .'

'Precisely, couple of pounds – which you told the old dear was really for the frame. And John, your father, and do please correct me if again I err, is, I believe, hoping for something in the region of eighteen hundred . . . ? Stealing, isn't it?'

'It's business. She was happy. Stupid old woman. You saw her – she was happy with her two pounds, wasn't she?'

'Yes but look, Adam – it's not really the two pounds I am talking about. Think about this – what if we had had the run of that house for the whole of the day? Uninterrupted. No longer the need to be fast and furtive?'

'There was a lot of good stuff in that house, I think . . .'

'Well exactly – my feeling too. You are beginning, I believe, to see what I am meaning. And another thing – why must we wait for them to respond to our advertisements? I mean to say – flyers . . . really rather primitive, no?'

'You really are a stupid bastard – do you know that? I get them done at the best printer around. Quality work, that is. Not cheap. Not – *primitive* . . . !'

'I do not refer to the artwork, Adam – but the technique. The approach. It's rather old-fashioned, don't you see? It's . . . slow. Why don't we simply select the most promising-looking houses and knock on the door? Are you really sure you won't take a glass of Chablis . . . ? It is rather fine . . .'

'No. Horse piss. And what if they won't let us in? Thought about that? What then? God, you really are just so thick I can't believe it . . .'

'Well in that case, Adam – we do what we're best at. We persuade them, yes? We practise the art of persuasion. And if they remain reluctant . . . well then we find ourselves in a position where we are rather compelled to insist, I'm afraid. Well now look – I really do think we ought at least to give it a try. Don't you? Nothing to lose, I should have said . . .'

'What did my father have to say about this? You talked to him, you said? Well what was his reaction, I'd very much like to know, to all of this dung that you're giving me . . . !'

'He was cautiously approving, is how I should interpret his words. Said I should speak to you, of course. Perfectly properly. Which, Adam, is currently my laboured endeavour . . .'

The very afternoon of this conversation, if so very stilted, one-sided and barely to be borne exchange should warrant even remotely so fulsome a term, I asked Fiona – she had been at the time enjoying what she was pleased to call a 'bubble bath' – whether she might and rather quickly care to knit for me a thick black balaclava. She expressed surprise, as well she might. Said, I remember, that it would crush the natural waves of my beautiful shiny hair, and that that would be a shame. Said too that she herself did not personally consider the climate to be sufficiently inclement to merit such a thing. But still she made no enquiry – she never ever did, she never does, concerning any of my whims and sudden enthusiasms, and in return for such rare and admirable continence on her part, she has always been the recipient of my sincere and undying appreciation.

There used to be in the old part of Henley at the time a rather pretty bow-fronted and quaintly old-fashioned little toyshop – for all I know, it well might still be there – and under cover of acquiring for Amanda the sweetest miniature china-faced doll, the chubby limbs suffused by lace (Amanda, she christened her Emily, and still she is very much cherished), I purchased also this rather garish large and coloured card alive with depictions of Wild West saloons, stagecoaches, covered wagons and desert cactuses, attached to which by means of a series of twists of wire were variously a pair of silvered cap pistols in their fringed and leatherette holsters, a sheriff's star, a pair of plastic spurs, a thin tin Bowie knife, and a bank robber's mask in the form of a black conceivably vinyl and elongated oval, and bearing a loop of elastic. This last item being all that I required. I detached it, and during the course of my amble back to the house I incidentally became the instrument of bringing considerable unanticipated happiness to a little schoolboy in blazer and cap, who highly optimistically was dangling over the parapet of the bridge and into the Thames a long length of knotted parcel string crudely tied on to a bamboo garden pole. At first he hesitated – almost palpably grappling with the echo of a long ago dinned-in parental warning concerning the necessity for rejection of any sort of gift when proffered by a stranger – and then with a whoop of joy, he seized with eagerness all of his cowboy loot.

Fiona being Fiona, the balaclava was ready and done in really next to no time at all, and rather a splendid thing it turned out to be: triple-ply cashmere, and so very gentle to the touch. And when, in my study, I placed it adjacent to the bank robber's mask . . . well of course I was quite perfectly aware of the apparent absurdity: for should I next be pressing into service a pillowslip and daubing on to it the word 'swag', that I might sling this across the shoulder of my black-and-white and horizontally striped jersey . . . ? Yes but more than this, I was very aware also that soon – though maybe not immediately – such disguise would become absolutely necessary. Not, of course, that I harboured even the slightest intention of conveying any such insight to the unspeakable excrescence that was Adam, my putative partner in crime. And I was quite intent too upon somehow ensuring that during each of our future escapades, I would manoeuvre myself with considerable delicacy and care so as never to be seen by him to be wearing these things, while also making similarly certain that no invaded householder should ever even so much as be able to glimpse me without them.

The first house we visited later in the week was a rather pleasing sort of Elizabethan manor house on the fringes of a village called Woodcote that I had noted during the course of a Sunday afternoon drive in the Bentley with Fiona. The house was easily old enough to offer the likelihood of treasures long untouched and forgotten by successive generations, yet the garden was unkempt and verging upon wildness, the ivy on the stonework quite rampant, the leaded glass mullions darkly clouded over and the guttering decidedly rickety: all of which suggested to me that the inhabitant doomed to reside here in perpetual chilly twilight and a martyr to even the very fundaments of upkeep might very probably be desperate for ready money. I always carried about me in excess of one hundred pounds, though extremely seldom was anything aproaching such a sum remotely required of me: the sight, however, of a thickish stack of fivers being riffled in my fingers was frequently sufficient to trigger in some or other skeletal and passed-over pensioner an eagerness to part with a proportion of his lumber. I swung the Bentley as close to the house as I could possibly engineer, while gunning the engine having drawn to a stop. This to render highly likely the rubbing of hard and ancient fingers against the grime of an upper window pane, followed by the dart of curious eyes. The sight then of a beautiful and famously expensive two-tone motor car, from deep amid the gleaming walnut and Connolly leather interior of which there now emerges with well-shod grace a pair of extremely hand-somely dressed gentlemen, the like of whom this sad and neglected pile cannot have played host to for at least a genera-tion. And so it did prove – I had no more than raised up the great and weighty bronze knocker on the close-grained oak and Gothic door, when it creaked its way open so terribly slowly, and from around the edge of it there gradually appeared the bright-eyed and enquiring scarf-covered head, then shoulders, and now the remainder of a diminutive and snow-haired old lady wearing a man's large military greatcoat, fingerless gloves, a Donegal slouch and mismatched galoshes.

'Ye-e-es . . . ?' she eventually managed, and so very tremu-lously. It occurred to me, I recall, that following how many long years of abstinence, she might so very easily have been struggling to remember quite how to speak. 'May I be of assistance to you gentlemen in any way . . . ?'

'Madam,' I said to her – my eyes so genial, the voice so very mellow and affable. 'I beg you to forgive us, my friend here and myself, for so outrageous and unwarranted an intru-sion upon your privacy in this, might I say, quite perfectly splendid example of rural Elizabethan architecture. How favoured you are, madam, to dwell in so indisputable a master-piece as this.'

Her invisible lips then fluttered into an unaccustomed smile of quite girlish pleasure as her fingers were straying towards the lank and powdery tufts of hair that had eluded the confines of her great and lovat hat.

'Oh . . . how exceedingly kind you are. It is a fine house, yes it is. I was born here, you know. So many of the family were. All gone away now, of course. Those that we didn't lose in the war, may God watch over them. Only me. Just me left, now. Would you, I wonder . . . perhaps care to view what we call the great hall . . . ? I expect you are most fearfully busy and so please do feel quite free to decline, should you think it at all an imposition . . . though I do feel that in particular the gallery might be of some small passing interest to you, should you be a student of the period. It is, I am informed, quite unique to the whole of southern England . . .'

'Oh my dear madam – I am overwhelmed, perfectly overwhelmed by your extraordinary generosity and hospitality. I can think of nothing I should care for more. My name is Arnold Barton, incidentally – please do call me Arnold. And my friend here – this is William Vyle. And I am sure I speak for him as well – yes, William? – when I say what a signal and enormous pleasure and honour it is to have met you.'

'Oh well in that case, come in – come in do. The state of the place is rather, um . . . well I no longer am really in the habit of receiving callers is the truth of the matter, don't you see? That side of things has rather fallen away, of late. So I fear you must take the house just as you find it. So unlike the old days. The parties we held here! Oh what fun! I simply can't tell you. They were famous throughout the county. Oh yes, that's right – you just leave your coats on the settle just there, if that is quite convenient. That's it. That's it. I do so

347

apologise for the cold. I haven't made up the fire. I tend not to, now. Seems rather silly, don't you know, just for one person. And then of course there is always the expense to be considered. These old houses, you know. Possibly you will take tea . . . ? Oh yes and how dreadfully rude of me – my name is Miss Myrtle Rivington, yes, though do please call me Myrtle, won't you? I am not too sure, however, now I come to think of it, that I find myself in a position to be able to offer you two gentlemen a biscuit . . .'

Proceedings thus far, I am compelled to admit, were entirely commensurate with the customary pattern. And as a consequence, Adam was raising his eyebrow in a thoroughly discourteous manner – wagging his head and baring his teeth as if in total and utter despair and contempt of me – though naturally, one would have expected hardly more. And so then it was evident to me that very soon indeed our Miss Myrtle Rivington, charming and so very tender though she most undoubtedly was, must perforce form the basis of my shining example: clearly I had to summon into being a demonstration, both swift and seamless, to convince this utterly vile and sneering young man with whom, for at least the time being, I was forced to cooperate, of our immediate and future direction. For a rapid glance about me already had assuaged any palpitating qualm over Miss Rivington's ancestors and periodically departing siblings having severally quite denuded the interior. Even to my less than tutored eye, here indeed was bounty. And so while Adam now deftly excused himself from the company, as was customary behaviour, I quite effortlessly waxed enthusiastic over all that was brought to my attention: the minstrel's gallery – a particular source of pride, perfectly evidently – with its finely carved newels and stringing . . . the escutcheon over the broad and massive mantel . . . a refectory table, Miss Rivington rather thought Stuart, around which in the glory days, they could so very easily accommodate up to twenty, thirty revellers, and even sometimes more. She seemed of a sudden so very much more youthful – well, less evidently aged, shall we say – this eager and birdlike guide of mine. And she continued to babble quite delightedly of the dark and dank little priest's hole so startlingly well concealed just the one step down from the upper half-landing . . . the tester bed that now lay wrapped and in parts in the ante-cellar, and within which, it had long been believed, one of the Henrys, she rather hoped the Eighth, had slept for the duration of just the one night, during the course of a county hunt. In the garden, beyond the parterre – alas, she regretted, now so terribly grown over – her grandfather had detected the foundations of a much earlier residence once upon the site, and evidence too of the likelihood of a moat. For my part, I had been concentrating – but subtly – upon a small vitrine set into a window bay, its surface of glass near felted with dust, this filled with a motley of what appeared to be beribboned seals, various badges, medals and other decorations – and also a cluster of oval portraits, the tiniest imaginable. While hard by the boot rack in the vestibule, there hung an umber oil no larger than a hand, and much of the type I had witnessed Adam pounce hard on before. And when that man returned – his eyes agleam with greed – I indicated to him in the agreed and tested manner those items which I considered to be of significant interest: he held my eyes, and nodded once.

'Madam – Miss Rivington . . . may I presume, upon the strength of so very brief an acquaintance, to be so bold as to tender a proposal . . . ?'

'Myrtle, please Arnold. I insist that you call me Myrtle. The tea, I fear, is gone quite cold. A proposal, you say . . . ? Why, what a thing. Whatever can you mean, I wonder? Ought I to make us a nice fresh pot . . . ?'

'Alas, madam – Myrtle, do forgive me – my friend and myself, we soon must take our leave. Now please, I beg of you, do not be in the slightest offended by what I am next about to say to you, for I earnestly assure you that I harbour at the centre of my heart none but the very best interests for yourself, and this very mighty edifice.'

'I see . . . well how very delicately put. Do please go on, Arnold, won't you . . . ?'

'Well, Myrtle . . . as you yourself have intimated, the upkeep of so grand a building as this . . . the concern, the responsibility, it must indeed be considerable, no? Ah yes – I see by your expression that indeed that is the case. Not to mention the continuous expense . . .'

'Continuous! Oh yes, yes indeed. That is so precisely the word! If it isn't the roof – and usually it is, I have to say:

quite like a sieve – then it is the plumbing, what little there is of it. Heating . . . well, nigh on impossible, if I'm being perfectly candid with you, Arnold.'

'Quite. I so understand. Then it occurs to me that you might then care to relinquish one or two of your possessions in order to realise some small capital for yourself, you know . . . ?'

'Relinquish . . . ? Oh – sell, do you mean? Oh no. I couldn't possibly. It has been suggested before, of course. Often by my sisters. And I cannot pretend that the money would not be most enormously welcome. But no. I feel, you see, less of a resident here, these days, and rather more of a, well – custodian, I suppose I mean . . .'

'And so attuned a sense of loyalty does you nothing less than the very highest credit, I do so assure you, Myrtle. But is one not forced to ask oneself . . . for whom, in fact, is the house in custody . . . ? Do you see?'

'Well of course it is true that I have no children . . . but I am an aunt, you know. Oh yes – many times over. A great-aunt too. More than I can count. So you see, even if I wished it, the things here, all these old things that surround me – they are not wholly mine to part with.'

'I see. Well in that case, Myrtle – I am going to behave as a friend to you. An outsider, yes of course – but a friend from the outside can very often be possessed of the sharpest vision. The way I now have come to view this . . . you owe it to yourself, Myrtle, to part with just a few little oddments, the occasional knick-knack – you would barely register their absence. You shake your head – ah but listen to me, Myrtle. Such small action on your part would at once so very hugely improve your day-to-day existence. A roaring fire – just think of it! Biscuits galore! And then would you find yourself in so far stronger a position, the better to be able to actively conserve the overwhelming remainder. Do you see the reason in it? Please do believe me when I say that I wish no less than the best for you, dear Myrtle. You do so very clearly deserve it.'

'You are kind. And I sincerely thank you for all your consideration. I am sure it is meant with the very finest intent. But I am firm, I am afraid. No doubt the mind of a foolish and old-fashioned woman, oh yes I have no doubt, who is spiting no one but herself. Ah yes – I can quite see that that is how it well might appear. But there – that is me. And so there's an end on it. And you say you must be leaving now, Arnold . . . ? How terribly sad. And you are quite sure, are you, that you won't change your mind about tea . . . ? No? Well I cannot tell you how much I have enjoyed the company of you both. I do so apologise, William – we barely have exchanged two words. Quite frightfully exciting to have callers again though, I must say. Oh yes, Arnold . . . why did you, in fact? Come here in the first place? Did you ever say . . . ? Silly of me, you know, but I simply cannot recall . . .'

This, in my experience, was an altogether singular circumstance. During the normal course of things, you see, the householder would naturally by now be quite wholly seduced, at least by the barest principle of trade. At which point it would become my task to bid with both eagerness and generosity for every manner of horror and nonsense that no doubt said householder anyway had long detested, solely in order surreptitiously to bag the one true prize. Although sometimes, rather annoyingly often as a matter of fact, there was no prize to be taken – whereupon we immediately turned and left, often with the now quite frantically avaricious owner in fervent and unseemly pursuit – imploring us to buy now for even just a handful of shillings that which I should not have deigned even to put to the torch. But in our Miss Myrtle Rivington we had a lady quite implacably opposed even to the very fundamental idea: she would not fall victim to the art of persuasion. Which did rather make things, I freely confess, just very slightly more awkward and provoking than ideally I could have wished for – and Adam by now, he was of course quite openly mocking: he had about him this very awful method of jeering me silently by way of his animal eyes, that acidic great twist of his ugly mouth. While on the other hand . . . this lady's quite blank rebuttal of each of my overtures could only render the eventual rout, my approaching victory over any such scruples, much the sweeter: ample demonstration of the total plausibility of all now that I was insisting upon. And so in the hallway, I simply was smiling down at her with considerable and not utterly feigned fondness, as she held out now to me my overcoat.

'Myrtle, dearest – did I really not inform you of the reason for my visit? How very remiss of me – I thought I had. Why – I called in order to rob you.'

Her action was momentarily arrested, though then she relaxed into an easy indulgence.

'Oh Arnold – really! What a thing to say! Isn't he awful, William? Perfectly awful. You really are a very naughty fellow, Arnold. Now tell me – do you have very far to go, the two of you? Your motor car is very handsome, I have to say. Daddy had one of the very same marque. Before the Great War, of course . . .'

'No distance at all, dear Myrtle. And as soon as young William here has transferred to the boot of my – yes it is, isn't it? Quite handsome motor car – the contents of this little vitrine here, then the rather – to my mind – lowering oil painting hanging just over there . . . in addition to, I do believe, some other little items of beauty which independently he has espied elsewhere . . . am I correct in this, William . . . ? Yes, I surmised so. Well then after all of that, we shall, I promise you, take up not one more moment of your time. I cannot tell you what a pleasure it has been.'

Still she seemed hesitant: her eyes were hedging the quite shocking novelty of this situation – rapidly deciding now which way they should jump. Then, as Adam was filling his pockets with the medals and seals, the badges and the miniatures, and while I proceeded to take down from the wall the small brown picture . . . the brightness in her eyes just immediately faded – her frail little chest beneath the bulk of the greatcoat, it really did appear to deflate. She touched my arm and looked up at me pleadingly.

'Arnold . . . please. You must not do this to me. Is it a joke . . . ? Some kind of I must say rather cruel sort of a joke that you are playing on me, yes . . . ? No . . . ! William – put those back this instant! Do you hear me? How dare you! Arnold – I beseech you! I took you to be a gentleman . . . ! They are honours – the family's honours! All of our history is in that case . . . ! Arnold – I beg of you . . . do not do this. Please . . . oh please, Arnold! How could you . . . ? How could you . . . ? I do not understand . . . I trusted you! I invited you into my house! Oh dear Lord, oh dear Lord . . . ! I would offer you money, but you know that I have none . . . !'

'On the contrary, Myrtle – it is I now, you see, who is to offer some to you. A parting gesture, if you will. Here we are, you see – a newly minted five-pound note. Yes? Oh do dry your eyes, dear lady – it is, after all, only stuff. Isn't it? You are old. And you have so very much more of it. And with this note, now you can have coal, do you see? Warmth, yes? Myrtle – it will buy you biscuits! Chocolate biscuits! One day you will thank me. And now . . . I think we are done . . . ? Yes, we are done – and so truly now we really must be away. Au revoir, my dear Myrtle – au revoir. I shall cherish the memory. And thank you so very much indeed for the tea.'

She was sobbing quite piteously by this time, of course – plucking ineffectually at the sleeve of my coat. But women, well – they will always tend to do this sort of thing. I was pleased though that she did not once attempt, as I confess I had half been expecting, her feeble and quite pitiable best to strike or try to in any way detain us, for then that would of course have had to be summarily dealt with, and I am not, unless it is essential, actually a brute. It was not until I had closed the great front door behind me . . . first it was the wailing to reach my ears – and then, soon after, a rather curiously discordant and quite jagged shrieking, this subsiding only slowly into some or other variety of low and vaguely farmyard mewling, which did seem quite insistent: yes, there would be weeping, then – and long into the night. Well there you have it.

During the course of our drive back to Henley, Adam quite suddenly was coughing out laughter. No – not laughter, for any of that must surely carry with it the airy implication of some element at least of humour, and a light enjoyment. Cackling is what he was doing – a hag-like expression of malicious delight in all we had freshly accomplished. And so this initial tutorial would have appeared to be complete. He insisted then that we go out again the very next day, an urgency to which I was most perfectly agreeable – I had been, indeed, upon the very verge of myself suggesting it – for then could I induct the man into the further and then ultimate streamlining of the entire operation: to dispense quite utterly with all of the rigmarole. No more silken flattery and idle grinning chatter – no mock admiration of some or other mean little gimcrack gewgaw: an end to the stirring of tea. We walk in. We take. If the tenant, the owner, the householder – however the damn person may desire to style himself – proves to be any more than meek, then he, she or they must immediately be restrained by whatever means necessary. And to this end, there soon and naturally evolved a scale of escalation. Usually no more was required than a firmly articulated word. Otherwise ropes. The warning of violence, or else its quick delivery. And because no longer central to the matter was a need for tact and delicacy, Adam now would be the first to enter – which he so did enjoy, the elbowing bully. I would follow, later and discreetly, and after he was done with his opening volley of barked-out intimidation – and only when he was rapidly mounting the staircase to gleefully ogle and ransack an upper floor – then would I deftly don my black and makeshift disguise. The dolt – never was he even aware of it. And nobody, not one of the marks at any time whatever, was witness to my features. So simple a plan was twofold: the protection of myself, perfectly obviously, and the extreme endangerment of Adam – whom now I hated with so appalling a power, and who, so very conveniently, was far too arrogant and self-absorbed even to glimpse it. And so from the repeated scattering of such seeds of remarkably mindless recklessness, there grew quite sturdily the flowering of his downfall. Together with, alas, though to varying degrees, that of every one of us. For although I had presumed a considerable knowledge of John Somerset, together with insight into his workings and character, still had I most woefully undervalued both the calibre of his determination, and the worth of his ferocity.

Stories by now were abounding locally, and all of them concerning a spate of domestic robberies perpetrated by a pair of itinerants, attempts at descriptions of the physiognomy of just one of whom, I felt quite perfectly sure, would by this time have been haltingly and tearfully proffered, and so many times over: an aspect of it all that seemed, somewhat strangely, not yet to have occurred to Adam. And so until the natural course of events might be seen to unfold, I remained, for the present, content to bide my time. The new regime, so to say, was now very thoroughly established and in vigorous and quite rude health, though it was not until many months later – while we were driving to what was to be, did either one of us but suspect it, our very last call to a country house – that Adam said something of a sudden to me that I freely confess to finding just a little unnerving.

'He knows, you know. My father. I told him. Oh yes. I told him. I expect he'll be wanting to . . . how shall I put it? Talk to you? Yeah . . .'

'Really? Well of course a conversation with John – as opposed to, say, well let me see . . . yourself, for instance – is always a thing to be relished. I do so look forward to it.'

'Don't pretend you didn't hear me, you bloody swine. I said I *told* him. Yes? He *knows* . . . !'

'Ah yes indeed – you did say that, you're quite perfectly

358

correct. Well then I suppose I must rise to it, mustn't I Adam? Told him *what* . . . ? All right? That response satisfy you, does it? Sufficiently melodramatic?'

'You won't find it so funny when my father's done with you. Telling you that. You won't be laughing then. You'll get it. You'll get it. And not before time. Sick of you, I am – you bloody crooked and stuck-up pig!'

'Crooked, yes. I think I am, you know – though you are too, of course. But you are aware of that. Stuck-up . . . ? An exceedingly bourgeois expression that tends to be bandied only by those who very well know and long have felt themselves to be most thoroughly inferior. And what about pig, now . . . ? No – I rather think not. Suits you though, rather. Pig. You really are one, you know.'

'You're a *fuck*, that's what you are. Thought you'd got away with it, didn't you? Thought you'd got away with all of it. Thought I didn't see. Oh stop all your playing around! The money . . . ? Oh yes – I saw you. I saw you, all right. Watched you do it, cool as you like. You've had it now. You've had it.'

'Indeed? You saw? How extraordinarily observant you are. I have to admit that I should never have thought it of you.'

And inside, I seethed. With anger, yes, and wholly directed at myself. How could I have been so very terribly remiss as to have permitted so extremely self-centred and virtually purblind a lout to witness any such thing . . . ? And so this will have been yesterday, then. At Pangbourne, in the little

Edwardian end-of-terrace. It must have been. For if he had seen me on any previous occasion, I surely would have been made most perfectly aware, and in tones no doubt as gloating and uncompromisingly threatening as those he is using to me now. For how many times had I got away with it before? It had long been my practice, while Adam was elsewhere in the building – snaffling the jewellery, stowing away some or other little bibelot – to don my doubtless rather alarming disguise and then gently, or, if necessary, not remotely gently, urge the latest slack-mouthed and palpably terrified victim to disclose the whereabouts of his money. The first time I did this, there was in my action hardly more than bravado – though on that occasion, rather to my surprise, a very large amount of cash was quickly thrust into my outstretched but barely expectant hands. Accompanied by almost a simpering gratitude, I recall – as if here were fair exchange for the sparing of his life. And subsequently I had discovered that more often than not there exists among older and rural folk a stout and inbuilt distrust for any of the banking institutions that younger and more worldly types will happily employ as a matter of course. And such is the pusillanimity of trembling people, that each of them gave it up freely. I did warn each of them never even to dream of speaking about the money, and not of my masked appearance . . . or else I should return, and silence them for ever. Thus far my threats would appear to have been taken very seriously – as, indeed, they were quite intended. And so in really next to no time, with recourse to such blissfully facile means, I had amassed a quite considerable fortune. My share of the proceeds from goods obtained had become really little more to me now than something by way of a bonus – because of course the money I obtained was always to remain mine, and mine alone. My little secret, you see. Though as of yesterday, it certainly now would appear, I have erred. My little secret . . . is out.

I drew up the Bentley quite close to the smartly colon-naded portico to this pleasingly compact and honey-coloured mid-Georgian rectory, that maybe not even so much as a fort-night earlier I had considered so very promising. I determined now to make it perfectly evident to Adam that I was very far from easy in my mind – though here was no mere subterfuge, I am bound to admit. I quite wildly understate the position when I say that John Somerset would not at all be taking kindly to this new and blistering information recently presented to him with more than a scent of coming vengeance, by this so loathsome son of his. Very rapid and decisive action was immediately required.

'You go in Adam, yes . . . ? Just should like briefly to collect my thoughts. I shall follow shortly.'

'Nervy, are you? Getting jumpy, you bastard? Don't blame you. If I was facing what my father's got in store for you, daresay I'd be on the jumpy side too. Thank Christ it's come. I said he should have got rid of you ages ago. The minute he found out about you and . . . my bloody mother, you stinking fucker . . . ! My bloody mother . . . ! And now you've been stealing from us, on top of it all. Cash. And for how bloody long, that's what I'd like to know. I'd happily have done you myself, more than happily, oh Christ yes – but he said no. He always said no. He was waiting, is what he said. Well . . . waiting's over. And today? Who cares what you do? Stay in the car, for all I care. Who needs you anyway? Cunt. Have one of your stinking cigarettes, why don't you? The condemned man's final smoke . . . !'

And more of his preposterous cackling, of course, as he swung himself out of the Bentley and was bounding up the three short steps to the door, as stupidly eager as a spaniel. I watched him as he arranged his face into the sort of expression he might even have imagined to be a smile – always the best he ever could muster – and saw him then gesticulate to almost a continental extent as the slight and elderly man before him was straining to understand, or even to distinguish the sounds. Admittance though – as ever – was quickly gained. I think 'grim' might very well be the word I now might select, were I with hindsight required to articulate my mood of the moment. There was stern work afoot – and with this I had so quickly to come to terms, as I eased on with scrupulous care a pair of thin and primrose soft kid gloves. Then I stepped out of the car, approached the portico and jangled the bell. When the door was opened no more than but a cranny, I rammed it back with all of my force and had got myself around it only just as the bony old fellow clutched at his empurpled brow, and was staggering down on to his knees. As his mouth hung open, he was gaping full at my face, his own shrunken features awakened into shock and an appalled enquiry: his having seen me, however, could hardly matter less. I had the man now by the abrasive lapels of his ancient tweed, and I was dragging the slump of him back into the hall. There by the mantel was a scuttle and fire irons – I drew out the poker, swung it about me and struck from the side a low and sweeping blow to the head. With the deadweight of a boulder dropped from out of the sky, he fell into a table which crackingly disintegrated into splinters, sending fragmented shards of blue-and-white porcelain fleeing into the corners. This brought the rumble and then thunder of Adam hurrying back down the staircase: he stopped still in an archway, and I permitted him just momentarily to be astonished by the tableau with which he immediately was confronted. Then, just one second before he would roaringly have emerged from his transfixion, I brought up again the poker and swung it hard and down into the crouch of his neck. The noise he made was guttural – his eyes rolled up and then over as he crumpled at his centre, before immediately collapsing in on himself, and then fell as a heap. I touched the redness to the side of his throat: a beat – sluggish, but palpably throbbing, which was all to the good. I then was forced to rifle his pockets in quest of a rather vulgar flick-knife with which fairly lately he had taken to posturing: it had a pale and nacre casing, the blade aroused by an evil swish and then clunk as it was springing erect from within its silver housing. I held the haft, traversing the floor towards the old man's rigid and contorted form. I remain to this day quite reasonably sure that already he was dead, but here was not at all the point. I turned him with the toe of my shoe so that now he lay flat upon his back. His white and withered face, I can hardly forget – although frozen, still it seemingly teetered upon the verge of eruption into hysterical laughter. I stooped to bring down the knife once, and then immediately again, deep into the centre of his heart – recoiling deftly from a bubbled upsurge of blood – extracted it perfectly smoothly, walked back over to Adam and tightly curled his fingers around the undeniable elegance of the thing: already, I observed, the gore upon the blade was the colour of wine, and crusting over into hardness. Then the poker had similarly to be placed into the old man's palm, his stiffened fist encouraged to clasp it . . . and finally now could I gather together a number of the sorts of desirable little items with which normally by this time we would happily have absconded – scatter them about the rucked-up kilim and Afghan rugs, then the brilliantly polished surrounding parquet, smelling very wholesomely of beeswax and lemons. Then I stood back, the better to collectedly appreciate all of my impromptu handiwork. It seemed to me to be complete. One might even say perfect. I turned to leave. And then I heard the noise.

Had I but left upon the instant. Had only the lady been just fleetingly aware of the blurred and distant brief confusion of rapid and shadowy movement – then the muted crunch of spat-out gravel as outside a motor car pulled away at speed. But no . . . but no . . . I lingered, gripped within a sort of fascination, though alert as a cat, for just that terrible moment longer. It was I whom she lit upon first – her head, with the neatly gathered-up and chalk-white bun, was cocked to the side in puzzlement, though at the fluttering hesitance of her lips, still there hovered the easy possibility of welcome. Then her eyes dropped down – her breath intaken at the sudden sight of Adam on the ground – though already had I reached her by the time she had shrilly whimpered once and covered her mouth with both her hands, when then she saw her husband. Her eyes were large and stricken, filled with the brimming of tears – I quickly spun around her feeble little body, for I did not care to see them. The merest twist to the softness of her gullet – no more exertion than if I were opening a bottle of ale – and then she was as a light and feathered broken bird, limp within my hands. The keeper to one of her earrings had passingly snagged the palm of my hand as she slid on down to the floor. I sucked at the graze, while inhaling the scent of her lavender water. Very nearly precisely four minutes later (for I timed it) . . . I found myself standing in a telephone box on a village green by a reedy pond, and by means of deliberately clipped and staccato sentences informing whoever at the local police station after a good long while had responded to the call that some or other constable there might well have an interest in imme-diately calling upon a nearby compact and honey-coloured mid-Georgian rectory, the one with a smartly colonnaded portico.

Now, though, there could be no time whatever for introspection. I was compelled to telephone Fiona and instruct her to prepare Amanda for immediate travel, together with only just so much luggage as was feasibly portable by the two of us. I should of course have preferred not to have endangered myself by returning to the house, but only I was party to the whereabouts of all my money, in addition to a very select cache of small but intrinsically cherishable things of very considerable value. While awaiting the taxi to Reading station, I remember that my eyes were darting constantly and uncontrollably, though to my fevered and quite indescribable relief, there came sign of no one. And so on that day, my father's rather lovely old house, a great number of my suits together with Fiona's costumes and gowns, and of course the beloved Bentley . . . all had summarily to be abandoned: only the lives of the three of us might now be considered to be of paramount concern.

And once in London – for to where else would one ever escape but the largest, most easily tolerant and crucially absorbent of cities – we stayed for a brief duration again at the Strand Palace Hotel. This though, clearly, was very far from ideal. I needed very soon a permanent dwelling and, by way of effective cover, some sort of extremely unlikely occupation, not to say a fresh identity. The advertisement for the butcher's shop in England's Lane I glimpsed in passing and quite wholly by chance in the *Evening Standard* while being attended to by the hotel barber. I had just instructed him, as he had lathered my face and now was stropping the razor, not to shave my upper lip: I of a sudden was determined upon a moustache. And then I thought, well now . . . butchery. I can, presumably, be apprised of the fundaments. And then could I proclaim my assumed identity for all to see on the frontage of the shop – and boldly, too. And this name shall be . . . what, now . . . ? Oh yes, I know – how had I that afternoon, and totally on the spur of the moment, introduced myself to that dear Miss Myrtle Rivington . . . ? Barton, wasn't it? Barton, yes – it's a good enough name. I fail to see anything wrong with it. And so from that moment on, the three of us – Fiona, Amanda and myself – would now be living as Bartons. And Fiona, well . . . she conducted herself throughout the whole of this really rather harrowing ordeal as quite the perfect angel. Undisguisedly hated the accommodation above the shop, of course – and coming from all that we had enjoyed, who, I ask you, could not? Though I had sworn to her that soon, one day, some time not too distant, we should reclaim our rightful position in the hierarchy of things. And such a future, you know, is very considerably overdue. I still have money. A fair deal. But how now can I dare to make a move, when I know that Somerset still is hounding me? Though nor can I remain: if the pig man found me, so soon will someone else. And here then is why I am compelled now and finally to draw all this to a halt. In the plainest of language, I am this very evening dispatching my man Obi to Henley, in order that he may seek out Somerset, and kill him – I care not how. It is the only way. And I imagine that the good people of Henley will never in their lives have set eyes upon one such as Obi: he will be stared at, pointed out – laughed at and feared by all of the children: an instant and abiding topic of conversation, obviously a figure of deep distrust, and therefore never ever to be forgotten. And all this is just so very good, you see: just so very good.

All these thoughts, though, and of so long ago . . . And still there remains just this one further thing, however . . . the other and quite key element of our living in Henley, and then finally decamping from it on that frenzied afternoon in so extremely unbecoming a scramble of haste . . . a factor which still I have yet to mention . . . because I cannot. For what, after all, could I possibly say? Because, you see . . . well had it not been for Fiona and Amanda, I of course would have faced him. Somerset. I should not have run from the man. But the instant removal of my wife and child had become quite wholly essential because I knew that he would have been murderous, quite finite in his expression. Though had it not been for them – had they been elsewhere, should they not even have existed – then I would have stayed, and fought him to the death. This not through any misplaced and reckless wave of bravado, but only for the glorious sake of the ultimate prize. Anna. Anna, yes of course. For the pain I had endured upon leaving her ... the spearing, ceaseless and seething hot agonies simply of missing her, day after endless day ... these, to me, seemed so very many times that much worse than dying. But rather to my shock, I had made my choice upon instinct: I absconded with my family while unaware that here even was my true intention. During the months that passed, however ... I thought of Anna constantly, my memories of love both sparkling and frightful – while I cowered away, shivering from the burn of all that I had caused her, by leaving immediately and amid a shameful silence destined never to be broken. Though subsequently ... with the rolling on of further time, the intensity of so obsessive and ultimately self-consuming contemplation ... it gradually dimmed ... so very slowly, it began to fade away ... together with the dulling of a stinging fear, and the stark white threat of apprehension.

And so things rather had remained ... right up until the arrival of the pig man. Prior to this quite alarming intrusion, upon only one single occasion had my cloaked and blacker chambers been flooded of a sudden by harsh illumination, and this at the moment when I knew from the wireless that Mr John Somerset, together with his son Mr Adam Somerset, both sometime residents of Henley-on-Thames, had that morning jointly been convicted upon forty-seven counts of variously burglary, fraud and aggravated assault, while the son alone was further found guilty of having committed what the broadcaster had elected to sensationally couch as the callous and brutal double murder of an innocent elderly couple. Just once more then did I dwell upon his mother: at that raw and glittering silver dawn which ripened into a marbling of indigo and vermilion, when Adam was hanged.

CHAPTER FOURTEEN

Are You All Right?

There was a time, you know – not really too terribly long ago, I suppose . . . although it does so very much seem to be, now. Such a long time ago. In the days when I was, well . . . at a time when I felt myself to be considerably more leisured. Than I am now. Easy in my mind. When I could after supper concentrate solely upon getting Paul all nicely tucked up in his bed for the night, while with such pleasant anticipation looking forward to when I would gradually unfold into that so very precious little particle of time that soon would be mine – that I could just have to myself. For by then I was so very well versed – and for how many years past? – in pointedly ignoring – secluding the whole of me safely away from any of Jim's more obnoxious or intrusive activities. Ticking off the minutes as patiently as possible before he'd heave himself out of that staved-in sofa with its feathering of fag ash, which so long ago had become that most wretched seat of his exceedingly awful and sovereign domain . . . and then would I suffer to hear him muttering one or other of his customary nonsenses concerning his so urgent need now to take the air, his ardent desire to stretch his legs. His arm was all he'd be stretching: ale is all he would take. Yet still was I expected to encourage quite cheerily this sudden and apparent whim, and in so twitteringly birdlike and thoroughly wifely a way – his bold and spontaneous response to an invigorating impulse propelling him towards an evening constitutional, the very impromptu mention of which you could nightly set your watch by.

And, in those early days, it now rather bitterly amuses me to recall, I actually did go so far as to rather sullenly resent it. Being left. I might even have considered myself to have been coldly abandoned. Why must you do it Jim. I'd ask him – and really quite plaintively. Why must you do it – night after night? You've got a bottle of Bass, haven't you? More than one. Here, in this house, in the cupboard under the stairs. And I've just brought you your cigarettes, haven't I? Room all nice and warm. And it's raining. It's raining, Jim. Can't you hear it against the windowpane? It sounds as if it's coming down really rather heavily. So why do you have to go out? Explain it to me, please. Why do you want to walk just a few doors down in the pouring rain to then be standing up for hours on end in your wet hat and coat in that horrid and stinkingly fugged-up place, drinking Bass and smoking cigarettes . . . ? Both of which you have. Here, in this house. Makes no sense does it, Jim? Makes no sense at all. But all he would do is grunt like an animal, tell me that 'women, they don't never understand' . . . and peremptorily leave. Now, of course, I thank the Lord for it. This nightly imbecility. Sometimes, it's all I can do to refrain from screaming from the rooftops and urging him to get a blooming move on. Oh go *on* Jim, is what I'm aching inside to shout at him. You've had your rhubarb and custard, you've slurped down your fourth cup of tea like a yak at a trough, you've ground out yet another Senior Service butt, and very disgustingly to the side of the saucer – so what on earth is *keeping* you? Hey? Get out of my sight – go to the blessed Washington, why won't you? Go on! Go on! Oh just *go*, you horrible man . . . !

Yes . . . but I don't. Ever say any of that. And soon enough, he's anyway gone. And there – when I used to hear the door clang – there was the signal, this was the trigger for that one single and utterly cherished moment in the day when at last I could gently uncoil – relax, yes, into finally being me. I'd hung up my motherly pinny – kicked off and into a corner just another poor and beholden skivvy's bespattered shackles – and now I could just be old Milly again. Just me, with something nice to listen to on the wireless – the Proms, or something – a cup of tea, a digestive and maybe then even a Craven "A", with my feet up on the pouffe. But all such moments, the sweet and lesisurely innocence of them . . . they seem lost to me now. Now . . . always there's something infuriatingly nagging at me. Something I long to do. Or something I so terribly regret not ever having done. Something I have to say.

Or else something I should so very obviously have said, and forcibly – then, and at the pertinent moment, now long passed. The appalling amount of money that still somehow I am owing to that perfectly loathsome and vulgar little tallyman, for all those ridiculous fripperies that I now know I'll never even so much as glance at again, nor ever dream of wearing. And he's not at all charming, this low and beastly man, now that I no longer am a subscriber to all of his leery enticements. Every Friday I pay him all that I can, and although I make very sure that always there is plenty on the table for both Jim and Paul every mealtime to enjoy, I myself have barely been eating so that I may somehow squeeze out just that little bit more from my pitiful housekeeping – and yet despite all of my deprivation, each and every Friday all he will do is rather horribly snarl at me, and tell me that now I am more heavily in debt than I had been the week before. How can this be? He shows me the columns in that dreadful ledger, and all these closely written figures – jabbed at accusingly by his manicured fingernail that yet somehow manages always to be grimy – they do appear to tally, though never intellectually can I make even the slightest sense out of them. You assiduously chisel away at any given obstacle, and then gradually its vastness will diminish – no? Well no not, it seems: any such action will serve only to stimulate growth. Oh dear. Oh dear. When and how will it ever end . . . ? Then there is the yearning – the yearning, then, that comes upon me for a certain individual . . . about whom now I hardly dare think – and cannot, coherently. Pain. My pain. The pain that still is deep within me, which sometimes will teasingly fade to the shadows where barely I still can distinguish its insidious nature, its loitering cruelty, nestled as it is in a soft and fugitive haven . . . which then, having lulled me, will and without warning twist up so viciously into a shockingly swelling and quite acidic nausea. Once or twice just lately I have been jarringly aware of sudden and tumultuous internal revolt – an involuntary heaving that alarms me into knowing that now I teeter on the convulsive and dreadful edge of retching quite violently . . . but no, nothing came. On each occasion, I was stranded agape and on my knees in the chill of the bathroom, eyes struck wide, my skin so clammy, the whole of my insides still shuddering with the ugly urge . . . but no . . . but no . . . nothing came. Which left me feeling jilted. Let down and taken in. As if even my own body, now, was lying to me. As a consequence, I do rather think, you know, that some time reasonably soon I might maybe be forced into seriously considering getting somebody to look at me. Oh I don't know, though . . . don't want to be seen to make a mountain of a molehill – it'll probably go away of its own accord. All these little things, they generally do.

This evening, however – and mercifully – it really isn't too bad at all, my now near-habitual pain. Perfectly tolerable. A sort of blessing, I suppose, because soon I just have to slip away for a moment. I don't want to, of course – honestly, I can think of nothing I would favour less. But goodness, you just should have heard him, the tone of his voice on the telephone. It went so very far beyond just simple concern, or even alarm. Stan, I feel sure, has come now to the point of desperation. He was barely sensible. Hardly even speaking comprehensibly, and nor did he seem able to respond to any of my quite insistent interrogation. I just had to, he kept on quite manically repeating to me, come round. Come over: I just had to. And then I would see. Christ Alive, then I would see . . . ! Well at first I had been more than concerned that all he was doing was yet once again, and perfectly unimaginably, intending to behave so very foolishly with me . . . but then his really quite frantic manner had quickly eradicated all those sorts of notions. I think that if anything awful had befallen little Anthony, then Stan would simply tearfully have told me. Clearly then, some or other element of Jane just had to lie at the root of all this — and had not that recent and very possibly misguided agitation of the abiding situation been solely due to my own insistence? Well: my responsibility also, then. And so — though still with considerable reluctance — I have agreed this evening to go round to see him. And of course it is Paul who is my primary concern, here — because yes I do know of course that he no longer may be said to be an infant, but still it is beyond me to help feeling so very deeply uneasy if ever on such very rare occasions I am compelled to leave him all on his own. But I see no other way. Because of course I could not possibly have gone, could I, until Jim was safely out of the way. Well could I? For Jim, you see . . . well I do now feel rather reasonably sure that he is, somewhere murky within his own very smudgily illegible and extraordinary nature, nurturing some or other I am sure quite wholly unspecific suspicion with regard to my recent behaviour – though for Jim to have registered even so much as a scintilla of just anything at all is more than ample demonstration, I feel, of just how lately I have become quite reckless. And always now there must remain the very distinct likelihood, an almost certainty, that a malicious retelling of Mrs Goodrich's mad and unfounded rumours concerning whatever she imagined she might have witnessed between myself and Stan, could well – by way of the flourishing grapevine, fed by ordure and bearing bitter fruit – finally now have reached him. And so therefore, in the light of all of this, I was hardly likely, following our supper, to casually suggest to Jim that he might this evening care to just slightly delay his pilgrimage to the pub, so that he may stay to keep a watchful eye on Paul. You ask me why, Jim . . . ? Because I am going out for a while. Where . . . ? I feel I cannot say. Why . . . ? Well you see, there is someone I have to speak to. Who . . . ? Once more, I am afraid, I must be silent. No. That – not to say his predictably full-throated reaction, this very feasibly to incorporate a barrage of typically colourful and foul-mouthed accusation – would have been considerably more at present than I could easily have borne.

And Paul too . . . though it fragments my heart even to think it . . . but Paul, he too – and I now know this to be true – he too has been sensing things. He has not escaped the web's sticky wickedness, and all of my own quite meticulous weaving. Might you suppose that here is merely the self-chastising projection upon the dear boy's white and treasured innocence of my own ungovernably blackening conscience? Ah . . . ! I would that it were . . . though alas, it is not. For I know my Paul, I know him so terribly well . . . and I have been wilfully blinding myself to the very self-evident truth of it that daily has been hanging before my eyes . . . and yes, although it makes me ceaselessly rock with hurt, I am afraid that now I know that it is true that he found himself no longer able to remain untroubled by myriad unknowable little things. I have seen it in the merest fleeting furrow of his sweet little brow. The flecks of doubt that would cluster within his eyes – and then, when I glanced at him, how they so very rapidly were darting away instead of sparklingly fusing with mine – yes, fusing with mine in the blissful bath of mutual love and the enveloping warmth of safety, just as always they used to. And although I was hourly quite terribly tortured by the conviction that now I . . . that now I . . . that now I am doing him harm . . . still I found myself so very far from prepared for all that he had to say when this very morning, just as I was busy clearing away the last of the breakfast things, suddenly he was speaking to me:

'Are you all right, Auntie Milly . . . ?'

It was the inflection, of course – there was nothing to alert me in the words. Or was there here no more than simply an observation? That clearly I am not. All right. But I must be. Mustn't I? For am I not a capable woman? Am I not the anchor? So I must be. You see. I just must. But the whole of my averted face felt pained and contorted in its strenuous efforts to contain the welling of hot tears of shame: for should he at this moment see me in that way, then all might truly be lost to him.

'Why of course I'm all right, Paul. What a thing to say. Right as rain. Of course I am. Why – are you not all right, then . . . ?'

My voice – I heard it – had been as forcedly lighthearted as that of a cornered and mendicant politician. Paul continued to hover in the area between the kitchen and the landing, as if poised upon an early escape – twisting to and fro the door handle, his eyes alighting upon anything but me.

'Well no . . . not really, Auntie Milly. I mean – I'm not *ill*, or anything . . .'

I bit my lower lip until it really did hurt me most fearfully.

'Well what's wrong then, Paul? Tell me. You know you can tell your Auntie Milly, don't you . . . ? Tell me anything, you can. You know that, don't you Paul . . . ?'

'I do. Well I used to. Not too sure now. Actually. Sometimes you don't sort of listen like you used to, so there's not much point. Sometimes I say something to you and you just sort of look funny at me afterwards. Like you didn't hear me, or something. And sometimes . . . your answers – when I ask you things, well what you say for an answer . . . it just doesn't

379

make much sense. Not always, I don't mean. Just sometimes, that's all . . .'

I rubbed my hands quite briskly on the tea towel: it was one of a bale, a bundle of six that I'd got on Saturday from Marion's. Only three-and-eleven, you know, which I really did consider to be most terribly reasonable. Each a different coloured check. This one was orange. I surreptitiously dabbed at my eyes with it.

'Well look, Paul – we've got a good five minutes till you've got to go off to school. Till you go to pick up Anthony, yes . . . ? So why don't we go next door and have a jolly good chat about it all. Hm? Yes? Good idea?'

'Oh gosh – it's nothing really. I don't really mind. I didn't want to make something big out of it, or anything. I'm only just saying, really, because you asked me . . .'

'Well, Paul . . . it is true that . . . well, your Auntie Milly has had a little bit on her mind, just lately. One or two things I've just had to think about. But it was very boring grown-up sort of stuff, you know, and now it's all over and done with. So from now on – I promise you: it'll be back to the way it was in the old days. Yes? How about that? And from now on you can ask me anything you like, and I'll close my eyes and stroke my beard and listen very very very closely, and then I'll give you the proper answer. Silly Auntie Milly. Haven't I been? Oh yes – and I'll try very hard not to look at you "funny" any more. All right? Happy now? Everything all right again?'

He nodded, Paul, though quite agonisingly slowly. And then he looked at me sidelong – his eyes still creased into a sort of confusion.

'Yes. Okay. It's just that . . . well, Auntie Milly . . . I just thought that maybe, I don't know – that maybe you just didn't love me any more . . .'

Never mind what I was feeling. Never mind any of that – everything I was going through, just you push, shove, jostle and shoulder all of that to the side, force it to buckle, and get it down on to its knees. Kick and stamp on it – smother it without mercy: leave it no chance to draw breath. I flung open my arms and simply called out to him. I was empty, and whooping with need.

'Come here – come over here, Paul, and let me give you a great big kiss . . . !'

And he rushed to me, my little angel . . . ! His eyes were glassy, his mouth sprung open into seemingly spontaneous glee. As I hugged him that closely, my eyes were so impossibly tightly compressed – and the tears, at last, they seeped out warmly before they tumbled, and I felt then so very utterly relieved – so loose, and quite unburdened. And when he pulled away from me, still he was beaming, and so very broadly. It appeared – oh thank you, Lord: thank you thank you thank you! – it really did appear as if somehow I had stemmed the tide: averted the sea that had risen to engulf us.

'Why are you crying, Auntie Milly . . . ?'

'Not crying. Not a bit. Just happy, that's all. Happy because

I love you, Paul – I love you, I love you, I love you . . . ! I have always loved you, and I always shall. How could you ever think anything else . . . ? I love you more than any single thing on God's sweet earth . . . ! And I am just so happy that you are happy too. You are, aren't you Paul? Happy? Yes . . . ?'

'I am. Course I am. Why shouldn't I be? I knew you loved me really . . . I know I said all that, but I didn't really think you didn't, honestly Auntie Milly – and I was telling that to Amanda. Not long ago we were talking and I said that to her. And she said she was too – she said she was happy too and she really likes it because her mummy and daddy, they both love her. She says they're always laughing and everything at home and there's always these really special and expensive chocolates that Mr Barton gets. He actually gets them for Mrs Barton because she really likes them, but Amanda's allowed to eat them as well. I think I know the ones she means – they're in the glass sort of counter thing in Mr Miller's, funny kind of mauve bits on top, and Anthony says they cost two-and-eleven a quarter which you could get thirty-five chews or seventy Black Jacks for, which I do actually know because we both worked it out. And he laughed, Anthony was laughing when I said it's just as well Mr Miller never lets big fat Sally from Lindy's anywhere near all those expensive chocs because she'd either eat the lot or else smash up the counter and then go and squish them all into the floor, like she always does.'

And even as I continued to hold my special boy so very very close to me . . . even as I still was wincing away from such poisonous barbs already pricking at and burning the warm complexion of my new-discovered joy . . . still, oh God help me, did I find myself most shamefully yearning for him, the smell of him, the touch of his hands all over my body: it was Jonathan still whom I longed to be holding . . . ! I gasped — I gasped, and I stepped away quickly, in the grip of such terrible shock. I had received my boy back into my arms, and all my thoughts were just to lustily grapple with a man who is lost to me. What vile manner of unspeakable she-devil had now I become . . . ?!

'And another thing Amanda said — and she's really right, but I hadn't thought of it before. Well I had, but I never said. It's that all of you talk the same, and it's really nice, the way you talk. I mean, you and her parents, obviously. Not Uncle Jim. Obviously. But you do, you know — you sound more and more the same. That's what Amanda and me think. I'd sort of noticed, but not really, if you know what I mean. It was only when Amanda said that I realised. I wish I knew all the words you know. The way you and Mr Barton sort of describe things. But I will one day, won't I Auntie Milly? Anthony says he's decided to become a famous author when he grows up, but I'd be better, wouldn't I? Don't you think? I'd be more famous, wouldn't I? Auntie Milly . . . ? Auntie Milly . . . ? You're crying again. What's wrong? Have I said something wrong? Didn't mean to. Don't cry . . . Please don't.

I really do like the way you talk. Both of you. I mean it. Honestly. I really really like it . . .'

'School, Paul. Yes? I've just got a weepy eye, that's all – must have got some washing-up soap in it. And you haven't said anything wrong at all. Of course you haven't. Tell you what – I'll go to the Dairies today, yes? Get you some more Corn Flakes. Yes – I thought that would please you. I know we haven't finished the last lot yet – but it's just the blue one that you're missing now, isn't it? Well maybe in this new packet, who knows? There might be a bright-blue submarine, and then you'll have the complete set! Won't you? Anthony will be green! And while I'm in there, I'll get some fish fingers. For your tea. You'd like that too, wouldn't you? And a Munchmallow for afterwards . . . ? Yes – I thought you would. Now hurry off then, Paul – you don't want to keep Anthony waiting, do you? Course you don't. And say hello to Mr Miller from me, will you? Yes? Won't forget? Good boy. Well off you go, then. One more kiss. There. Got everything? Satchel? All right, then. Bye bye, Paul. Bye bye. See you very soon. Just one more kiss . . . There. I love you . . . oh I do so love you . . .'

Well all that was a bit funny – bit odd, really. She keeps on crying all the time, I don't really know why. Well I sort of do, I suppose, because of what Amanda told me – but Amanda said she looked really happy, Auntie Milly, when she saw her, so I don't really get what there is to cry about, except that ladies do that because you see it on the television in things

384

like *Emergency Ward 10* which is on just before *Take Your Pick* which I'd really like to be on because they dole out piles of money if you don't open the box, and if you do open the box you win stuff, and then there's the yes–no interlude when if you say yes or no they bash a gong but if you don't, then they give you more money. I think it's better than *Double Your Money* though because on that you have to know the answers to questions but I like Hughie Green because he's funny.

We were on Primrose Hill when Amanda said it to me.

'Paul . . . there's something, and I don't know if I should tell you. God, you know – I'm absolutely *freezing* . . . ! Shall we move, do you think? Walk a bit?'

'Yes, if you like. We can go down the other side and then round the long way, if you want. So what were you saying about . . . ?'

'Well I was saying I don't know if I should tell you or not.'

'Tell me what?'

'Oh honestly, Paul! That's what I don't know whether I should or not. Tell you. Haven't you been listening?'

'Yes I was. Have been. I have been listening. I just don't know what you're on about, that's all. Do you want another sherbet lemon? I've got just two left.'

'Okay – let's walk, then. Feet are like ice. Well it's just that I saw your auntie. That's all. Thought you might want to know.'

'My auntie? You saw her? What do you mean?'

'With my daddy, I mean. In his office.'

'His office. I didn't know he had an office. But I suppose everybody does. In the Lane. Have some sort of an office, don't they? Uncle Jim's is like a dustbin. Did you say you didn't want a sherbet lemon . . . ?'

'No I don't. I don't really like them, actually. Haven't you got anything else?'

'Afraid not. I've got a Black Jack but the paper's half come off and it's gone a bit yucky. Don't think you'd like it. I did have some liquorice comfits, but they're all gone now. What was Auntie Milly doing in your dad's office, then? Paying for something, or something?'

'No – they were having a very nice time, it looked like. It's a jolly shame you haven't actually got any of those liquorice comfits left, Paul, because I really do like them, liquorice comfits. One of my favourites.'

'I can maybe get some more tomorrow. Not sure I want to go to Mr Miller's now though, what with Anthony the way he is. Oh and they're shut tomorrow anyway. Sunday.'

'Do you want to know about your auntie or not? I feel a bit better now we're moving. I was turning into a statue up there. Not literally, obviously. The branches of the trees . . . they look really lovely, don't they? All bare and black and wintry. I did them like that once in Art with charcoal.'

'Yes I do want to know. Course I do. What were they doing, then?'

'Well . . . laughing, and things. Having a drink of something.'

'Oh really? That's nice. I didn't actually know that they knew one another. I mean – apart from Auntie Milly buying our chops and chicken and things, obviously. But it's good they do, isn't it? That they know each other. Don't you think? Because we do, don't we? Know each other. So it's good that they do too, I think. Don't you?'

'Let's go under the trees, shall we? So beautiful. Yes and then they kissed. It was all very romantic. Like in those ancient films Mummy watches on Sunday afternoons. And her books. She reads all these books, and they've always got a man and a woman on the cover, holding each other and wearing really lovely clothes. Did you hear me, Paul? I said they kissed.'

'I . . . yes, I heard you. I just don't know quite what you mean . . .'

'What do you mean you don't know what I mean! I mean they kissed! They kissed! They gave each other a kiss. Do you know what that is . . . ? It's like . . . well look – close your eyes . . .'

'What . . . ?'

'Close your eyes, Paul . . .'

'What . . . ? Close my eyes? What for . . . ?'

'Close them.'

'But why should I close them, Amanda? You're not going to play some beastly trick on me, are you?'

'Oh God just close your eyes, can't you Paul . . . ! Right. At last. There, now . . . There. Did you like that, Paul? Did you . . . ? I did . . .'

'I . . . oh my gosh. You kissed me! You actually kissed me, Amanda . . . ! Oh thank you. Yes I did. I liked it a lot. Really did. Really did. Yes I really did . . . I'm really sorry I didn't close my eyes when you told me to, Amanda – it's just that you see I didn't know what on earth you were talking about . . .'

'Wanted to for ages . . . except that they weren't kissing like that. My Daddy and your Auntie.'

'They weren't?'

'No. They did it with mouths.'

'Oh right. Well what did you just use, then . . . ?'

'No – no, stupid. I mean mouths. Both their mouths. They did it on the mouth.'

'Mouth? Really? Are you sure? Because I don't think that's actually allowed, is it? Because they're not married. Well – they *are*, obviously, but not to . . . um . . .'

'Right on the mouth. With lips. Like this, Paul . . . like this . . . like this . . . yes, just like that. Are you all right? Are you? Give me your hand, Paul. Are you all right . . . ? Give me your hand . . .'

'I am. I am all right, thank you for asking. Are you all right, Amanda . . . ?'

'Give me your hand, Paul.'

'Why? I mean – right you are, then. Here it is . . .'

'Oh God, Paul – take your glove off . . . !'

'It's really freezing . . .'

'I'll make it warm. Come here, Paul. I'll make it warm. Promise.'

And she jolly well did – keep her promise, Amanda. She opened up her coat and I said but oh look you'll get cold Amanda, and she put my hand on her leg just under her frock and then she started sliding it – right up to her knickers, actually, which she said were her best and special ones – and I said oh my gosh, Amanda – someone might see us! Someone could be watching! And she said no, shh, no one's watching, nobody can see anything and so what if they can . . . and then she touched me at my front and I felt really sick inside, and that was just so great. Really really great – can't explain. And I've been thinking about it all. Well obviously. Haven't been thinking about anything else. And what I've decided is that it's really nice if Amanda and me are kissing, and her father and Auntie Milly are kissing – I think it's really nice. A bit like a Keats poem or something which we're doing in English. I asked her though, Amanda, what would her mother think about it, how she might feel, because she's married to Mr Barton, and she said that she already knows because she always does, which I don't know quite what she meant. And then she said that everybody in the whole of the Lane knows – that everyone does. So that must mean then that Uncle Jim, he must know too. Well I don't suppose anybody minds what he's feeling. Don't suppose he ever feels anything. Maybe Mr Barton will biff him on the nose and take him by the scruff of his neck and chuck him down the stairs and then dust off his hands afterwards: maybe now, me and Auntie Milly, we can get rid of him. He deserves it. Doesn't he? Of course he does. Because look – if he's so disgusting, why shouldn't my Auntie Milly go and kiss somebody who isn't? I don't know why it makes her cry, though. If that's what it is that makes her cry. Don't understand. Because when Amanda kissed me . . . and when I touched her like that . . . and then when she touched me . . . I didn't want to cry. It was such a freezing afternoon and I was so red and hot, and all I wanted was to laugh and laugh and laugh. And I had a secret now. A really proper grown-up secret. Everybody knows about Mr Barton and Auntie Milly, but nobody knows about Amanda and me. And I like that. Except I had to tell Anthony, obviously. I told him all of it. Knickers and everything. I did just because I wanted to, and there was nobody else I could tell. And he looked at me – just looked at me at first. And then he started crying. It was in the middle of break in the changing room, and he cried and cried and cried. I couldn't say anything to stop him. I tried to say that if anyone came in they'd laugh and say what a baby he is and maybe cuff him round the head and give him a Chinese burn and pinch one of his crutches and then go and tell everybody about it, but that didn't work. Nothing did. So I just left him, in the end.

'Stan . . . ? Stan . . . ? Hello . . . ? Are you there, Stan . . . ? Oh God . . . Look, I'm trying not to make much noise, because of Anthony. Yes . . . ? It's Milly, Stan. Where are you . . . ? Oh do come on, Stan – I can't go on whispering like this – I can't be any louder. And the light – the light on the landing, Stan. It isn't working . . .'

Oh Lord in heaven – this really is just too too typical of the man. He's on the telephone to me like some sort of a stuttering lunatic simply beseeching me to visit, and then when I – all right, yes, with quite some considerable reluctance, finally agree to it, does he then just decently thank me and politely replace the receiver? Oh no. He's pressing me then for a time: now, Milly? Can you come right now? Right this minute, yes? That would be prime. No? You can't? You really can't? Oh dear. Oh dear oh dear oh dear. Well when, then? Soon, yes? You will come really soon, won't you Milly? Oh Christ Alive, Milly – please God come soon . . . ! Yes well: I'm here now, Stan, aren't I? I've been blundering about downstairs in this awful perpetual twilight they do seem to so much enjoy here, I can't for the life of me think why. But now that I've somehow groped and clambered my way up to the top of this deathtrap staircase, it's pretty much pitch. So that single remaining and dimly miserable light bulb in one of the cock-eyed wall sconces must finally have surrendered, thus marking the end, then, of all illumination within the Miller ménage from now until quite possibly the whole of eternity.

'Milly . . . ? Milly . . . ? Is that you . . . ?'

'Oh – at last! A chink of light amid the gloom! Well of course it's me, Stan – who do you think it is? For heaven's sake! Who else might you have been expecting at this time of the evening? Cliff Richard and The Shadows? Honestly, Stan. Open the door a bit wider, won't you . . . then at least I'll be able to see where I'm going . . .'

'Sorry, Milly. Christ Alive, though – I'm that pleased to see you. And I'm sorry about the light. It went. It went pop, just like that, while I was down in the hall, telephoning you. I know I've got another one somewhere, light bulb, but I can't seem to put my hand to it, just for the moment. Have you been here long? I'm so sorry, Milly. Come in, come in. Now listen . . . I do hope you won't be too, well . . . I just think you ought to prepare yourself, that's all. That's all I'm saying. No no – that's all I'm saying. See for yourself, soon enough. Can't think why I didn't hear you earlier, though. I don't think I dozed off. No – fairly sure I didn't doze off, but I've been thinking a bit, you see. About this and that. In my mind, you know. Yes . . . I think it's fair to say that my mind, you see Milly . . . my mind, yes . . . well, it's been elsewhere.'

Yes: fair to say that. Because I've been up here with my Janey, just sitting here quietly, since the time I closed the shop. Even shut a bit early, which I'm hardly given to doing. Only just pulled down the blind on the door – about five-ish it was, I suppose, not too much later – and I'm hearing someone rapping away on the glass. Well I didn't open up again – ignored it, which fair amazed me. Ducked right down so they couldn't see me through the window – felt like a fugitive. Noticed a couple of crushed-up boxes of Jelly Babies while I was down there: that'd be Sally from Lindy's, then: Hippo. Yes so heaven knows which of my customers it was I offended, annoyed like that, but it just had to be done, you see. I'd had enough. I'd had enough, is the truth of it. Because up till then, I'd been keeping things fairly normal. Got Anthony up and off to school with a bowl of Shreddies inside him – was waiting for him to moan at me because it wasn't Corn Flakes with the bloody submarines inside, but he never did. He did seem a bit funny all round, little lad, but I don't think it was because he was, I don't know – sensing something, sort of style: I don't think it was anything of that order. And Paul too, when he turned up to fetch him, he didn't seem . . . well, what do I mean . . . ? He was happy enough in himself all right, but he wasn't so bright with Anthony as usual. Barely said a word to one another, the two of them, and in the normal way of things they're gossiping away nineteen to the dozen like a pair of old biddies over the garden fence. Offered Paul a couple of little bits off the penny tray and he says to me 'No thank you very much, Mr Miller – not sure Anthony would like it.' Ever so politely – but that was a funny thing to say to me, wasn't it? I thought it was. Looked over to Anthony, but he never spoke. So it all seemed strange, of course it did, but me – I had other things to think about, didn't I? I should say so. And my head . . . ! Christ Alive . . . ! I felt like I'd been hit by a truck. Little bit better after a quick nip of Scotch. And trying, I was – all the time trying to piece together bits of the evening, bits of the night. I remembered the scene in here all right. In this room. Then the Washington. Some of that, I can remember. Bloody Jim, and that friend of his – though I can't recall his name for love nor money. Lost in the mists, that is. Then we went down to Adelaide Road . . . and that's a bit sketchy as well. Except that she was a lovely girl, that Aggie. And yes I do remember her name, of course I do. Fine young woman. Very understanding. And she did me a very choice cup of Cadbury's Drinking Chocolate, which helped me out a bit. Don't ask me how much money I tore through: pretty much everything I'd had in the till, and it's not as if I can afford it, or anything.

And today . . . well I just sat in the shop, like I always do. It's automatic. Did what I do every day. The only thing different, apart from early closing, is that I didn't take Janey up her morning cup of tea. Didn't leave it on the bedside table, with a bit of toast. No. I didn't bother with that. Otherwise – like I say, just another day, really. Don't recall who came in, not all of them anyway. I slid the packets of cigarettes across the counter – always selling quite a few boxes of fifty and a hundred, this time of year; Player's, Wills, de Reszke, State Express – even Woodbines, they're all putting these festive sort of sleeves on them with robins and holly and all the rest of the palaver, and people do seem to like them. And I shook out of the rattling jars how many quarter pounds of every sort of sweet and bonbon and toffee – twisted them up into the little paper bags. Credited the housewives with their twopence on the empty against another bottle of lemonade, cream soda, Tizer, cherry cola. Delved into the fridge for a Wall's Family Brick, and then later on a Neapolitan. A rep came in from Rowntree's about some new line they're aiming to launch in a year or so, he was telling me – name of After Eight or something, I think. I couldn't really see it, if I'm honest – not with Clarnico Mint Chocs, Keiller's, Bendicks, Elizabeth Shaw all so very well established in the market. And I told him – they want to do something about that name, for starters: not catchy – people won't have it. So yes . . . just another day, really. Except it wasn't, of course. Because this was the day, wasn't it? The day for all these years I'd been waiting for. Dreading. Always knew it would come – just didn't know when, that's all. Nor its nature – only that it would be bad. And here it was. Now it was here. And when Anthony came home – hobbling a bit, he was: not looking so strong as he has been just lately, he maybe wants some cod liver oil or more of those iron tablets – I gave him all of these comics I'd got for him in Lawrence's when I nipped out for five minutes at dinner time to go to Victoria Wine for a bottle of Black & White: got a couple in the end, because I'm telling you – they just go nowhere. Yes and so I'd got him these comics because I wanted him well out of the way, didn't I? I would have tried to get him out of the house altogether, but I don't know anyone who'd have him. Except Milly, of course – but it was Milly, you see, I was needing to get over here, so that was no good. Yes – it was Milly, of course it was Milly I had to see – because who else could I talk to? No one. Don't know a soul. And she'd know what to do, Milly would. More than me, anyway – I haven't got a bloody clue. But Milly – she'll sort it all out, bound to. Capable woman, Milly is – and by God, do you need that. Yes so I gave him a Crunchie,

Anthony, two tubes of Smarties, handful of flying saucers . . . and that was on top of his tea. And I said to him, now listen: you stay in your room like a good little lad, eh Anthony? Yes? Because your dad, he's got one or two things to see to. Yes? All right? Are you all right, Anthony? Yes? You are? Good. Good boy.

Brighton. Isn't it funny? That's where I met her, my Janey. Never even been there before. Never since, now I come to think of it. It wasn't that long after VE Day. Lovely afternoon, it was: only ever seen the sea at Southend before then. Whole country was still full of it, of course, our whopping of Hitler. And I wouldn't have minded playing a part in all of that – well I was young, wasn't I? When the war kicked off I was – well, sort of young anyway. All I was doing up till then was helping my old dad out in the shop, so the thought of joining up, making something of myself, seeing a bit of the world – didn't strike me as a bad thing. My dad, he understood, bless him – would've waved me away quite bravely. He'd been through the first lot. Tommy. Mustard gas got him – pale, he always was. Eyes not too good. Little cough, all the time. Nothing hacking – wasn't bronchitic. Just a little cough, but he had it all the time. Well they wouldn't have me, the army. Right, I said – I'll go in the RAF. I wouldn't bother trying, is what they said to me. It's your lungs – you'll never pass a physical, son: sorry – that's the way it is. My lungs? My lungs? There's nothing wrong with my lungs . . . ! Smoke, do you . . . ? That's what they said to me then. Well everybody smokes, don't they? Pipe, I said – I smoke a pipe, but I don't even inhale. Well you might as well do mate, is what the orderly was saying to me next – laughing, having a right old time he was – you could inhale a bloody factory chimney, son, and it couldn't make those lungs of yours any worse than what they are now. Wouldn't even give me a desk job. Said I was a liability – more or less told me I wouldn't last the duration. So I went back to England's Lane What else could I do? Went on helping my dad in the shop. Hard times. Couldn't get the chocolate, nor most of the sweets, not in wartime. Then it was tobacco that was scarce: had to ask everyone to bring in their old packets so's the manufacturers could paste all these labels on, and sell them again. Air raids every night. Mr Lawrence – he copped it: bombed out, and just across the road. You wouldn't even know now, to look at it: it wasn't long after the war they rebuilt it all in keeping with the rest of the Lane. Funny. Didn't even know Milly back then. It's only when Anthony and her Paul started going to school together – that's when I got to know her. Made a vow to Janey that I'd get him a really good education, Anthony, and that's what I'm struggling to do. It's not easy, no of course it's not – but look: what is? You tell me that.

So my dad, out of the blue he comes up and he says to me – tell you what, Stan: you and me, we've been stuck in our little confectioner's shop for the whole of the war. So how do you fancy a good day out? Hey? Reckon we deserve it, don't you? A day in the country. Few ales, slap-up meal –

how does that sound to you, Stan? Yes – I remember now: a day in the country, that's what it was going to be – he'd even found out all about the charabancs. So I don't really know how suddenly we decided to go to the seaside – how it was we came to go to Brighton. But of course if we hadn't – if we'd gone somewhere else, Kent or Oxfordshire or something – then I never would've met my Janey. Because she lived there, you see. Hove. Her people were quite well-to-do. She's had ever such a good education. Me – one day I was at school doing my twelve times table, the next I was working in the sweetshop. Clever woman, Janey, and lovely to look at in those days. Tight little curls in her hair – that dimple I really always liked. Yeh – pretty thing, she was.

We were on the pier, my dad and me. And he was missing my mum, I could tell. Always went quiet, times like that. She would've liked this, he said to me, after a little bit. The air, the sea, all the view – oh yes, this she would've liked. TB is what took her – she didn't have much of a life. Short, you know. Anyway, there I was on the rifle range – we'd just both had cornets for twice the price we were selling them in the shop, but we didn't mind, not today, because we were on holiday, weren't we? And my dad, he was wanting to go on the dodgems and I said yeh okay Dad, but just let me have a go on the rifles, eh? So I was banging away there, and there was this little lot of girls, three or four of them, five maybe, just standing about and giggling. Anyway – I was quite good at it, the shooting. Won a big sort of a teddy bear thing, I did. Think it was a teddy bear. Oh yes – what am I saying? It was a teddy bear, course it was – still in Anthony's room, isn't it? And so I turned to them, these girls, and I said Well girls – which one of you would like a nice big cuddly teddy to take home with them then, eh? And one of them, she comes forward – little sailor hat she's got on her – and she says I would, me: I'd like a teddy bear. And I looked at her and I thought, well she seems nice. And so I said well look, I'll tell you what – you come and have a cup of tea with me, and then we'll see about giving you the teddy. And all the other girls were laughing away and nudging her and everything and she says to me well yes all right then: that seems fair. Yeh. So we went and had a cup of tea. And I gave her the teddy. And that was my Janey.

We wrote letters after that. She had beautiful handwriting – you should see my scrawl: it's diabolical. And less than a year later, my old dad, he gives up the ghost. So I wrote to tell her that, and she said she'd come to London to see me, come on the train to Victoria to see me, and I said oh no, you don't have to do that, not for me, I'll be all right – and she said no Stan, I want to: I want to come to see you – I'm doing it for me. And a couple of months after that, we were married. Couldn't tell you what she saw in me. She was quite a cut above. Could've had a . . . I don't know – Oxford don, say. Or a solicitor. Doctor – anything she wanted. Well maybe so, she said – but it's you, Stan: it's you I want. We were really so in love. I thought about her night and day. She lit up my life, my Janey – and oh, how she did love me back. Nothing she wouldn't have done for me. She'd be helping out in the shop, and still she'd have my tea all ready for me of an evening. Hard to credit it now, but that's the way it was. We had a really good laugh, Janey and me. And oh did she love her chocolate and her sweets! I used to say to her – I've twigged to it now, Janey: you only married me so's you could get your hands on all of the chocolate and the sweets . . . ! And she'd kiss me in that way she did, and tug on one of my ears: you're right Stan, she'd say: you're dead right about that. I said to her, you're mad you are – marrying a man whose lungs could give out at any moment. You know what she said? Do you know what she said to me? Tell you: she said . . . don't you worry about any of that, Stan – me, I can do your breathing for you. Yeh. That's what she said. Anyway – here I am. Still breathing: still just about able to do it for myself.

And what do they call it . . . ? Lingerie, yes, that's it – that was a thing she loved. Always so well turned out in the bedroom, she was. Silk stockings and lovely nighties – and she did like a nice negligee. I was very happy to get them for her. Anything she wanted, really. And very good to me, she was. I didn't know a thing about what to do – you know, in the bedroom department. Wanted it, but I didn't know how to go about it, sort of style. And she was a virgin, of course – well of course – but she had a . . . what is it? Instinct. That right? Think so. A sort of instinct, this sense of what to do. Yes – very good to me, she was. That all changed, though –

you know: after the incident. But in no time at all, little Freddie came along, little mite. Frederick Miller, yes – but we started calling him Freddie straight away. You just should've seen her face when she looked at him – when she was feeding him, bathing him, all of that. Yes. And then he was gone. Six months, bit under, and then he was gone. One morning, she looks in the cot . . . and that was it. He was gone. Snuffed out. No explanation. The doctors, the bloody doctors – they said to us yes well: these things do sometimes happen. Best try for another, that's the thing to do. But Janey . . . she wasn't my Janey any more, not after little Freddie went. We did, though – we did try for another, and every time we were doing it, every time we were in the bed and I was lying on the top of her, she was crying her bloody eyes out. I couldn't hardly stand it. Would break your bloody heart. And then after a bit, my Anthony was born. She was happy for a while – better, anyway . . . well we both were. But it was when she saw – when she saw him for the first time, after I'd just brought him back from the hospital with those callipers strapped on to his little legs . . . well . . . she just more or less went away, then. Gradually. Wasn't sudden. But more and more, she just left us to it. And then she went silent altogether. Just like she's been for the whole of another evening . . . and me just sitting here next to her, smoking my pipe and sipping a Scotch.

And then suddenly I'm hearing something – brought me right back down to earth, this has: must've been miles away. Something out on the landing, is it . . . ? Not young Anthony stumping about, I very much hope – if it is, then I'll have to get him back to bed pronto. Oh wait . . . ! Of course! How could I have forgotten that? It's Milly, isn't it? It's Milly – course it is. Christ Alive – it's only her I've been waiting for . . . !

'Stan . . . you are behaving most awfully mysteriously, you know . . .'

'No no. It's just that . . . well, come on in Milly. Come in.'

'Are you quite sure, Stan? Jane . . . she won't mind, will she . . . ?'

'I shouldn't have said so, no. Come in, Milly. That's it. You come in.'

I can smell the whisky on him from where I'm standing. I know it only too well from Jim, but I honestly never did consider our Stan to be a drinker. But there, it just goes to show, doesn't it? One of life's lessons that always and stubbornly one refuses to learn: the simple truth that never do you really know any single thing about anyone on earth. Do you? No you don't. Mmm . . . and wafts of other little odours too now, which just are tantalising – while with an awful reluctance and considerable amazement at my just even being here, I now find myself crossing the threshold of this deeply unwelcoming room, tainted as it is by the clogging of some unwholesome condition which, though maybe not diseased, still is in need of a disinfectant. That fustiness that I remember from the first time. That, yes . . . together with something else quite stale, but still somehow intensely and curiously sweetish. Impacted bedding, conceivably – and cold cream, I think it might be . . . some other sort of unction, and then an astringent mingling of unspecified medicine. And it is only now that openly I am wondering exactly what it is that I am hesitant to know. Extraordinary in itself, this – and so I can only think that I have successfully stifled within me even the smallest squeak of anticipation. I am left with the simple hope that she will not be shrill with me, nor accusatory. I am doing my best to bolster my resolve, though in the state in which I find myself, I know I could not bear anything in the way of a tirade.

The light from the bedside lamp is striking her oddly: all of her features seem to be so very hard and stark, their motion-less shadows still jagged, and eerily looming. I think though that I do not detect any malice in her eyes. The counterpane is stretched tight and so very neatly, her arms quite rigid on the top of it. Everything seems so terribly still. I hear, and acutely, a silent alarm . . . and just something chill now is gripping my heart . . .

'*Stan . . . ! . . .*'

I must be wild-eyed as agitatedly I am rushing across to him and clutching at his arm. His hand is softly patting mine: he's staring down at the ground, and very slowly shaking his head.

'It's sad, isn't it Milly? Yes it is. It's really very sad . . .'

'Oh Jesus, Stan . . . what has . . . what has happened here . . . ?'

'Well you see, Milly – oh, would you care to sit down at all? No? Well you see, Milly . . . and I never asked, did I? Rude of me. If I could get you a little something? Some sort of refreshment? Nice cup of tea, maybe? And you've already eaten, I expect, have you?'

'Stan. Are you *mad* . . . ? I asked you what has *happened* . . . !'

'Yes. Well I was getting to that. What has happened, Milly, is that sadly, Janey – my wife, yes? She has passed away. Yes. Janey, she's dead, you see.'

I consciously close my mouth. I do not want to go over to her, but that is exactly now what I find myself doing. The touch of her hand is cold beyond cold.

'When did this happen . . . ? Oh my *God*, Stan . . . !'

'Last evening. Last night. It's hard to put a time to it.'

'Last *night* . . . ! But Stan – have you called someone? Is anyone coming? Why isn't anyone here?'

'Well I called you, Milly. Didn't I? You're here. You would've been here sooner if you could've made it. I know that. But look – you're here now, aren't you? And that's the main thing.'

'No but I mean – *called* someone. Ambulance. Police, or something . . . !'

'Well I did think of it, yes, but you see – well, I really wouldn't know how to go about any of that sort of palaver. I'm not used to it. I rather hoped that you might, you know – do it for me. See to it all, sort of style. Awful to ask, I know . . .'

'Well I will – of course I will. I really ought to do it right now, hadn't I . . . ? But Stan – God's sake tell me! How did she . . . ?'

'Yes well. It's really quite a tale. Last evening, you see, I came in here to have it all out with her. Once and for all. Just like you told me to, Milly. Fancy you might have been proud of me. I was going to be a man about it. Remember? That's what you told me to do. Remember? It was you who told me to do it.'

'I told you . . . ?'

'Mm, you did. But anyway – much to my surprise, I found her to be quite chatty. I was bowled over, I don't mind telling you. Because like I say, Milly – can't really recall the last time she even so much as opened her mouth to me. Oh yes and by the way – it turns out she didn't eat all of those chocolate bars, you know. Fry's Peppermint Cream, Mackintosh's Toffee Cup – no no, never did it. Nor keep a diary. She was kidding you. Having you on. Her little joke, I suppose, though I can't for the life of me really see that it's funny, or anything. Someone's been bringing her food every day, is what she was telling me. Can't remember who – some young girl. And doing her hair. Look at her hair, Milly. Looks nice, doesn't it? Never noticed it before. So that was all of that . . . but then . . . well then she starts to . . . well: taunt me, I suppose is the word.'

'Taunt you . . . ? What do you mean . . . ?'

'Well, like – saying not nice things about me. Raking up

all old things from the past which she promised me she never would. Saying I wasn't a proper man, and everything – and it's . . . what is it? Ironic, I think. That right, Milly? Think so. Yeh – it was ironic, wasn't it, that? Because it's the very thing I'd come in here to be, you see. A man. For once in my life. Because I had to, see? It was you who told me, wasn't it Milly? Be a man about it – that's what you said. So that's what I was going to do. Have some gumption.'

'Stan . . . you mean you . . . ? Christ! You don't mean to tell me that you . . . ?'

'Hang on, hang on – haven't finished. Then she started saying that Anthony and me, we'd be better off without her. That she was . . . can't remember exactly – but that she was no sort of a mother and wife to us. True enough, of course. And then, well – it was then that she told me to kill her. Just like that. Commanded me to, really. She's done it before. Once, she did. While ago now. Kill me, Stan! That's what she said. Go on! Go on! Do it! Just do it! Kill me *now* . . . ! That's what she said. On and on.'

'Oh God. Oh God oh God oh *God* . . . !'

'Yes well I wasn't having any of that, of course. I wasn't going to be told what to do, was I? Not what I came in here for. But then, you see . . . well then she started sort of pleading with me, a bit. Really asking me very nicely if I wouldn't please, you know – do it. Kill her. Which was different. Wasn't it? Quite different, that was. Said it would be an act of devotion. A final act of devotion. Said it was the last thing we would ever do together. As a couple. That it would sort of make us one again, if you see what I mean. But I was angry, Milly, I make no bones. Oh yes – angry, angry. Because earlier, ooh – she's said some terrible things, I won't go into it. And now I felt the anger, see, but it was all muddled up with what she was saying to me about devotion, and all the rest of it . . . and then I thought she might be right after all. I thought I should maybe, you know? Kill her. I really did think it would be the right thing to do. So I went over to her, then – she was in the chair over there, look . . .'

'Stan. Oh Stan . . . !'

'And I stood right over her . . . and then I bent down . . . I bent down, and I looked her right in the eye – my hands come up . . . and I slapped her in the face. Really hard. I'm that ashamed. Never done such a thing before in my life. And then I just had to get out of there fast. Just had to. Needed a drink. Needed it badly. Shouldn't have left him, Anthony. Shouldn't have done it. Felt bad about that. But I did – I left him. Went to the Washington. I hate that place. Had a drink. Quite a few, as it turned out . . .'

'Stan . . . oh Stan, I'm just so confused . . . ! What exactly are you saying to me . . . ? Do you mean that you didn't . . . ?'

'What? Didn't what?'

'Well – you know . . . You didn't . . . ?'

'What? Didn't what?'

'Oh Jesus *Christ*, Stan! You didn't *kill* her . . . !'

'*Kill* her . . . ? Well of course I didn't *kill* her! Good grief! I'm surprised at you, Milly – what on earth do you take me for? I could never do a thing like that.'

'Well then . . . oh my God, Stan . . . well then, how did she . . . ? How come she's . . . ?'

'Yes well – fair point. I only came up to see her today around dinner time, you see. Normally I'll take her up a cup of tea first thing, sort of style, but I was still quite annoyed with her, if you want me to be frank with you Milly – and also . . . I did have one hell of a headache. Hangover, they call it. Not proud of myself. And that's when I found her. Just like this. I was standing there talking to her for the best part of ten minutes – felt ever such a fool. Well you do, don't you? If you're doing all of that and then you turn round and twig that the person you're speaking to's dead. And all these little bottles and packets and things all over the bedside table – see them, Milly? Left it all like it was. Haven't touched a thing. Thought I shouldn't.'

'Oh God yes . . . I didn't notice. Dozens of them . . . where did they all come from?'

'Allchin's. Boots, one or two . . .'

'No, Stan – I mean, why are there so many?'

'Oh well – doctors, you know. Bloody doctors. It's all they do, isn't it? Dole out pills. Kill or cure. She must have been hoarding them. Saving them all up. Planning it, maybe. And then last night, well . . . the day had come, in her mind. Once she'd seen I wasn't going to do what she was asking. One thing I've been thinking – maybe she was just wanting me to do that so's I'd get into trouble for it. I hope that wasn't what she was thinking. I don't really believe it, not my Janey – but you never know, do you? With women. I'm sad, she's gone. Difficult to sort of really think that she's gone. After all these years. Because I really did love her, you know Milly. Hard to credit, really – but I did, I really did. I loved my Janey . . . when she was still my Janey, I did. Yes. Oh well. Anyway. Um – she left a note. Do you want to read it?'

'She left a note . . . ? Oh my God, Stan – well of course I want to read it! I mean, well – you know, if you're quite sure you want me to. Oh . . . don't cry, Stan. Please don't cry. Poor, poor man. Should we . . . close her eyes, do you think? Would you like me to, Stan? Close her eyes? She'd be . . . more at peace. What do you think? Or maybe we should just leave things . . . But I really must now telephone the, um . . . well I don't suppose it's an ambulance we're really wanting, is it? Police, I think. I should imagine they'll send a coroner as well. Ambulance too though, now I think about it, because obviously they'll have to, um . . .'

'Coroner, Milly? Not sure I know what that is . . .'

'Well a coroner, he sort of certifies the death, I think. Honestly, Stan – I've had quite as little experience in all of this as you have. I had to attend to Eunice, of course, and her husband. Eunice was my sister, you know. Yes. But all that was a very long time ago . . .'

'Well I'm not sure we'll need a coroner, will we? I mean –

we know she's dead. We do know that. Don't need to certify it. She's dead. It's already certain.'

'Yes well I do think they still have to go through the motions. Here, Stan – here's a tissue. Are you feeling a little bit better now? Are you all right . . . ? Yes . . . ? Because what they have to do is, um . . . establish the cause of death, I believe the phrase is.'

'Pills. It was the pills, wasn't it? The pills that all the doctors shoved at her to make her better. It's all just jobs for the boys, isn't it really? Doctors, coroners . . . we don't need these people. Do we? They don't do any good.'

'Well I've still got to telephone, Stan, whatever you may think. Oh God – that landing again, and the awful dark hall . . . Oh and you'll have to explain to them why you didn't ring immediately. They'll want to know that.'

'Well – I was waiting for you, Milly.'

'Yes I know that, Stan – but maybe you should just say . . . I don't know . . . maybe just say that you were in a state of shock. That's probably the best. Do you think you can remember that, Stan? State of shock. Yes?'

'Got you. All right, then. State of shock. Whatever you say, Milly. I knew I could depend on you. But look – don't you want to read it first? The note?'

'I really should telephone, Stan . . . well . . . I don't suppose a minute or two can matter now, can it? After all this time. But you're sure, are you Stan? Because it must be quite . . . personal to you. You're really sure you want me to?'

'Oh yes. You're part of it all, Milly. I do feel you're a part of it. Not in any bad way, I don't mean. And anyway – you're in it.'

'In it, Stan . . . ? In what? I don't understand.'

'The note. In the note. You've got a mention.'

'I don't . . . I don't believe it . . . ! Let me see it, Stan.'

'Here you are, Milly. I've got it right here. Beautiful handwriting, isn't it? She always did write a lovely letter. I've kept them all, you know. All the letters she wrote to me before we were married. Oh yes. Kept them all. Every man jack of them. Add this one to the bundle now, I suppose. Because there won't be any more . . .'

'Really, Stan . . . ? You've still got all her letters? Oh . . . that's just so touching. Now – let me look at this . . . right, then. "Dear Stanley, the fact that now you are reading these words proves that I am finally dead. Unless I have significantly misjudged the dosage, which I doubt – though in that case I shall be in a hospital somewhere, and the subject of determined resuscitation, and clearly I do not wish for this. Nor do you. You have been through quite enough, more than enough, as it is. You might have thought my behaviour of late to be deliberately cruel – so frequently I horrified even myself. But no. I am – was – troubled. Disordered. Now though, we are both of us free of all that. I know that you will take good care of Anthony, just as always you have. Maybe one day – who knows? – your eternal optimism will prove to be not unfounded, and he might yet regain full use of his limbs. Let us hope to God. I am sorry to leave you with the inconvenience of my remains, but I feel sure that Mary will ably deal with all of the necessary undertakings: she appeared, as I said, to be a capable woman. We did love each other though – didn't we Stan? And now, I honestly do believe, we will again. Goodbye, my husband. Goodbye. Jane." Oh . . . Stan . . . just look at me . . . I'm crying now . . . ! Oh Stan, poor Stan, I just can't imagine how you're feeling. It's all just so, so sad. And . . . Mary . . . that's . . . ?'

'Yes, that's you. She did that. Ever since you called round to see her that afternoon, she called you Mary. I can't imagine why. She knew full well that your name is Milly. Can't explain it. She did have some funny ways.'

'Have you still got that tissue, Stan . . . ? Oh – what must I look like . . . ! Complete mess. Now listen – I have to see to things. It's what you both wanted, clearly, so I promise I shan't let you down. I'm going to dial 999 now – explain the situation. They will have dealt with this sort of thing before, I'm quite certain. You just sit here, Stan. Or would you prefer the living room, maybe . . . ? Can I get you something . . . ? Oh Stan – are you all right . . . ?'

'Yes yes – I'll be fine in here. I'll just stop with my Janey for a bit. Won't be here much longer, will she? I expect she won't. I'll have a bit of a drink and a last little chat with my Janey. I'll be fine.'

'I will make sure she's properly looked after, Stan – so don't you concern yourself about any of that side of things.

Levertons in Haverstock Hill. The funeral directors, yes? I've heard they're very good. We'll make sure we get nothing but the best for her. All right? Well look – I shan't be long.'

'But you'll be staying though, won't you Milly? You know – till they come, and everything.'

'Of course I will, Stan. Wouldn't think of leaving you. Of course I'll stay. Of course.'

'Thank you, Milly. Thank you. You're so very good to me, and I hardly deserve it. Oh and before you go downstairs – can I just give you this . . . ? Token. Little token present, if you like, for everything you've done for me.'

'Present, Stan . . . ? Oh good heavens – what are you thinking of! I don't want any presents, do I? I'm just here to help, that's all.'

'Well you might as well have it, Milly. You'd be doing me a favour, really. It's no good to me. Not now. And I've lost the receipt. Searched high and low for the blessed thing, but it's disappeared. Quite a mystery really – because normally I keep them, all of my receipts, in this old Sharp's toffee tin on the dresser. Not there, though. Looked and looked.'

'Well Stan . . . all right . . . what is it? Oh – John Barnes bag, that's always a promising start. Let's have a look then, shall we . . . ? But honestly Stan, you really didn't have to give me anything, you know. But still it's terribly kind of you. So . . . what have we here . . . ? Oh . . .'

'Remember it, do you? It's that negligee thing you tried on for me that time. Yes? Remember that? I went back for

413

it. Thought it might cheer her up a bit, my Janey. But, well – beyond cheering up now, isn't she? Well past that stage. And I know how much you liked it. How it looked on you, and everything . . .'

'It's . . . lovely, Stan. How sweet of you to think of me . . . and you say you've lost the receipt though, have you . . . ?'

'Vanished into thin air – can't understand it. Had that tin upended twice, all over the kitchen table. Not a dicky bird. Oh and there's something else, Milly, I'd quite like to ask you. If you've got a minute.'

'Oh Stan – I've really got to telephone now, you know . . . and God, it's so late . . . ! Have you seen the time, Stan?'

'Just a minute. Won't take more than a minute, promise you Milly.'

'Well . . . what is it, Stan?'

'It's just that . . . well – under the circumstances and all . . . I was just wondering if you'd consider, um . . .'

'What, Stan? Consider what? I've really got to go and do this now . . .'

'Well – us getting married. Being my wife, sort of style. Because I haven't got one any more, you see. You don't have to answer me straight off.'

I am holding now this nylon negligee, limply between my fingers. And I am staring into the wide and ingenuous eyes of a man whom I sincerely believe to be deranged.

'I'm going downstairs now, Stan. All right? To make the telephone call.'

'All right then. Milly. Like I say – you don't have to give me your answer now. We can talk about it later on. Chew the fat, sort of style. When everyone's been and gone. And Janey – when Janey's out of the bedroom. Be nicer that way. More polite. Don't be long though, will you? Christ Alive – it's funny, you know: you haven't even gone yet, and already I'm missing you. Isn't that funny? I think that's funny – don't you, Milly? So you will come back? When you've done all that, you will come straight back to me, won't you Milly?'

My inner pain, the flood of it . . . now, at this moment, it has chosen quite violently to visit me again. I am trying my best not to show it.

'I will, Stan. When I've done all that, that's what I'll do: I shall come straight back to you.'

CHAPTER FIFTEEN

All I've Ever Wanted

That night what just gone by – that night, I am not joking, it were just the last bloody straw, far's I'm concerned. I mean blimey – there's a limit, ain't there? Ay? Got to be a limit. Man can only be expected to take just so much and no more. And I reckon I been doing that, when it come to Mill – taking it. Yeh – I've took it square on the chin for just about as long as I can bloody stand it. I weren't happy before – no I weren't. But last night, well – that's just been and gone and done it. I mean it – I bleeding had it, now. What she reckon she up to, Gawd in bloody heaven? Ay? I come home from the pub – whole place in darkness. Funny, I thought – I ain't that late. Mill, fancied she'd be doing her knitting, or something – listening to the wireless, watching the box. Little bit of dusting, maybe – whatever she get up to. But no – she must've got an early night in then, looks like. So I'm tiptoeing about like a bleeding fairy – and I ain't too much cop at that at the best of times: it's my boots when I kicks them off, always makes one hell of a clunking noise on the lino, there – and then I thinks to myself . . . nah, ain't right, this. Something ain't right. She not here – I can feel it. So I'm thinking I hope the boy ain't been took poorly – she maybe had to get him up the hospital a bit sharpish. Looking about the place for a scrap of paper . . . maybe she's wrote to me what's going on. But there ain't nothing about, nothing I can see. So I sticks my head into Pauly's room, and there he are, look – dead to the world, all lost in dreamland, little lad. His candlewick woss-name's slid off on to the floor, so I sees to all of that.

Then I sits myself down on the settee, lights up a fag, wonders if I can go another bottle of Bass, and I gets to putting my mind to it. Because it ain't never happened before. Well of course it ain't never bloody happened before: you come in of a night time, you expect your missus to bleeding be there, don't you? Ay? Course you do. Not out gallivanting, not this time of the night. And what time were it . . . ? Yeh – gone eleven. Blimey. Don't believe it. And she gone off and left Pauly, that's the bloody amazing part of it. She ain't never done that. Not never once in the whole of his life. Yeh . . . but things ain't normal. See? Between the two of them, like. Because this morning, after I had my tea and a slice, I goes down the shop like I always does – thought I'd have a fag, little chat with Cyril, before I heaves out all of the gubbins on to the pavement – and then I'm thinking oh bugger me, I only gone and left them on the kitchen table, ain't I? My fags. So I goes back up, and that's when I'm hearing the pair of them talking. Don't pay it no mind, not at first I don't – because I knows it, don't I? Soon as I'm out the way they's both going Phew Thank Gawd – now we can have ourselves a nice little chinwag like we's Sir Lancelot or somebody and Lady Whatsername, once the fucking dragon's out the road. Yeh but it were different, this. They was upset, the two of them. Tell that. And Pauly, he were going to Mill that she don't love him no more. Well me, I were just behind the door there, and it were all I could do not to give out one hell of a big fat laugh when I'm hearing that lot, I'm telling you. Because if Mill don't love Pauly, well then my name's Stirling bloody Moss, that's all I can say. But see – he weren't really sort of saying what he's meaning, like. Only a lad – he don't got the words. Can't sort of think it out like what a grown-up do. But what he were getting at – well I knows full well what he were getting at, don't I? Because me, I been feeling it and all. Mill . . . she ain't got her mind on the job no more, is what it is. I mean yeh – she still seeing to all of the doings, I ain't saying that. Always got the tea on the table, house all nice and tidy, making sure I got a clean hanky . . . but all the time it like she, I don't know . . . like she sort of sleepwalking, or something. Always somewhere else in her mind, like. Yeh. Well so what am I supposed to do then, ay? What am I supposed to think?

Well I know what I'm thinking. Been trying not to. Been trying to stick two fingers up at it for – blimey, bleeding ages now. First there were that perfume what she got on: weren't lavender, were it? Ay? No – and it weren't no Lily of the Valley neither. Then she got a mauve sort of a brooch thing, what I ain't never seed before. Well: said nothing. Trying not to notice, weren't I? Yeh but I can't no more. Not after all of last night. Writing on the wall. Got to be faced, son: got to be faced. Because yeh – I knows I don't get sort of social with people in the Lane. Keeps myself to myself. Always done that. What's my business ain't no one's else's – and so far as their business go, well: couldn't give a bugger. Other people, though – they ain't like that. So I'm going to be hearing things, ain't I? Bound to. And then the way what they looks at you. Some of them, it ain't just looks what they give you – they don't care what they saying. Like that poxy Mrs Goodrich, for one. She come in the shop the other day for her Bryant & May long matches what she get for her stove. I says to her how many times in the past: Ever Ready, they doing a nice little igniter, look – battery last a good long time: telling you – saving, in the long run. But nah – she won't have it: Bryant & May long matches is what she's wanting, so I flogs them to her: no skin off of my wossname. And then she going in that la-di-da bloody voice she got – all bloody hoity-toity, she is – oh you are looking so terribly terribly well I must say, Mr Stammer. Blah blah blah. And I says to her, come again, missus? Your cheeks, she says – so healthy-looking: must be all that good red meat Mrs Stammer's always cooking for you. Forever seems to be in the butcher's, doesn't she? She does seem to love her pound of flesh. Sometimes, Mr Stammer, she honestly does appear to spend more time with Mr Barton than she does with you . . . ! Yes – and then she laughs, like. Making it so it's all a bloody little joke, ho fucking ho. I could've hit her with a spade: had one, just handy. Yeh, I says to her – I do like my bit of meat. Oh I'm sure, she says to me – something you have in common with your perfectly delightful wife . . . ! And other stuff I heard and all – don't want to get into it. It's only when I found that fag end that I started proper thinking about it. That time she gone and shut my shop, and it weren't nothing to do with having to get a Beechams Powder down her or splashing water on her face or whatever she said it were. She were in my back room with him, maybe getting up to all sorts . . . and him smoking one of them posh bloody black fags of his, bold as you bloody like – because I got it off of Stan later on: he only get them in for him, that Barton bastard. Well yeh: who else round here is going to shell out twice what it cost for twenty Senior Service just on account of the bleeding fags is black? I ask you. And she shut my shop – and I don't never do that. I never done that. And Cyril there . . . don't know what he must've thought about it all. Yeh – so she lied to me. Barefaced, it were. Now fair enough – I'd lied to her about the dentist, yeh fair enough. But it's only because I just had to see my Daisy, weren't it? Been ages. And it's different, anyway – I'm a bloke, aren't I? Different for blokes – everybody knows that. Women . . . they just don't do that sort of thing. Not proper

420

sort of ladies, they don't. It's disgusting, that's what it is. I can't hardly think of it . . . my Mill, doing it. I can't hardly think of it. It's disgusting. Oh blimey. All I know is, she never do it with me . . .

My first idea were I goes round there and I kills him. Leave Mill right out of it – don't say nothing to Mill, because I don't want no upset. Not at home, like. Ain't right for the boy. After that I'm thinking, I'll just go and duff him up, warn him off, sort of style. And then I thought but blimey – he's a fucking giant, that geezer. I'm round his gaff . . . he got knives, and that. Could get nasty. Yeh and after a bit – and by this time I were well into the Scotch, I don't mind telling you – I were blaming myself. No I were. Because I said it before, ain't I? Look at me. Go on. Just look at me. Yeh? And now look at Mill. You see what I mean? Course you bloody do – everybody do. Can't rightly blame the old mare, can you? It's someone like that toffee-nosed bastard what she should have been with from the off. Stands to reason. Woman like that. Her education. The way what she talk, and all. Well – she talk like him, don't she? Yeh. She talk like him. Still and all though, my Mill . . . if she thinking of jacking me in, giving me the old elbow sort of style, well then she could do a whole lot better for herself than a bleeding butcher. Because let's not go forgetting it: for all his poncing about, that's all the bugger is – he's only a bleeding butcher.

It hurt me, mind – I ain't saying it don't hurt me, nor nothing. But I maybe deserve it, you know? All that hurt. On account of I's common as muck, and she a lady. Sooner or later, it going to come out. Got to. Like chalk and wossname. And then I thought, well look — can't last for ever, can it? Ay? I mean it ain't like it's something in a book or out the cinema: ain't no bloody fairy tale. She'll get fed up of him, maybe. Yeh, she will. And then it'll be all right. She'll be my Mill again and we can forget all about it. So best for now I says nothing. And like I say — I weren't happy, I weren't happy about it, course I bloody weren't . . . but that's where we was with it. Yeh but after last night . . . well, all that's right out the window: it's changed now. Everything — it's all different now. Because when she come in . . . when at last she come up the stairs, and it weren't much off of midnight — she got a shiner on her like what you ain't going to believe . . . her stocking is all torn and there's a bit of blood there — and she holding her stomach like it been cut in half. And yeh — when I hear her come in the door, I were well ready to give her all sorts of merry bloody hell. Yeh . . . but when I seed her like that . . . I just says to her: you get up to your bed, girl. Getting the doctor round.

'Don't be ridiculous, Jim. You'll do nothing of the sort. Waking him at this hour . . . I'm perfectly all right. I'll just bathe my eye and . . . an Elastoplast for the shin, possibly. Right as rain. Is Paul all right? Have you looked in on him?'

'What sort of a bloody man is it, ay? Ay? Does this to a woman . . .'

'Oh heaven's sake, Jim! He didn't do this to me! Of course he didn't. It was an accident, that's all. I was careless.'

'An accident, oh yeh I see. So what – you walk into a door, did you?'

'No I didn't walk into a door, as it happens. I fell down a few stairs, and then I somehow very stupidly managed to hit my head, my face, on the newel post. It's nothing. I expect it looks far worse than it is.'

'The newel post? You hit your face on the newel post? What's a bloody newel post . . . ?'

'Thing at the end of the banister, Jim. I'll just go and clean myself up a little bit now, if that's quite all right with you. And yes I'm absolutely sure you have questions Jim, many questions, but I should be truly grateful if possibly you could contain them until morning. I really am most dreadfully tired. Is Paul all right? You didn't answer me. I'll just quickly go in and see him . . .'

'He fine. I seed him. And why you got hold of yourself like that . . . ? That weren't done by no mule post.'

'Newel, Jim. Indigestion. Just a touch. I'm going now.'

'Baloney, that is. I'm getting the doctor. What he paid for.'

'Oh Lord – how many times! I don't need a doctor. I just took a little tumble, that's all.'

Yes I did. And I would happily kick myself for having done so, although I do seem to be supporting quite sufficient injury as it is. It was stupid of me, hurrying in the dark, but by that time I felt quite simply desperate to be away from him – finally to be gone from this dreadful house and back out into the cold sweet peace of England's Lane. Though before all that –

while Stan's most recent and perfectly extraordinary behaviour had momentarily thrown me, I freely admit it – still by the time I had carefully negotiated my perilous journey back down the staircase and into the murky hallway, I was reasonably content to attribute it to shock and a temporary confusion. He had, after all, and only hours previously, happened upon the dead and horribly bright-eyed body of his wife: his mind very surely just had to be disturbed. I felt confident that simple common sense would soon be reasserted within his clearly fevered brain.

At what I imagined could probably by now be the foot of the stairs, I sent out exploratory and waggling toes to make certain, and then was feeling my way along the wall before opening the door to what I remembered was the stockroom – then groping about for the switch, and delighted to discover that it worked. And from amid the triangle of still barely ochre illumination that the now ajar door was grudgingly shedding, I bent to the telephone – perched as it was atop a pair of seemingly pristine directories, A–D and E–K, on the small hall table with its feathery bloom of dust – and then, very purposefully, set about my task.

Now it is the police I have to deal with. They answered straight away – which, on reflection, I suppose I cannot wholly have been expecting, for I found myself stuttering, and really quite badly, when all the time I had determined to be forthright. Eventually I managed to stammer my preference for 'police' from the proffered options, while adding on quickly that we might easily be requiring also an ambulance, though definitely no fire engine (and yes – even as I said it, I was shuddering from a flush of embarrassment). The switchboard lady's serene detachment was quite thoroughly admirable, but then I suppose they must be dealing daily, and more especially nightly, with every manner of very terrible events. I then explained as best I could to whomever else I was immediately connected the specific circumstance of this particular death – that here was a suicide, that there existed a note and so on – and then was required to confirm that the person in question was indeed dead, and this I straight away did (and on being further asked how I came to speak with such unswerving certitude, all I could say was, well – no breath, you see: Jane, she's no longer breathing). Anyway, within an alarmingly short time, the house seemed to be positively infested with this rather intimidating bustle of people who had brought with them the whip of cold from outside – and each of whom, I observed with approval, had very sensibly come equipped with large black torches which threw out a strong white beam – though I am quite sure that here was standard night-time issue, and that they could not possibly have been aware of Stan's exceedingly parsimonious attitude when it comes to the replacement of light bulbs. There was an older man with a neat white clipped moustache who busied himself with Jane – though whether doctor or coroner I did not care to ask – and as two, or actually it's three, young constables simply and very self-consciously stood about, a detective of some sort was putting to Stan a series of questions, fortunately of the most basic nature, each of which he fielded with surprising and almost masterful ease, though I did think that he might be appearing to be rather too cavalier (and I can't quite explain that). There were forms and signatures which I helped him to deal with, and then came the information that during the morning at a mutually convenient hour some other people would briefly be calling, and that private arrangements ought meanwhile to be made with a local firm of undertakers. Muttered consolation then was bashfully bestowed upon all bereaved parties, present or absent, and as suddenly as they had arrived, all of them were gone.

'Well, Stan . . . that didn't go too badly, did it? On the whole. I'd say. Are you all right . . . ? Oh heavens – the *time*, Stan . . . ! I ought to have telephoned Jim while I was down there . . . Oh bother – I just didn't think of it . . .'

'Oh good – so you've decided already then, have you Milly? Well I can't tell you how happy that makes me.'

'Oh dear . . . what on earth are you talking about now, Stan . . . ?'

'Jim. You were going to tell him that his time is now over. Yes? That he is in the past. That he must now make do with his floozy called Daisy. Did you know, Milly, that Jim has a floozy called Daisy? Oh yes. Big girl. And that from this day forward, you are to follow your heart . . . !'

'Oh *Jesus*, Stan . . . ! *Jesus* . . . ! Oh God oh God oh God. Look. Everything's been attended to. No more can be done tonight. I'm really very tired and I have to go home now. All right?'

'I perfectly understand, Milly. You'll want to be picking up all of your things. Well thank you for coming. I'm sorry you can't stay to have some tea or something. Cold cream. Would you care for it at all . . . ? Great big pot there, look. Shame to let it all go to waste . . .'

'I'm leaving now, Stan. This minute.'

'Right you are, then. Well what shall I do . . . ? Oh yes – I know. I think I'll just go and wake up Anthony.'

'What? *What* . . . ? What is *wrong* with you, Stan . . . ? I've only been thinking what a blessing it is he hasn't already been woken, with all these people traipsing up and down the stairs. He's asleep, Stan. He's got school in the morning. The little mite's at peace, for heaven's sake. What on earth do you want to go and wake him up for . . . ?'

'Well – I thought he might like to come in and say hello to his mother.'

I stared at him. I just stared at him wide-eyed, willing either one of us to blink.

'Say hello to his *mother* . . . ? Jesus Christ – she's *dead*, Stan . . . !'

'Well yes I think I do know that, Milly. Perfectly aware. But it hardly matters, does it? Because even if she wasn't, it's not as if she'd have spoken to him or anything. And anyway – I think she looks quite nice, just the way she is now. Don't you, Milly? I really do think she looks quite nice. It's her hair, you know. I never noticed it before . . . not before she pointed it out to me.'

That's when I turned. That's when I ran. For the second time that week I hurtled down that blessed black staircase before I even realised I was doing such a thing – and Stan was calling to me, his voice so plaintive: Milly . . . ! Milly . . . ! Come back – you've forgotten your negligee, look . . . ! And it was only at the very bottom of the stairs, God curse it, where it was completely and quite bafflingly dark, that in high confusion I was caught up into a welter of disorientation and totally lost my footing and . . . well: a badly barked shin – not to say a ruined pair of Bear Brand nylons that I'd bought from Marion's only last Saturday – as well as an extremely painful eye, due to its staggering and audible collision with an acorn finial. The pain in my stomach was really very acute, and the ice that hung in the air outside was forcing me to gasp. Never before have I shut behind me my own front door with such solidly heartfelt relief. I crept upstairs as quietly as my bitterly stinging shin would permit – I could hardly avoid a hobble – and I was desperate to know that all was well with Paul, while not at all hopefully hoping against hope that Jim would have long ago tumbled into his pit of oblivion so that I could in peace simply tend to my wounds as best I might, and then stop forever just *thinking*. Sleep then, oh yes . . . oh please God yes – sleep, just sleep . . .

But no. There was Jim. Of course, of course: there just had to be Jim. Words were exchanged, heated on his part, and all to no purpose. At last I could bear not a second more of it, and I escaped to my bed. Some time later – I have no idea how long – I think I might have been hovering with bliss amid that weird though lulling twilight of very nearly somnolence, when I was jarred of a sudden into total wakefulness by the door of my room being briskly swung open. As I winced away from the light on the landing, cowering under covers, at once all of my pains concertedly returned to me, and I braced myself against whatever new form of anguish there now was to come. Though very much to my surprise, here before me stood Doctor McAuley – round-faced, comfortingly overweight – the waistcoat of his three-piece suit, where the watch chain winked, very apparently under strain – this almost miraculous presence quite instantly and utterly reassuring. I exhaled with what I sensed to be a profound and long-repressed relief, and felt quite heady with joy: I knew absolutely that I was very pleased indeed to see him.

Yes. And all that was last night. He dressed my leg rather better than I had, anointed my swollen eye and laid across it a soft and comforting pad. He probed my stomach with sensitive care: the chill of the stethoscope, it made me flinch, and then it made me giggle. He assumed of course that I knew I was pregnant . . . ? And I suppose . . . yes, that I did, though I could hardly dare hope it. I implored him, however, to say nothing to Jim – please, Doctor McAuley, please oh please: you must now promise me – not a single word about it. Promise me, Doctor – promise! He smiled, patted my hand, and warmly gave me his complete assurance. He asked in return for no explanation, and nor did he seem even remotely perplexed by all such insistent beseeching. Very possibly – and in common with seemingly just every living soul the length of England's Lane – he knows, or fancies he does, all of my very most intimate secrets. And since he left me . . . I simply have lain here, and thought of nothing but my physical state. Nothing else at all, except the state of me now. Then, very early – I had lost the thread of time, but long before usually he opens up the shop – I was aware of him banging about on the landing, Jim, and then of his leaving the house. No doubt he will be stamping up the road, hell bent on confronting what he will soon enough discover to be the gibbering madman that now is Stan, and accusing him of all the most terrible things. I don't really mind. Don't mind at all, in fact. And anyway, the news of Jane will serve very well to bring him up short. Maybe Jim will strike him, before explanations are tendered. Maybe Stan will gabble to him in a rush of all his golden visions of the idyllic future that he and I are to share, if only amid the twisting avenues and profusion of kaleidoscopic flowers that bloom irrepressibly within the elliptical contours of his own quite delirious imagination. I don't really mind. Don't mind at all, in fact. I don't at all care what either one of them will be doing, saying, thinking. Nor – but of course – do I care even remotely about the existence or otherwise of the floozy called Daisy. Was I really meant to? How perfectly laughable. Moreover . . . and for the first time I can remember . . . nor even do I care about Jonathan Barton. For he is gone, you see – gone from me, has been for a good long while. No longer am I yearning, and nor am I dogged by the clogging of perpetual anxiety – its immutable core has crumbled into atoms, and then nothingness. The cowl that covered me has fallen away, and I wallow in a new-born peace, my pain a tangible comfort. And I glow now with all that I am cherishing within me: a future that annihilates the present, and so very far exceeds simply all that has gone before. And it is everything I have ever wanted.

It is fitting – the symmetry of the thing, its pleasingly plump and nicely rounded wholeness: I am satisfied completely. For how perfectly splendid – finally to hear it from the more than abundant lips of Obi: that now John Somerset, erstwhile colleague and adversary, is finally dead. And that the news of his so very devoutly wished-for demise was brought to me on the eve of this cold, bright and really quite excitingly bracing, exceedingly early morning – while happily I am engaged in packing tightly into yet one more of these coarse and greasy jute sacks of detritus, the final few fragments – the last and rotten dismembered parts of the oafish and ill-fated pig man. That beggarly messenger who so very far over-reached himself, as eventually will all such untried, raw and rapacious yahoos. He now, quite thoroughly, has ceased to exist. As too has his sender: the dispatcher is duly dispatched.

And when Obi had come to me last evening, primarily I

was most eager to stem at the outset any great rush of vocal enthusiasm – jubilation over his triumph, or even the barest detail: I wished to know nothing at all of the entire affair beyond the absolute truth, forged in iron, that Somerset now is dead. And of course I did wonder, during the really very surprisingly brief period of time that Obi has been away from London, how I could trust beyond all question the veracity of his words . . . and though I have no potent explanation for it, I implicitly do so. It is perhaps his literal simple-mindedness in which I so ardently believe: I imagine him to be possessed of a primitive and inherently slavish commitment to not just unthinking obedience to so evident a superior, but also the dinned-in sense of duty to complete a given task before any due bounty may be expected or bestowed – or else come cowering and crouched, to stoically endure the severity of punishment administered by the master. I believe Obi to be the blank-eyed personification of doggedness in his pursuit of an end, this in order then to justify the commensurate reward. It soon transpired, however, that I need not at all have concerned myself over any surfeit of eloquence: he uttered very few words, I rather suspect because there are pitiably few at his ready disposal, and those ejaculations that do break free – from amid much quite comical facial distortion – are extra-ordinarily difficult to accurately decipher. A good deal of what he utters truly does sound to be no more than mutedly furious and animal grunts – although gradually, by degree, one finds that with concentration one may usefully ally and conjoin this or that stray and passing consonant with a couple of broken-backed vowels, and consequently, with considerable delicacy and painstaking dedication, reasonably deftly construct a plausible, though yet conjectural, half-phrase that would appear to be not wholly without relevance. Ultimately I found it more reliably straightforward to put to Obi a set of perfectly simple questions, each requiring from him no more than an emphatic and affirmative nod, or else a shake of his big and bull-like head. The only factor that concerned me, of course, was positive and unequivocal confirmation of Somerset's death. I wished not to know of the agency – and neither do I mind in how subtle or warlike a manner Obi elected to fulfil his commission. Should he have been careless in his method of execution or else in its aftermath, then the consequence will be merely that a shambling and deeply suspect coloured stranger – witnessed by many to be of fearsome aspect, and with hooded and malevolent eyes – will actively be sought by whatever means and authority the town of Henley can muster. Whether, in cooperation with Scotland Yard, they track him to the capital – and I should say that I deem this to be doubtful . . . though should they, by way of fortune or good judgement, be successful in their endeavour . . . well that outcome too is quite perfectly conducive: for in custody, his continued sullen insolence or else a detonation of his physical power . . . even quite simply the colour of his skin – any of these will more than adequately measure to serve as his jailer, and walk with him subsequently the short way to the gallows.

And so just last evening, I paid him the money, quite as contracted. I adjudged that to have retrogressively haggled with the man, as comes quite naturally to me, would have been more than unwise. His hands are both large and strong – as is this patently disfigured though innate perception of correctness within him: earlier I alluded to this – and no, I do not feel wild in ascribing it to him. At the sight of the considerable roll of cash, his eyes betrayed no hint of light: he pocketed it without comment. I think that upon parting he might have attempted to convey to me his willingness to again be of service, should ever such necessity arise – I believe that it was some sort of valediction loosely upon those lines, though in perfect honesty it is most damnably difficult to be sure, many of the more guttural noises that emerge from him being open to any manner of interpretation. Smilingly and in return, I myself offered up an alternative selection of non-commital though thoroughly agreeable-sounding utterances, which did appear to content him. But of course we never again shall encounter – well of course not. Indeed, within a very short time, I fervently aspire to be no longer compelled to encounter nor consort with any other living soul, the length of England's Lane . . . for now, I have so very thoroughly outgrown it: I hear its stitching, ripping at the seams. The Lane – this ultimately tiresome though I suppose quite perfectly blameless little street, together with an amenable smattering of its more credulous inhabitants – has amply fulfilled its usefulness. And this is true too of my foray into butchery: so unlikely a diversion has well served its purpose ... and all such purpose, now and at last, is come to an end. For with the long and threatening shadow of Somerset's continued existence darkening no longer the sunlit uplands of what I hope and trust to be a far more golden future, I know that very soon, I shall quit this place: to begin anew, and somewhere fresh – finally, and in long and criminally overdue recognition of their sweet and saintly eternal forbearance, to be able to bestow upon my dear wife Fiona and my little girl Amanda ... the life more suited.

So ... I have tied up the mouths of the sacks with twine, and now I manhandle the pair of them to be propped against the gates of the yard ... when next there comes of a sudden, to quite mar the still and stinging cold of this perfect winter's morning, a staccato and determined pounding from without. The dirty and angular man – he who swings up at once and with ease to his shoulders these deadweight and unspeakable burdens, those which I am straining even now to drag along the ground, and then will shrug them away so very lightly and with insouciance into the rear of his cart: the very same who confided in me the baffling truth that the contents are 'all boiled down' – never before has he called this early, nor demonstrated such unmannerly insistence. But no matter: in the light of all, it is good, now – yes, it is fitting to be rid of the last of it. Ah ... but no, in fact – such a conclusion is not yet to be ... for as I haul wide the door, what of all things should I find to be festering upon the other side of it but a risible and shabby little ironmonger, seemingly in the midst of a losing though self-evidently strenuous struggle to contain within him all the spillage of his grievances.

'Ah . . . and there was I so sincerely believing this joyous and quite sparkling morning to be replete with goodness – though I do see now that I was quite thoroughly wrong about that . . .'

'Right. Let me in!'

'. . . for now we would appear to have your very good self as something by way of a supplementary benefit. What bounty. And how may I assist you, Mr Stammer . . . ?'

'Don't you try to keep me out, you . . . !'

'As you may see, my dear fellow – the door is quite open.'

'Yeh well – right. Right, you . . . ! And don't you start up with your bloody "dear fellow" on me, you bloody . . . ! You know what you are . . . ? You're a right bloody . . . ! . . .'

'You are regarding me in a highly pugnacious manner, Mr Stammer. Excuse me – I'll just shut the door behind you, if I may. Hardly need prying eyes, I think. Now from what little you have hitherto uttered, I am gathering that in some or other manner I have grievously displeased you. Should eventually you ever care to elaborate, then of course I should be more than delighted to, er . . .'

'Stop! Pack all that in! Had just about enough. You stop all of that! You and all these bloody other people – talking like you's the King of fucking England – and you ain't! You ain't! You's nothing! Same as what I am. But I reckon – what

436

I reckon is, I'm better! See? Better than you! Because I don't go twisting about. And I would've left you to it, if that's what Mill wanted – would've gone with it, you bastard! But nah! Ain't enough for you, were it? Ay? You got to go and . . . *beat* her, the poor little gel . . . ! She only little! I ain't never lifted my hand to no woman! Not never once in my bloody life. Let alone another man's wife, you . . . !'

'Do not approach further, Mr Stammer, I urge you – and please unclench your two little fists, else I fear I shall be compelled to strike you down. I have not the least idea what you are talking about. In this I am sincere. I too, Mr Stammer, maintain an inviolate rule where violence towards women is concerned: I never indulge in it, and have nothing but the most base contempt for any who does. With the exception, quite naturally, of the odd little harmless bit of horseplay, you know . . .'

'*Horse*play . . . ? What you fucking on about . . . ?'

'Oh – you know. Surely you do. Erotic diversion. Titillation, yes . . . ? Damn good spanking, sort of thing. You are English, aren't you? Surely at least you must have heard of it . . . ? No but then of course, I doubt whether you attended that sort of school . . .'

'I don't know what you on about! You disgusting! I ought to bloody *kill* you, you bastard . . . !'

'Why?'

'Ay? Ay . . . ? *Why* . . . ?!'

'Mm. Why do you feel you should? I am receiving the

impression that your dear wife Milly – please, Mr Stammer, do I pray you allow me to finish – that your dear wife Milly has been attacked by a person unknown. Certainly not I. And I am distressed to hear it. I should never wish nor visit upon her the slightest harm. Do you believe me, Mr Stammer? I sincerely hope that you do . . . you anyway appear to be modifying your behaviour. You have slightly quietened, at least . . .'

'You denying it . . . ?'

'Oh dear. I rather hoped by now that possibly we might have established that. Yes, Mr Stammer: I am denying it.'

'You never clock her round the eye . . . ? Belt her in the stomach?'

'Certainly not. Who could have perpetrated such an outrage? I cannot imagine who might be capable of such a thing.'

'Don't you try all that! Don't you do all that la-di-da baloney on me! Just talk to me straight: you saying you never done it. Right?'

'Oh dear God Almighty . . .'

'All right – all right, then: leave all that out of it, for the minute. And what . . . you saying what . . . ? You telling me that you and Mill . . . you and Mill . . . you never gone and done the dirty on me . . . ?'

'How very colourful your phraseology can be, Mr Stammer, once eventually you manage to utter any words at all. If I understand you correctly, you are asking me now whether I deny having consorted with your wife. Well no – I do not deny it in the least degree. Certainly we have enjoyed congress,

Milly and myself, though I fear I am behaving very much less than gallantly by making any such disclosure. You already do appear, however, to be apprised of the truth of it. Though I may say by way of an addendum that we have not encountered for quite some while, and never – and really I must forcibly reiterate this point, even at the risk of appearing tedious – never have I subjected her to physical abuse of any description whatever. Are you, er . . . feeling quite all right, Mr Stammer . . . ? You seem somehow pale . . . shaking, rather . . . trembling, yes. May I fetch you a glass of water? Something stronger, conceivably – despite the early hour. I have no brandy, I fear, though possibly I might be able to run to just a little soupçon of Benedictine . . .'

'My Mill . . . my Mill . . . so she really been and gone and done it . . .'

'Mm, I rather fear so. But brace up, old chap. It's all quite over and done with, you know.'

'Ay? What you saying? What you saying now? You mean . . . what you mean? She chuck you over? She ain't going to go with you? That what you saying?'

'Go with me?! Great heavens, no! What a thought. No no – there's simply no question at all of any such thing, and of course there never was. Indeed, Mr Stammer, you may well be encouraged when I inform you that come the new year, I shall in fact be leaving this place – leaving England's Lane. Oh yes. Closing the shop. Selling up. Whereupon my family and myself will be very pleased finally to be moving on. New decade, new beginning. I imagine this intelligence will hardly distress you. You might yourself, you know, do rather worse than to adopt a somewhat similar approach, yes? New decade, new beginning . . . ? Has a ring to it, don't you think?'

'You's off, you say . . . ? Leaving the Lane? What – whole bang shoot? That Amanda and all?'

'Why naturally, Mr Stammer. What a thing to say. I am hardly likely, I think, to abandon my daughter to fend for herself as a street urchin. She will be sorry, I daresay, to be forced to withdraw from the company of your boy – Paul, is it . . . ? Yes, Paul. Though I am guessing that such parting will not cause either one of us to shed too many tears. Am I correct in this surmise, Mr Stammer?'

'Ay . . . ? Oh yeh . . . yeh. Blimey . . . I don't know what to think. Can't think. Don't know what to think. Broken man, I am . . . broken man . . .'

'Oh nonsense, my dear fellow. You'll rebound. People do. For they must, you see . . .'

'I dunno. I dunno. I don't got nothing straight in my mind. Can't think proper no more. Still and all, though . . . just looking at you . . . me being here . . . fair turn my stomach, it do. I should . . . you know what I should do . . . ? Ay? You know what I should do . . . ? I should bloody knock your fucking block off . . . !'

'Well . . . I suppose I feel honour bound to encourage you to try, should you believe that such extreme action will in some small way serve to release a degree of your aggravation

. . . soothe your furrowed brow . . . however I feel it only fair to warn you that should you determine to resort to fisticuffs, I shall resist and retaliate with all means at my disposal. And I do fear that from such a contest as that, Mr Stammer, you would inevitably be destined, I think, to sorrowfully emerge as considerably the more injured party. In that I could, not to put too fine a point on it, snap you in half with the fingers of one hand. As I believe you are aware. But, having said all of that, if still you feel that you must . . . well, Mr Stammer, then you must, of course . . .'

My mind . . . I telling you . . . my mind, I just all in a tizz. Ain't had no kip – ain't had a shave. Feeling right rough. Ain't even got all of the doings out on to the pavement yet. Cyril ain't had his seed . . . And all these words what he giving me, this sod of a bastard . . . I ain't even sure what I got to be thinking about now. But it's Mill, got to be – that's all I cares about. I got my Mill, then I don't mind nothing. But him . . . just look at him . . . ponced-up bloody bastard. Wants taking down a peg. Yeh. Blimey . . . he fucking big, though. It right what he say: kill me, he could – don't even have to try. So I reckon I sling my hook. Get out of here. Can't do no good. Can I? What's done is done. Yeh – so that's what I got to do: get out of here. Stands to reason. Yeh it do . . . so I don't know why – don't bleeding go and ask me why – but I just gone up to the bastard, ain't I? Took one hell of a swing at him, and I got him right on the bloody jaw, look. His head, it jerk right back, it do – yeh, but he ain't going over, no not him. I don't follow it up. I don't follow it through. I'm just stood here. My hand, it feel like I broke it. He looking at me. He looking at me something terrible. Oh Gawd – I'm for it now. Can't run though, can I? I should cocoa. Not going to run. Can't run. No point hitting the bastard again though. He made of bloody iron. So I just got to take it, I reckon. Just got to stay stood here – wait till he get to me. Then I gets smashed to bloody bits.

'Mr Stammer . . . I do so thank you for calling. Sharing your views. And now I do quite earnestly and solemnly urge you just to turn around, and then walk out of here, please. While still you are able so to do.'

Because oh great heavens just look at him, won't you? This small and quite perfectly pathetic little oik, shuddering before me. Some slight show of bravado in the set of his shoulders, though still does he visibly quiver – and within each of his eyes there is sparking and alive the bright white pinpoint of absolute fear, just as in that of a snorting pig that senses the approach of a knife to its throat. And then behind that, a milky opacity – the quite dull glaze of acceptance of the soon to be here and grim inevitability: this I have witnessed so often in the slow eyes of a heifer, when first she is scenting the tang of an abattoir. There is no sense in slaughter, however – no, nor even retribution. For I am not a brute. I have wronged the man. He has struck me. Honour would appear, then, to have been crudely satisfied.

'Please, Mr Stammer, I should be so very much obliged to

you were you to do me the politeness of lingering no longer. There is, I do assure you, a limit to the breadth of my forbearance.'

In a tizz – I'm in a tizz . . . ! Don't know what I'm about. Can't think, that's the trouble – I just can't think proper. All what're on my mind are my Mill. Yeh. That all I know. Yeh. So that's what I got to do, then – right? Get back to her. Yeh. See what the doctor done. See how she feel. See she all right. Get out the sight of this bloody great bastard, yeh . . . before he bloody well kill me . . . that's what I got to do . . . and then get back to my Mill. On account of she my wife, ain't she? Yeh. That's right: she my wife.

And how many times since I gone over it in my mind . . . ? It's like now I were like . . . I don't know – two people, sort of style. Like my head, it never got round to telling my feet what it was I were up to. Because I'd flew at him, hadn't I? Yeh – I'd flew at him. And I were going to get out of there – all set, honest I were: I were on my way. Turned around, didn't I? Reaching out for the door knob, I were – think I even gone and said goodbye to the bastard. Next thing – I'd flew at him, and my hands, they's about his neck on account of all I wants is to throttle the fucking sod. And then I were thinking Christ Al-fucking Mighty – he smell of perfume, the bleeding ponce . . . ! Yeh and next minute I weren't thinking nothing on account of he pick me up like I's a bit of I don't know what and he throw me hard, right up against the bloody wall. My back and my head, they was bleeding killing me, I can tell you – my hands is useless, and I weren't even seeing straight no more. Then his great bloody fist – it slamming me right in the face and there blood all over, look, and I were feeling all bloated up and numb and yet I got all these terrible pains just bloody everywhere about me, and then I sees him pull back his bloody fist again and all I do is I just shuts my eyes – and when it come . . . yeh, when it come . . . it were like I were hit by a fucking train. My brain all rattling inside of me and my mouth is all gone like rubber and I hits the ground like I been heaved over and off of a mountain. Don't know how long I were down there. Next thing is water poured on to me – and I looks up, kind of, but I can't hardly see. And then I do . . . I sees him, yeh I sees him a bit – just standing there, he is, quite the thing: he straightening up his tie. He look fresh as paint. He look like he on his way to Buckingham bleeding Palace. And me . . . I got what I asked for, didn't I? My face, it do feel a funny shape – it don't even feel like my face no more. Lying here . . . my clothes is torn, reckon my nose is broke, and I shaking like I's made of paper. What it is is . . . I smashed to bloody bits.

Tried to creep into the house quiet, like. I'd just sort of crawled my way out of the Barton bastard's yard – just standing there he were, bold as you want, and he holding the door open for me for all the world like he that – what's his name . . . ? Yeh that Jeeves, is it, or something. Like he were going to be doling out to me a top hat and a pair of white fucking gloves. We never said nothing. Didn't meet no one in the

Lane, which were a blessing – Gawd alone know what I look like. It still were so bleeding early . . . yeh but I got to get the shop open soon, ain't I? Yeh – business is business, and I ain't never late. So what I done is, I come in the back – take the cover off of Cyril's cage, say hello like, poke him through a little bit of millet, and then I goes up the stairs, soft as I can. My face . . . I can't tell you. I looks in the mirror in the bathroom there, and blimey – I just can't tell you. I get a bit of water on it – and it do sting, and no mistake – and then I bungs on a squeeze of that Savlon – and yeh, all right, it look a bit better, feel a bit better. I touches my conk . . . and nah, don't reckon it are broke now. Big and bleeding red, though – and yeh, give me gyp all right. My eye – where he got me right square on the second doings – that more or less closed down. Going blue on the skin around it there, look – bit of sort of yellow and all: blimey – this rate, I'll be bleeding looking like Cyril. Then I hears Mill – Mill, she knocking about somewhere. Pauly – yeh, he will of gone off by now, pick up Anthony for his school . . . yeh so that's all right, then – he well out the road. But it's Mill I got to cope with now. Don't know where I can rightly start with it. Yeh well – no time to think: I turns round and she standing there, ain't she?

'Jim . . . ! Oh . . . Jim . . . ! Oh – your poor, poor face . . . ! He did that to you . . . ? I can hardly believe it. Oh Jim – why wouldn't you talk to me first? It's all just a huge misunderstanding, don't you see? I could have explained. But oh – look what he's done to you . . . I can't – I just can't believe

445

it. It must only be because he's . . . well I do think he might have become rather slightly deranged, you know. In the light of events. You didn't *hurt* him though, did you . . . ?'

'Blimey O bleeding Reilly . . .'

'No but what I mean is – he's not himself, do you see?'

'Yeh? Who the bleeding hell is he, then?'

'All I mean is, Jim, he's had a shock. He's very disturbed. Oh . . . but I am really so very very sorry for your injuries. It's just so untypical of the man. And also – well, he's such a weedy little fellow, isn't he . . . ? I just can't understand it.'

'Weedy, ay? You reckon?'

'Have you put something on that eye? Oh . . . just look at us Jim, though. The pair of us. Honestly – what a sight! It's really rather funny, don't you think . . . ?'

'Not really. No.'

'No but I mean our faces! We both of us look as if we've just gone ten rounds with, um . . . with, er . . . oh Lord, I don't know the names of any boxers . . .'

'Rocky Marciano.'

'Well, if you say so, Jim.'

'Henry Cooper.'

'Oh yes – I've heard of him, I think . . .'

'Freddie Mills.'

'Yes all right, Jim. That'll do, thank you very much . . .'

'Sonny Liston . . . Sugar Ray Robinson . . .'

'Oh dear God . . .'

'Yeh. Right. So, um . . . how's you, then? What the doc

say? You all right, are you? Here . . . tell me this though, Mill. I got to know. He really not hit you? That bastard? Because he says he never . . .'

'Well of course he didn't! I told you! I just fell down a few stairs, that's all. My own stupid fault. I'm fine. Never been better. Honestly, Jim – I'm completely fine. Although . . . there is one thing . . . just one little thing I should like to talk to you about . . .'

'Yeh well – I don't. Want to talk. Not about none of it.'

'Yes but there is just this one thing that we rather must. Talk about. I'm afraid.'

'Got to open the shop, ain't I . . . ?'

'Oh not now, I don't mean. This evening though, maybe. Yes? After supper?'

Well no. Couldn't face none of that, when the time come. So that's why, after I got my tea down me, I treats myself to a couple of stiff ones up the Washington, and then I got myself down here. See my Daisy. Yeh. And she been ever so under-standing. When she go and clock my dial, she don't say nothing like what every other bugger do – yeh and you should've heard them in the Washington: trouble and strife got the rolling pin on you, did she Jim? Aye aye – blind drunk again, was you Jim? One of them even gone and done that ten bleeding rounds with Henry bloody Cooper like what Mill done, you can believe it. Blimey . . . on and on, I don't know. But my Daisy, she just sort of look at me all sympathetic like, and then she kiss me where it hurt, yeh? And she say she make it

447

all go away and be better and everything. Yeh and I were ever so grateful. I weren't up for none of the usual, though: telling you – black and blue, I ain't kidding about. So she just kind of go and hold me, sort of style – sing a little lullaby, which is always favourite. And then she say to me – here, Jim: that pal of yours, he were down here earlier on. What, I says to her – Charlie, you mean? Nah, she goes – weren't Charlie, were that other one what you brung down here that time. You remember, don't you? Stan, weren't it . . . ? Oh yeh, I says – old Stan: how he keeping, then? Well, she says – weren't too chipper. And acting dead odd he were, that's what Aggie were saying to me. Odd? What sort of odd, I asks her. Well, she says – he give Aggie a right nice sort of a little nightie thing – negligee is what you might call it, I suppose. Yeh? Well that's handsome of him. Yeh I know, Daisy says to me – it were, but then you won't never guess what he come out with, Jim. Go on, I says – tell me, Daisy: ain't in the mood for no guessing games, gel. Well, she says – he only ask her to marry him, that's all. Said the first one what he ask today – she weren't having none of it, didn't want to know . . . so he go and ask Aggie instead . . . ! Blimey, I'm going – silly old sod: must have been plastered, weren't he? Couldn't say dear, Daisy says – but she laughing along with me, like. And you know what else he said, Jim? He said his wife, the wife what he did got, like . . . she gone and croaked. Just last night, that's what he were saying: that's a bit of a turn-up, ain't it? And Aggie – well, you know Aggie, Jim – she go to him,

Well I'm ever so sorry for your loss, my sweetheart, and it very kind of you, I'm sure, to ask me to be the next Mrs What Ever Your Name Is, dearie, but I don't really reckon I'm good for anyone's wife, you want the whole truth of it – but ta ever so much for the present all the same: ever so nice of you, Bert. And I'm laughing away there at all of that lot – and then I asks her, Daisy, what Aggie go calling him Bert for when his name is Stan, and she going oh search me, my lovely – maybe he want her to, maybe he tell her to: gentlemen what call, they will ask for the oddest things, some- times: they can be quite odd, Jim. And then she were doing that little thing what she do in my lughole, Daisy were . . . whispering she got a nice warm towel, and it all ready for me if I changes my mind and I wants it – fiddling about with me a little bit, you know – so yeh, I'm feeling all sort of funny inside . . . but still and all I'm thinking, ain't I? Thinking about it all. What Mill been doing . . . yeh well, take a bit of getting used to, that will. No denying it. Still – I got to keep her though, ain't I? Look like it. And at least now I found out about it. Got it all out in the open, like. And there can't be nothing else, can there? Ay? Not now. Nah. Done with. And Mill and me – we'll be all right, we will: we always was. And as for all them other bleeding old biddies in the Lane what's always with the gossip, and that – well bugger them, that's all. Can't give a tinker's cuss about any man jack of them. They soon get fed up with it – couple days, they be wagging their chins about some other poor old sod. Way of it, ain't it? Yeh. And then . . . and well then I gets down to thinking about me. All what I been through today . . . hard, it were . . . yeh but now I'm here – all nice and cosy, down here. And it right, you know, all what she say, my Daisy. Odd. It is. Proper odd. Things what men gets up to.

CHAPTER SIXTEEN

Spilt Milk

'It's the same every year, isn't it Mrs Stammer?'

'What is, Edie? And I'll need some more icing sugar, I think . . .'

'Christmas, I mean. You wait for it ever such a long time – talk about it, make your lists, all the extra work – and then suddenly: whoosh! It's right upon you.'

'Oh don't, Edie! I've still just so much to do! But I know what you mean, of course I do. All of a sudden, yes – you're perfectly correct, it's exactly what you say: you're barely aware, and then it's right upon you. Yes. Oh well. There it is. You know . . . I really don't think I'm able to resist a tin of that shortbread . . .'

'Oh I know what you mean, Mrs Stammer. They get them up so nice, don't they. All that tartan. Ever so Christmassy. The large one is it, Mrs Stammer . . . ? Right you are, then. And it's the same with Eat Me dates – got to have a box, haven't you? I can never decide if I like them or not. They're ever so sticky. And walnuts as well – but you do wonder, don't you? If it's worth all of the effort, for such a little nut. They don't even taste very nice. And you're picking bits of shell out of the carpet till doomsday. Oh I'm so looking forward to tomorrow, Mrs Stammer . . . ! The whole of the Lane is, far as I can tell. It'll be lovely in the library.'

'Oh I do so hope so, Edie. Council, you know – they've been making noises right up till the very last minute, officious little twerps. All sorts of by-law nonsenses, they've been quoting to me endlessly. But I told them straight: look here, my man, I said to this particular jumped-up little ass – Brumby, his name is – odious little man. Look here, I said – if you people can hold your Christmas party in the Town Hall which is funded by us, the ratepayers, then there's nothing to say we can't have ours in the library. That took the wind out of his sails. Goodness – it's only for a few hours. I didn't mention the group, of course – thought it might be unwise. Did you know about the group, Edie . . . ? Oh yes – huge excitements. Young Doreen's latest boyfriend – works in Woolworth's in Swiss Cottage, apparently, and he has one of these new sorts of guitar, she was telling me – you know, electric, you plug it in, like that fellow's in The Shadows, the one with the spectacles, you know? Yes and his friend, the friend of the chap who works in Woolworth's, he has drums and cymbals, and so on – Lord above! – and she sings, she's a singer, Doreen, or she says she is, anyway. Well I know. Anyway, I daresay it'll all be the most frightful row, but I'm sure it can't do any harm. It is Christmas, after all. Be fun. Add to the gaiety. And she's also bringing her Dansette, Doreen, and all sorts of Top Ten records, she was telling me – terribly excited about it all, she is. Older people will absolutely hate it, of course. I haven't said a word to Jim. He'll say it's all, I don't know . . . fuzzy-wuzzy jungle music or something, though hopefully not if the negroes are within earshot – not that they'd probably understand, I suppose. But we'll all be singing carols later on as usual, so that should please everybody, anyway. And Mrs Dent, she says she's perfectly happy to lend us her old upright so long as we can press-gang a few of the men into pushing it up the road, though she did warn me that it hasn't been tuned since just after the war – but then as it's only her who's going to be playing it, I can't imagine that it will matter very much: we're not really expecting Liberace, are we? She also asked me if she thought those same strong men might be willing to carry her over too, because apparently her feet are simply worse than ever, poor woman: always are, she says, at Christmas. Not sure if she was joking or not. And people did – finally, they did start giving a bit of money, though only within the last week or so: it was all terribly touch and go. So I think the food and drink side of things should be all right – and of course we're all so awfully grateful for your donations, Edie. Especially the cheese footballs – everyone loves those. Sally from Lindy's, she's doing the cake as usual – Paul said she'd eat it on the way over, which I told him was terribly cruel. Victoria Wine have been more than generous, I must say – and the Washington is setting up a barrel of Bass: I can't tell you how pleased my Jim was when he learned about that. Stan . . . poor Stan . . . he chipped in with fizzy drinks and sweets and crisps and things before he had to . . . oh well anyway – you know. And the people who work there – in the library, I mean – they're all quite cock-a-hoop about it all. I rather think because librarians, they maybe don't get invited to that many things, do they . . . ? Though that may be perfectly unfair. And, Edie . . . there'll be plenty of paper chains! I well remember your insistence about that. I've had Paul and Anthony licking them and putting them together all morning. Left them a great big jug of Robinson's Barley Water to keep their tongues wet. Which reminds me, Edie – I'd better take another bottle of Robinson's Barley Water . . .'

'Oh I am pleased about that, Mrs Stammer. I do love paper chains. And are there going to be those lovely little hot sausages, like last time? They're everyone's favourite, I think . . . Oh . . . sorry, Mrs Stammer . . . how awful of me . . . I really am ever so sorry, Mrs Stammer . . .'

'Quite all right, Edie. But no . . . I haven't actually, um . . . approached the butcher. But look – we shan't starve, I assure you.'

'Of course not, Mrs Stammer. And, um . . . balloons? What about balloons?'

'Old Mrs Jenkins from Moore's – you know Mrs Jenkins, don't you . . . ? Oh yes of course you do! Whatever am I thinking! You know everybody. Anyway – she's given us ten packets! All assorted colours and shapes. I think I'll have to get Jim to do those, though. Me – I'm quite out of puff as it is.'

Yes I am: and barely able to think. My goodness, my goodness – what a time this has been . . . ! And I do actually know exactly what Edie was meaning: you're planning and preparing, spending far too much money – and yes, that does, I am afraid, remain a somewhat sensitive subject – and meanwhile you're working all the hours God sends towards this colossal and important coming event . . . and yet something deep down just flatly refuses to allow you to believe that it ever will actually arrive. And then before you quite know where you are . . . bang! It's upon you. The party is actually tomorrow – I can hardly believe it. And then a few days later there's Christmas itself, of course . . . still a million things to see to . . . and then . . . yes well, I'm not yet really ready to think too hard about the coming year: 1960 . . . sounds so odd, everybody thinks so. And as for this year, of course . . . well, there has been so very much else to deal with hasn't there . . . ? Oh my Lord. And yes I could hardly fail to notice how Edie, poor thing, nearly bit off her tongue when she went and mentioned the sausages. Yes well. Everybody knows, of course. About all that. They have done for ages, it appears – and honestly, I hadn't the slightest idea . . . though I redden now to think it. It all serves as ample demonstration of how very completely one may wilfully blind onself: rather like children who cover

455

their eyes and so very endearingly believe themselves then to be invisible: not at all endearing, however, in one who would be seen to be an adult and capable woman. Ah well. There it is: spilt milk, if ever there was. And I have often thought, you know, during the past, oh, week or so: well, Milly – where on earth are you to begin? And of course I knew the answer to that: why, at the beginning, of course: chop-chop. And work your way quite doggedly onward until, with cold determination, eventually you come to the end. It's what we did in the war, isn't it? How we got through. And who said that, though . . . ? About beginning at the beginning, and so on . . . ? Was it someone in Dickens? Oh, you know – I rather fancy it was Alice: I rather believe it was. I sometimes think I wouldn't at all mind a convenient and fantastic rabbit hole to tumble down – a miraculous looking-glass I could idly walk through. And months ago . . . just months ago, when all I had been dreading was having to arrange this Christmas party – back in the days when still my everyday life was a blissfully humdrum affair – had I then but an inkling of all the coming upheavals quite on the top of that . . . well, I might truly, you know, have become a party to despair. It's quite as well in life, isn't it, that one never does know even so much as the nature of whatever is looming . . . ? Or else how could one dare to continue? But . . . one copes, doesn't one? One has to. Yes . . . though just lately, one has to admit that some matters have proved to be a great deal more difficult to deal with than others.

The funeral of Jane . . . that, thank the merciful Lord, at least now may be said to be over and done with. It was, of course, I who in the end had to attend to all of the dealings with the undertaker – because Stan . . . well, where to begin with the state of him, poor man . . . ? And quite simply, there was no one else. But Levertons, I must say they did behave quite thoroughly professionally: not, as I had feared, remote and cold-bloodedly mechanical, but suitably consolatory to the useless widower, while incidentally quite wholly comforting to me, simply by means of their confident demonstration of ability. During my very laboured endeavours to prise from Stan so much as an atom of information concerning her nature, it transpired that Jane, during the long distant days when actually she had dressed herself and then walked out into the street, had been a practising and semi-devout Catholic. For many years she used to attend High Mass at St Dominic's Priory each Sunday morning at eleven o'clock, as well as an occasional Benediction on a Wednesday evening. Stan did tell me though, during one of his rare quite lucid and rather more loquacious interludes, that it had to be a lifetime since her last confession. No service was held for her, however, for there was no one to attend: no parents, no siblings, no cousins, no friends. At the graveside in Hampstead Cemetery, there stood quite awkwardly only Stan and dear little Anthony, Jim, myself (both very much still the walking wounded) . . . and then Doreen, of all people on earth – I simply can't imagine why: I meant to ask her afterwards, but she already had drifted away. Edie had wanted to be there, but was vexed to be unable to find anyone that morning to cover for her absence from the Dairies. I had not thought it suitable for Paul to have to witness such a thing as a funeral at so early an age . . . and when Jim – yes, I suppose quite inevitably – had begun to prevaricate over his previous quite strenuous, though whisky-fuelled, promise to without a doubt be there, I was forced to put my foot down. And so with great reluctance, he placed in the window of the shop a hastily scribbled notice stating that he was 'Closed Due To Bereavement', this causing me, by simple recourse to my presence before them, the considerable embarrassment of days thereafter spent earnestly reassuring everyone in the Lane that I hadn't, in fact, quite recently passed away. And during the brief and ugly . . . well, what might one call it . . . ? Ceremony? No, I think not: hardly that . . . anyway, it rained. I had known that it would. Levertons had conjured up for us a priest, from whatever place it is that would appear to be brimful with clerics who are rentable by the hour. This balding, corpulent and, according to the thickness and virtual opacity of his tortoiseshell spectacles, seemingly purblind most holy reverend father – in prior exchange for a five-pound note (this, he rushed to assure us, to be contributed to the coffers of causes most dear to not just Jesus, Joseph and Mary, but all of the other saints as well) – had told us in solemn, evidently specious and I thought quite preposterous tones that our dear and departed sister would be absolved of all her sins that had been committed on this earth, and would at last find peace on the right hand of God. At which point Stan was heard to mutter quite bitterly Oh Christ Alive . . . ! . . . before sinking to his knees into the black and boggy ground, scattering upon the coffin lid first a clod or so of mud, and then a colourful selection of chocolate bars and sweets, each of which once, he was adamant, Jane had greatly favoured. Anthony had seemed quite perfectly detached about the whole affair – as if simply he were patiently awaiting the arrival of a bus. I beamed at him several times in what I hoped was a sort of collaborative encouragement, though simply he looked back at me blankly.

By the time we had all got back to the Lane, it was to a milling scene of truly great ructions – an ambulance and a police car a little way down, with everyone – Miss Jenkins from Moore's, Mr Bona, Edie, Sally from Lindy's . . . my hairdresser Gwendoline from Amy's, she was there, and so was old Mr Levy and the new woman from Marion's . . . even poor Mrs Dent – somehow, and doubtless horribly painfully, even she had managed to hobble along: all in the doorways of their shops, together with animatedly excited clusters of locals and passers-by, all of them chattering eagerly and arching their necks in the direction. Mrs Goodrich I saw standing at the rear doors of the ambulance with her arms very firmly crossed beneath her always rather daunting bosom, this not remotely diminished by a very ample Harris tweed coat – it was rather as if she had been appointed the official custodian of this vehicle, and should anyone think to approach without due and rigorous authorisation, then rest assured she would have a formidable deal to say upon the matter. I have to admit that at first it all did seem rather strange and unnerving to me . . . because the four of us – all dressed befittingly soberly – had been driven to England's Lane in one of Levertons' very glorious, lush, and almost impossibly glossy black Rolls-Royces, the bodywork dappled by a shivering of globular raindrops, and whose wings and running boards I thrillingly had thought to be a true and almost voluptuous delight. And now, of a sudden . . . the talk in the Lane was of nothing but death. It appeared that Mr Effingham, the man in Curios – that rather odd little old furniture and bric-a-brac shop – had less than an hour earlier been found in the customary stooped-over position in his rocking chair, the habitual curved pipe firmly jammed between his teeth, and the newspaper folded to the crossword on his knees before him – all perfectly usual – while seemingly staring vacantly into the cluttered and over-whelmingly brownish and ochre interior, quite as he has done every single weekday ever since I or anyone else can remember . . . although on this particular morning, however, he had ceased to breathe. Everyone agreed that there was consider-able irony in his discovery by a gentleman – a stranger to the area, who had just happened to be driving down the Lane on his way to visit Karl Marx's grave up in Highgate, is what someone later on had been telling me – when an African mask of some sort, I think it was, had glancingly caught his eye in the window. He had parked his car directly outside the shop, entered, asked to know the price of the mask — if mask it truly were — and after rather too much silence being the only forthcoming response, had gently tapped the man's shoulder, whereupon Mr Effingham — very alarmingly, I should imagine — had tumbled immediately to the floor, in a very heavy heap. The irony of course being that no one could recall the last time anyone had so much as thought even to walk through the door of that shop, let alone been desirous of actually making a purchase: none of us ever did understand how Mr Effingham managed to cope with his overheads. It was his heart, apparently: just stopped. Jim said to me — Blimey, dropping like flies: wouldn't bother with the Christmas party if I was you, Mill — this rate, won't be nobody about left to bleeding come to it. I considered the remark quite typically gross and insensitive . . . though, I have to confess, not utterly devoid of a fairly grim humour. It did not altogether surprise me that tacitly I had granted him this modicum of indulgence — for it has become increasingly plain to me quite recently that generally speaking — and initially, I confess, very much to my confusion — I am finding Jim, as each day passes, to be very slightly more, well . . . tolerable, I suppose is more or less what I am meaning. No . . . not what I am meaning at all: I see now immediately that this, of course, very considerably understates what it is that I am feeling . . . for while his countless very awful foibles, discourtesies and irritations still remain quite wholly undiminished — they coalesce, you see, into the very construction of the man — his attitude towards the current quite extraordinary situation in which we two now find ourselves . . . has been nothing short of overwhelming.

When, so gradually, I came fully to realise – and now I can but marvel at how unconscionably slow I was to see it – that just everyone in the Lane and doubtless beyond was thoroughly aware of at least the bones, if not the fleshed-out actuality, of my erstwhile relationship with Jonathan Barton . . . well then of course I was compelled to come to terms also with the inescapable fact that Jim, despite his determinedly ostrich-like manner, his proudly stubborn insularity . . . that Jim, well – he must know too. And – being Jim – he had not said so much as one single word upon the matter. And I really do believe, you know . . . that did I not find myself in this physically altered, new, and glorious circumstance, that I should certainly and for ever have maintained a parallel silence. For it is so often the way, I find: to insistently ignore quite implacably any little discomfort, a fleeting pain, a passing concern – to quell them, to deny them space to grow nor air to breathe, before quite coldly snuffing them out . . . it is more often than not quite wondrously effective: because after time, as well we know, all things must pass. As will my own much garlanded scandal: the brand will become less furious, though of course the very faintest scar will forever be upon me. But yes – my crime, if crime it truly were, will be superseded by the next great thing that comes around: before me there was the advent of the negroes; the suicide of Jane and the death of Mr Effingham can do me little harm.

I still do though feel so very foolish in imagining that all that might have reached the ears of Jim were Mrs Goodrich's mistaken and perfectly ludicrous assumptions concerning myself and Stan. Stan . . . ! I ask you . . . ! While all that time, the I suppose quite lurid reality had long been common knowledge. Rather interestingly, none has rushed to judge nor spurn me, which in turn has made me wonder. In the eyes of some women, I do detect the very outer edge of not maybe quite contempt, but certainly the mark of their own superiority – and at the edges of their lips, a hesitation that has all the makings of a sneer to come (while in Mrs Goodrich, both are open, animated, and quite unashamed). And all this has led me to contemplation. Must some women wonder what such a thing can be like . . . ? The illicit extramarital affair. Can others be remembering their own past indiscretion? Revelling in the memories of its blood-heat? And might not one or two secret liaisons yet be vibrant and alive? Or am I really the only woman in London throughout the whole of the nineteen-fifties to have done such a thing? Are women simply divided into those whose dalliances have been cruelly and shamingly exposed . . . and those others who thus far have eluded detection, camouflaged by the walls of the truly innocent, and so remaining for the present tightly swaddled within the impregnable warmth of decency? And during those days when my violated eye had shifted in shades from indigo to crimson before mercifully fading into a mild tangerine, how enthusiastic had been the debate over the identity of the inflictor? Could it have been the outcome of passion

463

from the virile lover? Or merely impotent recrimination from the woman's outraged and cuckolded husband, momentarily moved to violence? With the aid of such tinder, rumour is readily inflamed. And do not people so love to gorge on the burst of such bittersweet juice from the one and only forbidden fruit? Whereas in reality, of course, Jonathan . . . I always found to be gentle almost to the point of femininity – and Jim, not once has he ever raised a hand to me: a claim, I suspect, that few wives might honestly make. And for some reason I still am struggling to explain, I never did anticipate a confrontation with . . . you know . . . Mrs Barton. His wife. I never envisaged such a scene, and nor has it manifested. But all of this – and even that – is no more than periphery. There remained just the one matter that was truly of the essence – and, painful though it would be for him, it was Jim I had now to talk to. I very much had to. He and no one other. And he sensed it, I could tell. He would hurriedly pass through a room with shoulders hunched, as if to deflect the sudden swooping down of me, or at least be more prepared for when I did it. He did not know, you see, what next I had to tell him: nor did he want to. Yes yes – I was well aware of all of that: but still, though . . . but still, though . . . it simply had to be done.

'Jim . . . don't go out just yet. You know I've been wanting to talk to you . . .'

'Yeh well – just were thinking I'll stretch my legs a little bit . . .'

'Well you can do, Jim – but afterwards, yes? It won't take

464

long. Not long. It has to be now Jim, because there just isn't any other time, is there? Either you're in the shop or you're going down to the pub – or else Paul is still up and about. And it shouldn't be really, but it does seem even harder now that Anthony is here, and everything . . .'

'How long he staying? I ain't saying I mind, nor nothing. Just asking.'

'Well – it's quite hard to know. Not too long, I don't suppose. But the doctor did say that Stan has to have a complete rest. Utter exhaustion, apparently. I think he has undergone what they term a "breakdown", I think that's what it is. Like a motor car, I suppose: needs an overhaul. That would explain why he's been behaving really very oddly. And sometimes they just, you know – snap out of it. And other times, well . . . it can take rather a while, I gather. But he's no trouble, is he? Anthony. Poor little mite. I can't imagine all that can be going through his mind. All of a sudden, his mother's dead . . . his father's gone away. It must be so dreadfully upsetting and confusing for him. Mustn't it? Don't you think? I've tried to talk to him, but he doesn't seem to be very communicative. Responsive, you know? I've asked Paul what he talks about, and he says he's just like he always was. Well I don't know what to think, if that's the case. Because bottling it all up . . . well that can't be a good thing either, can it? Oh dear. Anyway – we'll do anything we can for him, obviously. I just have to remember about all his various ointments, and everything . . . I think I've got the hang of putting those awful things on to him, now . . .'

'He won't be too happy about the shop, will he? Old Stan. I should bleeding think not. Week off of Christmas time, and he gone and shut the bloody sweetshop! Dear oh dear. Were me, I cut my throat. And up the Washington, they got a penny a packet extra on your Senior Service: couple days, you down a tanner. I says to Reg there – it only criminal, what you doing: taking advantage. He just laugh . . .'

'It is awful about the shop – but well, it's hardly Stan's fault, is it? Didn't plan to go a bit loopy. Last thing in the world he wanted, I'm sure. Sally has said she can sometimes leave somebody else in Lindy's and go round to help him out a bit. But honestly, from what I've seen of the way she carries on, I'm not too convinced that it's altogether a good idea. When Stan comes back, he might take one look at everything she's done to his shop, turn right round and go straight back to the hospital. I suppose I might be able to do the odd after-noon . . . it's so awful to think of him losing the seasonal trade – and all those special Christmas lines, selection boxes and stockings and so on: not going to be much good to him in January, are they?'

'Got enough on your plate, ain't you? What with this party what you getting up. And now another kid to think about, and all . . .'

'Another . . . kid . . . ? What do you mean, Jim . . . ?'

'Well – you know. Anthony . . .'

'Oh yes. Yes I see. Jim – look, sit down, won't you? Shall I fetch you a glass of beer?'

'Well . . . it like I say – were going to go and stretch my legs, sort of style . . .'

'After, Jim. After. You just sit there. I'll get you a nice bottle of Bass from the refrigerator – or do you prefer one from under the stairs? Why don't you light up a cigarette, yes? Ah – you already have. All right, then. Fine. Well you just sit tight in here, Jim. Back in just a minute. And then we can talk.'

Yeh. Talk. That's what I bloody afraid of. On account of I know she been wanting to – busting to, she been. Women, that what they always doing – yakking away. Can't just belt up about it. And after all of the talk – what you got? Ay? What you got? You ain't got nothing, has you? Nah – you just ain't got nothing.

'There we are, Jim. I've brought you the less cool one, I hope that's right? I know how you say they can get too gassy when they're overchilled. Is it all right? Oh good. Good. That's good. Oh Jim – the button on your cardigan . . .'

'What about it . . . ?'

'Well – it's not there, is it? Have you got it? Do you know when you lost it?'

'Never knowed I lost it. Look – sod the bleeding button . . .'

'Well you can't go round with a cardigan with a button missing, can you? If it's lost, I can probably find a match for it in John Barnes. They do have quite a remarkable range.'

'Yeh. So that's all right then, ain't it? And so – well? Come on, Mill. You say you want to talk – so bleeding talk. I here now, ain't I? You want me to stop in, and I done it. So give it me. What you want to say?'

'Yes . . . yes, you're perfectly right, Jim. It's silly of me. I have been wanting to talk to you – wanted to for ages. And now that it's come to it . . . I don't know quite how to . . . um . . .'

'How to what? What you on about? Ay?'

'Well, Jim . . . it's rather hard. And I don't know quite how you will react. Well – the truth is, of course, I don't at all know how you're going to react. What you might think of me. Worse, even worse, than you already do. But anyway – the truth of the matter is, Jim . . . and it is all right then, is it? Yes? The beer . . . ?'

'Gordon Bennett . . . ! Never mind the bloody beer. Just get on with it . . .'

'Yes. Right. Well the bald fact is, Jim, that I'm . . . I'm, um – pregnant, Jim. I'm going to have a baby. Yes. There. Now I've said it. I'm going to have a baby . . . yes. And that's what I wanted to tell you. Jim . . . ? Jim . . . ? Did you hear what I said, Jim . . . ? I said . . .'

'I heard what you said. That it?'

'Is that . . . it . . . ? Well – that's enough, isn't it?'

'Yeh. It's enough. But I knowed that. Knowed that a long time.'

'You . . . *knew*? But you never said anything! How did you know, Jim? How on earth *could* you . . . ?'

'Seed my old Mum like it often enough. All what been

wrong with you. All with the stomach, and that. Yeh – I knowed. I knowed it.'

'Well . . . well . . . I don't know what to say . . . I'm so . . . I'm just so – surprised. And – relieved, I think. Ought I to be relieved, Jim?'

'Don't know what you mean. Happy – that what you ought to be. What you always wanted, ain't it? Kid of your own. What you always wanted. And now you got it. So now you's all right. Ain't you?'

'And . . . you don't mind . . . ? No – sorry, Jim. Stupid thing to say. Of course – of course you do. Of course you mind. Sorry – so sorry. What an absolutely frightful thing to say. What was I thinking of? Oh please do forgive me. It's just that . . . well, I don't want you to . . . hate me, Jim. Or the baby. I don't think I could bear it, you see. If you did that . . .'

'Right. So . . . you want to stop with me then, yeh . . . ?'

'I . . . yes. Yes I do, Jim. I honestly do. If you'll have me . . .'

'And . . . that ain't just on account of he pushing off, then?'

'Who . . . ?'

'You knows bloody well who . . .'

'Yes. Sorry, Jim. I actually wasn't aware of that . . . but I'm pleased. If that is the case, then I'm pleased. Very pleased.'

'I see. Right. Got it. Well I don't hate you, Mill. Won't never hate you. Can't, can I? Loves you, I does. Always I done that. Always loved you, Mill. And I bleeding always will. As to the kid . . . well – I done all right by Pauly, my way of thinking. So I don't see how I can't be doing it again. What you want, ain't it? As to having you, well – can't be doing without you, gel. Right lucky to have you. Always were. That's all I ever does it for. Shop. All of it. On account of I loves you, Mill . . . I loves you . . .'

My throat was stopped – I was close to strangulation. My heart was huge within me, the scattering of my brain quite utterly dizzied. I exhaled, once and so sharply, and was panting now from I think it must have been shock, and a nearly delirious gratitude: the sobbing which I felt just launching from my eyes, and tumbling away so freely, my lips an uncontrollable jumble. I just gazed at the man, and was gasping. I simply could not speak. And then on an unthinkable impulse, I rushed towards him and fell to my knees – held his hand, and kissed it with tenderness. I looked up into his wearied face that held for me no expression – a face that I had not even seen, and for so very many years. His lips were so firmly compressed, and in each of his eyes there trembled unfathomable tears.

It's great now it's the holidays and everything, but they did go and dole out piles of prep just like I knew they would because they always do. Madman Downes gave us the most because he's a stupid pig. And I know what Amanda said about getting it all done in the first weekend but I can't do that. Well – could, I suppose, but I'm not going to. It's the party today where everyone from the Lane goes which I always say to Auntie Milly I hate because it's all full of old people but I quite like it really – and there are children going, Amanda's going and other people from the council schools who she doesn't like because they're common – and Anthony, he'll be there and everything. I've been trying to be decent to Anthony, but it's quite hard because he doesn't really talk much any more. I thought it was because his mummy died but he says it isn't because he didn't ever see her anyway. And I said well what's wrong then, Anthony? Is it because you're living with us? Don't you like it? Your dad won't be away very long, that's what Auntie Milly told me. But don't you like it? Living here with us? I like it, living here. Don't you? What's wrong with it? And he said it isn't that – that he does quite like it, living here, and he really likes my Auntie Milly because everybody does and what she cooks for us and especially sausages and fish fingers and sometimes chicken which is best of all and he doesn't even mind Uncle Jim which is really amazing because I do. Aunt Milly, she's been quite nice to him lately, Uncle Jim – and I don't know why or anything, because he's just disgusting, like he always is. I hope she stops. I really do. Anyway I said so what's wrong then, Anthony? Aren't you looking forward to Christmas? Because I jolly am, I can jolly well tell you that. There's this tank I saw in Toys Toys Toys and it's really great because you put a battery in it like you do with a torch and it actually moves on these rubber sort of tracks which have got a special name but I can't remember what it is, and all these sparks come out of the gun bit and it turns around. I've told Auntie Milly about it heaps of times but I don't know if she's got it for me because it's forty-two-and-six which is very expensive I know, but it's really really great. That's what I really want but there'll be lots of other stuff too and some of it will be good but not things like V-necks which she knits and hankies and things. But I'll get the *Beano Book* and the *Dandy Book* because I always do and sometimes the *Topper* and the *Beezer* as well and I've said I want *Take Jennings for Instance* which is new so they won't have it in the library but we're going to the library now for the party so I can check but I don't think so. And I get a stocking from Santa which I know isn't really from Santa but it's jolly nice to get, and on television there's been all these commercials with Santa in and he looks really fat and kind and nice with his beard and everything and he makes me feel all excited and the commercials are only for pretty rotten things like Hoovers and Brylcreem and Woolworth's but he always looks really nice even if he's only black-and-white and not all red like you see on Christmas cards and things. I know he doesn't really exist, but maybe he does because nobody really knows.

And Anthony said he is looking forward to Christmas but he doesn't know if he'll get any presents because his dad's in a hospital somewhere but he knows where the spare key to the stockroom is so he says he can get us a Cadbury's Selection Box each – and the seven-and-six big one as well – and I said all this to Auntie Milly and she said that she was quite sure that Santa wouldn't forget him, which I told Anthony but he didn't say anything. And then I said can you get a Cadbury's

Selection Box which I can give to Amanda as well because all I've got for her is a slide for her hair with a ladybird on, but he didn't answer. And so I said it again and he still didn't answer and then I saw he was all sort of blubbing, like a little baby. So I said what's wrong now, Anthony? Why are you blubbing like a little baby? And I didn't expect him to answer me or anything, but he goes and says Amanda, and I go well what about Amanda? What's she got to do with you? And he says Nothing – she's got nothing to do with me at all and then he goes on crying which was pretty embarrassing actually and it's just as well we were at home and not at school because people like Robbins and Marshall and Hirschovitz would have tied him on to the pegs in the changing room and pelted him with inky blotch or something until he packed it in and if he didn't they would've poured water into his indoor shoes which they did to Handley the term before last.

Just thinking of Amanda, though – it's all been just so great with her lately, but I'm really really sad and it's the only thing that's really rotten. Because we'd been on the Hill again and she'd let me touch her and everything and she kissed me and everything and I get this really funny feeling when she touches me back on my thing and everything that I don't get when I go and do it myself because I tried it and it doesn't work. And then she told me that her dad had told her that soon, some time in the new year, they were all going to go away and I said what do you mean, Amanda? For a holiday? Is that what you mean? Why aren't you going in the summer because it'll be beastly and freezing in the new year because it always is and she said no Paul, not for a holiday – we're going away for good. Moving. Don't know where. And we're selling the shop and everything. And I said oh no that's terrible – but what about your school? And she said she didn't know. And I said well maybe you're not moving far away – like only up to John Barnes or something and he can be a butcher in there, your dad. And she said she didn't know. And so I told Auntie Milly and said I was really really sad and she said she was sad too. And I said but even if she does go away, Auntie Milly, I still will see her again won't I? And she said of course you will Paul. And I said well that's good Auntie Milly because I want to marry her, you see. Not yet obviously because I'm still going to school but when I do I've got to know where she is, got to have her address, haven't I? And she said I would. She said I would. And I'd already decided about that before, about marrying Amanda, because she's pretty and really nice and I'm obviously not ever going to marry Elizabeth Taylor because she's a film star which you're never going to meet in England's Lane because nothing exciting ever happens in England's Lane because everyone in it's so stupid and boring, and anyway she's probably quite old. Anyway – I'm going to see her now at the party – Amanda, obviously, not Elizabeth Taylor – and I'm really looking forward to that. She said she'd got a new dress for it with what she says has lilac ribbons on it and I bet she'll look really smashing in it. But still you know I don't get what Anthony's got to cry about. He doesn't even know Amanda.

'Paul . . . ! Paul . . . can you hear me . . . ? I'm downstairs . . .'

'Yes, Auntie Milly . . . ?'

'I'm going off now to the library, Paul. Got to see to all the little finishing touches before everybody starts to arrive. Oh heavens – do you know I've been there twice this morning already? Completely exhausted. One of the trestle tables that Mr Bona lent to us, yes . . . ? Chose to collapse just as Edie had put all the plates on to it. Can you believe it? Most of them were those Bakelite ones from Lindy's, thank the heavens, so there wasn't too much breakage. So anyway – can you and Anthony come along in about an hour, then? An hour, yes Paul? You can come with your Uncle Jim if you want . . . although he might be popping in somewhere else first, of course . . .'

'Yes. Washington. No – I'll just come with Anthony.'

'Right you are, then. And have you got your bow on? Do you need any help with it? My goodness – you're going to be quite the masher.'

'Of course I don't need any help with it. It's only clip-on. What's a masher?'

'A very handsome young man – that's what a masher is. All right Paul, my sweet. See you very soon, then.'

That's if I last that long: oh my Lord, I just can't tell you how over the last few days I honestly have come within an inch of being run off my feet . . . ! It's perfectly extraordinary – no matter how carefully, how very diligently you try to plan the timing of everything, it all just seems to come at you at once. This party – and I do so hope that it all goes well – yes this party, rather surprisingly, has proved to be the very least of my burdens. But then of course I have been so terribly lucky in having all of the girls helping me out – we've all mucked in together – and Edie and Gwendoline in particular: I honestly couldn't have managed it without them. And I did so laugh when Edie this morning so very eagerly volunteered to put up the paper chains: I think she felt that she just had to be certain they'd be there! The lad who works for Mr Levy, he'd already rolled across Mrs Dent's piano, and then he carried over two of the tallest stepladders that Jim had in the shop – and goodness, though: I didn't at all envy Edie being up there. It literally made me shiver just to look at her – because I've never been awfully good at heights, you know – and Eunice, she used to taunt and tease me quite mercilessly when we were little. At home, I couldn't even bear to look out of the attic window, though she forever was making me do it – and then she'd be urging me to climb up the big old conker tree we had in the garden, and she knew I just couldn't: it was all very naughty of her. In later years, we laughed about it all, of course . . .

And Doreen – she's been in the library all morning with her little Dansette and records and seemingly reams of sheet music . . . and also her very sallow and unsmiling young man – he it is who works in Woolworth's and is, she simperingly told me, called Derek. His guitar I have to say is rather beautiful – bright shiny red with lots of chromium detailing, rather reminiscent of those terribly long and swish American automobiles looking rather like spaceships that you see at the pictures. Derek, by contrast, is very drab indeed – dressed from head to toe in black, and possessing the dead air of a bloodless vampire. We can but hope that his alarming amplifier doesn't fuse the lights. The boy with the drums seems to be an altogether jollier sort of person, but the noise he was making during what he was pleased to term a 'tune-up' was quite perfectly dreadful, and horribly loud. I have told Doreen to limit the amount of time the group is actually playing because this room – already it's resounding with echo, and any conversation will be a complete impossibility.

Anyway – not long now till the off, and all is looking reasonably festive, I think. And it's just so wonderfully warm in here! All the radiators, you see (and gosh – what utter bliss it must be to have this central heating: just imagine to be rid of the freezing bedroom and the draughty hallway!). The tables, they have been pushed down to the far end – and when I saw them I did feel so terribly foolish because it had utterly escaped me that the library would of course be full of tables, but by then I'd already asked Mr Bona to lend us those trestles he uses in the shop, and so then I thought I had to go ahead and use them because he'd been to such a beast of an amount of trouble to clear them of all his boxes and barrels and everything, and I felt that if I didn't he could easily be offended. The chairs have been placed in little groups around the edges, and dear Mrs Jenkins from Moore's has in addition to the balloons also given us quite a few lengths of coloured crepe paper which I have draped in front of several of the bookcases, and Edie is attaching to them a series of stars and snowflakes that she has cut from a roll of cooking foil from the Dairies: the stars, yes they're really quite nice, though the snowflakes do not in the least resemble any snowflake I have ever seen, though of course I've said nothing to Edie. And those balloons – I had completely forgotten to ask Jim to blow them up (it was on my list, so I don't know how I came to overlook it) and so this very dingy Derek person is attending to them now: he looks so very pale and puny, you know, that the effort may very well do for him, which could easily be a blessing in disguise.

The keg of beer is looking horribly huge, the worry being that I have no doubt whatever that all the men will see it off with ease. Also on the table there, thanks to Victoria Wine, I can see whisky – two bottles of that – gin, cherry brandy, sherry and something obviously foreign and the brightest yellow that I am told is called . . . I think it is advocate: I do hope no rowdiness results. And Mr Levy has given us such a lovely tree – oh the smell! It is quite perfectly divine! – and both Miss and Mrs Jenkins have all the morning been very busy decorating it, and extremely beautifully too. It's so much larger than the really rather weeny little thing that late last night I finally got around to putting up in the living room, just to the side of the television set. And it's really so strange

– each year when I get out the old shoebox, yet one more little glass ornament is always broken – I just can't understand it because I always so very carefully fold them into tissue and then newspaper; I think I might this year have to buy one or two more, because it does look rather gappy. Usually I eke out the baubles with these little stacks of miniature chocolate bars each in a differently coloured shiny paper, and hanging from a little bow: we all eat them all up on Boxing Day. I used to buy them from Stan, but he didn't get them in this year. Paul loves it though, our little tree – and I've already wrapped this blessed tank that he's been on and on at me for weeks on end to buy for him. Fearfully expensive for what it is – it's only plastic, after all – but his heart was so set on it, little lamb. I'll put it beneath the tree this evening, but of course I shan't let on to him what it is. He loves his surprises on Christmas morning, and yet he's forever pleading with me to tell him what is in each and every one of the packages, silly little boy: by Christmas Eve, he's just so ridiculously excited . . . and I do adore it, to see it in his eyes. Anyway, I'll say to him it's something dreadfully dull such as socks, or to do with school. And although it seems that I've been running myself ragged over all these preparations at home, if I am being perfectly honest I do actually feel quite positively charged with energy: I actually am feeling it pulsing through me – it sometimes is almost as though I were lit up from within. Doctor McAuley, he told me the day before yesterday when I went to him for my check-up that this can often be the way, following all the pain and nausea that I was seemingly endlessly having to endure: thank the Lord all that's behind me. It did make me smile though when earlier this morning Edie said to me that I was looking 'radiant' – that was her actual word – because apart from Jim, I haven't told a soul. I suppose though as the new year progresses – 1960! I still simply can't get used to the sound of it – then things will begin to be quite apparent, but until such time I'd far rather keep quiet about it. My little secret. Big secret. And growing within me all the time . . . ! Can barely believe it – have to keep pinching myself. I haven't quite decided when to tell Paul . . . possibly leave it until he asks me why suddenly I'm becoming so horribly fat! Difficult to project quite how he might feel about it all. He'll just have to take a little time to get used to the idea, I suppose. Well – we all will.

And apart from this tank affair – and I do hope it isn't just a nine-day wonder, because it really did cost a small fortune: the battery alone was seven-and-six and weighs an absolute ton – I've also got for Paul his annuals and a handsome wooden jigsaw of HMS *Victory*, which I think he might like. And a drum of rubber building blocks called Minibrix that caught my eye while I was in Selfridge's: rather clever – they connect, you see, but then you can take them all apart afterwards and build something else entirely; and it's got roofs, you know, and little doors and windows – quite sweet. For his stocking there's a Matchbox car I know he hasn't got – I do hope he does still like them though, because I haven't seen him playing with them for simply ages – and a yo-yo, a multi-coloured biro that I saw in Smith's, a bag of gold chocolate coins, the usual white sugar mouse with pink eyes and his little stringy tail . . . and of course a clementine for the toe. And I've had to do similar for poor little Anthony: well I had to, didn't I? Though I was quite at a loss as to what I might buy him for his primary present: there I was in Selfridge's, surrounded by the bewildering mayhem that was the toy department, and my mind a complete and utter blank. I almost – I can't even say it! – I almost settled for a football and two little net goal-posts, and then I was just gasping in wonder at myself: oh my goodness, Milly – what in heaven's name are you *thinking* of . . . ?! I was covered in shame. So in the end I got him another jigsaw – this one of a racing car, so afterwards the two of them can swap about – and a rotating globe on a wooden stand. And the *Beezer* and *Topper* books. Haven't a clue as to whether he'll actually like any of it – but what was I to do? I don't know the boy, do I? And I couldn't ask Stan, could I? (and anyway – he's not allowed visitors: I do hope he's not terribly ill). There was such an endless queue for Santa's grotto – it went all the way out and around the shoe department and well into sporting goods – that I did feel rather relieved that this year I hadn't brought Paul along with me. He did so love it last time, though: Uncle Holly is his favourite, and he cherishes all the badges he's given him, over the years. And after all of that I was in the drizzle of Oxford Street feeling like a beast of burden and waiting for the bus, when I saw this stall on the pavement selling rolls of Christmas wrapping paper at very considerably less than in John Barnes and Smith's or even in Woolworth's, but when I got them home I was perfectly disgusted to discover that each of the sheets was virtually transparent . . . ! Great heavens – what do they imagine to be the point of decorative wrapping paper . . . ? You'd have to cover something in three or four sheets, or else there would be no surprise at all. So now I've simply spread them all across Mr Bona's trestle tables in the library to jolly them up a little bit, and ended up paying really rather a lot for some admittedly very good-quality rolls from John Barnes – holly, robins and Santa: all very traditional – and while I was there, I ordered our turkey. Hen bird – sweeter meat, I always find; usually I get it in the Lane, of course. I haven't had the time this year to knit for Paul a nice and Christmassy V-neck, but I did buy a new pattern and five balls of royal blue and primrose two-ply, so I'll have something bright for him at Easter. I daresay I shall be knitting other little tiny things too – oh what unimaginable excitement . . . ! And I know I shouldn't have, but I also got for myself one-and-a-half yards of nigger-brown corduroy which I think might make up into quite a pleasing little bolero: handy for the spring. It did make me remember though with a flood of guilt that I haven't so much as even begun on my winter tweed coat, and I've had the material for positively months. Which is why I'm still shivering in this old thing.

And Jim's stocking – because I do always make one up for

him, isn't it perfectly silly? – that's nearly done now too. I've got the socks and hankies (John Barnes) and a pack of playing cards which he probably will never use but they'd got on the backs a picture of a budgerigar which does look a little bit like Cyril, and you know how you can get quite desperate for any new little ideas, and they were only half-a-crown. But I haven't yet been able to buy the special Christmas box of a hundred Senior Service that I always get for him because, well – Stan isn't open, of course: but Sally has just told me that she's going to be there in the morning, so I can get them then (that is if she hasn't yet pulverised the entire stock of the shop). And then I'll round it off with the customary clementine. Normally I'll trim the stockings with little sprigs of berried holly that I cut from this great and overgrown thicket of it that I discovered on the Heath – but this year, honestly, I just haven't had a moment to get up there. I used so much to enjoy those rambles on the Heath – and Hampstead Village too: rather smarter than England's Lane and so full of charm, if occasionally just a little bit too, um . . . I think they call it bohemian, don't they? You do see some terribly intense young men and women wearing heavily framed spectacles and duffel coats, all striding about rather purposefully and boldly brandishing Penguin books as if they were weapons. I sometimes would sit outside The Coffee Cup in the High Street, watching the world go by and feeling dreadfully fuddy-duddy for only drinking tea.

The frock I am wearing for the party is quite a nice navy

shantung – full skirt, and a neat little Peter Pan collar of plum velvet, with cuffs of the same material at the three-quarter sleeves: soon, I expect, I shan't be able to get into it, for the belted waist is really rather nipped-in. It was the very last thing I ever acquired from the beastly tallyman, and I've never before worn it. I shall not see him again, that very vulgar and abusive little man – now that is a Christmas present, if ever there was one! I must be very dull, you know, for it had taken me rather a long while to comprehend that of course it is not the intention of such people that ever one should be rid of the shadow of debt – and should you come to approach such a state, well then you are first cajoled and subsequently bullied into pledging more and yet more in order to maintain a deliberately unsupportable level of liability. So upon the last occasion that he called – having firmly refused to allow him even to open his case of samples, much to his evident disgruntlement – I asked him quite coldly to write upon a piece of paper the entire extent of my accumulated folly. I tried not to intake my breath too audibly as I focused upon the figure, and then – I hope with a steady hand – I paid the man in full, and insisted upon a stamped and dated receipt. He was shocked – I imagine he has never before encountered such behaviour. His greedy pleasure in handling the notes was tempered by the realisation that the matter was at an end: that I was free of him for good.

And yes, it had pained me . . . to part with the necklace and earring set that once had belonged to my mother, and whose pearls and tiny emeralds Eunice had carried off to such very great effect. But they were hardly my style – and wherever should I have worn them? The Westminster Bank? John Barnes? The Dairies . . . ? I hardly think so. There is an evil little shop in Chalk Farm where such covert transactions may be carried out – Jim, he has termed it in the past 'the nest of Yids' – and I can only hope that the price obtained from the bent-over and somehow deplorable man there was a reasonably fair one. I anyway accepted it without demur, so eager was I by then to be away from the place. As he scooped in eagerly the jewellery and paid me quickly, however, I suspected that I had been rooked. Oh well – no matter. For now I have cast off the unimaginable weight of the millstone of debt – and I feel quite severed too from the being who was unstoppably propelled into the spiral of vanity and irresponsibility that so very nearly was my undoing. And with the money I had left over I have not just paid for all of Paul's and Anthony's presents, but also from John Barnes I bought a very smart blazer for Jim: brass buttons and a paisley lining – he has never possessed such a thing, and I gave it to him this morning. Selfish of me in one way – I just couldn't have him coming to the party in that perfectly hideous old jacket which he habitually wears. And I also gave him a tie – dark blue to tone with the blazer, and a fetching diagonal stripe in a paler blue and almost a saffron yellow. With his best white shirt which I've freshly ironed for him, he ought to be fairly presentable: while he's sitting down, at least – for his trousers, well . . .

they surpass all understanding. And I rounded off my Christmas spree with a gift box of Bronnley Lemon bath cubes and talcum for Edie, and for Gwendoline I bought from Moore's a Basildon Bond writing set – pad, envelopes, notelets and blotting paper in a rather attractive deep-green leatherette case with a zip fastener: the rather well fitted-out interior incorporates a loop that will happily accommodate a fountain pen, and also little pockets for stamps and space for an eraser. I feel sure she will appreciate it because she corresponds quite regularly with her two sisters in Bournemouth, as well as her cousin who is, I believe, somewhere in the north.

The staff of the library are loitering in clusters of twos and threes, all seemingly intent upon the parquet floor and eating rather a lot of cheese footballs. They appear either to be rather old ladies in twinsets and sensible lace-up shoes that survived the very worst that the Blitz could throw at them – their white hair in buns, and bristling with grips – or else lanky and very shy young men, generally ugly and apparently quite mortifyingly sincere, who are glancing rather longingly at the bottles of cheer being currently opened by that newish young lady from Victoria Wine. And oh look . . . Mr and Mrs Bona have arrived. And yes I am aware that their real name is in fact, um . . . what is it again? Schmidt, I think – but still I know I'll always think of them as Mr and Mrs Bona: silly, isn't it? And dear old Mr Levy is doing his pitiable best to usher in Mrs Dent upon his arm, look . . . with her feet turned in almost on to their very edges, and wearing a pair of what appear to be the most extraordinary sort of grotesquely misshapen and patent bootees, poor thing – and Mr Levy, he's none too steady himself. Mr Lawrence the newsagent – clearly relieved that this year his papers and magazines are quite safe from damage. Edie – and she'll be so annoyed with herself once she realises she has forgotten to take off her pinny – with Gwendoline, and having a good old natter: never stop chattering, those two, once they get together. Miss Jenkins handing a small glass of sherry to Mrs Jenkins who, following her exertions with the decorations, is enjoying a much-deserved rest in an armchair: they smile to each other so sweetly. Sally proudly standing sentry by her large and thickly iced Christmas cake with its forest of little fir trees, its top-hatted snowmen with red scarves and black buttons . . . while valiantly resisting devouring it whole. Oh and here's my Paul . . . ! Aaah . . . ! He does look nice, doesn't he? Makes me so proud. And little Anthony – his usual quite eager, though unreadable expression, and already looking around for a chair and somewhere to prop his crutches, little fellow. Well . . . all right then, Milly – I rather think that finally the party is getting under way. And now . . . oh yes – in she strides, in the manner of a general come to inspect the regiment: Mrs Goodrich, alone and unconquerable – for I don't think Mr Goodrich ever is actually permitted to leave the house – and I don't know if that was intended to be a smile of greeting towards me, but certainly I can see in it only the customary superior and contemptuous disdain: I think it can be the only way she obtains her pleasures. Doreen has put on some sort of a record, but it's awfully tinny and distant: Lord, though – let's just wait until the group strikes up . . . ! That'll give Mrs Goodrich something fresh to deplore. And now here's Reg from the Washington, and that unspeakable Charlie person: I don't think I've ever seen him when he's not drunk – quite as he is now – and Lord, he's only just arrived . . . ! Straight across to the Bass and whisky, of course. And so therefore Jim, I imagine, can hardly be far behind. Oh yes – here he comes now . . . oh my heavens, and at the same time as one of the negroes as well: Kelso, his name is, which I only quite recently discovered – he's the nice one, the one with the irrepressible smile . . . lots of pink gums, and simply acres of teeth. The other (who isn't here, for certainly you could hardly miss him if he were), he is called Obi, and I rather think everyone is terribly fearful of him. Children in particular, I have heard, will cross the road in order to avoid him – and I do have to agree that his hooded eyes, his scowling presence and highly intimidating bearing do come to rather epitomise the cannibal demon of legend, who gorges upon innocents and missionaries who hoped for something better. And now I can hear Jim's voice booming . . . something about Cadbury's Cocoa, and although dear Kelso appears to be thoroughly happy about it, more than that I truly do not care to know. And oh my heavens . . . ! Oh really! Oh no! That is just too bad of him . . . ! Jim – he is actually wearing his perfectly hideous old jacket . . . ! After all my trouble and expense – I simply can't believe it. Oh really – I just give up. What on earth can be *wrong* with the man . . . ?

Oh look: young Amanda. How very devastatingly pretty she is, and what a beautiful little dress. Paul, he will just be so very desperately sad when eventually she . . . when eventually they . . . leave England's Lane. And along comes Paul now – eyes so bright, ignoring me completely and practically running towards her. While standing just behind and a little away from Amanda . . . there is her father. I have been striving not to wonder whether he would come, while ruthlessly smothering all anticipation. And now that he is here . . . gaiety has abandoned me, and I deeply resent the kick to my heart.

I see myself now to be the deserving victim of my own complacency: I should have been alive to the prick of unease from the very first moment when I began to feel easy. For how many years in this accursed little street have I been guarded, watchful – judicious and justifiably apprehensive? How could I have failed to be aware of the rinsing of my wisdom away into a sluice? To have been so foolish as to have imagined that at last my sentence had been served, my ponderous punishment finally to be up? For this has been a day . . . just this one day has indeed proved to be fateful.

Though it began, as all the dull, wondrous or very most terrible days habitually will, quite perfectly normally. For never do we know. Here is at once the single most thrilling and quite chillingly terrifying factor of life: never do we know.

Why we continue, of course – hoping in earnest that bad will never come, aspiring the while to splendour. Always I recall a small and indistinct photograph which long ago I happened upon in a newspaper: the sodden and deadweight body of a drowned man, lugged by frogmen from the frozen lake beneath whose icy waters he had perished in his doubtless noble, though ultimately quite laughably stupid attempt to rescue a stranger's mongrel. I should have thought nothing of it, save for a detail that abides within me for ever: the watch. His wrists were dangling like two bent-over and sappy stems, and from one there glinted in the weak winter sunlight the bezel of his watch. His watch, which that very morning – once he had dressed, attended to his toilet, breakfasted . . . conceivably bestowed a kiss upon a loved one . . . he had strapped on to himself, quite as always he had done – though, unwittingly, for the very last time ever. Never do we know, you see. We must of course assume that any given dinner date, say . . . a summer holiday . . . Christmas itself . . . we must, we are compelled to assume that every such event actually will take place, and quite as anticipated, or else we might go mad. Because while knowing would derange us, unknowing can be quite as destabilising. We collaborate in our conviction that a thing is certain, though all is based upon prayer and an unthinking presumption. Gamblers revel in the wanton caprice of the rolling die, while the rest of us are forced unwillingly to play, having not the slightest notion even of so much as the nature of the game. Though as to its outcome, our instinct is true:

we lose. Of course. No matter the twists along the way — setback followed by jubilation, fluke superseded by flashes of art, pitfall, windfall, the inevitable tumbles and then such breathtaking escalation . . . in the end, we lose: every life can end only in failure, because at base it is all we have, it is all we are . . . and then it disappears. For some — possibly the fortunate few — that end will come with literal death. For such as myself, it arrives of a sudden, and devastatingly, when still there remains simply an eternity of nothingness, spiked by terror, all of which yet I somehow must endure.

Of course I had not wished even momentarily to be seen at this gaudy little annual beanfeast: a few I have attended briefly, while others I have successfully circumvented by means of some or other only very vaguely plausible pretext. This year, however, I was quite determined to shun it. I had been premature in informing Fiona that it was my intention that soon we should as a family quit this place (puerile behaviour on my part — I was eager to witness her rapture) and further had failed to caution her not yet to apprise Amanda of any such possibility, for then I knew — children being children — that the Lane would be alive to it in practically no time. So it has proved — and therefore of course I was anxious to side-step all of the horribly inevitable, not to say excruciatingly tedious questioning as to oh why, oh when, oh where . . . prattling, meddling and gossipy empty-headed fools that they all of them are. And then would come the whispered requests for assurance that still my premises will remain as a butcher

– as if I genuinely could give a tinker's damn in hell as to whatever it became, once I was away from it for good. I would sell at the highest price, and once I am gone for all I cared the shop could become anything from a rorty gin palace to a stinking glue factory, by way of a neon and sadomasochistic brothel.

And then also a matter of consideration, of course . . . there was Milly. The idiot child Doreen, simply I could snub . . . but Milly was rather a different concern. For it is not, after all, as if I dislike the woman, you see – oh no, quite to the contrary: I do find her really very personable. And had it been possible for things to have continued in the manner that rather blissfully, if briefly, they hitherto had been conducted . . . well then: all well and good. But alas, never can a simple affair manage to endure upon so agreeably even a keel. For any woman, eventually, she will of course want more – and never is there more – or else the glow of her pleasure must needs be outshone by the sudden and therefore astonishing dazzle that calls itself many things, though seldom is any more than merely bourgeois guilt; or the fear of discovery, and subsequent shame. This was not true of Milly, however – always she was rather better than that – but simply I became wary, just a little bored, and naturally shy of the declamations to come. And so one way or the other, such a thing will wither . . . a truth that never has disturbed me: it is not just the natural way of it, but a welcome detonation – a fond farewell, this quickly succeeded by a warm and cheery hello to something other, and altogether fresh. As, indeed, has been quite the way of it: a charming lady whom I encountered in a coffee bar in St John's Wood High Street – her name is Alicia, which I imagine to be fairly uncommon. She is some or other variety of press editor – features, conceivably – engaged by our local newspaper, the *Hampstead & Highgate Express*; I hardly ever see the thing, though I considered it rude to say so. She is articulate, slyly amusing, strikingly curvaceous and has about her an enticement, an air of curiosity: here is a more than adequate foundation.

But it was Amanda, you see. Fiona, perfectly naturally, had not the slightest intention of gracing this annual gimcrack embarrassment, into which the remainder of the Lane collectively and so very wholeheartedly will throw itself – and I hold in warm admiration her absolute carelessness for whatever this motley of her social inferiors might eventually think, say or do about that. But it was dear little Amanda, you see – so excited by her extremely pretty new dress, though she had made it quite clear to me that she didn't at all care to go there alone. I divined that it was not the very short walk that was concerning her so much as her subsequent and solitary entrance: she is of the age when a childish shyness vies for precedence with a new and far bolder pride in her appearance, this still tempered, however, by the need for parental endorsement: my heart was full when I saw it. So I determined to escort her to the library, quite as she wished, whereupon I should incline my head to the assembled throng, and

493

then immediately escape to Prince Arthur Road, where Alicia has rather a comfortable and alluring ... what you might easily term bachelor flatlet, I suppose, snug beneath the eaves of a handsome and substantial Victorian corner building. And here is precisely what happened: Doreen, the silly little thing, failed even to see me, so enrapt did she appear to be with a collection of musical instruments, each of which harboured a fearful potential, in addition to, seemingly, a reincarnated scarecrow. I then had to make perfectly sure that at the moment when there sprang into Milly's eye, as inescapably there would, that sudden light of something I did not at all care to interpret ... that then I should at once very closely be appreciating the intricacy of the moulding within the library's cornices, high above the ghastliness of all those raggedy paper chains, while actively retreating. And so it all quite satisfyingly came to pass: then I was gone.

The luncheon with Alicia was perfectly pleasant. She keeps the place just so, and I do rather care for it. Christmas decorations, I was gratified to observe, were confined to a cluster of greetings cards, a string of little green lights about the chimneypiece and a fine deep red poinsettia in a blue-and-white cachepot atop her wireless. I had brought for her a pendant necklace with a plain gold bevelled lozenge bearing an amethyst stone − a variety I am given occasionally to bestowing upon only a favoured few − along with a generous selection of chocolate pralines which I obtained from a rather well-appointed shop in Swiss Cottage by the name of Lessiters:

494

handsome and circular ribboned box, the confection itself so very much more sophisticated than anything one ever might acquire in that Miller person's tatty little sweetshop. He who, I believe, currently is enjoying residency in some sort of an asylum somewhere. It is maybe England's Lane that does this. Could this be a possibility? That insanity is our ultimate destiny – the only question remaining for each one of us being a simple matter of when . . . ?

Alicia had poached a salmon, and she much enjoyed my pleasure as she presented too a bottle of a more than decent Chablis that had been quite adequately chilled within the smallest refrigerator I ever have laid eyes upon: it squats within a redundant fireplace in what she is pleased to call her kitchenette. She later – with chocolates – was happy to sip some Benedictine, which also I had thought to take along with me. Intercourse was perfunctory, though no less satisfying for that – and from the way she was speaking to me later, as quite contentedly she lay within my arms, I divined that she is quite coyly eager to learn about the subtler sexual possibilities, and even one or two of the more diverting, if only very slightly dangerous, avenues and byways. Her breasts are the most copious I have experienced in a very long while, the nipples engorged and engaging; her fingers are highly adept, and it is her abiding regret that because daily she must utilise a typewriter, this precludes the growing of her nails, though still she does paint them both neatly and brightly. I did not tell her that our relationship was destined to be brief, due to my intention to soon move away. I did not tell her, no . . . and now, in the cruel white light of later events, I suppose I am rather pleased and grateful for that much. For now, at least, I shall have Alicia to return to.

I arrived back home still early in the afternoon – for when a woman is new, it does not do to overstay, to bestow over-much of oneself, for then she might easily though erroneously presume that here is a working template for any future occasion – when often a quite fleeting visit is all that I shall require of her. I had expected Amanda still to be at the party, and such – adjudging the silence – appeared to be the case. What I by no means expected, however, was to find Fiona in the drawing room – her face averted to the window, and stained by the traces of drying tears.

'Fiona . . . ? Fiona, my dear – whatever can be wrong . . . ?'

Her eyes, when slowly she turned them towards me, seemed filled with a passionate regret: how else am I to depict their profundity and ardour . . . and yet a melancholy longing, still that lingered within . . . ?

'Jonathan . . . dear Jonathan. I had no idea whether you would return . . .'

'Return, my dearest . . . ? I am at a loss to understand quite what you can, ah . . . why of course I have returned. Why should I not?'

'I thought, simply, that finally you had made your . . . choices. Choices, yes, that failed to favour me . . .'

'Fiona. Fiona . . . truly, all that you are saying is quite perfectly beyond me. I have delivered Amanda to the library, quite as we discussed . . . yes? The party in the library? And then I took a little bit of a walk. A walk, yes – and now I am here. So what has happened? I cannot bear to see you in such distress. Please, Fiona – explain to me why you are speaking in this way . . .'

'Ah. I assumed that you would know. I assumed that you had sent her to me.'

'Sent her . . . ? Who? Sent whom to you? Someone has been here? Well who? Who? Tell me please, Fiona. Who has been here and so upset you?'

'Your . . . woman. Your other woman. She said you would be with her. Yes – and for ever. And the moment I saw her, I did not doubt it.'

My mind was quite thrown into turmoil. I attempted to hold her gaze – wistful, she appeared to be now, and seemingly quite accepting – while concentrating hard and thinking rather desperately. My *woman* . . . ? Well which woman? It can have been none of them. It is completely impossible. And even were it not – none would presume: none would dare. None . . . no . . . with just the one sole exception under the sun. Oh . . . my . . . Christ . . . !

'She left for you a letter, Jonathan. It is there upon the table. Unsealed – I imagine deliberately, though I have forborne to touch it. I do not care to. Though before you read it, my dearest – and no matter what it might contain . . .

may I please speak? May I please make myself quite plain to you, Jonathan?'

'My dear . . . my dear . . . ! But you must understand . . . !'

'I should just like to say that whatever the eventual out-come – whatever may befall you – already I have arrived at a decision of my own. I have known – of course I have always known, that of all your women over the many long years, there ever was only one – just one who possessed the power, the aura, ultimately to take you from me. Well before such happens – no . . . please do allow me to finish, Jonathan: permit me to say everything that I must, for I never shall again. So . . . before such happens . . . I should like formally to release you. I am removing myself, Jonathan. Not literally, no . . . for where on earth should I go? I am quite without means, as well you are aware. But Amanda and myself . . . henceforth, we shall somehow be elsewhere. Elsewhere. No – please do not speak. And do not approach. Go now, Jonathan. Take your letter, and read it. No – I beg you: not a word. Not a single word. Leave me now. Please do go.'

Three or four times I attempted to speak, moved to interrupt, went to be near her . . . but no – she would have none of it. I left the room in a state of great agitation and considerable bewilderment. Though even as I threw myself into the chair at my desk, I knew that I would be bound to raise up the hammered vellum envelope . . . and while passing it slowly beneath each of my nostrils, close my eyes and shudderingly gulp down and deep into me the scent that I had known would cling there, its redolence and intensity within an instant storming the tumult of my brain, making me gasp, and making me giddy. And, while very gingerly I slid out the two thick sheets from the slither of the envelope's fuchsia tissue lining, already I was severely shocked by fear of all now that was to come.

Dearest Jonty,

Whether this is the first or the fiftieth time that you are reading this letter, please do know that you will carry its content within you for ever.

But how are you, dear Jonty? Less well now, I imagine, than formerly. It has been so very long, has it not? Since you left me without a single word. Since my son Adam was falsely accused and convicted of such terrible crimes, and subsequently paid your debt with his own young life. He cried as he stood upon the gallows: he cried out piteously for his mother. You do remember when I told you that no harm must come to him? Well now – despite our love for one another, Jonty, which always we knew would never die – harm must come to you.

I have, over the years, made more than one attempt to locate you. I was informed quite recently that my latest envoy had successfully picked up a scent, though never was he heard of again. How very clever you are, Jonty. How utterly ruthless. And yet . . . not always so clever, not infallibly so. For was it not you who sent Obi to me? How did you not come to see that one so corrupt must perforce be quite infinitely corruptible? It is due to his bought, though willingly delivered, intelligence that now and at last I have found you. Although he spoke no lie when he told you that my husband John is dead. Though he died many years ago, actually during his very first year of incarceration. One more outcome of your duplicity and despicable cowardice.

At first, it had been my simple intention to kill you. But now I have had time, so much time, to consider. All that I need you to know is that although we shall never meet again, always will I be with you. This last I said to Fiona's face, and, as by now you are aware, she will have completely misinterpreted my words, quite as was intended. For no longer will you have her: I have spoiled it. And just as no longer do I have my son, no longer will you have your daughter: I have spoiled it. But I am hardly done yet, my dear sweet Jonty. Whether you remain in England's Lane – and what a perfectly dear little place it would surely appear to be – or whether you choose to take yourself elsewhere . . . wherever you, Fiona and Amanda may roam . . . all of it is of no matter, for you know that always now I shall be able to find you. You are watched, Jonty: watched. I might, one day, have one of them executed. Your wife. Or your daughter.

Or even both – who can say? I might not, of course. Such a thing could happen this coming Christmas Day . . . ! Or not for many years. At Amanda's wedding breakfast, conceivably . . . ? Though possibly never, of course. But should it come, I promise that you will be alive to know it, Jonty: to be aware, and for ever. For surely now you see that never was it John who should have been your abiding concern, my dearest – the very dark depths of your fear, your dread anticipation. It was me. Just me. As still it remains. For between us, dear Jonty, there throbs such a passion that forever must bind us. I can feel us, Jonty. Beating.

My love, always

Anna

I sat in silence for a good long time – certainly the room was chill and quite perfectly dark by the time I could rouse myself into any sort of awareness. My fingers, now . . . they at last had ceased to tremble. And a letter such as this from any other woman in the world, I could quite easily dismiss as mere obfuscation and so much overblown oratory: no more than the spite and grudge of a slighted female. But this letter . . . ah . . . this particular letter had been penned in the blood of both of us by a spellbinding goddess – and eternal torment upon this earth in the shadow of the sword of vengeance . . . here is an agony that a goddess will inflict. Her finger now lingers on the trigger to insanity: for the rest of time I am cursed with insuperable disease so far beyond all human toleration: the venom of both knowing, and unknowing. There remains for me simply an eternity of nothingness, spiked by terror, all of which yet I somehow must endure.

And in the End . . .

'Happy Christmas, Jim . . .'

Yeh: and I looks at her when she say it – she sticking a cracker out at me, that what she up to now. Look a picture, she do: like the day I marry her. On account of I give that Gwendoline a bit of dosh – do her a perm, like, or whatever she get done. Yeh because Mill, she say to me – here Jim listen, do me a favour, don't be getting me no more of all of that lavender stuff, ay? Got a pile of it. So I says to her – yeh? Well, what you want then? Box of wossname? And she get a bit sarky and she go to me what's wossname, Jim? And I says to her well you know – chocolates, and that. And she go nah – tell you what I want: nice new hairdo. And then I do all of the sarky back at her and I says well I don't reckon I be much good to you on that side of things Mill, and she say don't be daft Jim: I mean Gwendoline, don't I? Yeh – so I done that, see . . . and she do look lovely. Shorter it is, the barnet – got a bit of red in it like what it used to the first time I seed her. As for me . . . I look like I been dragged under a bleeding bus, as bloody usual. I ain't been, nor nothing – but I feeling a bit on the doddery side, just lately. My face, that ain't looking quite so bad now – bit of dark around the eye, like – but the other day my plates gone again from under me: all of that Achilles wossname: you don't get no warning. They goes like it quite a lot, just lately. Yeh – so like I say, I a bit had it, sort of style.

Christmas Day, this is – and I'm in that blazer what Mill gone and got me. Ever so miffed I never wore it at her party. I were going to, yeh . . . and then I thinks – nah, it's a bit good for me, this: reckon what I'll do is, I'll just keep it nice. And after, she going so what you want to go keeping it nice for then, Jim? Nice for wearing at your funeral, that it? And I reckon she got a point – so I wearing it now, ain't I? She ever so pleased. Feel a bit bleeding hot in it though, on account of she got the fire going lovely: stupid, ain't it really? Being in a jacket when you's at home. Reckon I slip it off, later. Mill . . . she done us a lovely dinner, like what she always do: Trojan, it were – with the turkey and the stuffing and all of that plum duff what she gone and lit with a drop of my Scotch: prime, yeh. Pauly, he down there on the rug with Anthony, ain't he? Playing about with all of them doings what Mill gone and buyed them: don't know how she do it on what I give her – proper little housewife, and no mistake. Having ever such a time, them two boys is. Nice to see it. Weren't like that when I were a kid – never got nothing. So yeh: nice to see it.

But I knows, don't I . . . ? What bringing me down. Family matters, you might say. Family matters, yeh. Because it Cyril, ain't it? Course it bloody is. Fell off his perch, didn't he? Quite literal. Yesterday morning, I comes down quite the thing just like what I normally does, and he lying in his cage there, and all his little feet stuck up. Were ever so sad. Such a lovely little feller, my little Cyril were. Won't never be able to talk to him no more. And I reckon it were on account of me. Yeh it were. Them fumes. Mill, she were right all along about that. Can't go keeping a little bird, can you? Not with all them fumes. And it funny – yesterday, when I claps eyes on him, I gets it for the first time, them fumes. Before, ain't never noticed nothing – but yeh, stink like bleeding hell down there, it do. Can't do nothing about it. Way it is. And I don't know how she done it, Mill, of a Christmas Eve and all – but this morning, you know what she gone and give me? Well first off I got a pack of cards with a picture of Cyril on: you want to see it – spit bleeding image, I tell you. But that ain't nothing – because listen: you know what else she gone and got me? Canary. Yeh – little yellow canary. Ain't kidding. And after we bury little Cyril all nice and dignified in the yard in a old wooden box what once had Whiffs in, she must of gone and done up his cage – cleaned it all out proper, she had. Christmas paper on the bottom – robins, which is a bit funny – yeh and then she bung a bit of mistletoe up the top of it, like . . . and blow me down if that little birdie ain't coming out with his beak and giving me a smacker, right on my tache. Keep him up here, we will – all nice and cosy. Away from all them fumes. Ain't called him nothing yet. I says to Mill – how's about Yeller? And she go nah Jim – can't go calling no little bird Yeller: might take offence. She say Tweety – and Pauly, he go why don't you call him Sitting Bull, which is right plain bloody daft, you ask me. That kid, telling you – stuff he come out with. Ain't said nothing, but I think I going to go for William, when it come to it: look like a William, he do.

Yeh: my Mill, she done that. For me. On top of the rest of all what she done. Like that party of hers, for starters. Last Sunday, that were – don't seem like couple minutes back, that don't. Time, see – these days, it just go like wossname. Right good do, though – best we ever had, I reckon. Leaping about I were – like what all of them was: were a right old beano, telling you. That row what were coming out the lads and all that bleeding guitar and that – well, diabolical, go without saying. And them drums – bloody jungle music, that is. Yeh – and you want to see that Sambo, whatever his bleeding name is: jumping about like he on fire, or something. And all of them women – women what want knowing better, I'd say: like your Miss Jenkins out of Moore's, Edie out the Dairies – even that big girl what's in the cake place, Sally she called? Doreen, yeh – well you got to expect it off of Doreen, ain't you? She only a kid. But they all of them going: oh look at Kelso – yeh, that his name, Kelso, bloody stupid name – look at him go! Don't he dance good, they's all saying. Even Mill – she clapping away there. And I says to Reg and Charlie, yeh well – stick a poker up the bum of a monkey and you going to get dancing just as good as that, ain't you? They had a good old laugh about that, Reg and Charlie. But what I saying is, the music – you want to call it music – it didn't matter, see, on account of everyone were having a rare old time. Reg's Bass were sweet as a nut, and I bung a tot of Johnnie Walker into mine, don't I? Put hairs on your chest, that will. And we had Spam sandwiches and tomatoes and cake and jelly and all of that. Tell you what were funny – well two things, two things what was funny. That dog what old Mr Levy got – mangy old bugger it is – dozing away he were . . . and then all sudden like: going mad, he is. Running about and howling his bleeding head off and barging into all sorts – gels screaming, and that: orange juice, that go flying. Split my gut, I did. Turn out Charlie, he gone and slip the dog a bowl of ale, silly bugger – and old Mr Levy, he couldn't do nothing with him . . . and then just as sudden, bloody animal go to sleep again in the middle of the bleeding floor! Couple of the lads slide him into the corner, there – dear oh dear! Other bleeding funny thing what happened were when old Stan come wandering into the room . . . ! Blimey – stop everything dead, that did. Wearing a pair of bags what was far too big on him and a bloody pyjama jacket, you can believe it. Eyes all goggling about: look like the ghost of Christmas wossname, he did. Mill – she go and see to him. Don't know what it were all about. Never ask her. Yeh. And that Barton bastard . . . he never come. Leastways I never seed him. And that were a right good thing, tell you that. Because if he had done . . . if he gone over to my Mill, well . . . can't rightly tell you what I would've done then . . . because, well – had a few, hadn't I? What I would've done is probably got myself bloody killed this time round . . . so it just as well, really.

Because I been thinking about all of that, ain't I? Well course I have – got to. On account of next year, don't know when, well . . . my Mill, she going to . . . well – she going to be having a baby, ain't she? Ay? No getting round it. I mean – pleased for her, course. Why not? You just want to look at her: never seed her so good. And she all dead cheery, and that. So yeh . . . pleased for her, like I says . . . but it kill me, really. Inside, like. Not on account of what she done. Nah. I reckon she were owed. I don't care now – what she done. You married to a geezer like me, well . . . that what all of them smooth bastards is for then, I suppose. Nah – what kill me is . . . well . . . I wish it was me. That's all. What was – you know: bloke what give it her. Like what a husband ought. Still. Reckon I'll get over it. Get over most things, don't you? Give it a bit of time. Even Cyril. I'll get over it. One day. And little Willy – he help me no end, he will. Yeh – reckon I call him Little Willy: like that. And I got my Mill to thank for him. Like I got a lot to thank her for. She been good to me, that gel. And I loves her. Always done that. Always loved her. Yeh and I always will do, I knows that for sure. And the kid. Try my best, I will – try to love the new little kid more than ever I done with Pauly. Maybe it'll be a little sister for him, this one, ay? Mill, she go for that, she would. Make her all little dresses and knick-knacks and that. Yeh – she be happy with it. And here's a turn-up: she kiss me, the other day. Done it again this morning. Touch my hair, like. What I still got left of it. Yeh. Were nice. Got me wondering if . . . if me and Mill . . . you know . . . ever like could sort of get together again, and that. Of a night time, sort of style. Early days, course . . . And yeh I know she been with another bloke – yeh I do know that – but . . . I don't know . . . sometimes, I think of it, and it a bit get me going, you know? Can't hardly understand it. Like . . . last time I were down with my Daisy – when she were seeing to me, like, and singing in my lughole and all . . . I were thinking about Mill, and how she been and done it. Got me going a bit, you know . . . ? And Daisy, she go – blimey Jim! You getting younger every day, you! Yeh. Well. That's that. Ain't it, really? Most times, you can't hardly know what all are going on.

'Jim . . . ? How long exactly are you expecting me to continue standing here like a lemon? Are you going to pull this cracker with me, or are you not . . . ?'

'I am, Mill – yeh, course. Sorry, love. Miles away, weren't I . . .'

Yes, Jim – I can well believe it. I've noticed it in you, lately: very much more reflective, you appear to be. Well . . . I suppose that rather suddenly, you do have quite a fair deal to think about.

'Well pull the bleeding thing then, if you're going to . . . !'

'I am – I am pulling. I don't want to get too close because of the bang. Paul – here, Paul: come and help me pull this cracker . . . Oh . . . ! Oh . . . ! There it is! These crackers, honestly – they're the loudest I've ever heard. Here, Jim – put your hat on. We've all got hats on except for you. Look – it's a blue one. It'll go perfectly with your very smart blazer. There. You look very handsome, Jim. Quite the matinee idol.'

'Yeh yeh. Now listen – listen all of yous: I'm going to read out the joke. Ready? Here, Pauly – little magnifying glass we got in it, look. Want it? Here you are, then. Good lad. You can be like Sherlock wossname now, can't you? Ay? Now then: here we go: "The tallest structure in the world is the Empire State Building in New York City in the United States of America" . . . Yeh? So what? That it . . . ? Can't be. That it . . . ? Blimey. Well what's so funny about that, then . . . ?'

'It's not a joke, Jim. They aren't, all of them. Some of them are. The others are just, I don't know . . . facts . . .'

'Nothing bleeding funny about that, is there . . . ? Ay? Empire bleeding State . . . ? It don't make me laugh. Make you laugh, do it? Anyone laughing in here? Don't think so. Bleeding swizz, that is . . .'

'No, Jim – I've just explained . . .'

Oh dear. Some things, they don't ever change, do they? He's not a stupid man, Jim – oh no, far from it – though so very often he can appear to be distinctly obtuse. Though I'm hardly complaining. Am I? Honestly, he really has behaved rather impossibly well over the whole of the affair. Because of course there are many husbands who . . . well: if they knew their wives to be in my . . . shall we say, condition . . . ? Well then they would . . . beat her black and blue for starters, I can quite imagine. And then just throw her out. Many men, you know, that's exactly what they'd do. But from Jim I have had not so much as a word of recrimination. Not one single word. It's hard, of course, to quite know what he might be feeling. And I do care. I never used to – mind about what he was feeling . . . but I do, now.

We're having such a lovely day. Everything so far has gone quite swimmingly, I must say. Paul and Anthony have been up and about since dawn – I mean it! Quite literally since dawn! – banging about and yelping like puppies. It's nice for Paul, to have a friend to play with. Already, though, he is so missing Amanda – and she hasn't even gone anywhere yet. He wanted to ask her over later in the afternoon, and it did so hurt me to say no. But in the rather extraordinary circumstances, what else could I do . . . ? Anthony, though – little mite – he was just so thrilled with his stocking: said he'd never before received such a thing, except for those mesh ones that Mars do, apparently. And Paul – you should have seen his eyes when he tore the paper from that tank of his . . . ! They've both been playing with it constantly – apart from just before lunch when they did break off briefly to watch Mr Pastry on the television. I told them to go easy on it for the sake of the battery – and also because when it's trundling about and spitting our sparks, it does make a very beastly noise: but of course they've ignored me completely. Little souls. They've done the edges of the *Victory* jigsaw, and then I suppose it became rather more difficult, so that's been abandoned on the floor: I daresay they'll go back to it later. The drum of Minibrix I'm saving till after tea, or else the floor will be just covered with simply everything. That Matchbox car, though – that excited no interest whatever: I rather think they might have gone the way of the free gift inside the cereal packet, you know. It just must be faced: my little boy, he is beginning to grow up . . . which one day I suppose might please me.

And Jim – he does look so very different in that blazer, you know. Such a transformation – you'd hardly recognise him. I'll tell him to take it off in a minute, though – I can see that he's simply sweltering, poor man. But at the end of the Queen's broadcast, when he stood up to salute, he did look quite the English gentleman, I must say. And oh . . . he does so love that canary! I could see that immediately. I did rather wonder whether it was the right thing to do – but goodness, I simply couldn't bear the look of such deep sorrow that he carried in his eyes . . . ! He adored that little bird: Cyril, I honestly do believe that he was central to the man's existence. Well so I just had to do something, didn't I? I couldn't abide it – Jim, being heartbroken: no, not now. So yesterday – and I was up to my eyes – I took the 31 bus down to Camden Town where I had remembered there was a pet shop. Do you know – they had completely sold out of budgies, but they did have this beautiful bright-yellow canary. So I bought him – I just had enough left over from the necklace money. And I had to avoid the puppies and kittens – all so soulful and pleading – or else I just know I should have bought all of those as well. Jim – he keeps going over to the cage. Talking to him. He hasn't got a name yet. I'll leave it to Jim. Although I do hope he doesn't go ahead and call the little thing Yeller, as he threatened to do earlier – I don't know . . . it just seems so terribly dismissive, somehow.

And the lunch – that really did go awfully well. The boys being up so early was actually something of a blessing because there's always just so much to see to on Christmas morning. I've never wholly understood why cooking a turkey should always be so very much more of a business than any other sort of a meal – but there: incontestably it is. And the bird, it only just fitted into the oven – not an inch to spare. I always do worry about the breast – one so much doesn't want it to be dry – but it did turn out quite perfectly, even though I do say so myself. The stuffing too – not too much onion, and everybody seemed to enjoy it: Paul asked for seconds, dear heart. The roast potatoes, yes – they might have been just a weensy bit crispier, but no one seemed to mind. I've kept the wishbone . . . but do you know . . . it's just so perfectly silly, but I'm not sure I'll ever dare to pull it: a spell might be broken, along with the bone. And I had a small glass of sherry with my meal, which I suppose was quite nice if you like that sort of thing – though I don't, particularly. I did catch myself thinking in passing that some Chianti might be rather nice. Jim had beer, and the boys had Tizer. Anthony – he's well used to Tizer, of course, because of Stan. Stan, yes . . . Oh dear. Oh dear oh dear oh dear: poor, poor Stan.

I barely believed it when he walked through the door of the library. I had at the time actually been marvelling at a rather tiddly Sally – she was tottering atop her very silly shoes, and the smudge of far too heavy mascara had bestowed upon her the appearance of a rather gaudy giant panda: she was devouring with considerable intensity an unceasing quantity of her own jam tarts: she appeared to favour the yellow ones over the red. It had been no more than solely the shift in atmosphere that alerted me to something sudden and unto-ward within the room. Because right up until that moment – oh honestly, the party had truly been the very most jolly and merriest thing imaginable, and I was so very terribly pleased and relieved – because you never do know, do you really? I mean – you plan an event, you try to think of everything and to please people, but until they all actually arrive and the whole thing begins to get under way, well – you can never quite know just how it will be.

All I can say is that straightaway everyone started to properly get into the Christmas party spirit: surely there was festivity in the air. Doreen – at first she seemed to be quite content to play a few records, but even I was forced to concede that really her little Dansette was straining terribly within the yawn and vacuum of so very large a room. But when the emaciated Derek and the other one started up with their guitar and drums as Doreen began to trill away in time to it – well! The *noise* . . . ! I simply can't tell you. Mrs Goodrich happened to be standing quite near to me at the time, and oh heavens – it was so pure a joy to be able to witness her practically leap into the air as if she had been bitten! 'Oh my good *Lord* . . . !' she was wailing at me (and she did seem appalled, I am very pleased to say): 'What is that utterly dreadful *din*, Mrs Stammer . . . ?!' 'Well, Mrs Goodrich,' I then delighted in telling her, 'since you come to ask me, I do believe it is a song entitled 'What Do You Want?' Which as we speak is currently residing at the number one spot on the Top Ten hit parade. By a gentleman called Mr Adam Faith.' '*Indeed!*' she declaimed – rather taken aback, I hope, and having to raise her voice quite considerably. 'Well, Mrs Stammer – it most certainly is not what *I* want, I can very much assure you of *that* . . . !' And then she huffed away, ostentatiously clamping her palms to her ears – and doubt-less very eager to harass or patronise some other hapless soul. I was childishly pleased with my rejoinder, though: it just so happened that I had heard the record (and very dreadful it is, let us please be quite clear about that) just this very morning on *Housewives' Choice* on the wireless, otherwise of course I should never have known. And after they had mangled that number, beanpole Derek with the other one and Doreen fell into a rather too highly pitched version of 'Living Doll' – which everybody knows, of course, because it's Cliff Richard, isn't it? And The Shadows. Paul is humming it constantly.

And that's when everyone started to dance – even Jim was horsing around with the odious Charlie, but here was merely the outlet for the earlier stages of inebriation – I knew that, of course, but still I was pleased to see it. And Kelso . . . ! Oh my word! He ought to be on *Sunday Night At The London Palladium*, that one, he really ought – quite the professional. It's in his bones, of course – it's in the blood: from all the war dances or something, I suppose. Or is that Red Indians . . . ? Oh honestly – I just don't know what I'm talking about, do I? The other one though, Obi his name is, he wasn't there – didn't come, I can't imagine why. Maybe just as well though, because most people seem to be quite terrified of him – and I do have to admit, his general demeanour is more than somewhat menacing. Mr Lawrence – I heard him earlier declaiming that more or less their very existence was a downright disgrace, let alone the presence of the two of them in England's Lane: 'If we have a colour bar in this country,' he was saying really quite loudly, 'then will someone please explain to me why is it not *applied* . . . ?' Edie was sitting with Mrs Dent, which was kind of her, and they both seemed to be enjoying the Libby's tinned peaches with Carnation – but then, who wouldn't? And Paul now – he'd set down his dish of fruit cocktail (always he insists upon leaving all the little half cherries till last, dearest soul) and now he was starting to dance with Amanda . . . ! My heart did swell, I confess it. I think they were attempting the jive sort of thing, I do believe it's called, that Elvis Presley has popularised in America: they did look perfectly sweet, the two of them. Poor little Anthony, though . . . just looking on at them both, and with a fairly set expression, little fellow. Then I caught sight of Gwendoline chatting away to Miss and Mrs Jenkins in the furthest corner, and the shaft of milky light through the window, you know – it had caught her just so . . . and her hair, it was the loveliest and most delicate shade of auburn, quite like I used to wear mine. I determined on the spot to ask her to recreate it, and make my perm rather shorter and looser while she was about it. It was time, I felt, to display the truth that now I am changed: I only wished I had thought of it before the party, so that I could be flaunting my brand-new look to anyone who cared to glance in my direction. Anyway – I have had it done now, and I couldn't be more delighted with the result. I do think it makes me appear rather younger – but then, with all the energy at my disposal these days I honestly feel like a five-year-old anyway . . . though I suppose as my condition becomes gradually rather more apparent, I shall be recalling this time with both a languid nostalgia, and longing envy. Jim – he wasn't in the slightest bit put out when I told him quite plainly that I should simply expire from boredom if he gave so much as one more Yardley bath cube, and that instead I should like him to pay for a new coiffure.

The next thing that happened is that Mr Levy's dog, well – thoroughly inexplicably, he just went quite mad, so far as

I could see. Everyone was laughing, of course, as he was careering around and yelping – though I did spot the face of one of the old lady librarians rather cloud at the point when the jug of orange juice was spilt all over the parquet flooring. And then Mr Bona appeared with the most extraordinary-looking camera with a great big silver sort of bowl on the top of it, and everyone was shrieking and wincing as suddenly the flash bulbs were immediately dazzling them. I simply can't wait to see all the photographs – and he was so awfully good, Mr Bona: he made quite sure that everyone was included in at least one of the photos; I shall look awful, of course – I seldom take a good picture: always look an absolute fright. He must have used two whole rolls of film, I should think – and I well remember from the last time we took the Brownie to Bournemouth how horribly expensive they are. I saw him again just yesterday, Mr Bona, but he said that Boots had told him that they wouldn't have developed the pictures for at least another three-and-a-half weeks, because this and the summer are their busiest times. Bit of a disappointment – but quite something else to look forward to.

You could tell when the drink was beginning to have its effect on most of the men – raised and slurring voices, all the usual sort of thing – and I couldn't swear to it, but I rather fancy that some of the boys from the council schools might also have been tippling things that really they oughtn't. Yes and then suddenly these very rowdy boys, they were bursting balloons with cigarette ends. I know – cigarettes! And some of them can't have been much older than fourteen or so, I shouldn't have said. Well it's the parents, isn't it really? Serves them right. If you skimp on a child's education, that's the sort of thing you're going to have to expect. And here, I think, was the juncture when I came to sense the murmuring of a change of direction . . . the discordant arrest of the music, this quickly supplanted by the muttering masses. I turned with reluctance from the perfectly fascinating spectacle of the gorging Sally . . . and there I saw him: Stan – looking perfectly and tragically absurd in just a striped pyjama jacket and clearly somebody else's trousers. He looked about him briefly, and then was walking towards me with purpose, his eyes so very dark and zealous. Many now were glancing over to poor little Anthony, and I saw him quickly turn away.

'Hello, Milly. I'm sorry if I'm late . . .'

'Stan . . . ! Stan – what are you . . . ? Here, Stan – let's just go and sit in the corner, shall we? Just over there. Nice and comfy. Now can I get you something . . . ? Something to eat? A drink, maybe? Do they, um – know you've come? How did you get here, Stan . . . ?'

'Well yes, Milly – fair point, very fair point. Devil of a journey, you want the truth of the matter. Bus only got me so far. Then I had to walk. Why I'm rather late, you see. I do hope I haven't held you up though, or anything, Milly. I didn't want you to be holding anything up on account of me. Though of course I wouldn't have missed it for worlds . . .'

'No no – of course not, Stan. Well you're just in time, I assure you. So . . . you've come on your own then, have you? There's nobody with you? Well . . . does anyone know you're here?'

'No no. They said I mustn't leave. Quite firm about it. But there's all sorts of things, Milly, they say I mustn't do. It's less than friendly. I don't even know why I'm there. Why am I there, Milly? Do you know? I don't at all care for it. And the pills they make me take . . . ! I've never been a one for pills, as well you know. Look at my Janey. Look what the pills did for my Janey. Killed her. Didn't they?'

'And so, what . . . you've just been walking then, Stan . . . ? Dressed just like this? Oh but you must be absolutely freezing . . . ! I'll get you some tea, Stan.'

'Is a bit parky out there, I'm not denying. Lovely here, though. Warm as toast. Milly – never mind about tea for a minute. Something I want to say to you, see? Why I came, really. Here . . . what's everyone looking at . . . ? Staring. Why's everyone staring at us, Milly? Rude, I'd say . . .'

'Yes – quite right, Stan. Doreen . . . ! Doreen – can you hear me . . . ? Yes . . . ? Put on a record or something, will you? Nothing too jazzy. Thank you, Doreen. Come along, everybody . . . ! Lots of food and drink left . . . ! We'll cut the cake in a minute, and then we can all sing carols, yes? Yes? All right, then. That's fine. Now then, Stan . . . it's just us again. All right? But do let me get you a cup of tea – and possibly a sandwich, yes? Would you like that? A sandwich?'

'No appetite, if I'm honest with you Milly. But listen – first off, I've got to say I'm sorry.'

'Sorry, Stan . . . ? You've nothing to be sorry about . . .'

'Oh yes I have. Because I haven't brought you a Christmas present.'

'Oh . . . Stan . . . !'

'But I'm going to make up for it, you see, because I'm going to tell you where I keep the spare key to the shop, and then you can just go and help yourself to some of the special chocolates in the glass counter. Violet creams, maybe. Mint fondants, you might care for. The hazelnut whirls come highly recommended. Whole pound, if you like – I don't care. I would have gone there first and fetched them for you – make them look all nice, you know? But I didn't like to think I was holding up the party. It's good of you to have waited for me. Where's Anthony . . . ? Is Anthony here . . . ?'

'He's . . . yes – yes, he's here somewhere, Stan. Can't quite spot him at the moment, though. He's maybe gone to spend a penny.'

'Even that's a bit of a to-do for him, poor little lad. He well is he, Milly . . . ? Bearing up? Ever so good of you to, um – you know . . .'

'He's as good as gold, Stan. Really is. A pleasure to have around. And yes – he seems very, um . . . fit. Happy. Healthy. If you know what I mean . . . Um . . . Stan . . . don't you think I ought to telephone the, er – place? I think I ought to let them know where you are, don't you? They're bound to be concerned. Then maybe they can send a . . . maybe there's some way whereby you don't have to go all the way back on your own, yes? And in the cold.'

'In a minute, Milly. In a minute. Let me tell you what I have to, yes? Well first off – you remember that negligee, do you?'

'The . . . the negligee . . . oh yes. John Barnes.'

'That's the man. Well when I said I'd bought it for my Janey . . . well I hadn't. Not really. It was for you. Always meant to be for you, Milly. Never could forget how you looked in it, see?'

'Yes . . . I do see, Stan. Well . . . that was extremely thoughtful of you. Very kind. Thank you.'

'Yes. Except Aggie's got it now. Sorry about that. Aggie – she's a floozy in Adelaide Road. Very pleasant woman, as I recall. Not in your league, Milly. Goes without saying. You're a lady. Proper lady. Different class. But Aggie – she's a nice enough sort, I will say that for her. Lives with Daisy – your Jim's little friend. Well I say little . . . truth is – she's a big girl, Daisy. So anyway – she was ever so grateful for the negligee, Aggie was, but she didn't want to marry me. Take Janey's place. No she didn't. Which is perfectly understandable. Well – you didn't either, did you Milly? No blame in that. Perfectly understandable, course it is. Understand that of any woman. And the other thing I want you to know, Milly, is that I wouldn't let my Janey write all those bad things about you.'

'What . . . ? You wouldn't let . . . what bad things, Stan . . . ?'

'Oh – bad things. But I wouldn't have it. Wouldn't stand for it. Put my foot down. You would have been proud of me, Milly – I really was a man about it. Showed a bit of gumption. Well in her suicide note, you know . . . ? She wanted to accuse you of things. Wanted to write all that she says you were up to with Mr Barton, of all people – which of course I know was all lies, Milly. I do hope you understand that I know that. And then how you tried to take me away from her . . . and that was a lie too, more's the pity. Then kind of saying that you'd driven her to it, sort of style . . .'

'But Stan . . . I don't understand. How on earth could you . . . ?'

'Well she read it out to me, you see. That evening – when I'd just got back from Aggie's, in point of fact. I was quite tight, I don't mind telling you. Went in to see her. All was quiet. Quiet as the grave it was, in there. Peaceful as you like. And then a light came on. Bit of a shock. She was sitting up in bed, you see. And the pills all around her. Already she'd swallowed quite a few, I'd say. And she was just putting the finishing touches, I suppose. To her note, you know. And it was lucky, wasn't it really? That I happened to be there. Because when she read it out to me, I said: oh no, Janey – I'm not having that. You've got to rewrite it. I'm not having all that about Milly in there. So she did. Meek as a lamb, which was a fair surprise. She rewrote it. Stood over her while she did it. Like I say, I was quite a man about it. Fair deal of gumption, don't you think?'

'So Stan . . . you . . . *knew* . . . ! You *knew* she was going to kill herself . . . !'

'Did, yes. Well, to be fair – by the time I popped in to see her, she was well on the way, I'd say. I helped her along with the rest. Gave her little sips of water – because some of them, you know, they're ever so large. Don't know how these doctors are expecting you to cope. Held her hand. Seemed only polite. She was smiling at the end. Very serene, she seemed. Oh yes. She wasn't saying anything. But I was well used to that, wasn't I? Christ Alive – I should say so!'

Well of course I was perfectly stupefied. I put into Stan's hands a little bowl of gooseberry jelly – absurd I know, but it was the nearest thing to hand – made some sort of reassuring noises to the man, and then I quickly went over to Edie to ask her to sit with him while I went out to telephone the institution. I would simply say to them that Stan, as I trusted they were aware, had wandered, that he was safe, and could they please send an ambulance for him as quickly as possible. And I would upbraid them for their appalling carelessness in ever permitting such a thing, unwittingly or no: anything might have happened. And that is all I would say: that I had decided immediately. For whenever Stan would emerge from whatever it was into which he had so suddenly and very deeply receded . . . well then we simply couldn't have, could we, his then being taken off somewhere else, and so very much worse? For the sake of Anthony, if for no other reason. That little boy's future is so difficult and quite uncertain enough, I feel, without his father – already now with a history of mental illness – then being publicly branded as at the very least an accessory to a murder.

So I did all that – and the relief in the voice of the ward orderly, or whomever I was addressing, was as palpable and heartfelt as it was thoroughly undeserved; a private ambulance, he assured me, would immediately be dispatched. I then went in search of Anthony, who I felt quite sure was deliberately hiding. I understood the poor little fellow's embarrassment, of course I did – but this was his father, after all. And whatever may be set against Stan, no one could deny his strong and abiding love for the boy. And on my way across the room I threw a passing thank you to Doreen for having attended to all of the music side of things – for I did feel that undeniably it had added a very necessary dimension to the whole of the proceedings. She said she was enjoying herself, and so was everyone else . . . and Mrs Stammer, that Mr Miller over there – he all right, is he? Well no not really, Doreen: but he will be soon, I do feel sure of that. And then, well . . . she said something else . . . something that I am afraid has lingered within me. What she said was that she was pleased though that that Barton hadn't stayed. And I queried that, genuinely surprised: Mr Barton . . . ? Why, Doreen? Why ever do you say that? Because he's a right bastard like all men are, that's why – just takes what he wants, and then he buggers off: but then you know that, don't you? You know all about it, Mrs Stammer.

The ambulance did arrive quickly, and I helped Stan into the back of it: wrapped a large red blanket around his shoulders. He seemed to be stooped and rather thinner than he had been just a week ago – his eyes, ringed by shadows . . . enquiring, though still so very helplessly lost.

'So, then . . . what about Anthony . . . ? Did you find him, Milly?'

'I . . . no, Stan. I'm afraid I didn't. But you know what little boys are. Could be anywhere. Couldn't he? He'll be so terribly sorry that he missed you, though.'

'Yes. Expect so. Oh well. There it is. Well tell him a Merry Christmas then, will you Milly? From me, sort of style.'

'I will, Stan. Of course I will.'

'And you, Milly. You as well. I wish you a Merry Christmas.'

'Thank you, Stan. Thank you so much. You too. You too.'

'And a Happy New Year . . . !'

'Yes. Of course. Absolutely.'

'Will it be one, do you think Milly . . . ? Will it be one . . . ?'

'Oh I think so, Stan. I think so.'

The party continued quite a good deal longer, but that, for me, was the end of it. Though I did cut the cake – and very good it was too: moist, crammed with fruit, and eaten enthusiastically (most especially by Sally, its creator). The carols were lovely, as always they are – all the old favourites. Mrs Dent felt she could hardly do justice to the piano's pedals, though Mrs Bona happily stepped into the breach and proved to be more than up to the challenge. The men grew raucous during the Gloria choruses of 'Ding Dong Merrily On High', while all the children, bless them, were laughing their little heads off. Eventually – and at last worn out – I had concluded the day with a glass of Eno's Fruit Salts: I think it could well have been the marzipan that did it.

And now the future is looming. Well always it is, of course – though at Christmas time one seems to be most keenly aware of it: what with the contrast to the one preceding, if contrast ever there be. The reluctance to believe that twelve whole months can actually have passed. And always the awareness of a brand-new year – for the present just about content to be skulking in the shadows, though eagerly awaiting its grand and gaudy moment. 1960, then ... when my life will be changed, and as never before. For I, Milly, am soon to be a mother: that little thing. Well of course I have been that, a mother, a mother to dear Eunice's Paul, for quite a good long time: but now I really am actually to give birth. All that ever I desired. This morning, I fancy I felt a little kick; and I seem to be newly addicted to Tate & Lyle Golden Syrup, a thing to which before I was quite utterly indifferent – and also Craven "A": though the thought now of accompanying a cigarette with a Trebor's mint actively makes me queasy. And no, I cannot imagine quite how it will be ... the birth, you know. Doctor McAuley, he gave me a pamphlet – a flimsy and ill-printed little thing, which has left me none the wiser. And during early February, I believe it is, I am booked in to see some sort of a woman in the Hampstead General who, according to Doctor McAuley, is going to tell me . . . well I don't quite know what it is she is going to tell me. I daresay I shall pick it up. As women have been doing, though men will forget it, since ever time began. I do not know if it will hurt, the actual process . . . most mothers say yes, and I do rather hope that they are right: I just think that it ought to, somehow.

Other mothers of the very young . . . I have heard them talk of their child as almost no more than sort of a tangible consolation for the unforeseen slaughter of physical passion, or else a vanishing of the erstwhile partner. Though this, it seems plain to me, is quite utterly wrong: the baby, most surely, is the thing. The baby itself is the ultimate reward. The baby is the reason – whereas its agency, once and in whichever way it has passed, is as nothing. For within this I am sure lies the grand design: men and women must perforce come together in order to generate impact – and if such may result in not just progeny but a vast and enduring love, well then Gloria in Excelsis. Though it seldom seems to be. Those who appear to have been the happiest – Mrs Dent, say, or old Mr Levy – always they are split in two, and left to bleed. Mr and Mrs Bona remain bonded by the loss of that which still resonates as being the sole and very point of them: their son. While Mrs Goodrich runs her husband like a member of staff, brooking no distraction from any such uncertainties as children. As to myself and Jim . . . well, so very hard to say:

certainly no longer cut and dried, as for so terribly long it has been. I have decided to clean the window of the shop: remove everything that has lurked there, stacked in filth since pre-biblical times, and then polish the glass so brilliantly well that for the first time in eons, you will actually be able to see through it: this is quite a large thing. And the other day I kissed him, and that very much surprised me: Jim too, I imagine. Quite wholly a spontaneous gesture on my part . . . and the kiss . . . it didn't quite die upon my lips. This morning I did it again – but then I always do on Christmas Day: you have to, really. Though at present, obviously I cannot possibly think to more . . . and so do harbour a curious gratitude for the existence of this Daisy person, whoever she may be: big girl, according to Stan – not necessarily, these days, the most reliable of witnesses: but still. And as for Stan . . . and Jonathan . . . well: what is there left that I could possibly say? Then there are those who appear to be thoroughly content with a different sort of union, all of their own: Mrs Jenkins . . . and Miss Jenkins, her core. And those again who continue to wait and see: Edie, Gwendoline . . . even Sally can be the conjuror of dreams, I suppose. Doreen, of course – who never seems to wait too very long. And yes . . . I have ceased to pretend to have been shocked or surprised by her passing revelation: all that time ago, when Jonathan had emerged from his yard – covered in blood, and he held me . . . even as his most beautiful voice was assuring me of the utter innocence of so fleeting a liaison with Doreen, I knew it to be a lie. The need for no pain, though, and the continuance of bliss – they both quite willingly collaborated to stifle at once even so much as the muffled squeal of simple possibility. I don't care. About anything like that any more. Once, he was just so immense as to block out my light: now, he is barely visible to me. For I hold the prize. I have the very best of him. And I carry it within me.

Then there is England's Lane . . . this little island of ours: I used to think it would never change, and that nor should I. Why always in the past I have felt so very comfortable with the two of us, really. But my present altered state has heightened my awareness of a gentle shifting all about me. Curios . . . that shop – and I have only very recently learned this – is soon to be made into a coffee bar. Well there: it had to come, as they say. And of late, Gwendoline has developed a dreadful sort of eczema, I suppose due to all the chemicals that daily she is forced to handle. Poor dear Gwendoline – sometimes she will hold her hands beneath the cold tap for up to twenty minutes on end, and still they emerge so very raw, so very terribly inflamed: she binds them at night in gauze, though still the itching, it makes her distracted and she sobs as she tears at her bandages; Doctor McAuley has told her that it is just one of those things. So, then . . . for how long can Amy's continue, I wonder? Old Mr Levy too – at the end of each and every year, he always says to me that he has had quite enough: that he has been working for the whole of his life, and that now it is time to call it a day, pack up shop, and go off to live with his one remaining sister in Broadstairs. And this year, you know, I do believe he means it: he looked that sad. Maybe he has been spurred by an offer for his premises that arrived, he told me, quite out of the blue – and according to Edie, Mr Lawrence too is said to be considering an approach from the same mysteriously anonymous source, and that is rather something of a worry. Even more concerning is the fact that the two of them adjoin one another, you see, and this does rather strike me as ominous. And now of course there's the future of Stan's shop too to be considered. And another thing that Edie told me the day after the party is that dear old Champion the Wonder Horse is finally to be put out to grass: in the new year, the whole of the United Dairies is going over to electrified floats. And they're intending to install on the pavement outside the shop a machine which in return for sixpence will dispense a carton of chocolate-flavoured milk. I am not complacent: I cannot welcome any such things, for although they come dressed as progress, does there not also cling to each of them the whiff of erosion . . . ?

Well: I can do nothing about it. Can I? I shall, while rereading *Sense and Sensibility* for the squillionth time in my life, simply accept the winds of change – will them to amount to no more than a welcome summer breeze, and pray for no hurricane. I know that we shall be staying, whatever happens: myself, Jim, Paul . . . Anthony now, our little refugee, for whom grief, I fear, might patiently be waiting . . . and then ultimately . . . my baby. And I do see that it is not just England's Lane that begins to stir – it is England's every lane and borough. Newspapers and the wireless, they will insist upon exulting in the presumption that now we are standing poised at the dawn of a 'new age' . . . rather as if there were something wrong with this one. But we've already had that, haven't we? The new age. For our new age, it came with the end of war – and by God did we not grasp at it greedily, in exhaustion and quite tattered desperation? It is that very hard-won peace, the very heaven of unimagined contentment, that still we should be most ardently cherishing.

I, though, am not the person to run away from change. From anything. I couldn't. And I know that the most pointless and fruitless thing of all would be if ever I should attempt to run away from myself – as on occasion, if only fleetingly, has been tempting in the past – because I am so very aware that in no time at all I should so very effortlessly catch myself up. And so . . . along with every other living soul, I simply await the coming of another new year, and all that it brings to me. Quite undaunted, and ready to embrace it. For by now I am a more than capable woman.

COMING SOON

BOYS AND GIRLS

Joseph Connolly

'Connolly unfolds a rich and compelling drama of life'
DAILY MAIL

Susan wants another husband.
Which comes as a shock to the current one.

But not instead of you, Alan, my sugar – as well as. You see?

Yet once Susan has brazenly commandeered her boss's rich, elderly hand, Alan finds himself curiously cherishing the company – sharing wife, whisky and other, odder peccadilloes. Indeed Susan is forced to root out alternative amusements – and with their teenage daughter copying her disintegrating moral code, the complex machinery of their lives soon begins to break down.

Joseph Connolly plunges the reader into a tumultuous medley of inner monologues with keen, unabashed relish; exposing marital bedroom and male bonding in this biting, excruciatingly funny observation of men, women and adolescent girls.

PUBLISHED MAY 2013

Quercus

www.quercusbooks.co.uk

ALSO AVAILABLE

SUMMER THINGS

Joseph Connolly

'Connolly has established himself as a very English comic author, in the tradition of P. G. Wodehouse'

THE TIMES

Joseph Connolly's bestselling novel goes straight to the secret heart of that sticky promenade of lust, adultery and snobbery: the British seaside.

Casting aside rose-tinted sunglasses, he undresses the foibles and fears of the middle classes in a riot of one-upmanship, lechery and deceit. *Summer Things* is a novel that slips from one set of startling mishaps to another as easily as melting ice-cream from its cone.

Surprising, irreverent and hilarious, this new edition of *Summer Things* brings one of Connolly's best-loved novels to a new generation.

'Viciously funny'

DAILY TELEGRAPH

Quercus

www.quercusbooks.co.uk